Fire and Ice

"Sit down," said J.

I did. When he continued staring in silence, I raised my eyebrows and looked up at him as if to say, *What the hell is your problem?* But I tried to keep my voice neutral when I said, "I'm Daphne Urban. I was told to report to you."

"I know exactly who you are," he answered with a voice of steel and iron. "Now I'd like to get one thing clear. I didn't want you, or any of your kind, brought into this. I believe you are evil. But I also know that there is an evil in this world far greater than yours. And I will work with the devil himself to defeat it. I do not like you, but I will protect you. I do not care if you like me. But you need to listen to me."

His eyes held mine the entire time. And that was one big mistake. His words annoyed me to some degree, but I had been insulted by bastards more arrogant than this J. This little speech didn't scare me, or even impress me much. The real problem was that as J's eyes held mine, I felt as if I were falling into a cold blue place inside him, and it was so cold there, the cold burned. His soul was on fire within the ice, and I could see it. My skin tingled as if electricity started running across its surface. The air became charged like it does befo

BEYOND
THE
PALE

THE DARKWING CHRONICLES
BOOK ONE

SAVANNAH RUSSE

A SIGNET ECLIPSE BOOK

SIGNET ECLIPSE
Published by New American Library, a division of
Penguin Group (USA) Inc., 375 Hudson Street,
New York, New York 10014, USA
Penguin Group (Canada), 10 Alcorn Avenue, Toronto,
Ontario M4V 3B2, Canada (a division of Pearson Penguin Canada Inc.)
Penguin Books Ltd., 80 Strand, London WC2R ORL, England
Penguin Ireland, 25 St. Stephen's Green, Dublin 2,
Ireland (a division of Penguin Books Ltd.)
Penguin Group (Australia), 250 Camberwell Road, Camberwell, Victoria 3124,
Australia (a division of Pearson Australia Group Pty. Ltd.)
Penguin Books India Pvt. Ltd., 11 Community Centre, Panschsheel Park,
New Delhi—110 017, India
Penguin Group (NZ), cnr Airborne and Rosedale Roads, Albany,
Auckland 1310, New Zealand (a division of Pearson New Zealand Ltd.)
Penguin Books (South Africa) (Pty.) Ltd., 24 Sturdee Avenue,
Rosebank, Johannesburg 2196, South Africa

Penguin Books Ltd., Registered Offices:
80 Strand, London WC2R ORL, England

First published by Signet Eclipse, an imprint of New American Library,
a division of Penguin Group (USA) Inc.

First Printing, June 2005
10 9 8 7 6 5 4 3 2 1

To my sister, Corrine Boland.
I love you always, forever.
This novel has been as much
your dream for me as my own.

ACKNOWLEDGMENTS

I wish to express my grateful appreciation to the world's bats, those astonishing, maligned creatures who inspired this book. The victims of many myths, in truth they are not blind, they aren't rodents, and they don't get tangled in your hair. They are gentle animals who are meticulously clean and seldom transmit disease. Bats are essential to the balance of nature and deserve our protection . . . and our awe. To learn more about bats, please visit Bat Conservation International, www.batcon.org.

INTRODUCTION

I never wanted to be a spy. Of all the careers I've envisioned for myself in 450 years, secret agent never made my top ten. But fate doesn't give you a choice. At least it never offered one to me. . . .

CHAPTER 1

Uncle Sam Wants Me?

I was between relationships, 180-some years between relationships, to be exact. No long, sweet kisses, no I love yous, no moans of ecstasy or shivery release since the Greek rebellion against the Ottoman Turks. It had been a wee bit more than a dry spell. I called it the Sahara when I got into it with my girlfriends. You'd think I'd be used to a solitary existence by now. After all, being a female vampire tends to discourage long-term relationships because even a casual fling can have serious consequences. Indeed, my last affair nearly killed me, literally.

What put me off the whole man-woman commitment thing happened back in 1824, when I was a dark-haired beauty in Missolonghi. The affair had the potential to be a great love, one for the history books. Then, practically overnight, it ended badly. No, that's an understatement. To tell the truth, it ended *tragically*.

Talking about truth, let me tell you, do not believe for a moment the story that the great poet and revolutionary George Gordon, Lord Byron, died of a fever. I can't believe the public bought that, but then people believed Nixon when he said "I am not a crook." The real cause of Byron's death was a love bite gone bad—gone septic, to be medically accurate. I remember the incident as if it were yesterday.

We were strolling hand in hand near the inn where he had set up his temporary living quarters. We entered a rose garden arduously created by the innkeeper out of the swampy surroundings of this mosquito-ridden town. It wasn't the first time we had walked there, but it was to be the last. The April day had faded into a purple haze on the verge of turning into a black velvet night. A slight breeze stirred the foliage; the air felt heavy with the smell of flowers.

"Tell me more about London, George," I said, fanning myself feverishly, and not just from the warm temperatures. "Do you miss it? Is it difficult to be so far away from the parties?" I made sure I walked very close to him, my breath like a flower petal caressing his cheek.

"The parties provided an agreeable distraction from the rather frightening solitude of a poet," he said vaguely. Then he gazed out over the Gulf of Patras, lying flat and still to the west. A ship anchored far off the shore. I could easily discern it amid the scattered silver waves that leaped up and caught the last light. I don't know that Byron saw the vessel, but I think he did. She floated there at the starting point of a long journey, the shadows of her masts stretching eastward in the setting sun.

"So why did you leave?" I asked.

His face stayed turned toward the gulf when he answered. "I became tired of listening to hired musicians behind a row of artificial palm trees instead of to the single, pure-stringed instrument of my heart. I knew it was time to go."

Seeing him in profile, his face inexpressibly sad, I couldn't keep my eyes off him. Byron had a wide forehead, sensual lips, and long, dark lashes over bedroom eyes. He was as finely featured as a Greek god, certainly better-looking than his portraits, which I think make him look gay. In real life he was an unmistakably male, high-testosterone type, filled with energy, turned on by taking risks.

I admit that if I looked closely, dust soiled his clothes and grime blackened the inside of his collar. Deep lines fanned out from his eyes; his skin was sallow and dry. And when he became fatigued, his twisted foot pained him and his limp increased. Lately George looked especially worn out, dissolute from too much hashish and too many women. Yet, so little in life looks as pleasing under bright lights and cold scrutiny as it does by candlelight and heated glances exchanged over glasses of wine. Tonight Byron was incredibly handsome. I was enchanted. I fairly trembled to be near him. He could have so many women—he had had so many women—but for the past few weeks he had wanted me, only me.

Nonetheless, there were hours when he seemed far away in his thoughts, crossing some inner geography of his mind. "Let's not talk about England. Talking bores me," he said. "I'm much more interested in this." He pulled my face to his, kissed me hard and long, his mouth tasting of wine. When he stopped, he looked deeply into my eyes. "'She walks in beauty, like the night,'" he recited, "'of cloudless climes and starry skies.'" I virtually swooned.

This man, hard and hungry, had come to fight for Greek independence. He was a hero. I was starstruck. He was horny. I was flirtatious. He was thirty-six. I was a little over 274.

"Daphy," he said, "come on, sweet thing, give me a little. You know you want to."

Oh, yes, I did want to. I laughed and let him move the length of his body against me. I knew his reputation, and I knew what he was after, but I didn't care. He moaned, and whispered in a low hoarse voice, "Girl, you're going to be the death of me. It's been a long time since I've wanted a woman this much. There's something about you. Something . . . something mad, bad, and dangerous to know."

He clasped my hand. As he entwined our fingers, his ring bit into my flesh. The sensation made me tingle. He led me to a bench, putting one arm around my waist. I can still remember the feel of the hard muscles in his forearm through the thin silk of my camisole. He pulled me down onto his lap, his hand slipping up under my skirts. I didn't stop him. His mouth felt like silk as he lowered his lips to my heaving breast. My blood was racing, my head was spinning, and that was when the rising moon lit up the white skin on the back of his neck. I couldn't resist. I wanted to, I tried to, but I was carried away with rapture . . . and I bit him. Losing all control, I drank too much, too soon. He looked at me with stunned eyes, suddenly understanding, and then he slipped into unconsciousness. Poor George. And that's the truth about his death, but don't expect to hear about it in Lit 101. It still hurts me to talk about it.

After barely escaping from Missolonghi before Byron's comrades put a stake through my heart, I decided celibacy was the wiser course. But now even I, resolute as I am, have my limits. I was climbing the walls. A girl has her needs, and I certainly had mine.

And one of the needs I had was getting a new ID every twenty years or so. Vampires don't age. On the plus side, I'll never need Botox. In the minus column, I have to keep changing my birth date.

And that was how I got busted.

The earth turns on its dark side. It is winter.
You can get just about anything in New York City.

Even a vampire can get a fake ID, and when the time came, all of us went to Sid. He worked out of a wretched walk-up apartment on Ninth Street between Avenues B and C. The neighborhood gave me the creeps. And of course, I had to go there after dark. We all complained, but Sid just said, "And vhat do you vant? Park Avenue?" I knew I could get mugged. I just never expected what was about to happen. . . .

The day had been blustery, rain and sleet taking turns pelting the streets, and tonight the temperature was plummeting. As I trudged up the subway stairs onto the street at St. Marks Place I wondered whether spring would ever return. I shoved my hands deep into my pockets. The wind seemed to cut right through me. I have thin blood. I get cold easily. And tonight I had a feeling—a very bad feeling that wiggled around like a maggot in my gut. Something wasn't right. Something was dangerous out here tonight.

I've learned to listen to my instincts, so I kept aware of the people around me as I headed east on Ninth Street. It wasn't late, only around seven, yet the buildings already sat in murky darkness. The sidewalks glistened in the streetlights from the earlier rain. "Damn it!" I said out loud. "Damn it all to hell, it is frigging cold!" I shivered. The chilly damp was coming right through the thin soles of my Nine West boots.

I had gone two blocks when I heard footsteps behind me. Some black teenagers came up fast and passed me, elbowing each other and twirling around, laughing and jiving as they half danced, half ran down the block. But that wasn't what I heard. My hearing is extraordinarily discriminating. Behind me a different kind of footstep kept a measured, steady beat. Dread fell on me like a black curtain coming down.

I passed a fortune-teller's storefront. A Gypsy woman

leaned against the doorjamb, smoking a cigarette in the open doorway. *"Strega!"* she shouted at me and cringed backward, clutching the crucifix around her neck.

"Bitch!" I hissed back, showing my teeth. I gave her good scare, I think. I don't like Gypsies. They're all thieves.

I didn't slow my pace. I wanted to reach Sid's as fast as possible. I crossed Avenue A. I had to exercise self-control to keep from breaking into a jog. I made it to Avenue B. Another half block and I reached the stoop in front of Sid's building. I took the stairs two at time, stopped at the top, and looked back up the block.

A young man stood on the far side of a fenced-in basketball court, watching me. I knew without a doubt that his had been the footsteps behind me. He turned away quickly. I didn't see his face, but a ponytail of blond hair poked out from beneath a black watch cap. I didn't hesitate any longer. I ducked inside Sid's vestibule and pushed the doorbell for his apartment. No one answered. Fear was crashing down on me now. I kept pushing the button. *Damn it, Sid, where in hell are you?*

Finally the door buzzed and clicked open. I fairly flew through it. It shut and locked behind me. I took some deep, cleansing breaths. I told myself to calm down; it was nothing. The man was no one. He had nothing to do with me. I always get anxious when I have to see Sid. Needing to get an updated birth certificate rakes up a lot of my issues. It means another twenty years have passed, but I'm still the same. People I once cared about are gone. I'm still here. A yawning chasm of loneliness opens up inside me. I am always the outsider. Misunderstood. A freak. A monster. Unable to have the milestones that mark the lives of other women, I throw a pity party for myself. Yet, to be honest, I'm not alone. There are a lot of us who see Sid. A lot more than you'd ever suspect.

Relieved to be inside, I started up the stairs, unbuttoning my coat as I climbed. The hallway smelled of cabbage and urine. I never breathed deeply going up these stairs. Damn Sid for working out of such a dump. The lighting was dim. It was better that way. Sid's "office" occupied a tenement apartment on the fourth floor, the kind that has a bathtub in the kitchen covered with a board to make a table. He didn't live there. I don't know where he lived—a homeless shelter or Scarsdale, I never knew; he never said. When I got to the top of the stairs, I could see he had left his apartment door cracked. I pushed it open and went in.

"Sid? It's Daphne Urban, your seven-fifteen appointment," I said as I stepped into his apartment.

The light wasn't on. I felt a sudden panic as someone grabbed me. I was flung against a wall and held there with a hand between my shoulder blades. My arms were yanked behind my back, and the cold, hard steel of handcuffs bit into my wrists.

"Hello, Miss Urban," a silky voice said as I was shoved into the living room and pushed roughly down onto a hard wooden chair.

"Who are you? What do you want?" I began to shake from head to toe. From inside my coat came a sound like the rustling of fluttering wings. I started to rise up. A guy in a suit put his fat hand on my shoulder to keep me still. He had *cop* written all over him. Across from me sat another man. He was middle-aged, well dressed in a gray suit, clearly Saville Row and newly pressed. His legs were crossed, so I could clearly see he wore Gucci loafers, since one shoe was only about two feet from my knee. The man sat back in one of Sid's green easy chairs, the kind with wide armrests and a low, blocky profile, very 1950s. His face was lit by a quiet pool of yellow light from a table lamp. His gray hair was long, but pulled back neatly, giving him an artistic look. He was clean-shaven. His features were regular but bland, nothing notable, nothing unusual. His fingernails were short. He wore a silver wristwatch; I'm guessing it was a Tag. Everything about him was clean, neutral, and nondescript. The only thing out of the ordinary was that half of his left index finger was missing. Overall he seemed relaxed as he sat unmoving, studying me.

"Miss Urban," he said, making eye contact with me and not blinking at all, like a lizard or a snake. "I—actually we—have been watching you. We have been waiting to contact you at a time and a place where we have the . . . shall we say, privacy and anonymity to meet you without being observed. Why? To put it very simply, the United States government wants you. And I have an offer you can't refuse." He gave a half smile as he said that. But he wasn't being funny. "That's not quite accurate," he added. "You can refuse our offer. Of course you can. But your refusal means you're tired of living."

"I don't understand," I said. The man sat close enough that I could smell his aftershave. I think he was wearing Versace. I like nice things. I pay attention to them. It occurred to me that the man must hide a certain flamboyance beneath his plain exterior. No one subtle or conservative wears Versace. He was not what he seemed to be. I also noticed that the big cop next to me with his hand on my shoulder smelled sour, like fear. I knew that smell, and I knew he was afraid of me. But the thought just fluttered through my mind like a bat's wing. I was focusing on controlling my own fear. Fear is always the enemy. Once it blossoms into panic, reason flees. The primitive brain takes over, and it's flight or fight. Which? There were at least three men in this room. Two of them had grabbed me, one stood next to me, and one must be standing behind me in the shadows of the room. Did he hold a weapon? A gun? A stake? Something. To flee I had to get to the door or the window. They would try to stop me. I would choose to fight. Even bound by handcuffs I could fight. But should I fight? Should I transform myself into the monster I was within? I focused on my breaths to calm myself and waited for the seated man to answer.

"Miss Urban," he said again, pinning me with his eyes. "If you are thinking of trying to escape, don't. Listen to me. We know who you are—what you are. We are not vampire hunters. We haven't captured you in order to kill you. We need you, and we think you need us. We want to offer you a new life. A better life, we feel. One with purpose, with meaning."

Nothing he said made sense. I always feared that one day I would be caught. It would come to this. Cruel hands grabbing me, then a wooden stake causing me unbearable agony as it tore through my skin, broke my ribs, and pierced my heart. Afterward darkness, dust, oblivion. But what was this? Who were these men?

"I don't understand. What do you want from me?" I said as my body started to shake. I fought the urge to transform. The panic inched closer. In another moment I wouldn't be able to stop it. I would become the other thing, the thing with fangs and claws and animal instincts. The fat hand on my shoulder got heavier, tightening its grip.

"Miss Urban." The seated man's voice took on an edge of authority. "Let me be as direct as possible. I work for an intelligence agency of the United States government. I am what is called a recruiter. You are a vampire. People fear you. Some people hunt you down. But you are also a beautiful woman with extraordinary talents. This country—this nation—is at war. Our way of life, our very existence, is threatened by small groups of terrorists, both from within our borders and outside of them. They call this country the Great Satan. These fanatics take innocent lives in pursuit of their goals. They struck on 9/11. They will strike again—and if they succeed what they do will be worse, much worse, than what happened on 9/11. Our job is to make sure they don't succeed. We need you to help us stop them.

"You speak, we believe, thirteen languages and have lived in at least that many countries. Your IQ is so high you rank within the top one percent of the people on this planet. You are strong and cunning enough to have escaped detection and capture for nearly five hundred years. That, Miss Urban, is admirable. More important, your family—your mother, to be exact—has had a long involvement in international diplomacy . . ."

"Leave my mother out of this," I said, my fear receding in a burst of sudden anger. "Anything she did happened centuries ago."

The man waved his hand in a dismissive way. "As you wish. My point is that you are familiar with intrigue, taking it in with your mother's milk, so to speak. You have seen treachery and lies all your life. You have been betrayed and in turn betrayed others. The depths of human depravity and evil have darkened your soul and spirit, yet you have survived, and more than that—thrived. Your senses are superhuman. And, oh yes, you can fly. What we want from you, Miss Urban, is for you to be a spy. For us. For justice. For goodness."

"A spy?" I was dumbfounded. "A spy? For the United States? You're joking."

"Miss Urban, I have never been more serious. We have caught you. We can, and we will, terminate you right here, right now, if we have to. That's your Hobson's choice. You can take what we are offering—or nothing at all. By nothing, I mean the end of your existence. Death. Extinction."

"In other words . . ." I said, beginning to feel cold, defeated. Like midwinter ice, I was becoming brittle, lifeless, and still. "I work for you or I die."

"You are partially correct," the man said, leaning toward me. "If you choose to work for us, we need you to *want* to work for us. To believe in what you are doing. Choosing not to die is not enough. You have to choose to commit. You need to make a total commitment."

I laughed; it wasn't a pretty sound. "Commitment? To you? You are forcing me to do this. You tell me I can either work for you or you will kill me. Now you tell me I should feel this is my lucky break, a new career, a chance to fight for truth, justice, and the American way." I laughed again, and it sounded almost like a sob, my voice like breaking glass. "You want me to believe I can be a superhero for the U.S. of A. and a villain no more. Be serious. I can't just throw a switch inside me and suddenly change who I am."

The man across from me seemed to grow larger, to exude energy, to become almost incandescent. He held me still with the pure power of his words, the words of a true believer. "Miss Urban. Are you happy? Have you ever been happy? Are you fulfilled? Does your life have meaning? I'll answer for you. No. To every question. No. No. No. No. Why? Because you have lived a frivolous life. A wasted life. You have done nothing of consequence *in nearly five hundred years*. You live for your next nail appointment, for shopping, for romantic dreams of love, or for the momentary pleasure of good sex. If you can't have that, you settle for the latest movie at the cineplex or watching an episode of *The Sopranos* on HBO. You have so much to give. And you give nothing. You make—you have made . . . no difference in this world. You have wasted not one lifetime, but ten lifetimes."

I couldn't find my breath. I felt as if I had been

slapped. I knew all that he said was true. I had always known it. It haunted me in the night. Whenever I let myself ponder my existence, I felt frightened. I felt empty. I had neither love nor work. I believed in some vague ideals, but I had passion for none. I felt no pride in who I was or what I did. I was ashamed, disgusted with my needs and with the acts I had committed. And except for the horror I had inspired and the grief I had caused, I had done nothing of consequence. My life was meaningless. Had I thought of ending it? Yes. Had I ever thought about commitment? I had, for a short while, once long ago tried to make a commitment to a man. I had failed so abysmally that I had hardened the shell around my heart. But a total commitment to something bigger than the individual, to something larger than one's puny self? To a cause? To a government? Whoa. I had problems with committing myself to a government. I had seen too many governments come and go.

"Miss Urban." The man was talking again. "I believe you are capable of being much more than you are. I believe, and many of my colleagues believe, that you have the potential for greatness. Not all of my associates agree. Some of them feel you are a risk. Amoral. And dangerous. I don't believe that. I think, given the chance, you can excel. You can save not just your own soul, but this nation as a democracy and millions of people from injury and death. I'm not asking you to commit to a government, Miss Urban. If you were thinking that, get rid of the idea. I'm asking you to give yourself to the greater good. To the ideals upon which this country was founded. To the truths we hold as self-evident. To the right to be free. To goodness, Miss Urban. To life. We are offering you the chance to leave behind the darkness, the black desires, the blood urges that torment you. We know you fight them. We know you have not killed in decades. That is why you are sitting here and are not already a lifeless piece of garbage on the floor with a stake through your heart. We know that inside you, Miss Urban, is something pure and good. You can be a flawless diamond, not a shrouded thing of the shadows. You can be a more genuine hero than your Byron could ever have been . . . had he lived."

"How do you know about that? How did you find out everything about me? You know my past. You seem to even know my thoughts," I whispered. I felt strange. My heart was pounding; my breath caught in my throat. It was like the feeling I get in that last second before I transform: an eerie hesitation, a great pause between two existences, a wild expectation, then a bursting free.

"We *do* know everything about you, Miss Urban," the recruiter answered smugly. "The truth about the past may never reach the history books, but it is almost always recorded down to the smallest detail. As for how we know about you and your life . . . Your lack of logical deduction disappoints me, Miss Urban. Do you think Byron's followers didn't talk amongst themselves? They knew what you were. They pursued you. They tried to kill you, did they not? You escaped by the skin of your teeth. And is it not probable that someone who was there, troubled in his soul, fell on his knees in church, and in fear and trembling told his story to his priest? And afterward, Miss Urban, the priest did what? Wrote to his bishop? And the bishop did what? You get the idea.

"So, yes, Miss Urban, information about you—and countless others—is always written down by someone. It may be put in a file. The file may be hidden in the catacombs of Rome or locked in a Vatican vault, but it is there for those who have the power to obtain it. And we have our ways of finding those files, Miss Urban. We are very good at what we do. We know who and what you really are. And we have chosen you."

I was shocked by his words. I had been blind not to realize how visible my trail had been.

"And one more thing, Miss Urban," the recruiter said in a harder voice.

"Yes?" I said, still reeling from his last revelation. The dark of the room crowded in on me, flickers of panic chased through my mind like shadows, and I was, for one of the few times in my life, truly afraid.

"Do not even think about agreeing to our offer and then fleeing," he said, his words like flint striking rock, each one uttered with a sharp crack filled with sparks. "We have been watching you 24/7—in order to recruit you. We will continue to monitor your every move 24/7—in order to terminate you if you run. You have been visible to us for a long time. Please understand— and listen to me carefully—*there is nowhere you can go, no place you can hide, where you can escape us.* Do you hear me?"

I stammered. "I have to think. I need some time. You are asking more than anyone has ever asked of me."

"Unfortunately, Miss Urban, the one thing I can't give you is time to think. You are standing on a cliff and the wild beast is closing in behind you. You need to make a leap of faith, and make it now."

In that moment, I knew. I had to jump off the edge and free-fall into something I knew nothing about. I had been in New York City on 9/11. That day and the days that followed the destruction of the World Trade Center, I had felt helpless and grief stricken. Now I was being given a chance to do something that I couldn't do then. I could stop another attack. I could be important in a magnificent, positive way. A new door was opening for me. A new path was before me, if I took it.

"Okay." I said. "Yes. I'll be a spy." And I stepped onto the road to a different life.

CHAPTER 2

The leap into the abyss . . .

I was told to show up at six P.M. the following evening at 175 Fifth Avenue—otherwise known as Manhattan's Flatiron Building—and I was to proceed to the office of ABC Media, Inc. There I would meet my handler, get my assignment, and begin orientation. I was told to call my handler J.

Then the men let me go. They simply allowed me to walk out of Sid's apartment. Of course I was followed. Of course I was watched. I knew now that they would never let me go free. But what of it? I have never been free, always being hostage to fear or anxiety and the rigid "rules" of my very existence.

Once back in my Upper West Side apartment, I didn't make my way to bed even when the time grew late. After the sun sets, vampires do not sleep. We prowl the night. I remained indoors this evening, however, and through the wee hours I paced like a tiger in a zoo and thought far too much about the past. I was deeply troubled that a dossier existed on me, and had existed for centuries. Finally I realized I had no means to eliminate it, and I needed to accept what I could not change. I turned on the Turner Classic Movies channel and watched an old Hitchcock film. The hours crawled by slowly. My mind wandered although my body remained still. Sleep eluded me even after the rosy fingers of dawn began to stain the night sky with streaks of red.

I pulled the blinds tightly closed, and during the daytime hours when I usually rest I scrubbed the bathroom floor, cleaned out the refrigerator, and rearranged the living room furniture. Women, filled with nervous energy and faced with waiting, do not stand around looking out of windows or staring blankly into space, as do men. We must be in motion. Even while we're waiting for the microwave to heat a cup of coffee, we wash dishes, wipe off the counter, put clothes into the washer. We know a lot can be accomplished in two minutes.

All day long, while I scrubbed and cleaned, I thought about the job. And the more I thought, the more excited I became. Soon bubbles of anticipation buoyed me up, lifting my spirits. I realized that I wanted to do this; I really did. I didn't need the salary, of course. I had no need for outside income. My mother generously settled some of her considerable fortune on me centuries ago. My Swiss bank account was fat, my properties secure, my stocks healthy. However, over the years boredom or the need to fit in and appear like a normal human had led me to hold many jobs. Some had been mildly interesting to me. This one, despite the circumstance of my "hiring," filled me with expectation and hope.

That afternoon I spent hours getting ready for the meeting. I went through my closet. Jeans were too casual. A suit too businesslike. I finally decided on all black as appropriate spy attire—black gabardine slacks, a black cashmere turtleneck, and black Donald Pliner stretch boots with three-inch heels. Contrary to popular belief, I, and all the vampires I personally know, rarely dress in black. Our skin is far too pale. I think black makes me look cadaverlike, and that is *not* a good thing. Furthermore I'm not into Goth. I don't do piercing. The disaffected, mad-at-the-world, dead look is not the image I hope to convey. I've had to work too hard at blending in and looking normal. And I do not even own a cape, or at least I haven't for the past hundred years. Vampires aren't like the Amish or the Hasidim—or Count Dracula. We aren't required to dress in the style of our forefathers. I shop at Bloomingdale's here in New York, and I order from the Neiman Marcus catalog when I can't physically get to the Galleria in Houston, Texas, which I prefer over the Dallas store. The Houston Galleria is my absolutely favorite mall. I get a shopping high just thinking about Dolce & Gabbana, Gucci, Kenneth Cole, Nine West, teuscher Chocolates of Switzerland, all together, all in one mall. Whoever designed the Galleria deserves a Nobel prize in shopping. I could gush on, but I digress.

For my meeting with J, I put an Italian scarf in deep scarlet and gold around my neck to soften the harshness of the black. Red is a favorite color of mine. I consider it a power color, but I don't discount that it may subconsciously appeal to my libido or my appetite. I also added a wide, ornate belt in a mahogany red. Being bone thin, I don't have much of a bust, but I have a tiny waist. If you've got it, flaunt it. I kept my makeup subtle, but I knew I looked like a million dollars. As a final touch I put on a favorite ring, made during the Renaissance in Florence. It's two panther heads created from pavé diamonds, one panther head set in white gold facing one set in yellow gold, and each has green emerald eyes. It's not a subtle ring, but then I never put much stock in subtlety. As outerwear I chose a three-quarter-length black leather coat. I felt confident, self-assured, and raring to go.

Until I met my boss.

At 5:45 that evening I emerged from the subway at Twenty-third Street and Fifth Avenue. As I came out of the dark tunnel into the fading light of day, what I had agreed to do fully sank in. Anxiety dampened some of my enthusiasm, giving me as much of a chill as the plummeting temperatures predicted for that night. I pushed through the glass doors of the Flatiron Building, fought my way in through the crowd of departing workers going out, and entered an empty elevator car. It creaked and swayed upward.

A legitimate New York publishing house occupies the highest floors of 175 Fifth Avenue. ABC Media was a phony company on a much lower floor. I found the office, pressed the buzzer, the lock clicked open, and I walked into a long, narrow conference room. There was no one there.

Three closed doors lined the left wall. A square wooden table took up the center of the conference room where I now stood looking around, letting my instincts react and alert me to any potential danger. From behind one of the closed doors I heard a radio playing something from *Phantom of the Opera*. I sensed there were living beings nearby, but felt no lurking evil. All I smelled was stale air and the musty odor of cardboard boxes. An empty coffeemaker, a jar of Carnation powdered nondairy creamer, and a plastic cup filled with sugar packets sat on a little table near the windows, which were nearly opaque with grime. These windows filled the right-hand wall, which canted inward toward the front of the building, making the room a trapezoid. A door marked DIRECTOR was ajar at the end of the conference room.

The Flatiron Building is shaped like a huge wedge of cheese. Considered the oldest existing skyscraper in New York, the building comes to an apex in the front at the corner where Broadway crisscrosses Fifth Avenue. In that triangular corner, like Captain Ahab at the bow of his whaling ship, the *Pequod,* the man I assumed was J stood still as a statue, staring out of a window, his back to me. He didn't move as I approached.

I knocked on the doorjamb alongside his open door. Without turning to greet me, the man said, "Come in," and I did. I stood there as a long minute passed. Finally he looked over his shoulder at me. His blue eyes, cold as a glacier and hard as marbles, were filled with pure loathing.

"Sit down," he ordered.

I did. My face remained expressionless. If this was a game, I intended to win it. But when the man returned to gazing out the windows, rudely keeping his back toward me, I raised my eyebrows as if to say, *What the hell is your problem?* I was getting an attitude fast, but kept my voice flat and neutral when I said, "I'm Daphne Urban. I was told to report to you."

"I know exactly who you are and why you are here," he answered in a voice of steel and iron. He slowly moved away from the windows and faced me, but he kept the desk between us. He remained standing; I was sitting. Since he was a good six-foot-two or -three, he towered above me. It was a classic power move.

He continued talking and sounded to me like a pissed-off drill sergeant. "Now I'd like to get one thing clear from the start. I didn't want you, or any of your kind, brought into this. I believe you are evil. But I also know that there is an evil in this world far greater than yours. And I will work with the devil himself, if that's what it takes, to defeat it. But understand—my job is not to hold your hand or be your friend. Now that you are officially part of this operation, I have one job and one job only— to make sure you succeed. Lives are at stake here, Miss

Urban, potentially millions of innocent lives, and the American way of life itself. So I am putting any personal bias I have aside. I expect you to do the same. I do not like you, but I will protect you. I will do anything it takes to keep you alive. I do not care if you like me. But you need to listen to me and trust me. We need to be a team. I will be tough, but fair. I expect you to give not just a hundred percent to this operation but one hundred ten percent, one hundred twenty percent, or whatever it takes to bring down the bastards we're after."

His eyes held mine the entire time. And that was one big mistake. His words annoyed me to some degree, but I had been insulted before by more arrogant bastards than this J. And I don't intimate easily. I've been screamed at by a pope and held my ground, so this little speech didn't scare me, or even impress me much. The real problem was that as J's eyes held mine, I started to connect with him. I felt as if I were falling into a cold blue place inside him, and it was so cold there that it burned. Within the ice his soul was on fire, and I could see it. My skin tingled as if electricity had started running across it. The air became charged like it does before a lightning strike. This was a chemistry I hadn't experienced in decades, a sexual dynamite that could complicate my life beyond imagining.

I think he realized what was going on, because he stopped abruptly and looked away. He got busy at his desk as if searching for some papers, but not before I noticed a flush creeping up his neck. What can I say? Necks are an erogenous zone to me. His was muscular and thick and tempting. I tried to stop the thoughts edging in from the shadows of my mind.

"Let me introduce you to the others," he said, not looking at me. "Then we'll get started."

"Others?" I said. "What others?"

Now he did look at me, and his look was condescending,

almost pitying. "Did you really think you were the only one they recruited? Yes, Miss Urban, there are others."

"But I thought—" I started to say.

"You thought you were special," he said, cutting me off. "You thought you were the chosen one. They tell that to every vampire they recruit. But if it makes you feel any better, they don't recruit many of you. Most of you they simply terminate. So consider yourself lucky. You made the grade, or shall we say you made the final cut. You're still alive." Then he walked out from behind the desk, brushed past me, and went into the conference room. I followed.

He opened the first door to the right. "Your office," he said. I stuck my head in through the doorway. I saw nothing except an old metal desk with a laptop computer on it, a wooden chair, and a document shredder. A fluorescent light buzzed overhead. That was it. A real palace.

"You look surprised, Miss Urban. Yes, you'll need an office. You'll have paperwork to fill out occasionally, and you'll have classified material to review. And what happens here, stays here." He left the door open and told me to take a seat at the conference table.

As I sat down, he tapped lightly on the next door after the one to my office. "Miss Polycarp, we're ready to start," he said. The door opened and a stunningly beautiful blond woman appeared. She had luscious red lips, a deep tan, and a blinding smile. Something about her fairly twinkled, she was so radiant. "Okay, boss man, I'm a-coming," she said irreverently to J, who was already knocking at the last closed door. "Mr. O'Reilly? Please come join us," he said.

O'Reilly? I thought. I knew a vampire named Cormac O'Reilly. He'd been in the chorus line of a dozen Broadway shows, but he never seemed able to get his "big break." He was self-indulgent, self-absorbed, and totally superficial. I was surprised that he would have been recruited.

The blonde came over and slid into a chair next to mine. "Hey, girlfriend," she said with a thick Southern drawl. "My name's Benny Polycarp, short for Benjamina. What's yours?" She rolled her eyes in J's direction, then gave me a wink, saying quietly, "And what do you think of our fearless leader?"

"Daphne Urban. My friends call me Daphy," I answered. I couldn't help but grin back at her as I lowered my voice and said sotto voce, "I think he's a by-the-rules, by-the-book man, and I think he must have ticked off somebody big time to have gotten stuck with us. And this is a little off the subject, but do you mind me asking you a personal question?"

"No," she whispered back, "go ahead. Shoot."

"How the hell did you get such a great tan?"

"Oh, sugar! It's out of a bottle. I go to a day spa that gives a treatment called Buff 'n' Glo . . . a massage and application of a self-tanner in one delicious session," she said, and laughed. "As a blonde, I'd look like an albino with this fish-belly-white skin we all have. Not that it doesn't look good on you," she backpedaled quickly. "You have gorgeous black Irish looks, if you don't mind me saying so."

"Thanks for the compliment," I said, "but I thought those tanners would make me look yellow, sallow, you know. I never saw any that looked this good. I was chicken to try it. I figured I'd look like I had a liver problem. But no kidding, you'd never know yours came out of a bottle." J started our way, and I quickly whispered a request for the name of her salon.

Meanwhile a slight young man quietly slipped into the seat at the end of the table. It was Cormac, but before I could say anything, J sat down at the head of the table, glaring at Benny and me. Evidently chitchat was verboten.

"Mr. O'Reilly and Miss Polycarp have already been introduced," he said. "And from what I understand, Miss Urban, you already know Mr. O'Reilly."

I looked at Cormac and said, "We've known each other for quite some time." Then I turned my head away from J and mouthed silently to Cormac, *What are you doing here?* He just looked sulky and didn't respond.

J picked up a cardboard carton off the floor and put it on the table in front of him. From it he took out three thick packages.

"May I have your attention. Your team name is Darkwing. The package I am passing out to each of you will tell you about your assignment. It contains a computer disk with a complete dossier on the individual target and/or organization with which you will be involved. After you have a chance to review the information, I will meet with you individually to answer your questions and give you instructions. Miss Urban, I need to meet with you tomorrow night, here, as near to five P.M. as you can. I know you have to wait for sunset. You have your work cut out for you between now and then. I expect you to review the dossier and come prepared with questions. Your operation is of particular urgency."

I hadn't gotten a chance to open my package, but Benny and Cormac had already pulled a black binder out of each of theirs.

"What is this?" Cormac said as he opened to the first page of his. "You can't be serious. I'm supposed to be a spy, risking my life to save humanity. I can't be reading this right."

"If you thought you were going to be James Bond, Mr. O'Reilly, unfortunately that isn't what we had in mind for you."

"Well, hell, yes. I want to be a secret agent who leaps into action, doing battle with the bad guys. But what I'm reading here, you want me—and you have to be joking, because I have this thing about crucifixes—you want me to infiltrate a Catholic order—one that advocates a spiked chain worn around the thigh and use of a knotted rope for whipping? I read about these guys in *The Da Vinci Code*. Kinky, but not exactly my preference for a good time." Looking disgusted, Cormac slammed his binder shut and pushed it away.

"This job isn't about pleasing you, Mr. O'Reilly. It's about doing what needs to be done. Your area of operations is indeed Opus Dei; its new headquarters is here in Manhattan. When you go over the material, you'll see what we want you to do, but Mr. O'Reilly, stick with the factual material in the dossier and forget *The Da Vinci Code*. Since your assignment has a more generous time frame than either Miss Urban's or Miss Polycarp's, we don't need to meet right away. I would like to see you a week from today, right here in this room, at six P.M. And Mr. O'Reilly, I am aware that you have special concerns. We will work around them. Since you'll have some time, please use the coming week to disengage from your obligations—and personal entanglements."

"Oh, that's really rich," I couldn't help but say out loud. "Cormac, in a Catholic order. The same man who hasn't been able to keep his pants zipped for more than twenty-four hours at a clip in the past three hundred years."

"Shut up, Daphy," Cormac said. "You're still mad because I stole that sweet boy right, shall we say, from under you in Venice."

"We have an agenda here," J broke in. "If you two have a personal problem, take it up later." He shot a stern glance at both of us.

"Miss Polycarp," J continued. "I'll need to meet with you in forty-eight hours, here, as close to five P.M. as you can handle. Your assignment, like Miss Urban's, needs to have an agent in place as quickly as possible."

"Yes, sir," Benny said as she gave him a dazzling smile and a mock salute.

"Also in your package is the CFR, Code of Federal Regulations; 'A Federal Employee's Emergency Guide'; and several other publications from the OPM, Office of Personnel Management, containing detailed information about your status as a U.S. government employee. If you are issued a government uniform at any point, please remember that you cannot use your position or uniform for personal gain or profit. You will also find some forms that you need to complete and get back to me. Miss Urban, you do not have to finish them by tomorrow, but get them to me as soon as possible.

"As I said, I will go over your assignment in detail with each of you one by one. But in general there is one unbreakable rule. What you do as an operative is secret. You discuss nothing, and I mean nothing, about your assignment with anyone but me. You will have a cover story to tell your relatives and associates. Stick to it. Do not deviate from it. Confide in no one. If you see a psychiatrist—Mr. O'Reilly, I believe you do—you need to stop. Break your next appointment and don't go back. The agency will provide you with therapeutic support if necessary."

"What?" Cormac practically shrieked. "I have an anxiety attack when my shrink goes to the Hamptons for a weekend. I think I'm going to hyperventilate."

J ignored Cormac's dramatics. "You are agents operating in what we call deep cover. Each of you is in a black operation. That means even other government agencies do not know about it, nor do the watchdogs in Congress.

Officially your operation does not exist. You do not exist, as a spy. On paper, for the purposes of your salaries and benefits, you are GS11's step eight in the Department of the Interior. On paper, you are technical advisers on a historical restoration project for the National Park Service."

"How droll," Cormac said. "Maybe we can work on restoring your mother, Daphy. What is she, eight hundred years old by now?"

"Shut up, Cormac. If there's a body in need of restoration, it's yours. Talk about a sagging butt . . ."

Cormac's face contorted in fury as he opened his mouth to reply.

"Miss Urban, Mr. O'Reilly," J said in his drill-sergeant voice. "I'm not going to ask you to be quiet again. We don't have much time. I need to complete this orientation within the next fifteen minutes."

"Wait a minute, wait a minute," Benny said, jumping up from her seat. "Wait a minute! *This* is the orientation? When are we going to learn to use explosives, and run through a maze memorizing objects and remembering passwords, like on that TV show, *Spymaster*? I want to learn *cool* spy stuff."

"Yes," I chimed in. "I thought you'd be sending us to boot camp or something."

"You mean we're not going into basic training?" added Cormac. "I'm not going to see all those yummy young tight asses in fatigue pants?"

By this time J's face had turned a fine cherry red. I thought he was going to stroke out right in front of us. He slammed his fist on the table.

"Miss Polycarp, please sit down. All of you, be quiet and listen to me. Now! You're not going to be Navy SEALs, you're not going to be in Special Forces, and this is not a TV show! You all have photographic memories, and I don't think it's even an issue whether or not you can remember a password. You are already experts in several types of martial arts. Mr. O'Reilly, you have won awards in kickboxing. Miss Polycarp, you have taught tae kwon do. And Miss Urban, you were a ninja in feudal Japan at one point in . . . in . . . what the hell would you call what you do? Your *career*?"

J was practically foaming, he was so worked up. He started to talk even louder as he went on. "And besides your prowess in the martial arts, once you change, you have fangs and claws and are three times human size. You've each got longer kill histories than any soldier I have met. And quite frankly I cannot imagine how the need to blow up *anything* would arise when you, Miss Polycarp, are going to be working as a diamond special-ist, you, Mr. O'Reilly, will be in a religious order, and you, Miss Urban, will be dealing in aboriginal art.

"Everything else you need to know *for this orientation* is in your folders. Miss Urban, I'll see you in twenty-four hours. You're dismissed," he growled. With that, J stood up, picked up his folder, and stormed into his office, slamming the door behind him.

"Ohhh, somebody just had a hissy fit," said Cormac.

"I don't think he likes us," said Benny. "Too bad; he's sort of cute. Not my type, but cute."

I wasn't touching that remark with a ten-foot pole. I figured I'd change the subject. "Before we get out of here, Cormac, answer me—how did you get into this? I never figured you for a spy."

"Daphy, dear, I got into this the same way you did. They set me up. They arranged a phony "date" for me with this yummy bodybuilder in the steam room at the athletic club. Then slam, bam, thank you, ma'am, I was in handcuffs before I knew what hit me. I thought I was going to suffocate before the whole ordeal was over. I as-

sume you were offered the same options I was—sign on,
or *sayonara*. I was going to fight them at first, but you
know, I have been so incredibly bored lately. My acting
career is going absolutely nowhere, and if I go to one
more audition where the director tells me I'm too short,
I'll lose it—I really will. At least these folks recognize
my thespian talents. That's why they chose *me*." He
tossed his long hair back dramatically. "I can't imagine
why they picked *you,* Daphy."

"Oh, sure, Cormac," I said sarcastically. "You were
picked for your *thespian* talents. Everybody knows you
haven't danced professionally in years, and your last appearance on Broadway took place *behind* the set of *Cats,*
where you were screwing the casting director. And you
still didn't get the part, so I guess you were *too short* once
again."

"*Bitch!*" Cormac shrieked, standing up and starting
around the conference table to attack me when Benny
yelled, "Hey, you two! Cut it out!"

Cormac halted in his tracks and looked at her. Benny
continued talking. "That's better. Y'all have to remember,
we're in this together. We need to help each other. I guess
you two have a history, but whatever it is, forget it. I'm
the new kid on the block. They brought me in from Branson, Missouri. A vampire in Branson—isn't that just a
hoot? To be honest, I'm scared. If I screw up, not only
may umpteen people die, but I'm going to be terminated.
And honey, I like living. So let's try to get along with
each other."

"Amen, sister," said Cormac. "You're right."

"Agreed," I said. "Truce?" I said to Cormac.

"Truce. Come on, give me a hug, Daphy," he said as he
came over to me.

"Don't push it, Cormac," I said, but I let him pull
Benny and me into a group hug. Then we grabbed our

packages and exited the building together. All in all, I was feeling pretty doggone good. My first day as a spy, I had something dicey going on with my boss, wasn't bored, and didn't feel down about myself. I was looking forward to getting back to my apartment and popping into my computer the disk with my assignment.

New York straphangers know that there are two subway entrances at Twenty-third Street. The entrance to the downtown train abuts the Flatiron Building's western side, the Fifth Avenue side. To get to the uptown line, a passenger has to cross Broadway on the building's eastern side, a wide six-lane expanse with cars, taxis, and buses careening south from the junction of three different streets. Tonight it was fairly empty—desolate, in fact. I walked briskly across Broadway and nearly flew down the stairs to the subway. As I descended, I thought I heard the train coming into the station, so I pulled the Metrocard out of my pocket and pushed through the turnstile like a madwoman. When I stepped onto the platform I could see the downtown express on the center tracks blasting through the station without stopping. It wasn't my train. But in my hurry I had forgotten my own security measures, rule number one of which is to look around before I entered any confined area. It's a New York thing as much as a vampire survival tactic.

Now I stood there in the dim light, in that eerie underground environment that felt like a cave and awakened ancient stirrings I wanted to forget, to ignore, to smother unborn within me. I looked up and imagined hanging batlike from a rock ceiling with chirping all around me, awaiting the flight that came with sunset and that anticipation arousing my hunger—and blood desires. I shook my head and tried to chase those thoughts away by concentrating on some colorful wall ads for an HBO series. I tried to ignore the strong smell of fetid rainwater lying in puddles between the rails, the odor of stale urine where drunks peed off the platform onto the tracks, and the squeaking of rats far back in the tunnels leading uptown out of the station. But my senses were being pulled to the dark side and the night wanderings that haunted my soul.

Resisting that pull was partially why I stayed in the well-lighted area within sight of the transit worker in the booth on the other side of the turnstiles. I had especially strong feelings churning through me tonight. I looked impatiently at my watch. I walked toward the edge of the platform to peer into the darkness of the tunnel, hoping to spot the yellow headlight of a coming train. That was when I noticed a man not more than thirty feet farther down the platform from me, waiting for the train. I swore he hadn't been there a moment ago.

He wasn't looking at me, not then anyway. He gazed aimlessly across the wide expanse of tracks toward the downtown platform on the other side. He wore an expensive-looking brown leather aviator jacket and jeans. He stood with a lazy arrogance, his hands in his pockets, his feet slightly apart. But what startled me was his black watch cap and blond ponytail. My first thought was that this was the guy who had followed me to Sid's. My second thought was that I wasn't sure. As if he knew I was watching him, he slowly turned to face me. He looked right at me, intently, deliberately, his eyes burning with intensity.

My body tensed. My heart started to thud in my chest. Feelings were crashing over me like waves. My instincts warned me to be careful, get ready to run. My rational mind took notice that he was drop-dead good-looking, almost fashion-model pretty, except for a puckered scar along his cheekbone. Almost in the same moment I realized what was setting off the alarm bells in my gut. He had clenched his fists, and his face looked . . . I wasn't sure what—angry, perhaps predatory. Whatever it was, it didn't feel friendly. The hair on the back of my neck stood up, and, unexpectedly, I felt a fleeting urge to transform. Reason overrode that reflex, and I thought I would go back up to the busy street above and hail a cab. But even as I was making that decision, the man moved. I took a step backward toward the turnstiles. I thought he was coming toward me, but instead he did the strangest thing. He looked around until he spotted the revolving iron bars that led off the platform and bolted toward them. In an instant he smacked them with his hand and spun through them, exiting on the other side and running down the passageway toward the far stairs, his ponytail making one last flash of brightness before he was gone.

I stood still as a stone. I let out the breath I'd been unconsciously holding. Was it the same man who followed me yesterday? It must have been. He could be a stalker, but I figured he was from the agency, keeping an eye on me. I'd ask J tomorrow. There was a roar as the R train pulled into the station. I barely waited for the doors to open before I got on and dropped into a seat. Suddenly I felt tired to my very bones. And I couldn't get that man on the subway platform out of my mind.

CHAPTER 3

Merchant of Death

My target was called by one name, sort of like Cher. His name was Bonaventure. A synopsis of his dossier was on the disk:

> Bonaventure, age thirty-three, was born in Moscow and trained with the Russian Air Force. According to Interpol he holds five international passports in the names of Johnny Danza, Juan Duarte, John Bono, John Best, and John Good. His nickname is "Mad Dog." A recent UN study calls him the world's leading merchant of death, being the principal conduit for planes and weapons systems from Eastern Europe supplied to insurgents in Africa and terrorist groups including Hamas, Hezbollah, and al Qaeda. Within the last sixty days Bonaventure has purchased in excess of $16 million worth of antiaircraft guns, 122mm propelled canons, antitank rockets, antiaircraft missiles, and mortar bombs—all from Bulgaria. The sales were registered on end-user certificates from the African state of Togo.
>
> The UN report also identifies Bonaventure as the spider who weaves a web of shady arms dealers, di-

*amond brokers, and other operatives. He owns a
network of enterprises—from an aircraft repair
company in the United Arab Emirates to a charter
company in Miami, Florida. As one of the owners of
Air Fair Liberia (registered in equatorial Guinea
with headquarters in Sharjah, United Arab Emirates), he maintains one of the largest private aircraft fleets in the world. He conducts his business
primarily from the gulf state of Sharjah, which is
part of the United Arab Emirates.*

*Bonaventure is currently in the United States,
supposedly to buy pieces for his collection of New
Guinea tribal art. Bonaventure is said to maintain
a primary residence in the Balkans with his wife,
Alicia, and her father who, according to the UN report, "at one point held a high position in the KGB,
perhaps even as high as a deputy chairman." Rumors persist that he is estranged from his wife, and
that she is seeking a divorce but they have been unable to come to settlement about property. That has
not been confirmed. His personal fortune is esti-
mated to be in the billions of dollars.*

*In addition to his compound in Sharjah, UAE,
Bonaventure maintains an office at a small airport
in the same country. He also has a penthouse apartment in Manhattan on the Upper East Side. Besides
his passion for aboriginal art, which approaches
the level of an obsession (see footnote thirty-three
for an FBI profiler's explanation of this fanatical
drive to collect masks designed to protect the owner
from black magic, and statues of males with huge
penises), he is a devotee of Japanese sushi.*

I printed out a hard copy of the entire file, all two hundred pages, which included the entire UN report on

Bonaventure, a *Washington Post* investigative feature article, and a British MI6 report on his activities with the Taliban in Afghanistan. Along with the narrative, the disk included a picture that looked as if it was taken with a telephoto lens. It showed a powerfully built man of medium height standing next to a four-engine prop plane belonging to Air Damal. Bonaventure was dressed in khakis, and his face was obscured by a bush hat, a dark beard, and mirrored aviator sunglasses. Big frigging help if I had to pick him out of a crowd. I thought he looked like a malevolent frog, one that the kisses from even a hundred beautiful women couldn't turn into a prince.

The dossier didn't say anything about why Bonaventure was my target or what I was supposed to do. I guessed I'd find out when I met with J the next night, which was just as well. I had enough to cope with at the moment—my mother.

I had been paging through the materials when Marozia Urban—known to her friends as Mar-Mar—showed up at my apartment around two A.M. I'm not sure what image most people would have of a woman who had been lover to one pope and the mother of another (my half brother, Pope John XI, long since departed from this world). Some church history books, in scurrilous accounts, accuse my mother of seduction and intrigue. I can well imagine her dreaming up schemes, but depicting her as a femme fatale was pure fiction. In real life, my mother was a thousand-megawatt ball of energy standing about five feet tall in Birkenstocks, bell bottoms, and a tie-dyed shirt. She looked about eighteen years old. A peace sign around her neck gave testament to that inescapable fact that Mar-Mar had loved the 1960s, embraced "Make love, not war" with a vengeance, and decided that she had found a fashion statement she wanted to keep making. Tune in, turn on, drop out. During those days when the air smelled of marijuana and the streets rang with shouts of "Hell, no, we won't go," Mar-Mar with all her "eccentricities" of haunting the night, sleeping in a coffin, and shunning all foods with garlic had been accepted without question for the first time in her life. As a result, in her mind and in her lifestyle, she was staying right then, right there. The embarrassment she caused me during the preppy 1980s still makes me blush. Inexhaustible, irrepressible, and determined to meddle in my love life (or lack thereof), she is my cross to bear. . . .

The doorbell downstairs buzzed and Mar-Mar yelled through the intercom, "Beam me up, Scotty!" I barely had time to hide the dossier before she was at my door. I opened it, and she fairly exploded into the room. "Hello, babycakes! How's it hanging?" she chortled. She plopped down a carryall filled with organic veggies on a nearby chair and caught me in a bear hug around the waist. The top of her head came up to my chin.

I cringed and gently extracted myself. "I'm fine, Ma," I said. "How are you?"

"Everything's copacetic. You don't mind if I smoke?" she said. I did but just handed her an ashtray. She flicked her Bic and lit a joint she had taken from a pack of innocent-looking Camel nonfilters.

"Oh, Ma, you're not going to smoke *that*," I said in dismay.

She laughed, and in between deep drags of pungent-smelling Mary Jane, she started singing, "Ain't No Sunshine When She's Gone." She has never gotten over me getting my own place—and it's been two hundred years. She still tries to control my life every chance she gets. At the present moment I watched as she spotted the mail I left on my dining room table. She casually walked by me to position herself near enough to the stack of letters to read the envelopes. She even brushed her hand—

accidentally, of course—across the pile to get a look at the items near the bottom. She was incorrigible.

I ignored her snooping but I couldn't overlook the weed she was smoking. "You know I hate your getting high," I said.

"Yep, it's downright annoying, isn't it? Listen, sweetie, it relaxes me, and it's healthier than alcohol. Not that I object to that either. 'Candy is dandy but liquor is quicker,'" she said, and grinned at me. She was impossible. I gave up and braced myself for what was coming.

"So have you met anyone lately?"

"No, Ma."

"You know," she said, "my friend Zoe has a son. He's single and—"

"And he's a vampire," I finished for her. I remembered other times she had fixed me up with someone and pictured a pale, effete creature who still lived with his mother.

"Yes, of course he's a vampire. You know how I feel about dating outside of the family. It's a recipe for heartbreak. Who else can you trust not to betray you, except one of your own? Who else can know who and what you are, and still accept you? Trust is the basis for any successful relationship. Living a double life with a lover is the kiss of death, no pun intended."

"So why didn't you take your own advice?" I responded with sarcasm in my voice. Although I love my mother, she pushes my buttons, and I nearly always end up saying something I regret later.

"Oh, honey," she said with a catch in her voice and sadness creeping in. "There were other considerations when it came to Giamo. Your father was a mere mortal when we met, but he was such a wonderful man. I made an exception for him, and, well, he needed me. He had such plans, such dreams. And I never lied to him. At least after the first time I bit him, I never lied to him. He loved me even more after he came over to us. We were such an amazing team, until he was betrayed and . . ." Her eyes began to well up. "I'll never stop missing him. We were soul mates. And he gave me you." The tears started rolling down her cheeks.

I never learn. Any mention of my father, Giambattista Castagna, and the waterworks start. I have never learned much about him from her. She raised me on her own, and we were in hiding a great deal of that time. If I dared to ask what happened to my father and why he wasn't with us, she simply began weeping. I believed her tears were genuine, but it was an effective way of ending the conversation. When I asked about her life before I was born, she usually said something like, "We must live in the present. Focus on the *now,* dearest. The past is gone." It bothers me a great deal that she has kept so much from me. All I really know for certain is that she was born in Italy—in the tenth century. She never mentions my grandmother or any of her first husbands. I discovered she was married many times (under many aliases) before she met my father by researching her in libraries around the world. Everything I have read has only deepened the mystery around her.

"I'm starting a new job tomorrow," I said, hoping to distract her before she really got bawling.

She sniffed and the tears vanished. "Oh really? That's wonderful, sweetie. Who are you working for? What will you be doing?"

I had memorized my cover, but the real test would be whether she believed it. "I'm working on the cataloging and restoration of nineteenth-century theatrical artifacts. For the National Park Service."

A look of something—suspicion?—flickered across my mother's face. "How did that happen?" she asked.

"A fluke," I said, and went toward the kitchen to get a

drink. "Do you want a glass of mineral water?" She nodded yes. "*Frizzante* or *naturale?*" I asked her, using the Italian for water with bubbles or without them.

"*Frizzante,* with a slice of lemon if it wouldn't be too much trouble," she said, following me. "What kind of a fluke?"

"You remember Cormac O'Reilly?" I opened a bottle of Pellegrino, took a piece of lemon from a dish in the fridge, and handed the glass to Mar-Mar.

She took it from me and said, "You mean the dancer? The one who was in *A Chorus Line* twenty years ago? I thought you two weren't speaking."

"Well, we weren't, but I ran into him a while ago and we made up. He's working on this historical theater project and thought I might be good at it too. It's definitely an advantage when you've seen the items actually in use." I grinned. "The NPS was still hiring—it's just a temporary position—so I got the job. I think it will be interesting. I've been bored lately."

"Idle hands are the devil's workshop," Mar-Mar muttered. "You know you can always work with Greenpeace."

"Someone else is going to have to save the whales, Ma," I said. "This job is enough for me. And I can work at night."

"As long as you're happy," she said with a sigh that meant she wasn't, and got back to the point of her visit. "You know, it wouldn't hurt to go out just once with Zoe's son. At least try it. He seems like a nice boy."

"I don't think so, Ma."

"For me. Just do it for me. Look, you don't even have to go out on a real date. Come by my place next Saturday night. I'll have Zoe and Louis in for drinks."

"Louis?" I said.

"He's French, from Louisiana. It's *that* branch of the family, you know, but he's quite nice."

I really didn't know anything about *that* branch of the family except some nasty rumors. Although I didn't care about Louis's lineage, I was sure I wouldn't like him. I am not attracted to most vampire men. In any case, I knew my mother wouldn't give up until I agreed. I gave in. "Sure, Ma, drinks will be fine."

A brilliant smile lit up my mother's face. Her mission accomplished, she quickly finished up her mineral water and announced that she was meeting friends in the East Village. After bestowing a quick kiss on both my cheeks, European style, she left. I must admit that my apartment felt empty once she had gone.

After a few hours of meditation and listening to Bach's Goldberg Variations, I fell into a deep sleep at dawn. When I finally heard the alarm—I must have hit the snooze button five or six times without regaining full consciousness—twilight was falling. I had less than an hour to get dressed and down to Twenty-third Street. I threw on a sweater and a pair of jeans. I didn't mind being rushed. Where there had once been a dull ache in my heart, I felt light and giddy from both adrenaline and optimism. I could be a great spy; I just knew it. Whatever J wanted me to do, I felt confident I could handle it. It wouldn't be long before I realized how self-deluded I was at that moment. But ignorance is bliss, and I never again felt so happy as I did that day. I never again slept so soundly or so long.

J was waiting for me in the conference room. A grin on my face, my footsteps light and quick, I burst through the door. Seeing his grim face felt like hitting a brick wall.

"Sit down, Miss Urban," he said flatly. I did.

"We have a lot of material to review. You will meet your target tomorrow, so you don't have much time to prepare." He avoided my eyes. I sought out his, but failed to make contact, so I stared at his strong jaw, noted the shadow of a beard beginning to show, watched the movement of his mouth. I began to imagine how those lips would feel tracing down the center of my naked back. A warm, shivery feeling chased up and down my spine where his lips left little kisses. . . .

"Miss Urban, when you contact us," he said roughly, stopping my sweet dreams, "you should use your code name, Hermes."

"Ah, the Greek god. The messenger. And what is yours?"

"Ringmaster."

"So you're calling the shots."

"Whatever. I don't pick the names, Miss Urban," he said. "Now, to get on with this. You represent a private collector of aboriginal art. The collector is real. The art is real. Bonaventure knows of the collection and very much wants to purchase items from it. The collector refuses to have direct contact with him. Bonaventure has tried. He has been turned down. Finally the collector has agreed to work through a middleman—you. This gives you entrée into Bonaventure's apartment. You have an appointment tomorrow at seven thirty P.M."

"What's the address?"

"It's in this file." He picked up a nine-by-twelve brown envelope and handed it to me. "In there is all you need to know about the collector and the art you are going to sell. Read it, memorize it, then destroy it. And by destroy I mean burn it." I slipped the envelope into my Louis Vuitton backpack. "You need to insinuate yourself into Bonaventure's life. That is where you can put your beauty and charm to use."

I finally managed to look him in the eyes. His held mine for a brief moment; then he deliberately looked away. It was enough. The chemistry was there. He knew it, and I knew it. I pulled my attention back to my coming assignment. "What am I supposed to do, exactly?" I asked.

"Your first task is to plant some listening devices inside Bonaventure's apartment. We haven't been able to pick up much from outside the building. We think he's jamming our directional mikes."

J handed me a small box. "The devices and the instructions about where to plant them, and how, are in here. Again, memorize your instructions, then destroy the paper and this container. Transport the bugs themselves in with your pocket change. Their cases look like dimes. The devices inside the case are much smaller." He handed me the small package. I dropped it into my backpack.

"Now, your second objective. We need you to get information on the recipients of Bonaventure's next big weapons delivery. We already know they belong to a terrorist cell operating in this area, somewhere near New York City. And we know they will pay him in diamonds. . . ."

"Ah, the Benny Polycarp connection," I said.

"You're very quick, Miss Urban. Yes, that is how your fellow operative will be connected to this mission. She will be called in to evaluate and appraise the payment. We've worked hard setting this operation up. You're the linchpin that holds it all together. You are going to be our means to identify the terrorists and stop them."

"What does 'stop them' mean?" I said. "Am I supposed to kill someone?"

"Probably not. You're not there to terminate anyone, just to get us information. The art deal gives Bonaventure the need for major cash, and fast. You might look at your role as a conveyer of knowledge. You plant the listening device. You pick up information on who is bringing the cash to Bonaventure, who is getting the weapons, and when the exchange will take place. Anything beyond that will be a bonus. Other members of our agency will prevent the terrorists from getting the weapons and arrest them. Maybe we will be able to turn one of them to our side and make him a double agent. We haven't had much success in infiltrating these groups. But that's not your job. Your job is to make sure we have enough data to interrupt the exchange and catch the buyers.

"As for Bonaventure himself, there will always be merchants of death like him. Frankly he is more useful to us alive than dead. We know his weaknesses, and through you, we hope to be able to control him."

"And what are his weaknesses?"

"Greed, for one. An obsessive personality, for another. He is a collector and he'll go to extraordinary lengths to obtain an item he wants. Don't make it too easy for him. The quest is part of what gives him pleasure. The art collection you represent has pieces he desperately wants to acquire. Some of them were used in New Guinea witchcraft rituals. Most people would find them repugnant, but Bonaventure likes that sort of thing. He also likes beautiful women, and that is another weakness you will need to exploit."

"Do I have to sleep with him?" I said, my voice hardening.

"What you do to get the information is up to you," J said, and looked at me as if to measure my reaction.

"Well, I won't have sex with him," I said, glaring at him. "I'm not a whore."

"I never implied you were, Miss Urban," he said more softly, almost kindly. "What you do in the course of the mission—what any of us do—we do in order to get the job done. I believe you will do whatever it takes. But how you win Bonaventure's confidence, how you capture his trust, to the extent he ever trusts anyone, will be your decision." He was still looking at me then, and a hot wind seemed to stir my blood. I was drawn to J as if a golden wire reached out from his soul and wound around my heart, reeling me in. Such feelings could lead only to hurt and pain, I knew. But at that moment I thought of nothing but of having his mouth cover mine. I wasn't thinking very clearly. No, that's not true: I wasn't thinking at all.

I leaned closer to J. He didn't draw back. "In other words, sex is a weapon I may choose to use. Or not." I could feel his breath touch my face. I knew his desire was rising up to answer mine. I expected him to kiss me. . . .

Instead a flicker of something like surprise crossed his face. He pulled back as if he had been burned. His eyes changed, becoming flat and angry. "Let me get something clear, Miss Urban. We will be working closely together, but *my* relationship with *all* Darkwing team members is the same. It's a professional one. I am your team leader. Nothing less, and certainly nothing more."

Liar, I thought to myself. *I know you feel the same pull I do.*

He stood up and pushed his chair back. "Furthermore, and I will not repeat this again"—he spit the words out—"what you are disgusts me. A whore would be more moral. You are a monster, not a woman. I know about the vampires' magnetism and the magical attraction that pulls humans to them so they can satisfy their lust for blood. You are depraved. All of you are nothing more than beasts. And no matter what your powers, I would never—do you hear me?—never so much as touch you."

Something snapped in me then. An emotional gate opened and white-hot anger poured through. He had rejected me as a woman, and more than that, he had demonized my entire race. His arrogance and his belief in his *human* superiority pushed me over the edge. I returned his words with ones of my own, hard as adamantine. "You are right, J. You are so, so right. I am *not* human. I *am* a monster." I paused for moment and slowly got to my feet. "I am a *vampire,*" I hissed. "You need to know exactly what that means." To his shock and amazement I pulled off my sweater and shimmied out of my jeans as fast as any quick-change artist. And then, having committed myself to what was about to happen, I let the transformation into my bat shape begin. . . .

A dark veil began to swirl around me, blurring the very air. I felt myself hover between two worlds before a jolt of energy surged through my blood. I grew taller, I saw my nails extend and become claws, I felt wings spring out from my back with a rustling like a death rattle from infinity. My white skin metamorphosed into a dark, soft pelt. I felt immeasurably strong; power surged through my veins as a laugh escaped my throat. I rose up then, above the floor, suspended in the air, a creature more beautiful than a bird, more terrifying than a bat, sleek and shining, a dark phantasmagoria, glistening with rainbow colors that broke forth from prismatic silver crescents clinging like water droplets to my fur. A glow surrounded me as I ascended. My head came close to the ceiling. As I extended my magnificent bat wings, they reached from wall to wall. When I spoke, I knew J could see my fangs.

"Look and fear me, human," I said in a voice of silk and flame.

J had moved away, his back pressed against the room's front wall. His face held a mixture of awe and terror. To his credit, he did not tremble or faint. Many had. Many had wept and pleaded. Many had voided their bowels as they sank down onto their knees in abject fear. J, unlike them, looked up at me with something like admiration.

"I didn't know," he whispered. "I had heard, but I didn't really know. You look like . . . you look like something, not a bat . . . an angel."

"A dark angel," I said with a voice that seduced and mesmerized. "I am the reality of myths and nightmares. I am ancient desires come alive to haunt you." And with that, as he stood spellbound and unable to move, I flew closer to him. I landed lightly on the floor before him. His eyes closed, then snapped open and looked deeply into mine, which were dark and fathomless, filled with melancholy. I leaned forward. My lips brushed his. He moaned. The man who had vowed never to touch me devoured my lips with an unmistakable hunger. I broke the kiss and moved my lips to his jaw. His eyes closed as I went lower and touched his neck, softly, gently with my teeth. I nipped yet did not bite. He stiffened but he didn't resist. Without total surrender, yet submitting, he offered himself to me. No human can resist a vampire's seduction.

At that moment, however, I pulled back, and I laughed a cruel hard laugh. He stood there as if frozen. He had guts; I'll say that for him. And now he understood in the very fibers of his being what I had: power.

Suffice it to say I then grabbed my clothes in my talons and managed to get myself through the door of the office and out into the lobby in front of the elevators. It was far from a graceful exit. Huge in my bat form, I had to squeeze through the door, and one wing got stuck on a hinge. I hurriedly tugged it free, swearing all the while. At least I didn't fall on my face. As soon as I slammed the door shut behind me, I changed back to human form in a blast of light, dressed nearly as quickly, fled to the stairs, not the elevator, and rushed down to the first floor. As I ran across the lobby and pushed through the heavy glass doors to the street, exhaustion and anxiety washed over me. I had made a mistake. I had shown myself, revealed my true being, and let J live. I hated him. Or did I? I felt confused about that. But what was done was done. Nevertheless, I had exposed too much.

There were sure to be repercussions when J reported this. Would the agency think me unstable and a threat to them? If J conveyed that I had threatened to bite him, I would probably be terminated with the same cold deliberation with which animal-control officers shoot a rabid dog. Even so, in practical terms, the agency probably wouldn't eliminate me until after this urgent mission was over. If I was the linchpin, then they couldn't replace me overnight. At least I had time to figure out what to do. Right now I was so angry and upset, I had to do something to calm down.

It was too late to shop, but I had the address of the salon where Benny got her Buff 'n' Glo. I hailed a taxi. The Middle Eastern driver took off like a rabbit. While he raced in and out of traffic, he continued a loud conversation on his cell phone. He was speaking Pashto, a language used by some Northern Afghanistan tribes. I had known Ahmad Shah Abdali of Kandahar, founder of the Durrani clan and invader of India back in the eighteenth century, and I had learned a powerful lesson in cunning from him. It was not a pleasant memory. The driver made some remarks about me into the cell phone, basically saying, "You should see the babe I just picked up; she's definitely fuckable." *Yeah, sure, in your dreams,* I thought. I repaid him in spades when I got out. I handed him a tip and said, in Pashto, something like, "You stink like a camel and my uncles would enjoy your tiny private part like a cocktail frank." He turned pale and pulled out into traffic so quickly that he nearly hit a bus.

I walked into the salon and lucked into an appointment. An hour later I emerged a new woman—one with a tan!

The night was young, and I felt good again. Screw J. I was an idiot for letting myself feel something for him. It just had been too long since I was involved with a man. Hell's bells, it had been years since I'd even dated. The loneliness, not to mention the horniness, was making me vulnerable. What I needed was some nice, no-strings-attached sex, just to take the edge off. Unfortunately I didn't have any "hot prospects"—Zoe's bloodless son Louis or Cormac were not even worthy of a second thought. I certainly wasn't about to go to a bar and try to get picked up. That wasn't my style. I had to get myself back under control and find something to keep myself busy. The first thing that popped into my head was to take a cab to Bonaventure's address at Park Avenue and Seventy-fourth Street and case the joint, so to speak. It would be a damned good idea to find out what I would be walking into tomorrow.

Bonaventure's place looked like all the other Park Avenue solid-stone apartment buildings whose maroon awnings and liveried doormen scream *money*. I exited the cab and I walked past Bonaventure's building without pausing. I saw enough with a quick look. The building was narrow, and I figured it contained one apartment per floor. Glancing through the doors I could see a small jewel box of a lobby, sparkling with lots of gilt and crystal chandeliers. There was a graceful Louis XIV desk holding a phone. At the far side of the room was a single elevator. Near the front door stood a doorman in a fancy gray uniform. An older man, he was busy on a cell phone. I didn't want to draw attention to myself, so I quickly walked to the corner and crossed the avenue. I wandered one block west to Madison, hoping to find a late night Korean deli. Mostly I was thirsty, not particularly hungry, and I needed a bottle of water. I was also much too wound up to go home.

Like many other women, I have a habit of surreptitiously looking at my reflection in shop windows while I'm walking. There is a widely held old-wives' tale that a vampire doesn't have a mirror image. That's just misinformation. It is ghosts that don't reflect, being just ectoplasm and spirit. Ergo no body, no reflection. We vampires, on the other hand, are solid as flesh and blood. We *are* flesh and blood. I would have had a hell of a time putting on makeup for the past five hundred years if I couldn't see myself. I need a mirror when I do my hair and makeup. And beyond the vanity factor, I surely would have been nailed, or more accurately, *staked,* long ago if I passed by a looking glass and nothing was there. But I applaud the notion that most people—even the so-called experts—believe that vampires are so without substance or so magical that we can't be seen in a mirror. It's saved my ass more than once.

Right now I was so delighted with my tan that I was positively preening as I walked down Madison. Whenever there was a mirrored back to a window display and I got a clear view of myself, it was a wow. I stopped in front of a jewelry store with a full-length one behind the display. I couldn't get over how good I looked— healthy, perpetual pallor gone. I no longer fit Sir John Suckling's lines, "Why so pale and wan, fond lover, prithee, why so pale?" I radiated outdoorsy good health.

No doubt that was why I was so preoccupied that I didn't notice the man coming up behind me until it was too late.

CHAPTER 4

What looks like an appealing offer may not be.
                    —A fortune cookie's fortune

A gun barrel poked me hard in the middle of my back. I froze. A strong hand gripped my upper arm and pulled me against a hard-muscled body. Inches from my ear a low voice said, "Stay away from Bonaventure. He's mine."

I stood rigid and unmoving. My heart was pounding. I tried to keep my voice from shaking. "I don't know what you're talking about."

"Yes, you do. I've been following you. You're one of J's people."

Adrenaline was pounding through my veins. I felt every inch of the man's powerful chest against my back, and suddenly I realized I wasn't frightened. What I felt was excitement. This was no mugger. I figured he was another spy, albeit from a rival country or agency. Suddenly I felt exquisitely alive, all my perceptions heightened. I looked up at my reflection in the jewelry store window and recognized the man with the gun—it was black watch cap, blond ponytail! He *had* been following me on the subway platform. I stared at him arrogantly in the glass and said with no fear in my voice, "If I'm one of J's people, who are you?"

"Not one of J's people. Let's leave it at that," the man answered. He stared back at my reflection.

Suddenly the whole thing struck me as absurd. I wasn't a career spy. If anything I was a rookie spy who'd made a mess of everything my first day on the job. Maybe I'd risk running away from the whole deal and change identities again. Despite the recruiter's warning, I bet that I could. On the other hand, maybe, just maybe, I could redeem myself from my earlier faux pas. It might be fun to see if I could be a real spy by finding out who the blond ponytail really was.

Unlike me, though, this guy was dead serious, and he was really full of himself. He sounded like a bad movie. But he certainly was good-looking, and his well-muscled body was like steel. Ripples of anticipation started low in my belly. Blond Ponytail had been playing games with me. Now I was going to play games with him—even though I hadn't made up my mind what kind of game it might be.

"Well," I said, lightening my tone, "that's the most original pickup line I've ever heard." We stared at each other's reflections.

Unexpectedly the man laughed. The hard poking in my back disappeared, although he still held my arm so firmly it hurt as he spun me around to face him. In intimate proximity, I could see him clearly in the store's light. He smiled at me. If Brad Pitt were taller, he could have been this guy's twin. My heart skipped a beat. I guessed he was in his thirties, his face unwrinkled except for a few lines on his high forehead. His eyes were hooded—bedroom eyes, I'd call them. His brows were dark and straight. But it was his lips that were really sexy. The bottom lip was full and almost pouting. The more I looked, the more my thoughts lingered. This guy was hot. I gave myself a mental slap. *And he could be dangerous,* my rational mind said. *He followed you. He scared you. Find out who he is and stop thinking like a trollop,* I reminded myself.

In fact, my conscious mind was being sabotaged by the smell of leather and soap, fresh-washed hair and citrus aftershave. And underlying those aromas was an animal muskiness, a scent that was unmistakably male. He still wore his distressed-leather bomber jacket, and jeans that fit him like a second skin. I'd wager big money he wasn't wearing underwear. His long blond hair remained tied back in a ponytail, but the watch cap was gone. It might be unwise, but I was attracted to his physical appearance. Now that I was reasonably sure he was a "colleague" of some sort, I was letting go of my former fears completely.

And while I was looking at him, he was looking at me as if he could eat me up like ice cream, one lick at a time. The air fairly buzzed with the instant attraction between us. It must be the adrenaline, I thought, and my vulnerable state.

A horn beeped on Madison Avenue. The light changed and traffic roared past. But suddenly everything seemed to stop for me. I looked into his eyes. Before I knew what was happening, he pulled me closer and kissed me while we stood right there on the sidewalk. His lips, soft but demanding, felt as good as they looked. The world tilted, my head spun, desire rocketed right up my spine. But when I got over the surprise, I pushed him away and said, "Hey! You followed me, you stuck a gun in my back, and you threatened me. If you wanted to meet me, you could have just asked me for my phone number. You want to introduce yourself? And then do you feel like telling me what the hell is going on?"

"Darius," he said. "You can call me Darius. Maybe I handled this all wrong."

"You mean acting like a stalker or a mugger wasn't the best way to meet a woman?"

"Look, we need to talk. Let's go somewhere." He didn't ask; he just told me. That pissed me off.

"Why should I talk to you? Because you have a gun? Or because you kissed me?" I refused to move an inch.

Darius gave me a look of exasperation. "Look, I'm sorry. All right? I know an all-night Chinese restaurant near here. I'd like to get off the street and someplace more private."

Before I answered, he tightened his hold on my arm and was escorting me down the block. "What the hell do you think you're doing!" I said, and was pulling back when he put his lips near my ear and whispered, "Please. I need to get out of here. You do too. It's not safe. Come on, and hurry." After that I went along without a fuss. He never let go of my arm, but his touch was gentler. We walked a few blocks east and south to Peking Won King. We stepped into a harshly lit room and slid into a booth. We were the only customers in the place. Darius sat opposite me, positioning himself so he could watch the door. The waiter came over. Darius ordered a pot of green tea.

"Now talk," he said.

"Me? You wanted to talk, so go ahead, talk. Tell me why I shouldn't get up and walk out of here right now," I said, my voice steady and controlled, but my insides doing somersaults.

Looking like a high school teacher whose pupil had just mouthed off in class, Darius opened his mouth to answer, then stopped as if he were considering what to say. For a moment he watched me. I returned his stare without flinching. "Okay, you're right. It's my party," he said at last. "Let me tell you what I know and what I think.

"Twice I've followed you when I was watching to see who J was running. The grapevine says he's after Bonaventure. Well, Bonaventure's mine. And beyond that, there are rumors he's handling vampires."

My heart did a flip as I made sure to keep a poker face and hide my inner trepidation. I rolled my eyes as if to say he had a screw loose, and I said, "Vampires? You have got to be kidding. Vampires aren't real."

Darius pushed a loose strand of hair from his face as he glanced away from me, collecting his thoughts again. Then he came back to my eyes with his, his voice low, as if he didn't want to be overheard—although there was no one around, not even the waiter. "Look, maybe you don't believe in them, but let me tell you, vampires do exist. They are real, and they're right here in New York. They walk the same streets you and I do. They sit next to us on the subway. And in the dark of night they kill innocent people just to satisfy their need for blood. If J has started using them, I want to know about it. I need to know."

"So you thought I was a vampire?" I tried to sound mocking at the absurdity of his words.

"Yes. No. I mean I did, but I wasn't sure." Darius sounded frustrated. "You know, I thought you might be when I first saw you. You sort of had the look. And I couldn't find out much about you from your neighbors besides your name, and some of them didn't even know that."

"You were asking my neighbors about me? What the hell? You have some damned nerve. You also sound nuts. You know, I think I'd better get out of here." I stood up and started out of the booth. His hand came down on my arm like a vise.

I glared at it and then at him. "Let go of me or I'm going to start screaming my head off," I said.

"Wait. Let me explain. Give me a chance to finish, will you?" His voice was pleading, his face open and sincere.

I didn't move. "Why should I?" I said.

"I might know things you should know. About Bonaventure. About your boss. About what you're mixed up in."

I looked into his eyes, which seemed to see right into my mind. They were nice eyes, in a handsome face. The hand on my arm held firm, but he was taking care not to hurt me. In fact, his hand felt warm and good. Finally I sat back down.

"You've got one more chance to convince me you're not a lunatic," I said.

"Listen, about the vampire thing," he said. "I tell you they're real, and for a couple of reasons I wasn't sure about you. Then you went to that spa. You came out looking as if you just flew in from the Caribbean. Vampires can't handle the light of tanning beds. They'd end up dust bunnies blowing in the wind. That did it for me. I'm convinced you're not one of them."

Damn, this guy is clueless, I thought. *He's never heard of self-tanner? Where's he been?* One thing I'd bet on—he hadn't been around women in a while, that was for sure. *So thank you, Benny,* I thought. *You just saved my ass.* I said in a nasty tone, "Gee, thanks for the vote of confidence. By the way, have you been living outside the U.S.?"

He look at me suspiciously. "Who told you that? Why do you want to know?

"Idle curiosity," I said. "Let's say you're a little short on the social graces."

He laughed without mirth and said, "Yeah, where I've been there wasn't a lot of polite conversation going on." A darkness passed over his face, and I felt a profound sadness emanating from him. Silence fell between us. I fiddled with my napkin. He looked down at the table. He sighed and continued talking with pain audible in his voice. "Look, Daphne Urban, I saw you come out of J's office yesterday. I spent some of today asking around about you. You're pretty much a mystery woman. Then again this evening you were back at the Flatiron Building, so I assume you were meeting with J again. I hung around and followed you when you came out. You ended up at Bonaventure's. It stands to reason you are working for J and the agency, and you're connected to their plans for Bonaventure. You know, you're messing with the world's biggest arms dealer." His voice took on an edge. "And lady, you're stepping on my toes. Let me give you a friendly warning. You're in way over your head. J's people don't have the brains or the balls to deal with Bonaventure. And a woman sure as hell can't cut it in this business." He growled that last bit.

I didn't like his tone of voice, and my own was equally hostile when I said, "Look, you Neanderthal. I don't know who you are, but you *think* you know who I am. You don't, and you have about ten seconds to tell me why I should sit here any longer. After that I'm leaving. And I mean it."

He started talking fast. "Look, Daphne, J and I go back a long way. How well do you know him? You know, he has a habit of using people and not giving a damn if they get killed or not."

"How well do *you* know J?" I asked, using what I call "the Jewish defense" of answering a question with a question. I had a very good teacher in Kiev long ago.

"So you admit you do know him," Darius countered.

"Granted. Though 'know' is too strong a word."

"Okay, you're working for him, then."

"Well, who exactly are you working for? And what do you really want from me?"

He looked at me for a hard moment. Suddenly I felt a sexual tingle that raised the stakes here. Darius was clearly sizing me up. Something was going on below the surface of conversation. The air was zinging with electricity. It was buzzing like the fluorescent light over my head. Darius started talking again. "I guess we should stop tap-dancing around. I work for a U.S. intelligence agency—but not the same one as J. And he's not going to mess up my operation again."

"And that operation is Bonaventure?"

"Bonaventure."

"Well, Houston, we have a problem," I said.

At that point the waiter showed up with tea and asked to take our order. I wasn't hungry, but it would be smart to eat something. Another old-wives' tale is that vampires only drink blood. I need to eat my veggies same as anyone else. Without fiber I'd be in some bind, pardon my pun. "Buddha's Delight," I said.

"Steamed shrimp and vegetables, and O-O soup. You want soup?" he asked me.

"No, thanks," I said.

"That's it," he said to the waiter.

The waiter repeated back our order without writing anything down, gathered up our menus, and left.

"You a vegetarian?" Darius asked me.

I was sipping some water and choked. "Sorry, went down the wrong pipe." I managed to get the words out between coughs. When I could speak normally again, I said, "I avoid eating anything with a face." *Biting anyone with a face is a different story altogether,* I thought. "And you? Any dietary aberrations?"

"I try to eat 'clean' since I'm working out." *That explains the hard body,* I mentally noted. "But I confess to having a weakness for Ben and Jerry's ice cream. My favorite flavor is Cherry Garcia."

"I'm with you on the ice cream," I said. "My favorite Ben and Jerry's is Phish Food. I like anything with gooey marshmallow and chocolate and caramel." I figured I'd try to find out something about this guy's past. "By the way, are you a Dead head? You know, Cherry Garcia and all," I asked.

"No." He laughed. "They were a little before my time. I just like the ice cream. When it comes to the music of my misspent youth, I was into Nirvana and grunge rock. But that was long ago and far away. Like I said, where I've been there hasn't been much chance to listen to pop music. When I was lucky, I could find some classical stuff on the radio. I guess Nirvana was the last group I liked enough to buy every CD they made."

"As for Nirvana, me too," I agreed. "I've always had this attraction to the doomed, tormented type of guy with the soul of a poet. When Kurt Cobain killed himself, I felt like I'd seen it all before," I said as my thoughts drifted to the past. *Get hold of yourself, girl,* I reminded myself. *You're on the job here. Make polite conversation and see what you can find out.* So I went on: "I've also listened to Emmylou Harris for years. Annie Lennox, too, and Johnette Napolitano; you know, her group was Concrete Blonde. Oh, yeah, for a long time in the nineties I was crazy about a group called October Project."

"You're kidding," he said, his face lighting up and looking a lot younger. "Me too. Favorite song?"

"'Ariel.' You ever go to any of their concerts? They had a Northeast tour in the mid-nineties. Johnette also did a concert with the Talking Heads here in New York; I think it was in 1996 or 1997. Were you in the city then?"

"No," was all he said.

"Where were you living?" I pressed.

"Here and there. I moved around a lot," he answered vaguely. Then he looked at me again, holding me with his gaze. My stomach gave a little squeeze. "You know, you're a beautiful woman. All chiaroscuro shadows playing in your face, your hair, your eyes. You've got the most amazing eyes," he said. "Do you mind me asking if you're in a relationship?"

Being rejected by J had hurt more than I wanted to

admit. Now Darius's words poured over me like honey. He could have been handing me a line, but it felt good anyway. "Not right now," I said. "I haven't been seeing anyone special lately. I'm still getting over a bad breakup. What about you? Married?"

"No. I'm single. I'm not with anybody. My job keeps me tied up a lot and doesn't give me time for a relationship."

"And what's your job exactly?"

"Classified," he answered, and gave me a lopsided grin. "Same as yours."

"So we're both, shall we say, spies?"

"Some people might say that."

I tried a different tactic. I looked down at the place mat, which was a chart of Chinese astrology. "What year were you born?" I asked.

"Nineteen seventy-four," he answered, and I wondered if that was the truth.

"So that makes you how old?" I asked quickly.

"Old enough," he said.

I was getting nowhere. I found 1974 on the place mat. "Ah, the Tiger." I read aloud, *"'The Tiger is highly regarded in China with his almost magical powers to keep thieves and ghosts at bay. A Tiger person is born to command and not to obey. Tigers are charismatic and dynamic. They are courageous and respected even by those who oppose them. Tigers are fighters and stand up for what they think is right. Best matches: Horse, Dog, Dragon. Beware the Monkey.'"*

"And what year were you born?" Darius asked as he started reading the place mat, too.

"It's impolite for a gentleman to ask a lady her weight or her age," I said as I quickly scanned the mat. I tried to remember how old I was on my latest ID. I was about to choose the year of the Dragon. Meanwhile I knew exactly what astrological animal I'd be if I used my real birthday.

No doubt about it; I was the Monkey. If I believed in signs, that one would set off alarm bells.

Fortunately the silent waiter reappeared and wordlessly plopped down Darius's bowl, obscuring the place mat below.

Saved by O-O soup, I thought.

"Let's get back to J," he said.

"Why?" I asked.

"I think you're being set up," he said.

"Why do you say that?" I asked, feeling a little nervous. It's true I had mixed feelings about J. Maybe I was being thrown to the wolves. He said he hated vampires. He acted like a real bastard too. Like all women scorned, I was ready to trash the scorner. "Do you know J well?"

"I wouldn't say *well*. But I've butted heads with that SOB more than once."

"Doesn't sound like you like him."

"I'm not a fan. Why do you want to know?"

The rules were that I wasn't supposed to discuss my job with anyone. But maybe I should just get out of this whole mess while I could. More information about what was really going on would help. Darius could be an important source of information for me. I intended to survive, and Darius was right; I didn't know if I could trust J. I didn't know if I could trust Darius either, but he wasn't threatening to kill me if I didn't work for him. I had some deep-seated resentment about the coercion the agency had used to recruit me. So I decided to answer with most of the truth. "I do work for J. And to be frank, I've already had a run-in with him. Do you think he has a problem working with women?"

"I don't know about that. I do know he's ex-military. Special Forces. Has a reputation as a by-the-book kind of guy. To quote Churchill, 'He has all the virtues I dislike and none of the vices I admire.'" Darius looked at me, studying my reactions. "He's got no sense of humor, but he's not a bad guy, from what I hear. Fair. Unless you cross him. So did you cross him?"

Uh oh, I thought. "In a manner of speaking," I said.

"Well, from what I've heard, there are no second chances if someone screws up. At least, that's his reputation. He's a real hard-ass. I never liked the guy. Nothing personal. Some of his people were friends of mine. They ended up dead. I know what I'm talking about, Daphne. Part of the problem isn't J himself. Officially our agencies don't communicate. The upshot is we duplicate efforts and get in each other's way, like on this Bonaventure thing."

"Yeah, the Bonaventure thing. Look, Darius. I can't get out of this assignment. But maybe I can rub your back, if you rub mine." The words were out of my mouth before I could stop them. All I meant was that I was a rookie and could use all the help I could get. The sexual innuendo had brought a smile to Darius's face.

"You know, that sounds like a good idea. What do you have in mind?" I felt his foot touch mine under the table. I could have pulled away and ended the overture. Instead I put the toe of my boot behind his calf and rubbed. Our eyes met. Things were starting to heat up, and I should have been keeping my mind on business.

"Well, what do you know about why Bonaventure's in New York?" I asked bluntly.

"Daphne, no offense, but he's out of your league. Bonaventure is a wicked dude. He doesn't have a conscience. He'll sell weapons to anyone who has the money, no matter what they plan to do with them. And he's a Russian. I'm not putting the Russian people down, but Bonaventure is a Soviet-style Russian. Ruthless. Eliminates anyone who gets in his way. Loves money above all things. A true VBM."

"VBM?"

Darius laughed without humor, "A Very Bad Man."

"That's really cute, Darius. But what's your interest in him?"

"Sorry, Daphne. That's classified, too. And yours?"

"Ditto."

"All right," Darius said between mouthfuls of soup, "assuming we both are after the same thing, how can we each get what we want?" Again there was a double entendre. He put down his spoon, reached out, and took my hand. He started playing with my fingers. Sensation ran along my skin and a tingling shot up my arm. I pulled my hand away.

"Why should I trust you, Darius? Why would you want to work with me, and what am I going to get out of it? And right now, can you prove to me we're working on the same side?"

"Proof? Daphne, in this business there is no proof except a shared history: people you've trained with and people who watched your back when you needed them to. When you don't have a common past, you have to take others at face value because you trust your instincts. That's a risk, but as you know, this business is all about risk. You find informants. You get information. You use your gut to weigh whether it's reliable or not when you can't verify it from another source. I'm following my instincts with you. But here . . ." He went into a pocket inside his coat. He pulled out a wallet and flipped it open. He threw it on the table in front of me. "That's my identity card. No, it doesn't say, 'Darius della Chiesa, spy.' What does it say, Daphne?"

I picked the wallet up. On one side of the billfold I saw a New York State driver's license. It listed a Queens address. Darius's birthday was February 8, 1974. Damn, he was telling the truth about that. On the other side of the fold was a government ID card. The agency was the Department of the Interior. His position was "Exhibit Specialist." Shit, that sounded familiar. That was what my cover was. Bureaucrats have absolutely no imagination.

"I've seen plenty of fake IDs, Darius. This means nothing," I said.

"That's the point. Are they real?" He picked up his wallet and put it back in his pocket. "It comes down to instinct, Daphne. And risk. Weigh them. Look at me. What do you want to do? You can walk out of here right now. I won't stop you. But I think we can help each other. Do you trust J? What do your instincts tell you about him? What is your gut saying about me?" His words came fast; he didn't let go of my eyes with his. His face looked open, honest, totally sincere. If he were lying, he was a master at it. I examined my feelings and let my antenna pick up every vibe he was sending out. He hadn't told me much. He had been evasive. But my bullshit meter wasn't registering anything. I believed him. And I felt we were at a turning point. We could be allies . . . or enemies.

I made my decision. "Look, Darius. I have a meeting with Bonaventure tomorrow night. You want to meet up afterward? I'll be in a better position to see if we can collaborate after I know more." As I looked at Darius, my pulse sped up. I was losing control of my hungers. My physical needs had become a tide pulsing through my blood. I was rushing toward the dark side. The long resisted temptation of intimacy with a stranger, of overpowering him and drinking from him, started to drown out my reason. Right now the only position I wanted to be in with Darius was under him. Or on top. I'd enjoy him either way.

He was looking at me with frank sexual desire. An understanding passed between us. He wanted me too. Our feelings bypassed words. It wasn't an unusual thing. Men and women meet in bars, they have a few drinks, and they go home together for a night of pleasure, no strings, no commitment. It happens all the time. I really had nothing to lose except my growing sexual frustration. I certainly had nothing to fear.

At that moment the waiter showed up with our order and we broke eye contact. We passed the rest of the meal making small talk about the food. We compared Chinese and Japanese cuisines. He talked a bit about restaurants in Thailand. I admitted I spent time in Kyoto. All the while my foot was going up and down behind his leg. He asked if I wanted a taste of his dish. I nodded. He asked for my chopsticks, and I handed them to him. He delicately picked up a shrimp and brought it to my lips. I steadied his hand with mine as I took it into my mouth. The sensations when we touched spoke volumes.

"I'm ready to leave," he said. "What about you?"

"I'm ready too." The meaning behind my words couldn't have been clearer.

Darius insisted on hailing a cab and taking me home. I didn't argue. I insisted he come up for nightcap. He didn't argue. As soon as we stepped into the elevator and the doors slid closed, I turned toward him, wrapping my arms around his neck. He backed me up against the elevator wall, his lips coming down hard on mine. All thoughts stopped, my mind spinning off into a welcoming darkness of pure sensation as our bodies collided. His hand went up under my blouse, found my nipple, and stroked it with his thumb. I groaned. We could have slid down the wall right then onto the elevator floor, but I lived on only the tenth floor. The car stopped and the doors parted. I opened my eyes, blinked, grabbed his hand, and pulled him into the hall. We got to my apartment door without detouring into another kiss as I fumbled through my bag for my keys. Darius stood behind me, pressing his body into mine, his dick firm against my ass. I managed to unlock the door, and we just about fell together into the dark hall. I didn't turn on the light.

Darius pulled up my sweater and trailed kisses down my chest, the stubble on his cheeks rough against my breasts. My head went back against the wall and I made a soft, happy moan.

His lips touched my stomach above the waistband of my jeans. His hands were around my waist; then they were lifting me. He swung me into his arms. The living room held the soft illumination of the city lights, enough to show Darius where the sofa was. He carried me there. He put me down gently. I half sat up and struggled out of my coat, ripped off my sweater, and threw them both on the floor. Darius slid out of his leather jacket, his eyes fixed on me.

With my sharp night vision, I could see him clearly. I took in every tempting inch as he peeled off a tight-fitting T-shirt. He undid his jeans and stepped out of them. No underwear. I had guessed that earlier and wasn't disappointed to find out I was right. I definitely wasn't disappointed with Darius. I couldn't wait to touch him.

He knelt next to the sofa and removed my boots. Then he undid the button of my jeans and carefully pulled them down. They went on the pile. My black lace panties joined them in an instant.

"Are you comfortable?" he asked. I was half reclining with my back propped against a sofa cushion, looking down at his face.

"I couldn't be better," I murmured, and meant it.

"Yes you could," he said with meaning, and spread my thighs apart with his hands. Next thing I knew his tongue was running over me, tasting me and making my stomach clench and my breath come in gasps. With sensations going to my brain like the bubbles of fine champagne, a sweet dizziness took me in spiraling circles upward. He added little nibbles to his tonguing and I just about lost my mind. I could not wait any longer. The yearning and frustrated longing of all the years rushed forward and demanded to be satisfied right now.

"Please fuck me," I moaned, writhing beneath him.

"I want you to come first," he said.

"No, please, I need you in me now," I pleaded.

He stood up. He picked up his jeans and pulled out a condom from a pocket. He put the rubber on and then found my sweet spot with the head of his penis, teasing me for a moment by rubbing against my clitoris before plunging inside me.

"Oh!" I said, pain and pleasure combining as I remembered what it felt like to be with a man.

"Ohhhh," he said. "You are so hot, so good," he whispered. He leaned down and kissed me as he buried himself deep within me. I could taste myself on his lips. I was rushing off into an oblivion of no thought, where everything was feeling. I had to rein myself in. If I lost myself completely I could bite him before I realized what I had done. Yet oddly, so far with Darius I felt no urge to drink from him. No moonlight lit up his neck. No dark urges overwhelmed me. I just felt consumed with the joy of this eager, handsome man taking me with all his strength to the top of the mountain and higher, ever higher toward the stars.

Now I kept my eyes open and watched the ecstasy on his face as we moved together in perfect rhythm. I pushed hard against him until he buried himself deep inside me over and over again. He was positively incandescent, glowing with passion. He pulled out. "What—" I started to say.

"Shh," he said, cutting me off. His powerful hands

went behind my knees and pushed my thighs up against my sides. The movement opened me wide, exposing my most private self to his steady gaze. He leaned forward and brushed my clitoris with his tongue. I groaned.

"Oh, my impatient girl," he said as he stood up again. "I have more pleasure in store for you."

He slowly, tantalizingly pushed his cock into me, farther and farther. With my knees drawn up, he was able to go incredibly deep, his throbbing dick buried inside me. My pleasure soared. I was coming to a climax quickly.

"Now," I said. "Come now."

He increased his pace, pounded his body against mine, and I came as if red-hot sparks from a raging fire rained down on my soul. As I was coming, he came with a deep satisfied groan, and for those moments we were joined as one in the eternal dance. Our beings merged and the other became the self. We were somewhere together, far away from the place we had begun.

Then reality—the dark room, the cool air—came back. He was sweaty on top of me, but he was careful to hold most of his weight up with one muscular arm so as not to crush me. With his other hand, with strong, smooth fingers, he pushed my damp hair back from my cheek, and said, "You are so beautiful." He kissed me tenderly on the cheek, and with that he said, "Thank you."

"Thank you too," I said. Suddenly my eyes were bright with tears in the dim light. One spilled over and ran down my cheek. I had been alone for so many years, with no man telling me I was beautiful and with no healthy release for all the passions locked up within me. In the deepest recesses of my heart I had secretly feared I might never feel myself aroused by a man again or have another lover. "It's been a long, long time," I said to Darius.

"I guessed it might be," he said, and leaned down to kiss away my tear.

He might have guessed I hadn't made love in a while. But in his wildest dreams he never could have figured out how long. Totaling up the decades and all those celibate years, it had been nearly two centuries. And what would he have thought if he knew George Gordon, Lord Byron, had been my last lover? George, wild, intemperate George, was a hard act to follow. George had been all angles, all hardness—sinewy legs and long strong fingers that teased and stroked until I screamed. Thin to the point of emaciation, he was far from muscular, his narrow chest crisscrossed by the terrible scars of a lashing.

I will never forget the urgency of his lovemaking. Even as he took me, he seemed in a hurry, as if his time were running out. And it was. He was sometimes rough. He purposely hurt me just a little, just to increase my desire. Yet always a gentleman, Byron insisted on satisfying me with his hands after he finished first. We had never climaxed together. That simultaneity is a rare gift, and Darius had given it to me. I was satisfied. I was content—for the moment.

Darius sat up and leaned his head back, closing his eyes. I lay there listening to him breathe, neither of us saying a word until Darius blurted out, "Maybe we shouldn't have done this."

I felt as if cold water had been splashed on me. "What do you mean?" I had just been thinking that we should be doing "this" again, preferably as soon as possible.

"It can complicate things if we're planning to work together. It will be distracting. Bonaventure is dangerous. If I start worrying about you getting hurt—"

I cut him off. "I can take care of myself."

"Yeah, right," he said with sarcasm dripping from his words. "Look, you're a woman, and—"

My words fairly exploded from me. "*You* look, Darius. You don't know me or anything about me. I'm a woman, all right, and I can handle myself just fine. I have for nearly five hun—" I stopped myself just in time. "For many years. If I couldn't, J wouldn't have sent me on the assignment." I reached over to the pile of clothes and found my sweater. I angrily yanked it on. I was reaching down for my panties when Darius went to grab for his T-shirt. Our hands touched. He squeezed my fingers gently, then let them go.

"I didn't mean to put you down. I'm sorry," he said. "And I don't want to ruin this night." He picked up his shirt and pulled it on over his head. He leaned back, staying nude from the waist down. "And, you're right. I had no basis for what I said." I looked at his muscular abs, hard thighs, and spent cock, and he knew I was staring. He started talking again, watching me watching him. He spoke soft and low. "I'm just having doubts that we should keep doing this while we're on this mission. Wanting to fuck you all the time would make it really hard for *me* to concentrate. And Daphne, if it's always this good, I would want to fuck you every chance I had," he said with a smile in his voice.

Suddenly I wasn't at all mad. I felt happy and very naughty. "Darius, let me show you how good it's *always* going to be." I moved toward him and gently touched his cock, making it stir beneath my hand.

Darius groaned. "Daphne, didn't I satisfy you?" he asked.

"Yes," I said. I leaned toward him and tongued his ear. "But the night is young, and as you noticed, I had been waiting a long time for what we just did. So I'm being a greedy girl and asking for more."

"And when do you want more?" he said, taking me in his arms.

"How soon can you handle it?" I said as our lips touched.

"How's thirty minutes or so?" he murmured.

"Let me see if I can convince you to make it fifteen," I whispered playfully as I leaned down to kiss his belly, and listened to him moan as I began to lower my lips toward his cock.

"Fifteen it is," he sighed.

It was around dawn when we made love for a third time. After that Darius yawned and said he'd better get going. He left his cell phone number and told me to call after I finished up with Bonaventure that evening. We decided to meet on the steps in front of the Metropolitan Museum, which was within walking distance of Bonaventure's place.

I was sore but satisfied. After Darius left, I moved a tall bookcase away from the wall, unlocked a hidden door, and entered a small room. There I climbed into my coffin. Within moments I had tumbled into that world of dreams that lies across the boundary between existence and death. I saw a firefly swept away on a blue wind. I saw Byron walking far in the distance, climbing a green hill. He looked young and boyish. He stopped and turned around, waving at me, smiling, and as I slept, I am quite sure I was smiling too.

CHAPTER 5

Let they love in kisses rain
on my lips and eyelids pale.
　　　"The Indian Serenade" by Percy Bysshe Shelley

When I woke it was my morning, the start of an early winter evening for everyone else. I sat up languidly, pushing my hair back from my face. A strange unease possessed me. I felt as if I had either ended or just begun a chapter of my life. I didn't know how to tell the difference. There cannot be a beginning without an ending. My self-imposed celibacy was over. Would I put my memories of old love away in some recessed part of my mind like flowers pressed between the pages of a book? What in my life had begun? Had I found merely a night of desire, now over? On one level I hoped not. My senses, now reawakened, wanted more of him. On another level, I had wished for a fling with no deep emotions or commitments attached. In my circumstances, as both a vampire and a spy, an intimate relationship with Darius would be dangerous for us both.

My answer to my questioning mind was simply not to think about it. My meeting with Bonaventure was just hours away. I assembled the information I had picked up from J the day before on my dining room table and sat down with a steaming cup of black coffee. I had to become familiar with the eavesdropping devices that J had given me. That wouldn't take long. More difficult was internalizing the information about the art collection and its owner. My mind began curling around the problems ahead like a snake around a stick.

How could I not only represent an art collector I had never met, but then negotiate the sale of art I had never seen? I didn't think much of J's so-called plan. His directions seemed loose and careless, hastily contrived and just as hastily thrown together. I suppose if the intelligence about the arms deal was recent and extremely urgent, it hadn't afforded J, or whoever masterminded this scheme, the luxury of time.

In my papers it said the collector's name was Douglas Schneibel. A Soho address and phone number were also listed. J said the man was real. He said the items Bonaventure wished to acquire were also genuine. I debated contacting Schneibel for about two minutes before I picked up the phone and made the call. I figured I had already broken the rules—hell, I had smashed them—in the scene with J and then my indiscretions with Darius, so I might as well break a few more.

A man answered, his voice carrying a heavy German accent. "Hello?"

"Mr. Schneibel?" I asked.

"Ya, who isssst this?"

"My name is Daphne Urban. I work with . . . um . . . with J. He . . . well, he asked me to act as your agent in the sale of part of your New Guinea collection. I'm making the contact this evening. Is it at all possible that I could meet with you first so I can see the pieces the buyer wishes to acquire?"

There was a long silence. I thought the man had hung up. Then he said slowly, "I ssssuppose you sssshould." His Ss seemed to draw out in a hiss. "I sssshould have known you would want to examine the collection. When do you want to come?"

I didn't have much time before my meeting with Bonaventure. The subway downtown would be quicker than a cab, but it would still take me a good half hour just to get there. I calculated quickly. "Would six be okay? It would give us an hour together before I have to leave."

"Asss you wissssh. I assume you have the street address. I am on the third floor. No buzzer downstairs. I watch for you. Stand in front of the entry door and look up."

"All right. At six, then."

"Yessss," he hissed, and then the phone went silent.

My next phone call was to Bonaventure to confirm our appointment. He didn't answer, of course. Someone—a woman, I assume a servant—did. Russian accent this time. Yes, I was expected at seven-thirty that evening. The doorman would announce me, she said, and hung up abruptly. I always confirm appointments. I learned that elementary rule in my first century of life after I appeared one too many times at a shop to discover the merchant had left for the day or met with a trader, only to find he'd already sold the object of my quest. Fool me once, shame on you. Fool me twice, shame on me.

My Prada boots with their four-inch heels were not made for walking. However, I was supposed to be a sophisticated art agent, so sneakers were out. I wore a slim suede skirt in loden green and a white cashmere sweater accented by a thin black belt. I topped the outfit off with a wool Davos coat made in Austria that I had ordered from the Gorsuch catalog. My hair was pulled back severely into a chignon; I added to my ears tasteful gold loops accented by diamond teardrops. I wore my favorite leopard head ring, of course. I tucked a small black Bosca handbag under my arm and also carried a black Bosca briefcase, which should be suitably impressive, as it was handcrafted in premium-grade Italian leather.

I believed that costume was essential when playing a part. For most of my life I had to pretend to be someone other than I was: I was a merchant's young widow in medieval Florence; I posed as an Amsterdam trader's daughter in the seventeenth century, a Swiss herbalist in the eighteenth, a lady in waiting in Empress Josephine's court. I was Byron's earthy Greek a half century later, then, in the uprising of Easter 1916, I was a fiery Irish revolutionary in Dublin and a friend of W. B. Yeats. I had been a spiritual seeker in India; later I transformed into a wanderer—some said a witch—through the Caucasus Mountains and into Afghanistan. I had so many other identities, too. I never "died"; I just disappeared and reappeared somewhere else as someone else. Come to think of it, with all the identities I had donned and all the lying I had done, I had been training to be a spy for several hundred years. I should be damn good at it.

Barely forty-five minutes later I stood as instructed by Douglas Schneibel before the battered green-painted doors of a loft building right off Canal Street near the Holland Tunnel. I looked up and trained my eyes on the third floor until finally a hand extended out a third floor window and dropped a key attached to a hefty, sawdust-stuffed lozenge of cloth. "Hey!" I yelled as it narrowly missed my head, and I jumped aside as it splatted to the ground. I picked it up and opened the door. An open-sided freight elevator waited inside, the kind where a pulley opens a top and bottom gate. The area was harshly lit by a bare hanging bulb. I got in the elevator, which could have held twenty people, closed the gate, and moved the brass lever to the number three. The elevator ascended slowly with creaks and moans past one set of iron doors before jerking to a halt before another.

As I stood there, the iron doors parted, and a plump, short man wearing wire-rimmed glasses waited in front of them to greet me. I could see the pink of his scalp through his thin white hair. I opened the elevator gates, stepped through the iron doors, and found myself in a cavernous space. A white rat sat on the old man's shoulder. It squeaked at me.

I like rodents. White rats make good pets if you get over the American culture's unreasonable prejudice against them. They're smart and affectionate. This one stood up, alertly staring at me with his little pink eyes. His nose twitched excitedly. The man reached up and gently grabbed him.

"*Komm,* Gunther, into your *haus,*" he said as he removed the rat from his shoulder and deposited it in the pocket of the old tweed jacket he wore. The rat peeked out of the pocket's top, riding like a first-class passenger, but stayed put.

"Mr. Schneibel? I'm Daphne Urban." I would have extended my hand, but he had already turned his back toward me.

"Thisss way," he said, his gait heavy and slow as he moved forward into the gallery.

"Is this your exhibition space, or do you live here, Mr. Schneibel?" I asked as we entered a dimly lit loft.

"A private gallery. For my collection only," he said, his voice quavery and his speech a bit slurred. He stopped and flipped a light switch and bright spotlights set some areas ablaze with light and left other areas in darkness.

We were standing in a large, open space filled with freestanding walls that made an octagon. In the center of the room sat a huge doughnut-shaped bloodred seat. Artwork, lit by track lighting suspended from the high ceiling, hung on the display walls or sat on pedestals in front of them. I felt as much as saw them. I had encountered such malevolent creations only once before—in North Africa, in a witch doctor's longhouse. Like the objects I saw there, these were primitive totem pieces created to cast bad spells and kill opponents. They were as much weapons as a machine gun.

I could feel the evil radiating from the freestanding crude wooden objects, squat stone figures with hideous faces, and very old ceremonial masks with huge staring eyes. There were some other items as well, pale heads and bulbous statues that appeared to be made of bones and feathers, sticks and leather . . . or perhaps human skin. I wouldn't call any of them beautiful, though some of the masks were exquisitely made. They were undeniably totems or magic items and, in their own way, fascinating.

"*Bitte,* pleassse, ssssit down, Miss Urban." Mr. Schneibel gestured toward the crimson seat at the room's heart. He remained standing in the shadows. "My collection is well known among connoisseurs of aboriginal art. I can display just a small portion, but these are some of the most desirable pieces. At least, they're desirable to certain people, who know what they are and have a taste . . . or, shall we say, an affinity for them."

"What are they?" I said as I sat down. The seat was in the shadows, all the light in the room concentrated on the art, much like a theater stage.

"They are ritual amulets and totems. The New Guinea tribes are cannibals. Were you aware of that?"

"Yes," I answered. Talking about cannibalism made me uncomfortable, being a variation on my own practices of blood drinking and the taking on of another's life energy.

Herr Schneibel seemed to be lost in memory as he went on: "Some of these figures incorporate the victims' hair and bones. They carry powerful magic. The ones with the huge phalluses are to confer fertility. Others impart magical powers and superhuman strength. The

masks were used in dances, celebrations, healing cere-
monies . . . or their opposite, rites to bring death and disease to one's enemies."

"And do they?" I interrupted, wondering if he had real
evidence that these "powers" were more than the power
of suggestion.

"Yes, Miss Urban, they do. Not on their own, of
course. If a tribal witch doctor uses them in ancient, tra-
ditional ways, they can affect a person's behavior or
health. They can even bring death. It isn't just psycho-
logical, if that's what you are thinking. They have a force
that operates whether the target is aware of it or not.
Without a witch doctor, or someone else trained in magic,
their power isn't as precise. But it is still there. Can you
feel it?"

I shivered, but I lowered my emotional shields and let
myself fully perceive the energies darting around the
room like piranhas in a tank. Dark waves of evil rushed
past and around me, searching for vulnerability and
nearly sucking my breath from my lungs. I gasped out my
reply. "Yes. I feel it. It's like the presence of death."

He walked toward me then and touched my shoulder
reassuringly with his hand. He said, "I thought you did.
Not everyone does, at least consciously." He stood by me
then, as if to offer me the protection of his presence. I
wondered if he wore something to ward off the negativ-
ity of being near these objects. "Most people who view
these pieces will suddenly feel sick or anxious."

"How charming."

"Charming? No. But just as Western religions use art
to inspire awe or to make the viewer feel small and pow-
erless in the presence of an all-powerful god, these items
had a spiritual purpose. They inspired fear and respect for
the tribe's shaman. They helped him exert control over
the tribe."

"Are these what Bonaventure wants?" I said, and looked into the old man's face.

"Yesss," he answered, and closed his eyes, almost as if gripped by a stab of pain. "He wants them badly. To the point of a mad obsession." He opened his eyes and looked at me with a piercing gaze. "And, Miss Urban, I agreed to let your people make Bonaventure think he can get them. But he must never possess them, do you understand?"

I heard the urgency in his words and said, "It would help if you explained."

"Bonaventure—and his name carries with it a terrible irony, since it means a good or great arrival—wants their power. He is a man who likes being an instrument of death, although he prefers to let others kill and terrorize. It's more than a profession to him. It has made him very rich, but it's more than the money. He relishes being feared."

"I've known others who liked it," I said, and thought, much to my shame, *including myself.*

"Yesss, Miss Urban, history has seen untold numbers of tyrants and monsters. Bonaventure is one of many. But I won't aid and abet him. I will destroy these pieces before I'd let him have them." His voice was loud and the quaver gone. An iron will was in his tone. I caught a glimpse of the young man he had been once. He nearly shook with rage.

"Herr Schneibel," I asked, "how did you come by these things?"

He paused a moment, as if to collect himself. In a calmer voice he said, "It is a long story, too long for our short time today. It would be good for you to know some of it, however." His earlier outburst seemed to have exhausted him. He sat down heavily, near me, to tell his story. I could hear the rat squeaking in his pocket. Schneibel himself smelled of Scotch.

"I was never a solider, merely a secretary to one of Rommel's officers in Africa. I hated the Nazis, but it was hardly safe to say so. Much to my relief I was taken prisoner by the Americans, and, in the course of my internment, I met a GI who had been previously stationed in the Pacific, in New Guinea. We struck up a friendship. He told me of the things he had seen. I come from a family who owned many art galleries in Germany before the Nazis took over. We had a large collection of African art, which was very popular in Europe early in the century. Picasso, Matisse, the Fauves, they all were influenced by the art we displayed. Our business was soon gone once the war started. The Nazi elite simply took what art they wished for their private collections, and no one else had money for luxuries. Some of my family relocated in Switzerland. So I had the experience, you see. When I heard about the art of the Western Pacific, I thought, correctly as it turned out, that aboriginal art would also become immensely popular.

"After the war, I made my way to the islands and began shipping native art to New York. Spirit figures. Hunting charms. Shields, woven masks, wooden yam masks. They are extremely beautiful and interesting. *Ja,* so interesting. I befriended several tribal leaders. I stayed mostly with the headhunters of the Papua. Even though they liked me and allowed me to come and go freely, it was a dangerous thing to do. I had many close calls. Michael Rockefeller, the son of Nelson Rockefeller, disappeared there, you know. He was visiting the Asmat tribe. The official report was that he drowned. It was easier for the family to believe that. But these are tales for another time."

Schneibel sighed heavily. He removed a handkerchief from inside his jacket and wiped his brow, then noisily blew his nose. He slowly returned it to his pocket and went on.

"I was able to settle here in New York. I became a citizen. Because of my background I have had what you might call an association with U.S. intelligence people. In the beginning I dealt with the OSS. Then it became more complicated, with so many agencies, each operating with its own staff. Yet over the years I have been able to be of assistance to your government. Recently my contacts in Malaysia and the Philippines have had information that I passed on. But I am old and getting tired. I cannot deal with Bonaventure. He is too slippery. And he is Russian. I am German. There is already an antagonism there. And I have had dreams recently . . . Never mind." He fell silent for a moment. "I feel the end is coming for me. But what of it? Few will miss me except my little friend Gunther. And death is inescapable. Everyone dies, Miss Urban."

I didn't respond, but I thought, *Not everyone, Mr. Schneibel.*

I made it to Bonaventure's by seven thirty, but just barely. I decided to take a cab uptown from Schneibel's gallery. My feet were already aching in the boots. The thought of clomping up and down subway steps made me risk hailing a taxi and getting stuck in Manhattan's unpredictable street traffic. During the ride I did my breathing exercises, trying to shut out the lurching of the cab. I prepared myself for the performance ahead. I didn't think my physical being would be in jeopardy, but I did fear not being able to accomplish my mission, or, if discovered, that I might have to kill. That would not be a good thing. My karma is damaged enough. Should I ever pass over to the other side and then return to earth, I no doubt have a wretched life of penance and suffering to look forward to.

When I arrived at Seventy-fourth Street, I was accompanied through the lobby to the brass birdcage of an elevator by the white-gloved doorman. He respectfully held it open for me, pushed the button for the penthouse, and allowed the door to close. As the car slowly rose upward, my emotions were mixed, excitement with an undercurrent of anxiety. I was entering the unknown, where I could influence but not control events. Control is of tremendous importance to me on many levels, and the paradox of my life is that when I am the most powerful—in vampire form—I am also the most out of control, operating on a knife edge between reason and blind desire. That realization made me shiver. My hands were like ice. I silently repeated an affirmation that often helped me bolster my confidence: *I have the willpower and discipline to do anything I desire.*

I had repeated that like a mantra ten times by the time the elevator stopped. As the door opened, I presented myself as a self-assured professional woman whose imperious manner and straight posture bordered on arrogance. A maid was waiting. I treated her like the servant she was, handing her my coat before she asked. She took it and indicated that I follow her. Two doors opened into the small space where we stood. One, drab green on the left-hand wall, was clearly a service entrance. A service elevator paralleled the one I had just used. The other door was part of a painted trompe l'oeil of a medieval town that covered the entire wall. I thought I recognized the cobbled street that led into San Gimignano, in Tuscany. The whole effect was quite clever. The door, painted in faux stone, opened into Bonaventure's lavish penthouse, its brightly lit interior gaudy in the extreme. The last time I saw so much gilding and satin was in Donald Trump's apartment. Obviously the message being delivered was, "I have so much money I don't know what to do with it all."

The maid was a middle-aged Slav built like a refrigerator. Her thick ankles, wrapped in support hose, peeked
out from beneath the skirt of her black maid's uniform.
She led me through the apartment and into a back room,
evidently a library. The books looked purely decorative;
the conference table was in an ersatz French style, white
and gilded. The chairs were also white and gilded, with
pink satin seats. Not to my taste, but definitely pricey.

The maid gruffly told me that "the master" would be in
shortly. She pulled out a chair for me to sit at the conference table. As soon as she left, I opened my purse and
took out a lipstick and a mirrored compact where I had
concealed the listening devices. I flipped open the compact and slipped two of the devices into my hand as I applied a coat of lipstick. Then, having practiced my rusty
skills of sleight of hand, I planted a listening device under
the edge of the table as I returned the compact to my
purse. Even if I was being electronically observed, and I
assumed I was, what I had done was imperceptible unless
someone replayed the recording tape in slow motion.
Under a table was not the most original spot for a bug, but
the only instructions I had were to avoid placing the tiny
dot near a heat source.

I opened my briefcase and took out a folder containing
photographs of Schneibel's collection. I pretended to spot
a book of interest and stood up, casually walking over to
the bookcase. As I reached up to pull down the book, my
other hand grabbed the lip of a shelf, and I was able to
plant another bug. I took down the book which looked as
if it had never been opened. It was Butler's *Lives of the
Saints*.

As I stood there, book in hand, the door opened and
Bonaventure walked in. Two men accompanied him. One
of them, Caucasian, bulky, huge in size, with oily slicked-
back hair and a pockmarked face, stared at me with frank

interest. The other was an African, bald-headed, dark-skinned, sour-mouthed, and poisonous. Sunglasses covered his eyes, but they didn't hide the look of pure hate he sent my way. We disliked each other on sight.

Bonaventure, a toad in a tuxedo, gave me a wide, toothy smile. "Miss Urban, it is a pleasure. Come, let us sit!" His appearance had changed considerably from the figure I had seen in the photo. He had shaved off his beard and had gained some weight, giving him a paunch. He swept his arm expansively, then pulled out my chair and waited for me to cross the room. His two companions took their places standing on either side of the room, observing.

Having hastily replaced the book and radiating my best smile, I said, "Likewise, Mr. Bonaventure. May it be both a pleasant and profitable evening for us both."

"Just Bonaventure, Miss Urban. May I get you a beverage? I am having vodka, of course!" He laughed a booming laugh. With that, almost magically, the maid opened the door and set a tray down containing beautiful etched crystal glasses, bottles of mineral water, slices of lemon, and a decanter filled with a clear liquid that I assumed was the vodka. Like the jewel in a crown, a plate of small toasts encircling a mountain of black caviar occupied the center of the tray. Sour cream and red caviar also sat on delicate porcelain plates. The silverware was ornate and highly polished.

"Mineral water would be delightful," I said. The maid arranged a large glass of straight vodka and another of mineral water in front of Bonaventure, who sat at the head of the table. Then she poured me a glass of water, added a slice of lemon, and put it in front of me. She ignored the two bodyguards as if they did not exist. "Anything else, master?" she said.

He looked at me questioningly. I said, "This is fine."

"Good. That will be all, Tanya." And she silently exited the room.

The hair on the back of my neck fairly bristled. Every one of my animal senses was on hyperalert. The standing men smelled of blood, and I suspected they had killed recently. Their eyes glittered, their every movement was edgy, taut, and they both watched me as a stalking cat does a bird. Outwardly I made sure that I appeared delighted with my company. No sweat betrayed me, no smell of fear. Yet so great was my perception of danger that I had to fight the instinct to transform.

Gracefully, with the studied movements gained in the courts of kings, I turned toward Bonaventure and said, "Mr. Schneibel sends his regards."

"Ah, Herr Schneibel. I have heard he has not been well of late. How do you find him?" He took a long, smooth drink of vodka. The alcohol fumes were visible as they wafted upward from his glass.

Diplomatically I said, "He is as his age demands. But well, thank you. Sound and youthful in mind if not in body. A great gentleman."

"Let us drink to his health then." Bonaventure laughed again and took another long drink. He was drunk in the way a heavy drinker is drunk, saturated with alcohol in order to function. "And you, Miss Urban, have you worked for him long?" He reached out and piled a toast with caviar. He sucked it in noisily, piglike. Some dribbled out and down his chin. He dabbed at it with a pink damask napkin. He motioned at the plate to me.

"No, thank you," I said. "He uses my services when he needs them."

Ignoring my refusal, Bonaventure took a plate and scooped caviar on it. With his stubby fingers he added a few rounds of toast. He pushed it across the table toward me. "You must not refuse. It is the best. Extraordinary. A rare treat. I insist. And does your appointment with me mean he is willing at last to sell?"

I pulled the plate toward me. There was always a power play with men like this. I put a small amount of caviar on a toast and ate. The eggs popped in my mouth, tasting salty and complex. "Excellent. You were right to insist," I said carefully. "And yes, I have brought a portfolio of the works he thinks you wish to acquire."

"I would prefer to see his collection in person."

"Of course. But as you know, Mr. Schneibel rarely makes the pieces accessible to anyone other than museum curators and researchers, and then on a very limited basis. None of his pieces has ever gone on the open market."

"But he has sold some."

"Granted. And that is all I am at liberty to discuss with regard to that. His buyers are private and anonymous, as you know."

"Yes, Miss Urban. That is how I learned of Mr. Schneibel. I saw a large statue in the possession of an associate. I was taken with it. It was far beyond anything I had, and my own collection is extensive. My associate was reluctant to tell me where he had acquired it, but eventually he did. And eventually he sold it to me. I can be very persuasive, Miss Urban," he said in a smarmy way. He looked at me, drinking in every one of my features rudely, openly. I looked back, my gaze as unblinking as his, straight into his yellowish, demonic eyes. A look of something—recognition?—passed over his face. My heart squeezed in my chest. I wondered what he saw in my eyes. I knew what I saw in his —something beastlike and inhuman, touched by a dark energy that seemed to originate in the depths of hell. I knew right then that Bonaventure had embraced evil as his preferred dish and had swallowed it whole.

The caviar I had eaten suddenly left a bitter taste in my mouth. I took a sip of mineral water; then I pushed the folder of photographs over to Bonaventure. Time to cut to the chase. "Here are the items Mr. Schneibel would consider selling. You have until Monday to consider whether you are interested in any or all of them. Write your offer on the back of the photograph of any piece you wish to purchase. The amount, however, can be no lower than one million dollars—per item. Mr. Schneibel is not eager to sell, as you know. If you wish to be persuasive, please keep that in mind."

"I would prefer if Herr Schneibel would simply name his price."

"That is not *his* preference, however," I said.

"I also want to see the collection before I bid. We are talking about a great deal of money, Miss Urban." He shuffled through the photos, pausing occasionally. "There are, what, fifteen photographs here?"

"Sixteen. And indeed, very few individuals can afford to purchase these items. You among few others know their true worth. Pieces like this simply do not exist elsewhere, not even in New Guinea, not for the past forty years. So this is Mr. Schneibel's offer. Take it or leave it. You can see the pieces after you purchase them."

"But that is unheard-of."

"Unheard-of, yes, yet it happens often," I said evenly. "That is how Mr. Schneibel does business. He guarantees that the pieces are authentic, genuine, and as seen in the photographs. You know his reputation in this field. Please don't insult him further."

A small flush had started up Bonaventure's neck. He was not used to someone else calling the shots or being in control. Especially not a woman.

Before he could answer there was an urgent tap at the door. Tanya's head popped in. "Master, excuse me, please, but there is a problem with—" And with that the door flung open and banged against the wall.

"I can speak for myself, Tanya." A pretty woman in a satin nightgown stood there holding a white cat. The long hair that cascaded down her back was yellow like ripe corn. She was thin to the point of fragility, and she would have been prettier but her mascara made ugly black smudges under her eyes, and her bright red lipstick ran in a crazy zigzag across her lips. She was also most obviously drunk. The cat looked at me, hissed, arched its spine, and bounded out of the woman's arms.

She screamed, "Princess!" The cat's claws left scratches on her arm. I couldn't help but notice the bright blood appearing on her milky skin. "Tanya! Get her!" The maid scrambled off in pursuit. Then the blonde turned back to Bonaventure. She was on the verge of hysteria. Her whole body was shivering, and her eyes were wild.

"Ohhh, I knew it! Always a woman! You don't love me. You've never loved me," she began sobbing.

I used this distraction to open my purse and extract my compact. I opened it and took a quick look in the mirror, and as I pretended to rearrange a few tendrils loosened from my chignon, I slipped another listening device into my hand.

Bonaventure had stood up quickly, reached the crying woman in a step, and put his arms around her as she collapsed against him. With more gentleness than I imagined him capable of, he said, "Hush, Catharine, you don't feel well, do you, darling? My pet, this is a business meeting. Just business." Despite his soft words, I could see he held her in a way she could not escape. He looked over at me. "Miss Urban, please excuse us. Would Monday at seven thirty be convenient, yes? Good, I'll see you then. Bockerie, come with me. Issa, show Miss Urban out." The black man gave me a final venomous look, left his post, and followed Bonaventure and the woman down the hall. There was a great arrogance and no fear in him. The other man, Issa, came and stood by my side like a prison guard as I closed the briefcase and stood up. I waited until Issa turned toward the door before picking up the briefcase and allowing my small purse to remain on the chair.

I had hopes of planting one more bug in the front hall near the phone. It was going to take both luck and superb acting to pull it off. Issa stayed close, invading my private space as we walked through the apartment. With a coquettish smile, I said, "Have you been with Bonaventure long?"

"Long enough," he said.

"If he needs muscle, you certainly fill the job specs," I fairly simpered. Gag me with a spoon, as the Valley Girls once said.

He flexed a bicep, then, showing crooked teeth, he grinned at me. "I was a weightlifter. I was on the Olympic team for my country. Nineteen eighty-four."

"And your country is . . . let me guess . . . Bulgaria?"

"You are very smart. As smart as beautiful. Yes, Bulgaria." He was so pleased he strutted.

By that time we were in the vestibule near the front door. "I have traveled there. It's a lovely country."

At that moment the stolid Tanya rushed up with my coat. "Here," she said. Issa took it, and she scurried off without another word, perhaps still involved with the drama of Catharine. I stopped, and like a gentleman Issa helped me on with my coat. Now was the perfect time for me to look around and down, fabricating a look of confusion. "Oh, my purse! I left it on the chair, I think. I'll have to go back for it."

"No. I fetch. Just wait. Not long. I hurry." Issa lumbered away like a bear.

Alone in the vestibule I pretended to have a problem with my boot. I picked up one foot, wobbled, and felt for the wall to steady myself. My hand slid and brushed the ornate mirror above the table holding the phone. The bug was deposited. Perfect. I was awfully good, even if I say so myself. Finally my hand rested on the table as I still balanced on my leg and examined the heel of my other boot. Apparently satisfied, I put my foot down gingerly as if testing the heel, just as Issa returned with my purse.

"Thank you *so* much," I gushed. He grinned, looking dumb and self-satisfied. My knight in shining armor. He opened the door and leaned toward me, but I slipped through it before he could get too close. The tiny elevator was standing open and I quickly got in, making sure I gave Issa a cheery wave with one hand. Despite holding the briefcase, I managed to press the lobby button with the other. I kept in character all the way down. I looked impatiently at my watch. Then I stared straight ahead, keeping a poker face. I'm sure cameras were everywhere, and I'm just as sure they detected nothing unusual about me. Nothing at all.

CHAPTER 6

Down by the salley gardens my love and I did meet.

—William Butler Yeats

Unwilling to walk more than necessary in four-inch heels, I asked the doorman to hail a taxi. The cabbie gave a snort of impatience when I told him to take me to the Metropolitan Museum. The few blocks made the fare hardly worth his time. Too bad. I would have tipped better if he'd been more gracious.

I pulled out my cell phone and called Darius. He answered on the first ring. "I'm on my way," I said.

"I will be waiting," he answered. "*Ciao.*"

Now that I'd accomplished my mission without a flaw, adrenaline was pumping through my veins, and my heart beat a fast staccato. Adrenaline is every bit as addictive as heroin, and that's the truth. The rush is a tidal wave of excitement pushing one up and over the top of feelings. And for me, such rampant passions are dangerous. My mask may begin to slip and the hungers within me threaten to emerge. I had to calm down and get hold of my emotions before I was lost to a lust for blood that made me reckless and uncaring about the consequences of a bite . . . until it was too late.

The cab pulled up in front of the museum. Spotlights blazed against the stone facade, making it look as grand as the Temple at Luxor or the Parthenon. Wide stone stairs swept majestically up to the tall fluted columns before the huge front doors. A few steps up from the sidewalk Darius stood, turned away from the street so that he didn't immediately see me. I gave a little gasp when I saw him. Gone were the jeans and leather. He looked elegant in a long topcoat and Italian loafers. A silk scarf hung around his neck. He was gorgeous with a capital G. Suddenly the building's grandeur seemed puny. I could see only Darius. The anticipation of sex mingled with the adrenaline, and along with my physical desire, dreams were awakening that I had suppressed long ago. If I were honest with myself, I would admit I wanted someone special to care about, and I wanted to be loved.

It didn't matter that I had just met Darius and that he was an enigma. I knew almost nothing about him, and what I did know might be lies. Yet the night we had spent together had been sweet and satisfying. It had brought my sexuality into blossom after decades of dormancy. And in truth, Darius—mysterious, dangerous, intelligent, and driven—embodied all the men I had loved and lost. I didn't know who he was, but my heart knew who I wanted him to be. I threw some money at the cabbie and exited the taxi.

Darius turned and saw me, and his face shone. The rest of the world faded into gray as I filled up with joy. I don't remember walking the few steps to his side, but suddenly I was in his arms and he was kissing me. The aphrodisiac of adrenaline carried me away. I felt so good and exquisitely alive. His arms were strong around me; his lips were soft. Their touch against mine lit a Fourth of July sparkler in my brain, and glittering lights exploded all around me. When he broke the kiss, Darius looked into my eyes and asked, "Are you all right?"

"Now I am," I said.

"I want to hear all about your night. But first, have you eaten?"

"No."

"Are you hungry?"

Not for food, I suddenly realized. *I'm hungry for blood.* I pushed the thought away. "Yes," I said.

"Good. We can go across the street to the Stanhope."

"Perfect," I said. The Stanhope Hotel's restaurant is excellent, and the clientele chic. I used to see John Kennedy Jr. there, before his unfortunate marriage and too early death. The Stanhope—staid, quiet, and tasteful—is my favorite New York hotel. Another favorite is the old Waldorf Astoria, whose excellent service never fails to live up to its reputation, unlike the Plaza, which is overrated and a tourist trap. However, as Darius took my hand and we crossed Fifth Avenue, the crisp, clear evening like cool water around us, I could have eaten sawdust and thought it a divine idea.

As Darius walked, he reminded me of his Chinese sign, the Tiger. Tall and lithe, he moved with catlike power, a hunter on the prowl. He conveyed authority, from the dignified black coat he wore to the way he looked other men square in the eye, with the attitude that he was an alpha male, the leader of the pack. Not cocky but self-assured, he was intimidating, conveying strength and command. Darius didn't so much enter a room as take it over.

Now, as we entered the hotel's dining room, the maître d' hurried over, called him *sir*, took my coat, and seated us immediately. A waiter rushed to our table for our drink order. Darius ordered a single-malt Scotch. Near to losing control when I was stone cold sober, I stuck with mineral water. I avoided alcohol most of the time because I was afraid to lower my inhibitions. Tonight especially it was taking all my willpower to resist the thoughts tugging at me to drink blood. Giving rein to my vampire traits with Darius would at best ruin everything. At worst . . . I didn't want to consider the worst that might happen. I had vowed I would never go that route again.

Focusing on the soft ambience of the room, all candle glow and rich brocade, I settled into my seat and let myself feel warm and safe. Darius reached across the small table, took my hand, and rubbed his thumb across my knuckles in almost an absentminded way. His touch was like being brushed with an electric wire that sent small shocks up my arm. He smiled at me again before releasing my hand, and he seemed to be expecting me to say something. I guessed he was anxious for me to talk about what had happened with Bonaventure, yet I wasn't ready to jump into business. So I stayed silent, and so did he. The lack of conversation soon felt awkward and uncomfortable.

I was relieved when the drinks arrived and the waiter asked for our order. Impulsively I ordered a steak, hoping to take the edge off my growing taste for blood. I asked for it rare. Darius raised an eyebrow. "I thought you didn't eat meat," he said.

"Tonight's an exception," I said. "I'm starving, and I think I need the B vitamins."

I was starving—for him. I craved his mouth, his voice, his hair. I wanted to lick his face and nibble on his shoulders. I wanted to bite him and suck him with a soul-deep hunger. To paraphrase the poet Neruda, I was pacing around, sniffing the twilight, hunting for his hot heart.

Darius, on the other hand, seemed focused on telling the waiter he wanted salmon, grilled, and steamed vegetables. I thought he was oblivious to my unvoiced longings, yet when he finally raised his eyes to look into mine his desire was naked there—for a second. Then a door slammed shut behind his gaze and he demanded, rather than asked, "Tell me about Bonaventure."

Anger flashed through me, along with the suspicion that I was unimportant to this man. In that moment I felt that the sweet words, the hot sex, and now the elegant dinner were all just to butter me up and get information from me.

"Maybe I'd like to eat before we discuss business," I said, thoroughly pissed off.

"Daphne," he said, and reached for my hand. "I was only thinking of you. Once we get that out of the way, you can relax, and we can just enjoy the rest of the night together."

"Oh, puh-lease," I answered. "I don't believe that. Don't make things worse by being phony."

"Women!" he said, and dropped my hand. He seemed to be struggling to control his temper. He took a long drink of Scotch and thought a moment. Then he looked at me and said carefully, "Daphne, I apologize. I really do. I thought it might be best to ask you some questions about what you saw and heard while everything was fresh in your mind. I thought—I really did—that dinner might be more appetizing with the subjects of terrorism, weapons, and related nastiness out of the way. But when would *you* like to talk about Bonaventure?"

I looked back at him and gave what he said some thought. I hated to concede he was right, but I did. "Since you put it that way, I can see your point. Okay, let's start over. What do you want to know? If I think I can tell you without compromising my mission, I will. *But* it has to be a two-way street. You need to share information with me as well. Is that agreed?"

"I never thought it would be any other way," he said.

I wasn't sure I bought that, but I said, "Go ahead; what's your first question?"

"What was Bonaventure's mood and attitude?"

"Drunk but in control."

"Who was with him?"

"Two bodyguards, one an African, the other Eastern European. Do you know who they are?" I said this slowly and deliberately. I wanted to see how much Darius was really willing to share.

Without hesitation, he answered. "The African is Sam Bockerie, also known as General Mosquito because he sucks the life out of his enemies. He's from Sierra Leone and is more than a bodyguard for Bonaventure. He's a middleman in the exchange of diamonds for weapons. He's dangerous, inhumanly vicious, without conscience."

"He disliked me on sight. Why?" I asked.

"I doubt if it was anything about you," Darius said. "Bockerie dislikes everyone on sight. He's like a mad beast that snarls at the wind. He's reputed to be magic, protected by charms and spells or even transformed by them into some sort of supernatural creature. Probably that's a rumor to scare others into doing what he asks. Even the mention of his name strikes fear in the jungles where they mine the blood diamonds of Africa. Watch your back around him."

I nodded. That description fit the man I saw. "And what do you know about the other bodyguard?"

"That sounds like Issa Mingo, a strongman who knows Bonaventure from Russia. They've been together for years. He's not as dumb as he looks."

"You could have fooled me," I said with a laugh.

"Well, he likes good-looking women, and he thinks of himself as a ladies' man," Darius said, his voice low and serious.

"I figured that much out all by myself," I commented.

"Well, don't get yourself in a position where he shows you what he likes about pretty women. He's as cruel as he is crude. Did you notice anyone else?"

"The only others I saw—and there could have been people in the apartment who remained unseen—were the maid—her name was Tanya—and a young woman, also drunk and in a bad state. Bonaventure called her Catharine."

Darius nodded. "She's Bonaventure's lover. By all accounts she's practically a prisoner. Did you notice any security?"

I shook my head. "I didn't see anything. I assume there is camera surveillance, but downstairs there's only the doorman to screen visitors. No guns were out in the open, but both bodyguards were carrying them, I'm sure. Why do you want to know?"

Darius didn't answer my question. Instead he asked, "When are you going back?"

"Monday. Same time as tonight," I said, and, feeling annoyed, I asked again. "Why do you want to know? Darius, don't play games because I'm not going to play along."

"I might need you to help me get in that night. Let me think about it," he said dismissively.

"No! Let *me* think about it. Why should I help you get in? What are you planning? What do you know that I don't? I told you this has to be a mutual exchange, or it all stops here."

Darius didn't answer right away. I knew he was using me for his own ends when it came to Bonaventure. But then I was using him. I felt like J had thrown me to the wolves. I didn't have any backup. My instructions were sketchy at best. If I got out of this alive—and if I could help stop this potential terrorist attack—it would be by my own wits and cunning. So far Darius seemed to have better information. J's dossiers didn't include anything about Bonaventure's bodyguards. I was beginning to trust Darius more than my own boss. I really wanted to see how much he'd tell me.

Darius leaned forward, closer to me, and said very quietly, "We've had Bonaventure under surveillance since he arrived in New York. He's setting up a major weapons sale with men we believe to be terrorists."

"Tell me something I don't know," I whispered back.

"The buy is something beyond the ordinary. We expect it to happen early next week. We think Bonaventure has already brought the weapons into this country. We think we know how. We need to know exactly where the weapons are and who is getting them. We need to take possession of whatever it is Bonaventure is selling, and we need to capture the men who want it."

I felt disappointed. I sat up straight and looked at Darius. Maybe I was making a mistake in setting up this "side deal" with a rival agent. I shook my head. "So far, Darius, that is old information. J told me about the same thing. What have you to do with this that he doesn't? I know there's something else involved here. Come on, convince me I should help you. How can you help me?"

Darius sat back in his chair as well, staring down at his glass of Scotch. He picked it up and swirled the liquid around. It seemed a bit oily against the side of the glass. Finally he looked up at me. "Okay, here's the bottom line. J is dealing purely in the intelligence end of this. He wants people taken alive. His agency wants to turn the terrorists into double agents, or simply empty them of useful information. My agency disagrees. They want to hunt these people down and kill them. You might say I'm in the cleanup end. Certain people are my special targets. Certain people my agency is convinced should not be left alive."

"Who? Why?"

"Look, Daphne. There are things you are better off not knowing. It doesn't concern you." He hesitated. "Or you and me. Yes, it's totally screwed up that every intelligence agency does its own thing. I know that. And if you don't know it, you should. One benefit you and I can get out of coordinating our efforts is that we won't get each other killed. And right now you can help me big-time. You can be my ticket into Bonaventure's apartment."

"I don't see how."

"Don't worry your pretty head about that. I'll set everything up."

A patronizing tone had crept into his voice. That is something that pushes my buttons. My tone swung over into the red zone on the annoyance meter. "You know, Darius, you're pissing me off. This *pretty head* has a brain in it. And it's telling me you want to call the shots. That's not going to fly. Either you level with me and we act as partners, or I finish this glass of water and go catch a taxi."

Darius snapped back, "I would level with you if I thought you knew what the hell you were doing! Do you have any idea how brutal these people are? If they even suspect you're setting them up, they won't just kill you. They'll make sure they have fun killing you." Darius was keeping his voice low, but I could see his muscles tensing, and he was spitting out his words like machine-gun bullets.

"I told you, Darius, I can handle myself. Why do you have such a hard time believing that? Is it because I'm a woman?"

"Damn it, Daphne, yes, that's part of it. More than that, I'm beginning to have feelings for you. Maybe you think I'm handing you a line and that we hardly know each other. Well, there are things you know about a person by instinct—and by screwing them three times in one night. Look, I think there's a good chance one of us can get killed before this all over. I want to try to get both of us through it alive."

I was stunned by his words. We had been really good together, but our sex didn't have any strings attached. We were practically strangers when we fell into bed. We made no promises to each other. I had admitted to myself I could really fall for Darius, but I never expected him to talk about his feelings. My voice softened a little, but I wanted to stick to my guns. "Well, I don't want you to get killed either. But helping you enter that apartment is probably going to be a risk of huge proportions. So far I don't have any reason to do it."

"I think you do. Daphne, I'm going to enter that apartment with you or without you. I'm going to do what I've been sent to do. If we don't work together, we might get in each other's way. Worse, you could walk in on something or end up being a hostage. I don't know what might happen if we keep each other in the dark. But if we work together, I do know we'll be safer. It's just common sense to coordinate our two operations. And there's so much at stake. And like I said, I know J. He'll leave you hanging out there if it's between saving you and salvaging his operation. He's a coldhearted bastard, Daphne. I'm not. I promise you that."

A lot of what he said made sense. I still had doubts, though, so I said, "Let me think about it."

"There's nothing to think about, and you know it."

My eyes got huge. I was ready to dump my water on him and tell him to go to hell when I saw he was grinning at me. "Gotcha," he said as the waiter brought our food. I dug in and downed the steak quickly, as fast as I could get the bites into my mouth. Once I saw Darius looking at me. "What?" I said before I took another bloody forkful.

"You weren't kidding when you said you were starved," he said.

I couldn't resist another zinger. "*I* mean what *I* say," I countered.

"I'm beginning to believe you do," he said. We both cleaned our plates. Under the table my foot had ended up against his leg again. The contact felt good, sexy, and it was beginning to feel familiar. I liked it more than I was ready to admit.

"Let's get coffee and dessert," Darius said with a rakish grin, and signaled to the waiter. Then he looked at me.

The sizzle started in my toes and went straight up to my stomach, which did a little flip. Not many men have given me that sensation. The chemistry between us was explosive, and I definitely didn't need to think about *that*. "And then what?" I said, my voice full of meaning.

"Then we can go upstairs—*if* you want to. I'm not presuming anything, but I'd like to spend time with you. I'd like to be with you. The suites here are beautiful."

"That would be extravagant."

"You are worth the extravagance, Daphne. You are extraordinary, fiery and strong, gentle and lovely. And the seduction of a sophisticated woman requires a certain ambience. And I guessed you would like the Stanhope."

"You guessed correctly. But is that what you intend to do, seduce me?" The banter between us was making me excited. My breath was coming faster. I was beginning to want him badly.

His eyes glittered. "Yes, Daphne Urban, I intend to seduce you and love you as certain dark things are to be loved, between the shadow and the soul. I want to find the hidden places within you like a traveler following twisting roads through the mountains that lead higher and higher till they vanish in the clouds."

I'm a sucker for a man with a poetic imagination and a silver tongue. My legs were going all jelly again. I didn't know if I could stand up to get out of the restaurant. I wasn't so foolish as to think he hadn't used that line before, but I liked hearing it. It showed me a part of Darius that appealed to me a great deal. And I wanted sex with this man, as much as he obviously wanted sex with me. We were two adults doing an adult thing, and I intended to enjoy it thoroughly.

Fortunately for my reputation, the waiter brought me a crème brûlée laced with white chocolate and raspberries accompanied by a cup of decaf. It was sinfully good. Darius had cheesecake and espresso. He ate like a truck driver, with gusto and no regard to calories. I asked him about his family. He said he came from a large Northern Italian family who settled in Brooklyn. His father and uncles ran a bakery.

"And how did you end up a spy?" I asked.

He took a long breath and put down his fork. "I was in the military, a Navy SEAL. After a point I just wanted do my time and get out. I felt we were fighting pointless wars and losing lives stupidly. Then my youngest brother was murdered. I took it badly. My whole family was grieving, but I was burning up from the inside out. I just wanted to get the bastard who did it. I was approached by someone who offered a chance for me to do just that. It changed everything."

"Did you avenge your brother?" I asked.

"Yes." Darius's voice hammered the word like an iron nail. Then he pressed his fingers against his eyes and paused a minute before going on. "Yes. I did. And then I was given another assignment by the person who first approached me. He was a recruiter, probably much like the one who must have recruited you. Same shit, different day. But my life suddenly had purpose." Darius let out a sigh. "It seems like all that is ancient history." He looked at me. "End of story." He shrugged.

"I appreciate your telling me that, Darius. I really do." I reached over and gently touched his face. He took my hand and raised it to his lips, kissing my palm.

Then he said, "If you're ready, let's go upstairs." He pushed his chair back, then came over and held mine. A waiter rushed over with the check. Darius smiled as he signed it.

"Don't you have to go book the room?" I asked.

"I did this afternoon," he said.

"You what!" I exploded.

He pulled me to him and whispered, "Just in case you said yes. And I was so hoping you would."

"You're incorrigible." I laughed. "And I did, didn't I," I whispered back, nuzzling his ear.

"Okay, let's get out of here." He grinned.

I was very ready to leave, and I was glad Darius's hurry saved me from having to talk about myself, my past, my family, my becoming a spy, because anything I said would have been a pack of lies.

At first I thought it was because the Stanhope is a staid old lady of a hotel that we didn't kiss in the elevator going up to our room, although I was burning with desire. Darius stood just far enough away so we didn't touch, and he didn't look at me even though he was smiling. And then I realized not touching was intensifying the expectation, and that Darius was playing at something. I wanted to see what. We didn't kiss outside the hotel room door. When we entered, we didn't touch. A sitting room lay to our left. The bedroom lay to the right. My coat was already hung in the closet by some efficient member of the hotel staff. Darius walked in front of me to the bedroom and switched on the light next to the bed. The bed, opulent with a brocade cover and huge soft pillows, was high enough to need a little step stool to help a person get into it. I stood in the doorway. Darius crossed the room and sat down in a wing chair near the windows. He obviously knew the layout well, and it crossed my mind that he must have brought women here before. He stretched his long legs out in front of him, crossed them, and clasped his hands across his stomach. He looked at me with sultry eyes.

"Would you take off your clothes for me?" he said.

"Yes," I said softly, ready to go wherever this scenario led.

"Would you take them off slowly?" he said. "Yes," I answered, and I did. When I stood there naked, he looked at me from head to toe. My nipples were hard. The air was warm and caressing. I stared back at him. He got up and walked to me. When he touched me, my life stopped. Time was suspended. He encircled my arms within his embrace, pinning them to my sides. He kissed me deeply. The wool of his jacket rubbed against my breasts. The softness of his sweater touched my stomach. He said, "Your body is as smooth as marble, as smooth as stones in the water."

"Yes," I said, seeking his lips with mine.

He pushed me back toward the bed and made me lie down with just my torso on the bedspread, my legs dangling over the side. He stood between them while his hands stroked down across my stomach and held my thighs, his touch leaving a trail of shivery wonder. Darius was breathing harder now. He took his thumbs and parted me, rubbing and circling as my breath caught and made little gasps. Then he stopped.

I heard more than saw him unbutton and unzip his pants, and then I realized he didn't get undressed. I propped myself up my elbows to see what he was doing. He stayed fully clothed while I awaited him, totally naked. I watched as he slipped his cock out of his pants and held it in his hand. He rubbed it against me, and I could feel its hardness. I arched expectantly. But I didn't anticipate the force with which he thrust himself into me or the depth to which he penetrated. I moaned loudly, stunned. His arms on either side of my waist held his body above me. I looked up into his face as he pounded against me. He watched me as he did it. He pushed hard. He pushed deep. I saw his face begin to change from consciousness into an enraptured trance. After that, I doubt if he really saw me. He just thrust into me again and again. It went on for long minutes, a rhythmic motion that hypnotized and aroused us both into a Tantric ecstasy.

Using the techniques taught me long ago in the empress's court, I tightened and released around his cock with my pelvic muscles, matching the beat of his movement. I was very strong. He groaned, carried away with pleasure. But he was strong too. He balanced on one arm while he reached down with his hand and increased the sensations rocking me. Someone long practiced in the art of love must have taught him how to prolong a woman's pleasure, for he did things with his fingers and his cock that had me gasping. I started to groan and then to thrash about, until he leaned over and with one hand grabbed my hair. He pinned me down and held me still while he drove me wild with ecstasy. "Do I please you, Daphne? Tell me how it feels when I fuck you," he whispered. "Does it feel good?"

"Yes." I gasped. "It feels so good, Darius. Hot and hard. Rock hard, Darius."

He covered my mouth with his, kissing me hard as he fucked me hard. The bed rocked, and I was coming. Half-conscious, I was lost in sensation. I wanted to scream but his mouth muffled my groans. I was losing control; I was rising and flying.

I reached up with my hand and clasped his neck. I started to pull him down toward my mouth. I wanted to drink his blood and feel the ecstasy that was greater than an orgasm as streams of light coursed through my veins.

Something inside me tried to hold back, but it was too late. I saw his jugular vein blue under his skin and couldn't resist, my teeth becoming fangs as I leaned toward his flesh to bite and—

I didn't. Darius pulled away suddenly, arching his back as he exploded within me, his neck far from my reach. And that snapped me fully conscious, fear coursing through me at how close I had come to taking him to the realms of the undead. He pumped against me some more; then made me climax again with his fingers. I screamed; I know I did. Only when he had withdrawn and lifted my legs up onto the bed, turning me and putting my head on a satin pillow, did I realize there had been no condom between us. I'm immune to disease, it's true, but vampires can conceive. Conditions must be exactly right for that rarity to occur, and I doubted that I would, but I wondered why Darius had taken such a risk. The only reason that came to me was that he believed this mission was not one that he'd finish alive.

He climbed into the bed then and lay beside my naked body, still fully clothed. It was exciting to feel his clothes against my flesh, but also disconcerting. He turned my head toward him and kissed me. In the darkness he recited to me. It sounded vaguely like something Charles Swinburne might write. " 'Thine eyes blind me, thine tresses burn me. I could eat thy breasts as honey, and drink thy blood as wine. Thy sharp sighs divide my flesh and spirit with soft sound . . . that from face to feet, thy body were abolished and consumed, and in my very flesh thy very flesh entombed.' " He leaned down and kissed each breast between each line he said, then, when the poem was over, ran one hand idly over them before his fingers came up to stroke my face.

I sighed and again wondered if he said those words to other women he took to bed. He was either a player or a true romantic. I just didn't know him well enough to decide which.

"What are you thinking?" he asked.

"I was wondering where you learned to recite poetry. In college?"

"In a Chinese prison," he said bitterly, and rolled away.

Me and my big mouth, I thought. I shifted onto my side. "I'm sorry. I'm sorry for whatever you went through. No matter where you learned it, the lines are beautiful." I was silent for a moment, then said, "Can I ask you to do something for me?"

"What?" he said, the mood broken and a tension growing in his body.

"Would you please take off your clothes?"

He did, and we both got under the covers. Within minutes he had fallen deeply asleep. I stayed still for a while, smelling him, listening to his soft snores. I wasn't sleepy, and besides, I couldn't spend the night. I had to be back in my coffin before first light. I slipped out of bed and washed up in the bathroom, put on my clothes, and came quietly back into the bedroom. I looked at Darius lying there, the tangled sheet around his waist, one strong leg exposed. Even in sleep his fists were clenched, his jaw tensed, his brow furrowed. He followed dream spirits into battle. He slumbered but didn't rest. I hoped I wasn't making a serious mistake by trusting him and, after tonight, I thought, truly caring about him. I knew this was a driven man and I was not his priority.

It was different for me. I never had an urgency to complete anything. There would be always time to dream and create, time for all the nights of work and days of leisure, time for a hundred visions and revisions. I had eternity before me to do what I wished. Darius, the clock ticking, dashed ahead at full tilt, bringing his private demons with him as inseparable companions. The finality of death stayed with him like a shadow at his side. I looked at him once more.

My heart didn't want to go. I took my coat from the hall closet and let myself out, being careful not to slam the door. Over the centuries I too have memorized poetry and the words of my Irish friend, Billy Yeats, haunted me as I left: *In a field by the river my love and I did stand, And on my leaning shoulder she laid her snow-white hand. She bid me take life easy, as the grass grows on the weirs; But I was young and foolish, and now am full of tears.*

I hoped the words weren't prophetic, but a chill passed through me as I stepped back onto the Fifth Avenue sidewalk. With the cold air snapping me into a pellucid awareness, I was unhappily sure they were.

CHAPTER 7

*Cruelty has a human heart, and jealousy a
human face.*

—William Blake

I arrived home, my body satisfied, my mood pensive,
my soul troubled. And knowing full well that the person who phoned me most often was my mother, I knew
the message light blinking on my answering machine
didn't bode well.

It was worse than I thought.

First message, Ma's cigarette-and-whiskey voice: "Hi,
sweetie, I didn't know you were going out. Are you seeing someone? Don't forget: Drinks tomorrow night. No
excuses. Sevenish. Look pretty. Love you. And power to
the people."

Next, totally unexpectedly, was Cormac: "Sooo,
you're not home on a Friday evening, well, la-di-da. At
least one of us seems to have something—or *someone*—
interesting to do. And it sure isn't me, you little devil,
you. Have you been kicking ass? Catching bad guys.
Playing Mata Hari?

"Don't ask what I've been doing. I'm just a glorified
concierge. Dry cleaning deliveries. Oh, my God, you
would not believe how many times an evening I'm calling upstairs to the rooms, 'Brother Johnson, your gar-
ments from Pure and Spotless are at the front desk.' And

nonstop, all night long, they pipe in Gregorian chants . . . in Latin. I had enough of that in the Middle Ages, thank you! I swear, I could just scream. I've been wearing earphones so I can listen to Madonna.

"But here I am, chattering on about me. I called to tell you that I saw our mutual friend tonight, and he is surly, surly, surly. I don't know what you did to piss him off, but oh, my, are you on his shit list. You'll have to give me all the juicy details ASAP. Don't call me, I'll call you. Kiss, kiss."

Third message: "Hey, there, girlfriend, it's Benny. I just have to tell you what I'm being sent to do. I am as nervous as a long-tailed cat in a room full of rocking chairs. Give me a jingle! Till then, tie a big knot in your rope and hold on. Well, I'd better get back to my rat killing . . . that's hillbilly slang for taking care of business. Call meeeee!"

I had to smile. *Sure, J, mum's the word. We won't discuss a thing about this secret spy operation. Right.*

And then the kicker, message *numero quatro:* "Hermes. This is Ringmaster. Get your butt down here. Now."

I had been ordered around enough for one night. "In your dreams," I yelled at the machine. Okay, I guess I was in deep trouble. Was this about Bonaventure? Was this about my . . . shall we call it my indiscretion when I left him the last time? Whatever had him ticked off, I wasn't about to jump and run. Instead a scheme formed in my mind, and I called Benny. She answered on the second ring.

I told her I had only a minute to talk, but was she free tomorrow night and would she mind stopping by my mother's for cocktails? She said she'd love to. I told her I would swing by her place around six thirty to pick her up and that she should dress sexy in case we wanted to do the club scene afterward. She said she would "go whole hog and pig crazy." Her relentless good humor almost made me forget I had to face J before dawn. But I wasn't going anywhere until I showered and changed. Besides, I was suddenly dead tired, and I hoped the water would slap some life back into me. A nice big glass of blood wouldn't hurt either.

Did I think about Darius? Oh, yes. He was a wisp of smoke filtering through my mind, shading everything with the thought that what I had done with him had complicated my life and entangled me in cords that I might never be able to break. Yet I couldn't wait to see him again.

I showed up at J's office a little before four in the A.M. I had scrubbed myself with a loofah, washed my hair, and thrown on tight jeans. I pulled a pair of snuggly warm UGGS onto my feet, and for outerwear I chose a vintage World War II navy pea jacket.

The street was empty of both traffic and people when I left my apartment building. I had to walk down the block to Broadway to find a passing cab. New York is a city that never sleeps, but on the Upper West Side, in the middle of the night, it dozes a bit. The streetlights glare, but sounds are muted, as if they're wearing bedroom slippers.

The temperature had started to fall again. I shivered and jammed my hands deeply into my pockets, unhappy that I had to be outside again. With the sky inky black above, ancient urges hummed inside me, tempting me to duck into a shadowy doorway and transform, and once transformed to fly, swooping along looking for another lone walker, to drop down, embrace him, and drink.

I hated feeling like that. I hated the monster inside me. I didn't choose to be what I was. No matter how beautiful I was, or kind, or good, it made no difference. I was a vampire. That was reason enough for people to hate me and all my race. Didn't I have the same senses, affections, and passions as any other woman? Didn't I feel the warmth of the same sun, the cold of the same winter? Didn't I cry when hurt? Didn't my heart break when my love left me, just like any woman? Didn't I yearn for understanding and acceptance, for tenderness and compassion, just like any woman? And if you wronged me, didn't I yearn for revenge, just like any woman?

A cab with its on-duty light on finally pulled over. I got in and told the driver to take me to the Flatiron Building. New York cabbies don't ask questions, and if this one wondered what the hell I was doing out at that hour, he didn't say. As indifferent as the city itself, he probably didn't care.

When I arrived at the building, the night watchman unlocked the door and held it open for me as if he were waiting for me to show. Upstairs, J was wearing thunderclouds when I strolled in. From the way his lips were pressed together and his brow creased, it was pretty clear without his saying a word that he was really ticked off. I looked at him coolly, uncaring. I didn't let his fury bother me. I figured J was a man with anger issues. He probably exploded two or three times a day. I didn't think he was going to stake me, so what else did I have to worry about? Would he fire me? Nah.

My sauntering in with an attitude really fueled his inner fires. His anger seemed to heat the air around him. "Sit down," he said, and motioned toward the conference table. "I have to talk to you."

I plopped into a chair and threw my backpack down with a bang onto the floor. "Good evening to you too. And before we start, I'm parched. I need something to drink. Is there a Coke machine on this floor?"

"No, no Coke machine," he said. He seemed to be talking through clenched teeth. "You know, this is not a joke."

"I didn't think it was," I said as I shrugged out of my jacket. His scowl deepened. I rattled on. "Do you mind if I grab that bottle of water over there? It's probably warm, but that's okay." I got up and sauntered over to a table. I picked up the bottle with maddening slowness, twisted off the cap, and took a long swallow. I wiped my mouth off with my hand before I went back to my seat. "That's better. So, J, what's so important it couldn't wait until tomorrow? Is this about my going to Schneibel?" I said, all wide-eyed and innocent.

"No, we expected you to contact Schneibel. It fit your profile. What we didn't expect was this." He pulled out a snapshot and slapped it down on the table in front of me.

The photo showed me kissing Darius on the steps of the Metropolitan Museum of Art. We were in quite a clinch.

I was shocked that I had been followed and didn't know it. My stomach started churning, but I kept my voice light and unconcerned. "It's me and the guy I've been seeing. So?"

"So? So! You've been seeing Darius della Chiesa. How long has this been going on?" J's jaw was so tight I thought he was going to splinter his molars.

"A while. What's the big deal?" I said. My anger was growing to match his.

"Don't bullshit me," he bellowed. "It had to start after you were recruited. He's an agent and you damn well know it. He picked you up to get information from you. What did you tell him?"

"Nothing. Absolutely nothing. And how do you know *he* picked *me* up? Maybe I came on to him! We met; we had great chemistry. It's nothing to do with business. End of story." But what J said had put words to my own suspicions. My distrust of Darius came back in full force, and yet I no longer believed J either. I felt manipulated from both sides and getting angrier by the moment.

As if picking up on my unspoken thoughts, J said, "You can't believe that. We know he's been keeping Bonaventure under surveillance. His people won't talk to my people. I need to know what he's told you."

I decided right then that I was shutting J out of what I was doing until I found out who was on *my* side, if anybody. "Nothing," I said. "He told me nothing. I told him nothing. As you can see from the photo, we weren't doing a lot of talking."

"Stop being a fool. He's using you. How far has this gone? Are you sleeping with him?"

I felt as if I were a criminal being interrogated. I stood up, grabbing my jacket and backpack. I had had enough, and I was leaving. "That's none of your business," I spit at him. I opened the door, but before I knew what was happening, J was in front of me, forcing me back into the room and slamming it shut again.

"It damn well is my business," he screamed right in my face, "if he's using you to get to our target, and I'm sure he is. Answer me, damn it. I need to know."

This was getting out of hand, and before I got into a shoving or shouting match with J, I decided to pull back. Taking the shrillness out of my own voice, I retreated a few steps and said calmly, "Look, we met. We kissed. We progressed from there. It was as good for him as it was for me. Sex is not love. Don't worry about it. Darius told me he was an agent who was keeping surveillance on Bonaventure. He's been totally up-front with me. He's got his thing, and we have ours, and there's no problem."

J just shook his head, his anger deflating like a spent balloon. He said with disgust, "If you've slept with him, you've already compromised the entire unit."

My feelings were still churning, although I was using all my will to control them. I was being treated as if I was an idiot without an ounce of intelligence. Despite my efforts at calming down, I started to yell again. "How can you say that? I told you I didn't tell him anything. And we just have a physical thing going. Good sex, but nothing more. No strings attached."

Suddenly J was like a volcano about to erupt. "You're a woman, God damn it. For a woman sex *always* has strings attached. It *always* means something to you. From the looks of this picture, you've already fallen for him. You cannot know what you're doing!" J was now Vesuvius in full lava flow. "You idiot! Don't you understand? Darius isn't just 'an agent.'"

I was shaking with fury. I threw my jacket down on the table, my hands on my hips as I squared off in front of J. I thought this kind of sexist crap went out in the 1980s. I was about to give J a real piece of my mind when the last thing he said registered. I stopped in my tracks. "What do you mean, Darius isn't just 'an agent'?"

J glared at me. "Darius della Chiesa is a loose cannon. Unpredictable. Even his handler can't control him. He has his own agenda. And damn it all to hell, Daphne, tell me you don't know—he's a vampire slayer!"

I felt the blood draining from my face. My hands turned to ice. The room spun. I thought I was going to pass out. Somehow I managed to keep my voice from betraying me. "I can't believe that. Do you know that for a fact? Where's your proof?" I spit the words out.

J looked at me. He seemed to be struggling with what he was about to say. Finally he said, "I don't have any proof. But it's more than a rumor. It's what people who are in a position to know are saying. He has a personal vendetta against vampires. We can't take the chance that it's true. You may have already endangered the whole team. He can use you to find them all. You have to stay away from him."

My mind was racing, internally reviewing everything Darius had said and done, searching for clues I could have missed. There were red flags I should have spotted, yet a small voice inside me was warning that I just couldn't trust what J said. It was exactly what he would make up to hurt me, to get even for my transforming.

"I don't believe he is a vampire slayer. I would bet my life that he isn't. I repeat, what goes on between Darius and me is none of your goddamn business. What is your business is my meeting with Bonaventure. On the way down in the cab I wrote up a report. Here." I reached in my backpack for a folder. I threw it on the table. "That's exactly what I heard at Bonaventure's, what I saw, and what I did there. I'm scheduled to meet him again Monday night. The bugs are in place. What else do you want me to do?" I sat back and folded my arms across my chest.

J picked up the folder and started reading my report. He said, "We've already picked up some information from your plants. Things are moving fast. I'll have instructions for you by Sunday. Don't be out of touch." He glared at me. "And don't see Darius della Chiesa again," he ordered.

My eyes flashed, and I was ready to tell him to go take a flying leap into the ocean, when, no longer yelling, he added in a gentle tone, "It's too big a risk. I mean it, Daphne. If he finds out what you are, he won't hesitate. He'll put a stake through your heart." I almost believed he was truly worried about me—for about a nanosecond.

"Go fuck yourself, J," I said. I got up slowly, put on my jacket, and swung my backpack onto my shoulder. "I'm tired. I'm going home to bed. If you need to get in touch with me in a hurry, call my cell phone like everyone else.

I'm sure you have the number. But if it's turned off, it means I'm busy. Or in bed . . . with whomever I damn well please." I threw my backpack over my shoulder and walked out. I left J standing there staring after me. I don't know what he was thinking, but I bet it wasn't a pretty thought.

As for Darius, I didn't know what to believe. But I'd be watchful. The worm of doubt was already burrowing deep into the heart of the rose.

CHAPTER 8

The Cocktail Party

For our Saturday evening out, Benny had gussied herself up to the nines. She was wearing a Betsey Johnson fuchsia number with a slit up the side that went all the way to Honolulu. She had applied glittery body makeup and added gold sparkle to her hair. The heels on her mules were so high that I didn't know how she walked. She'd put on a full-length white fox coat. She wasn't subtle, but she looked good.

Reflecting my somber mood, I wore brown leather pants and a brown jersey halter top under a Harley motorcycle jacket. I had on square-toed Frye boots and didn't do much with my hair. I looked like a brown wren next to a peacock.

Arriving at my mother's—she lived in Scarsdale despite her counterculture proclivities—Benny and I were greeted at the door by a pimply-faced girl in a miniskirt and cowboy boots. She held a martini glass containing a clear liquid garnished with olives, no ice. "I just got these ready. Want one? Vodka martini. Or would you rather have gin?" she offered.

"Neither. No, thanks. Not for me. What about you, Benny?" I said.

"I wouldn't mind, sugar," Benny said. "Just to take the edge off."

"Stoli or gin?"

"Stoli."

"Anything in it?"

"Olives. And just rinse the glass out with vermouth, honey, if you don't mind. But I think I'd like to get my coat off first."

"No problemo," the girl said. "Just leave it on the chair and I'll hang it up for you. I hope it's fake fur. You know it's cruel and inhumane to kill animals for their pelts."

What about for their blood? I thought. What I said was, "By the way, who are you?"

"I'm Sage Thyme. I'm in your mother's Save the Trees: Stop the Deforestation Group."

"I didn't know the forest primeval still stood in Westchester. Logging and clear-cutting? What are they building, another mall?"

"You silly," Sage Thyme said as she downed her drink. "You are just like your mother said you would be. Very biting. I mean satiric. The logging's upstate in the Adirondacks. It's terrible, but I'm sure you knew that. You were just pulling my leg, weren't you? You know, you are so lucky. Your mom is really something. So much energy." Sage gave me a puzzled look and added, "She sort of looks younger than you." Then she shrugged and downed the rest of her drink before saying, "Well, she *is* a vegetarian, and after all she was a teen mother in the slums. She told us all about how she was no more than a child when she had you, and how she had to claw her way out of poverty and her culturally deprived beginnings. She has such courage. What a wonderful role model for all of us!" Sage flashed me a loopy grin and went scurrying off toward the kitchen, and it was all I could do not to roll my eyes.

"Oh, she's a role model, all right," I murmured to myself, "if someone needs a mentor for making up big fat lies." The real story was that my mother had been over six hundred years old when she had me. She lived in a doge's palace on the outskirts of Rome at the time and had already amassed enough gold and jewels to make her one of the wealthiest women in the world. The "clawed" part might be accurate, however.

On cue, my mother sailed into the hall, dressed in an inky-black floor-length gown that had a wide leather waistband and leather lacing up the front. I thought it could double as a wedding dress for the Bride of Frankenstein. The collar of the dress draped back into a huge hood that hung down the back nearly to the floor. Around her neck she wore her peace sign. She looked positively Goth. I'm lucky she wasn't wearing a nose ring. She clapped her hands at our arrival and said in an earsplitting voice, "Daphy, you look . . . you look very nice. And you've brought a friend!"

"Yes. Mar-Mar, this is Benny Polycarp, a colleague from my new *job*." And I surreptitiously gave Benny a pinch to remind her that my mother didn't know about our real job. I had rehearsed what she should say on the drive up here, and I hoped she didn't blow it. "Benny, this is Marozia Urban, my mother."

"I am so pleased to meet you," Benny drawled. "It's such a homey-time feeling to visit with family again. Being alone in New York City makes me nervous as a whore in church, and that's the truth."

For the sake of appearances Mar-Mar had forgone her usual ganja for the more respectable high of alcohol. However, even with one foot in happy land, she narrowed her eyes at Benny in close scrutiny and gave her a careful once-over. "Where are you from?"

"Branson. Branson, Missouri. It's real country down

there. Not like here. You have such a beautiful house, Marozia, and Scarsdale looks just so pretty. On our way here I saw that you have a Starbucks and a Barnes and Noble, and all the good department stores. It looks just like heaven. Back home my house was so far out in a holler they had to pipe daylight in. Not that I wanted daylight much after I was turned."

Mar-Mar gave me a questioning look.

"Yes, she's a vampire," I whispered.

"Oh, right on!" Mar-Mar gushed. She put her arm around Benny's shoulder and steered her toward the living room. "But how in the world did a vampire end up in Branson?" she asked, softly, in a conspiratorial voice.

Tagging along behind them I could hear Benny start to tell her about a bluegrass banjo player she met back in the 1920s, and he was just so sweet-talking, and the next thing she knew he was showing her things . . . why, she never dreamed people did that . . . and one thing led to another, and it just got out of hand, and her daddy would have just about kilt her if he found out, but he didn't find out, of course. . . .

I had tuned out the conversation, however, because I had spotted the languid young man sprawled on the sofa. He had to be Louis. I nearly giggled as I took in his outfit. No straight man wore a shirt like that, lavender silk with French cuffs undone and dangling over his hands. He had a ring on every single finger, and I never could handle going out with a guy who wore more jewelry than I did. But it was his paleness and the brilliant green eyes that were almost incandescent that almost made me gasp. He noticed me staring at him, and looked back at me. The hair on my arms stood up, and I felt like something had walked over my grave. I swore I felt singed by his stare. He tossed his head, and dark curls tumbled over his brow. I couldn't make up my

mind if he looked more like a young Keith Richards or
RuPaul. His leather pants were so tight, it was obvious
his "package" was either stuffed with a sock or very impressive. *This* was my mother's choice of a mate for
me? She had to be kidding. If the man wasn't gay he
was at least bisexual.

Louis stood and gave a little bow toward the three of
us. He was very tall. He smiled at me and gave me shud-
ders. But as luck would have it, I didn't have to worry. He
took one long look at Benny and never again looked anywhere else. He extended a white hand, and when she
grasped it, he took hers to his lips and kissed her fingers
one at a time. His mouth was very red. "I am Louis," he
said, pronouncing it the French way, as "Looey."

"Your accent?" Benny said.

"Louis'ana. And you?"

"The Show-Me State, sweetie," she purred. "Missouri.
Why, we are practically kin."

Their eyes met and locked. They sat down on the sofa
tight against each other, laughing and talking as if no one
else existed. Mar-Mar looked nonplussed. Her best-laid
plans had gone kaput for sure.

I couldn't have been happier. Giving up without a
fight, Mar-Mar towed me over to meet Zoe, Louis's
mom. Zoe was a bony harridan who must have been sev-
enty when she was turned, because eternal youth eluded
her. The thought of some young vampire lowering himself onto her wrinkled neck did not bear thinking about.
She wore a boxy Chanel suit, held a cigarette holder in
her fingers, and reeked of gin. Swaying as she rose from
her chair, she gave me a long-toothed grin. "You look exactly like your mother!"

I repressed a snort, but just barely. My mother and I, a
Mutt and Jeff duo, don't even look related. The woman
was three sheets to the wind and probably couldn't see

straight. Sage Thyme walked up with her tray. "Not another of those dreadful concoctions!" Zoe shrieked. "Get me a martini made with Bombay Sapphire, girl. Now that's what a real martini drinker prefers. And as Mar-Mar can tell you, I'm a real martini drinker."

Mar-Mar laughed and said, "Right on! Now, Zoe, tell us that story again—it's my favorite one—about being up in a tree with the maharaja. The story about the tigers."

"You missed the point completely, Marozia." She smiled a bleary smile. "There *were* no tigers. *That* was the point." Zoe turned to me, stabbing the air with her cigarette holder, and tried to focus her eyes in my direction. "You see, Daphne, Louis and I had gone off to India . . . oh, it was back before the war." She stopped and drifted off for a moment. "Which war was it? I think it was the first? Was it the first, Mar-Mar? Well, whenever it was, the maharaja, the old devil, had only one thing on his mind. . . ."

The evening went downhill from there. I stuck it out for an hour before I suggested to Benny that we head back to the city. We could go clubbing if she wanted. She whispered to me that she hoped Louis could come too. She looked so happy I couldn't say no. I called a car service and we said our good-byes. Mar-Mar kissed the air beside my ear and made some sniffing sounds while murmuring something about always hurting the one you love. I was saved from a further guilt trip when her John Lennon CD started skipping and she rushed over to rescue it. The sound of Enya singing "Only Time" soon filled the room. Talk about hurting the one you love. Sage Thyme yelled from the kitchen that other members of Save the Trees just phoned and were on the way up. They wanted to hear the story about the boy who could hear bats calling. Should she mix more drinks? Where was the bag of Pirates Booty? All in all I didn't think Mar-Mar would miss me. Benny, Louis, and I slipped out without provoking tears.

A whole vampire club scene exists in New York City, but I usually avoid it like the plague. Just because they are vampires doesn't mean I have anything in common with the men who hang out there, besides the whole bloodlust thing. They're almost all party animals, getting drunk or high, following their favorite music groups, and competing for the best-looking women. I've never met even one who wanted to discuss books or stroll through a museum. Their idea of culture is movies and television, the latest drinks, and the fastest new cars—and lurking in the background is always the quest for their next bite. That's exactly what I don't want to be around. And to tell the truth, it wasn't even nine o'clock and I was feeling totally down, missing Darius.

We had no sooner climbed into the Lincoln Town Car that arrived to take us back to the city, when I made up my mind to call him from my cell phone. I knew it was unwise, having read that best seller, *The Rules,* a while ago to see if anything had changed in two hundred years. It hadn't: Men still want women who are hard to get. The worst thing a woman can do is act needy, pushy, aggressive, in control, outspoken—or honest. And I was about to break one of the top ten rules: Don't Call Him and Rarely Return His Calls.

All day my thoughts about my relationship with Darius had been bouncing back and forth in my brain like a Ping-Pong ball: He didn't ask what I was doing on Saturday night. On the other hand, he had already dozed off when I left him the night before. Then again, he could have called. He didn't, and I checked both my cell and home phone messages every hour on the hour. Conversely, I had to factor in that he was a spy in the middle of a dangerous mission. Maybe he didn't have time for social calls. Unfortunately the bottom line was inescapable: If he cared about me at all, he would have wanted to know if I got home okay, if it was as good for me as it was for him, and if I was free to see him again. It wasn't a good sign that he hadn't phoned the minute he woke up.

Canceling out the bottom line, however, was the fact that I had stayed celibate for nearly two hundred years. I was now in hormonal overdrive and deaf to reason. My rationale for making the call, not that it really mattered, was that Darius and I needed to talk about our next move with Bonaventure.

I turned to Benny and Louis. "You guys mind if I give somebody a jingle? See if he can meet us?" I said.

"Why would we mind, sugar?" Benny asked.

"He's not one of us," I said. "He doesn't know about us. If that's going to be a problem, let me know."

Benny looked at Louis. "Doesn't bother me," he said.

"You go right ahead, Daphy. We'd love to meet him," she said, as Louis put his arm around her and gave her a squeeze.

I was taking a hell of a chance. If Darius was a vampire slayer, I could be endangering all our lives. But my thinking was being short-circuited by my sex drive, by being alone on a date night, and by the fact that the later it got in the evening, the greater my desires grew. Once again I feared the ancient yearnings within me would always batter my soul, putting my high-minded resolves at war with my base instincts, driving me with hungers that originated far back in misty time, when wolves howled on the Russian steppes and the Gypsy wagons of Romany moved restlessly across the land, traveling south to warmer climes and camping outside our city, on the Roman plains.

I sat in the jump seat of that Lincoln with the cell phone in my hand, ready to make the call. Instead I looked out the window at the darkness and remembered how it all began for me.

Centuries ago, with the ground mist swirling around my slim ankles, the full moon rising, I received that fateful bite in the arms of a Gypsy king. Poor Mar-Mar, she had tried to protect me for so long. Perhaps if that caravan hadn't camped so near our palace, if I hadn't been merely eighteen with my hormones raging, and if I hadn't seen Florin, his shirt open to the waist, a bandanna around his neck, standing there in the shadows holding the reins of his gray pony, perhaps it would not have happened at all.

I had been picking flowers there at the edge of the woods. My arms were filled with trailing blossoms. I tarried later than was prudent. In truth, I had seen him there before and had come looking for him. From the moment I had stepped into the meadow I knew he was there waiting, and I moved self-consciously. I bent down amidst buttercups and daisies until my dress became damp at the hem from the grass. The skirt pulled against my legs as I moved, outlining my young body. I kept bending and plucking the flowers as the twilight lengthened. I felt no fear at all. All the while I was gathering the blooms, he was smiling as he watched me, and when I finally straightened up and stared back at him, he beckoned for me to come. Me, foolish girl, so curious and so attracted to those dark devil eyes, walked into the shadows. He took my hand and boosted me up onto the back of his pony. Then he led me off. My flowers were soon crushed beneath me in the bed of my damnation. I have often thought that if I had chosen another path that day, perhaps my life would have been different. Or perhaps that meeting had been my escapable fate, writ somewhere on my soul by a ghostly hand.

Weak and pale after that long night, nearly dead from loss of blood, I awoke in my own bed, Mar-Mar weeping in a chair nearby. She called in doctors and chanted every spell she knew. They applied poultices and plasters, and still I raved with delirium. My fevered dreams were hideous, fantastical, and erotic. I remember them still. And I remember crying out over and over for my lover, screaming his name until my voice was a mere rasping croak. I called to him even when no sound came from my bloodless lips.

Florin returned for me again that night, landing on my window and hissing at Mar-Mar that she knew it was already too late. My sunken eyes looked up at him as if he were a god. I rose from the bed, my white nightgown billowing out behind me like a fairy's wings, and I went to him despite Mar-Mar's desperate pleas. He gathered me in his arms and we flew away to a fog-shrouded wagon sitting under the tall larch trees. All too soon my white gown was stained with red and the deed irrevocably done.

I shook myself out of my reveries, looked at the cell phone again and dialed Darius's number. He answered on the first ring.

"Darius?" I said, "It's Daphne."

"Hey," he said, his voice soft and low.

"Hey, you, too. You busy?"

"No, I just finished up. Tell you about it later. I was just going to call you."

"Yeah, sure you were."

"No, really. I couldn't stop thinking about you."

I felt annoyance that he thought I'd believe him so easily. If he were thinking about me so much, he would have called me. "Whatever," I said, disgust clear in my voice. I nearly hung up right then, but my libido kept me from pushing the disconnect button.

He must have heard me loud and clear, because he was almost pleading when he said, "Daphne, honest, I was in a location where I didn't have reception on my cell phone since before dawn this morning. I really wanted to talk with you. Can we get together tonight? I have some things to run by you."

"That's why I called you," I said. "I think we need to get our plans straight." I knew I was lying. A business meeting wasn't at all what I had in mind for a Saturday date with Darius. I kept talking: "I'm with some friends headed back into the city from Westchester. You want to meet us? Hang on a minute." I hit the mute button and interrupted Benny and Louis's conversation about foreign films, specifically whether Fellini's *Nights of Cabiria* was better than Truffaut's *The Four Hundred Blows*. "Look, a vampire club is out for me," I said to them. "Do you mind hanging out for a while at the Library Bar at the Hudson Hotel? It's on West Fifty-eighth Street."

Benny said, "Whatever you want; it's fine with us."

I told Darius and approximated the time when we'd get there, then clicked off.

"Don't you think a person's taste in movies splits according to gender lines?" Louis asked me. "There are chick flicks and guy flicks."

"Personally I think it splits according to IQ points. Films that demand a brain and those that don't," I said, not giving a good goddamn about the discussion.

Louis ignored my indifference. "Let me guess. You also like Fellini, but you prefer *Juliet of the Spirits*."

I sighed. Louis and Benny were so into each other, they didn't notice I wasn't fired up about discussing film. I didn't want to be a party pooper, so I said, "Fellini's okay."

Benny chimed in, "What's your favorite movie?"

I laughed at her question. My taste runs to the quirky

and offbeat in just about everything. *"Caro Diario,"* I answered.

Louis raised his eyebrows and looked at Benny. She shrugged. He said. "I never heard of it."

"Me neither," Benny said. "Who's the director?" I noticed that the two of them were now holding hands.

"Nanni Moretti," I answered.

"The Italian Communist?" Louis squealed.

I cringed inwardly at his tinny voice, but pasted a smile on my face. "Yeah, I guess Moretti is a Communist. But it's not his politics I care about. He's funny, and I prefer comedies, that's all. Even dark ones."

"Come on, Daphy, name another one. See if we know it," Benny begged.

"An Everlasting Piece, directed by Barry Levinson," I said.

"Got me again," Louis said. "Your choices are pretty oddball, if you don't mind me saying. What made you like this one?"

"It's Irish, set in Belfast during the Troubles," I said. "It's pretty recent, and not dark. It has a great sound track. It's full of irony and very funny. Life has enough tears. I don't need more at the movies."

Benny and Louis exchanged glances. Louis rolled his eyes. Benny giggled.

"By the way," Louis said, "I've been admiring your ring all night. May I see it?"

"Sure. It's Florentine. Renaissance." I took off my leopard-head ring and gave it to him.

Louis turned on one of the car's interior lights and held the ring close to it. "Exquisite," he said. "I have a thing for rings, as you can probably tell," he said, and held up a bejeweled hand. "The design of this ring is highly unusual. I can see there's a maker's hallmark inside."

"May I see?" Benny asked, and Louis handed it over.

Benny examined the ring closely in a way only a jeweler would. I could see admiration on her face. "It's lovely. I've seen real Renaissance period rings only in museums, never up close. After all, Daphy, I'm soooo much younger than you," she said, shooting me a wicked grin. I responded very maturely by sticking my tongue out at her. When we stopped giggling, she took another look at the ring and said, "Daphy, honey, do you know one of the emerald panther eyes is loose in the setting?"

"No. Let me see." She handed it back. I couldn't see well, but I could feel that it was.

"If you don't mind my taking it, I'll have one of the jewelers fix it when I go into work on Monday. Don't worry; I won't let it out of my sight. I can return it to you Monday night."

"That would be terrific," I said. "I'd hate to lose a stone. These emeralds are as close to perfect as they ever get." I handed the ring back and Benny put it in her tiny purse, which was firmly attached to the belt of her dress by a golden chain. She might look flighty and careless, but that was just part of her "dumb blonde" persona. I had seen enough of her to know that Benny Polycarp was smart, meticulous, and shrewd.

"Thanks, Benny. I appreciate it. Not to change the subject," I said, "but you wanted to talk, and this may be the only chance we get." I wasn't worried about speaking in front of Louis. Vampires excel at betrayal—outside the vampire family. Within our race we follow unwritten rules. One of them is not to snitch or to "out" anyone to humans. We close ranks and circle the wagons to protect each other. Persecuted throughout the centuries, we know our survival has depended on close family associations. There is *us*, and there is *them*. Unlike many other minorities, we can't become part of the mass culture. We can convert others to our race; we can't assimilate into theirs.

"Oh, yes. Daphy, I don't know if I have the nerves for the spy stuff, I really don't. They recruited me partly because I have a degree in gemology. So I'm supposed to be working for a firm in the Diamond Exchange. The place is crawling with intrigue, I tell you. And that just has to do with who's boffing who. They've been dealing with Bonaventure for years, ever since he's been insisting that certain buyers pay him in uncut diamonds. My firm regularly appraises the deliveries to make sure he's getting what he's promised. The head of my firm has been "convinced," you might call it, to cooperate with U.S. intelligence. I'm being sent up to Bonaventure's Monday night to certify a large payment in African diamonds from Sierra Leone—blood diamonds, they call them."

"Benny," I cut in, "I was wondering about how the weapons exchange for diamonds worked. Do you know?" I asked.

"Well, the way I understand it," Benny started, "it's done under the counter. You know, illegally. The terrorists smuggle the diamonds into the country, which isn't very hard to do. They turn them over to Bonaventure in exchange for the weapons. Actually they get a key or something like that that gives them access to the weapons. And yes, he always is on the up-and-up about that, but Bonaventure isn't about to physically turn over *anything*. The terrorists take all the risks, and he keeps his hands clean. He has complete deniability."

"He must be extremely cunning and cautious," I said, feeling very uneasy about the agency's scheme. "He's going to be suspicious of anything that seems unusual. I hope J knows what he's doing."

"You and me both," Benny said, and shivered.

"So how does Bonaventure convert the diamonds into cash without the banks tipping off the U.S. government?" I wondered out loud.

"It's pretty simple, really, Daphy. My boss is the one who actually converts the diamonds into cash—at a very nice discount, so it's worth his while. The cash is in the form of a cashier's check drawn on a numbered Swiss account. The Swiss give no one, not even U.S. intelligence agencies, the identities of account holders, nor reveal banking transactions."

"So Bonaventure sits on a fortune and there's no way to trace how he got it?" I said, sounding surprised. I was being disingenuous with Benny now; I had a Swiss account of my own, as did my mother. We've had plenty to hide over the centuries, and governments can follow a paper trail, so we've taken precautions not to leave one. The Swiss have always been very cooperative, since my mother is an extremely rich woman.

Benny was talking a mile a minute now. "Well, Daphy, that's why I'm getting so wound up. I'm supposed to show up Monday and appraise the diamonds, then give Bonaventure two cashier's checks, made out to cash, totaling *two hundred and fifty million dollars.* Then I transport the diamonds back to my company. Now, honey, there's no safer courier on earth than a vampire, so I'm not worried about getting mugged or anything." She stopped for a breath, then plunged ahead. "I am worried about Bonaventure smelling a rat. A new person being sent for this major deal . . . I mean, the head of the firm is supposed to handle this kind of exchange, not a blonde from Branson, Missouri. And the thing is, I have to be there when the diamonds are actually handed over. Bonaventure won't accept them unless I certify them. So J wants me to photo these guys on the sly and make sure the bugs you planted pick up the transaction."

I was thinking about J's scheme, and it was full of holes. "Benny," I asked, "you're sure this is happening at Bonaventure's apartment?"

"Yes. He doesn't go to his clients. They come to him."

"I have an appointment with him Monday night. I'd like to know how he's putting this all together."

"I'm supposed to get there at eight thirty," Benny clarified.

"After me." I stared out the window in silence for a few minutes.

Benny looked at Louis, who had listened without interrupting. "Benny, I think you're in a world of trouble," he said.

"Well, what do you think, Daphy? Can we pull this off?"

"Maybe," I said. "Here's the way I see it. Bonaventure is going to get out of New York City as fast as possible after the terrorists get the weapons. But he also wants my client's art. If anything catastrophic is planned for the city, he won't take the chance on its getting destroyed, so he'll want to take possession of it ASAP after the diamond exchange. My guess is he'll make a bid on the art and have it ready for me Monday night. He'll ask me to confirm it with Schneibel, the collector, while I'm right there at the apartment. If Schneibel agrees to the sale, Bonaventure will pay me on the spot—that's why there are two checks—and then arrange to pick up the art, all within the next seventy-two hours. Maybe the time pressure will make him less cautious than usual and more vulnerable to J's plan. Unfortunately, I don't think we can count on it."

"Do you really think terrorists are planning another attack on New York?"

"I don't know. I hope not. But if these guys with the key, or whatever they pick up, can be followed and they are stopped before they take possession of the weapons, we can make sure there won't be."

Louis broke in. "Let me get this straight. The safety of millions of people and the greatest city in the world rests on two female vampires. Pardon me for saying this, but we're fucked."

"Louis!" Benny said. "That's not nice! Besides, we have lots of backup, don't we, Daphy?"

"Oh, sure we do," I said sarcastically. "Except that we've never met any of them besides J. We don't know who they are or how many of them there are. Lots of backup? Uh-uh. Benny, I think we are screwed. And I'm beginning to believe we're expendable in J's eyes. I planted the listening devices, so whatever else I do is probably a bonus. Once the terrorists show up with the diamonds at Bonaventure's, J's people can start tailing them. You're a Judas goat. The bad guys are sure to show up before eight thirty because the diamonds have to be in Bonaventure's possession before you arrive with the money. J should be keeping Bonaventure's apartment building under surveillance, and he'll take his own damned photos. I bet the regular diamond guy was too scared to do this deal; that's why J needed you.

"He's been blowing smoke up our asses, Benny. And from what I've seen of his agency's operations, I don't think he has a snowball's chance in hell of catching these terrorists before it's too late. I think we'd better plan on handling this ourselves." I felt taken in, betrayed, and damned mad. *I wasn't going to take it anymore,* I thought.

"Can we handle it?" Benny said, her doubt evident and her big eyes like saucers.

"Transformed into vampire form we can," I said as if putting down my trump card.

"Oh, shit!" she and Louis said in unison.

"Well, yeah, it's a radical idea—vampires to the rescue of humanity." My fists were clenched, and my voice was strong. I meant every word. "Damn it, Benny, if we can't do this, nobody can."

"Wait a minute," Louis said. "I'll probably regret saying this, but count me in."

As it turned out, he was all too right.

Benny, a small-town girl in the big city, went all starry-eyed on the way up the steep, tall escalator that rose from street level to the Hudson's hotel lobby. At the top of the escalator she stood there openmouthed, staring at the mammoth chandelier, and I had to drag her past the huge disco bar with its illuminated floor and queue of hip young singles waiting to get in. The rest of the Hudson's main floor sits in a cozy gloom, with walls and ceilings painted black and the lighting very dim. It was perfect for illicit assignations and intrigue. My high comfort level here no doubt relates to its cavelike ambience.

The Library Bar, quiet and classy, sits in the rear of the hotel to the right of the bank of elevators. We walked in, and I spotted Darius waiting for us. He had commandeered the sofa by the fireplace, and since the place was packed, I figured he'd given a good tip to the bartender, a tall, thin Rasta with dreadlocks.

"Ohhh, yummy," Benny said when she spotted him waving at us. "He looks just like Brad Pitt. Don't worry, Daphy; Louis and I will have just one drink," she whispered to me as walked. "Then we'll split. Let's you and I talk again late tonight."

"Sure, Benny—why don't you drop by my apartment?" I whispered back.

"Cool. I'll give you a jingle when I'm on my way," she said sotto voce; then she was walking toward Darius, her accent dripping with honey, saying, "Why, sugar, it's so nice to meet a friend of Daphne's. I'm Benny from Branson, Missouri, and this is Louis. He's from N'awlins. We're just two out-of-towners in the big, bad city."

Darius grinned at her, and I caught him eyeing her cleavage. It would have been hard to miss. Benny didn't react, and I figured she was probably used to it. "My pleasure, I'm sure," Darius said to her, and shook hands with both of them. He held up his glass. It looked like Scotch. "What are you drinking?"

"Stoli martini, straight up, olive," Louis said.

"The same," Benny agreed.

"And you?" he asked me.

"Pellegrino, no ice, slice of lemon. Thanks." I was sticking to my no-alcohol rule, especially around Darius. My control slipped dangerously whenever he was near me. I had almost bitten him last night, and I felt a jolt of fear every time I remembered that.

Darius disappeared in the direction of the bar, and we vampires three sat down in front of the fire. Darius was back quicker than I expected. He took a seat on the arm of the sofa next to me, and a waitress showed up shortly afterward with the drinks.

"Are you in town on vacation?" Darius asked Benny and Louis. It occurred to me that not one person here could answer anything about themselves with truth. The normal social exchanges between strangers would be a fabrication created of lies and misinformation.

Louis said he was visiting his mother, which was a stretch, since according to Mar-Mar he was now living with her in Scarsdale. Benny said she was in New York for a job interview, and I said we three were friends from way back. Darius told them he was in the import-export business, bringing in electronics from China. We suffered through this farce for about ten minutes, until I said, "Benny, I know you and Louis would really rather be back at the Hudson's main bar with the music and dancing. Darius and I have some things to talk about, so it's okay, really."

Relief was obvious on both their faces. They grabbed their coats and said their good-byes. Darius went and sat at the opposite end of the sofa and we just stared at the fire for a few minutes. I fiddled with the lemon in my mineral water; he sloshed the Scotch around in the glass. With Darius right here next to me, I thought again that J's accusation that he was a vampire hunter came from spite, and maybe jealousy. Yet I felt cautious and closed. I was watching every word I said.

"So how are you feeling?" I asked stiffly.

"I'm fine, a little tired. It was a long day. How are you?" he said.

"I'm fine." I looked at him, wondering what was going on in his head. As if he read my thoughts, he said, "Look, Daphy, I would have phoned you this morning, I really meant to, but I was ordered in for a conference first thing."

I looked at him without reacting and said flatly, "Okay, you don't have to explain. But I have to be honest; I thought it was shitty that you didn't call."

"Look, I'm sorry, I really am. The whole day has been nuts." He moved closer so we wouldn't be overheard. In a low voice close to my ear, he said, "There's a lot of intelligence chatter being picked up; things are moving very quickly. We are pretty sure Bonaventure's weapons are in Port Newark. On a container ship. But there are dozens of ships and thousands of containers. We could find the right one, but not quickly enough. We need to spot the terrorists when they go to pick them up. It's the only sure way. I assume J's people have the same information and a similar plan."

My heart was beating fast, partly from what Darius was telling me and partly because his breath was caressing my ear as he talked, and it was exciting me. I tried to block my rising desire and concentrate on the spying operation. I said in all honesty, "I don't know what J's plans are, but it sounds as if we might be duplicating efforts."

Darius nodded in agreement. "Yeah, but this time it's a good idea. It means at least one team should be successful."

I turned my face to look at him. Our lips were very close. Neither of us could resist, and he kissed me lightly before I said to him, "How does this new information affect *your* plans?"

"It makes breaking into Bonaventure's apartment Monday night even more urgent."

"Darius, if I'm going to help you do it, I want to know what you're planning to do once you get in."

He moved away from me and looked toward the fire as he said, "I have something to take care of."

I leaned toward him and turned his face toward me. "Darius, I want to know. What's going to happen?"

He took my hand in his and looked at me intently. "Daphne, I'm sorry, but I told you before: It's safer if I tell you nothing. What you don't know, you can't be forced to tell or accidentally give away. Believe me on this. And all I need you to do is to open the service entrance door. From the inside."

I left my hand in his and moved my body closer until we touched. "Is that it? Why do you need me at all? I thought you people knew how to pick locks."

"We do," he answered, putting his lips on my hair and stirring the fires banked inside me. "Unfortunately, the service door is the only other way into the apartment besides the front door, and it has one of those safety bars you see in older apartments, the ones that hook into the floor then lever against the door. There's no way to get in without using an ax, and I don't think that would be quiet enough."

I put my head on his shoulder. I felt so comfortable and

content. I mused that what we were talking could wait a couple of hours. Maybe Darius and I could book a room here and go upstairs. I had lost interest in spying for the moment. "Darius," I said, "maybe we can find a more private place to carry on this conversation."

To my dismay, Darius said, "Can you sit up? I want to show you something." I sighed and moved away from him. The chance of any hot sex tonight was fading fast. The mood was broken, and I was beginning to feel frustrated and edgy.

"I brought you a drawing," he said as he took a folded piece of paper from his pocket, opened it up, and put it down on the coffee table in front of us. It was a layout of the apartment. I wondered why J hadn't provided me with one. I guess he didn't have it. I wondered what agency Darius actually worked for. They certainly had excellent resources. I decided right then that I needed to find out. I'd start by asking J, and I tucked the idea away in the recesses of my mind.

"Here is where you come in," he said, taking one of my hands in his as he pointed with the other. He touched me as if it had become second nature to him, and I liked it. He went on showing me the map. "The living room is straight ahead; the dining room is off to the left."

I pointed to the library. "This is where we had our meeting," I said.

"Okay. You can see it's toward the rear of the apartment, where the bedrooms and some other rooms are. The kitchen is here, closer to the front entrance, on the far side of the dining room. Behind the kitchen is the maid's room with her bathroom. There's another small room on the other side of the bathroom, which is basically a corridor between the rooms. And here"—he pointed to a passageway marked in red—"is a hall running off the kitchen to the service entrance. Your biggest problem is going to be the maid. Make sure she's busy somewhere else. If anyone sees you in the kitchen or servants' quarters, you can always say you got lost on the way to the bathroom or decided to get a drink of water on the way back from a potty break."

"What about the cameras? Do you have any idea how I can avoid being spotted?"

"I'll take care of that. Those cameras will be having technical difficulties for a while that night. Don't worry about them."

I pulled back and disengaged my hand. "Well, I am worried about them and how I'm going to pull this off. Look, Darius, I can't screw up my dealings with Bonaventure. I'm not thrilled about doing this. Say I do succeed. How will you even know the door's open?"

"I just have to trust you," he said, and looked into my eyes. His sincerity looked forced as he added, "I do trust you. I'm counting on you, Daphne. I don't think you'll let me down."

"I don't buy a word of what you just said, Darius," I said, glaring into his face. "I may not know you well, but I think I know you better than that. You don't leave much to chance. Level with me here. How do you know I'm going to get an opportunity to open that door?"

He hesitated a minute, then said, "Because your girlfriend Benny, the one you just introduced me to, is going to show up at eight thirty to appraise the diamonds, and nobody will be paying much attention to you."

My mouth dropped open. I was taken aback completely. "How do you know that?" I asked.

"That's classified," he said brusquely.

"No, that's bullshit," I countered. "How do I know you're not spying on me? How do I know you didn't plant a listening device in my apartment the other night? I warn you, Darius, I'm ready to call it quits right now."

I pushed myself up from the deep cushions of the sofa, not gracefully, but faster than Darius could stop me.

I was so pissed off, I was ready to leave and not look back, and I intended to get home and make sure my apartment wasn't bugged.

Darius got up right behind me and caught my arm, pulling me toward him. "Daphne, wait," he said. "I didn't bug your apartment, I swear. Think about it. I didn't know I was going to end up there, did I? How likely is it that I'd be carrying technology like that around with me?"

I was steaming. I yanked my arm away. "All right. Then tell me how you knew about Benny. And don't lie, because I swear, Darius, if I catch you in another lie, it's over. You. Me. And any chance we can work together."

"We bugged the offices of the diamond dealer she works for."

"That's it?" I said with a little skepticism and a great deal of relief.

"That's it. And that's the truth. And J's bugged them too, only he did it with the owner's knowledge. You ought to warn your friend."

"I will, thanks. But damn it, you should have told me right from the start," I said. "Are you ever going to tell me everything, Darius?"

He held me next to him and looked deeply into my eyes. "Daphne, you have to understand that I can never tell you everything. It would betray the trust of others, and it would be dangerous to you and to me. All I can promise is that I'll tell you what concerns you directly. Will you accept that? And you can do the same for me. Agreed?"

I thought about it. I reached up and touched his face. I was beginning to feel we were linked in ways that went beyond the sex we had shared. What he offered to tell me was more than I had any right to expect. We were *secret* agents, after all. I knew he saw me as less than an equal, but in the spy game I was the beginner and he was a veteran. I had to give a little, since he had no way of knowing about my powers. It was smarter to let him think he was top dog, at least for now.

"I need you, Daphne . . ." he began and my heart skipped a beat before he finished his sentence, "to get that door open for me at eight thirty. I'm really sorry about asking you to do this, but it's important."

I shook my head. "Darius, I'll still be in the apartment, the men making the exchange are going to be showing up, the bodyguards will be there, Benny will be too, and who knows how many others. The apartment is going to be swarming with people. I don't see how you can accomplish anything."

Darius didn't hesitate to answer me. "I'll be in that little spare room until I make my move. You'll be long gone when I do. And Benny will be out of there before anything goes down. I'll make sure of it."

I decided to see if he knew anything else. "Darius, do you know who is bringing the diamonds?" I asked.

"No, but it's not likely to be the terrorists. It will probably be middlemen. And Daphne, that's as much as I know."

My mind was racing. I had to decide what to do after I met with Bonaventure. I hoped Benny wouldn't be too hungover to think about it too.

I turned my attention back to Darius. I felt a little guilty about lying to him on so many levels when I was throwing a hissy fit because he was lying to me. A sadness came over me. He was staring at me. "What?" I said.

"Daphne, I . . . well, I want you to know I do care about you. And God knows I want you. Just standing this close to you is arousing me."

I glanced down and saw the bulge in the front of his trousers. "You might say that." I smiled.

"I can't exactly hide it from you." He grinned. "But seriously, for the next couple of days I think we need to keep our distance, except if it concerns Bonaventure. We need to focus on this mission and stopping the terrorists. And realistically, we don't have the time to spend together. But when this is all over, I want to see you again, if you're willing."

I knew what he said made sense, and I wished I didn't feel so disappointed. "Assuming we are both still standing when it's over," I said bitterly. "You know there's another way to look at this; that we should take advantage of every moment we can because one or both of us may be *dead* when this is all over."

"Daphne, I've spent a lot of time training and learning how to stay alive. I've been in dangerous situations before. I can't tell you not to worry. It would be better if you didn't, though. Worry doesn't accomplish anything. I'll do everything I can to succeed. I can say that much. I also wanted to say that I think you have a lot of guts."

"Thanks, Darius, that's just the kind of compliment a girl likes to hear," I said, softening my words with a half-hearted smile.

He smiled right back at me, and my heart did a little flutter. "I could give you lots of other compliments, but we might end up at the front desk, hoping they have a room open. I can't risk it."

"I'd like to take the risk, but I'm getting the message," I said. "So if we're both alive and in one piece after this assignment, then what do you have in mind?"

"Long walks beside the river. Sunsets at the beach. A movie on Friday nights. Let's take it one step at a time."

I was surprised by the rosy picture Darius painted of us as a couple. Our passions exploded as soon as we touched, but who knew if we had enough in common for more than an affair? We had so much against us—his being a spy and my being a vampire, just for starters. But I didn't voice my doubts. There'd be time to face those problems after we stopped the terrorists. And I suspected that, despite his assurances, Darius thought there was a good chance he'd be killed. From what had happened the other night, when he didn't use a condom, I was convinced he wasn't planning on a future—and at best he was deluding himself that there could be an "us." At worst he was handing me a line to string me along. That realization sent a stab of pain through me.

"Darius, I don't know what to say," I responded honestly.

"Daphne," he said, encircling me in his arms, "don't say anything. Think about it. We can be good together."

The fire was warm, the room was dim, I was in a handsome man's arms, and I felt good for the moment, so why not dream? I knew in reality that a relationship between us would be difficult, maybe impossible. I looked at him smiling at me and didn't smile back. "Okay," I said, "let's see what happens. Then I'm willing to take it one step at a time."

"That's all I'm asking for, Daphne." He sounded a little disappointed. I pressed closer to him, and I remembered the major reason I was here in the first place: Darius turned me on.

"Don't try to get out of it by getting yourself killed, okay?" I said, and put my head against his chest and heard his heart beating. Right now Darius was alive. All I had was the moment, and I wanted him tonight, not tomorrow or the next day. I could feel his cock pressing into me. He groaned.

"Daphne, you're killing me." He broke our clinch, stepped away, and sat down on the sofa, pulling me down next to him. "I need a drink." He laughed.

Obviously I wasn't going to be able to seduce him, so I laughed too, and said, "Darius, if we're going to start dating, can I ask you something personal?"

He looked at me cautiously. "What do you want to know?"

"What's your favorite foreign film?" He gave me a blank look. Whatever Darius thought I was going to ask, that wasn't it. "Really, Darius, I want to know. Isn't that a typical 'dating' question?"

"Yeah, I guess so. Do you mean a foreign film or a classic? When it comes to movies, I'm more a Western fan."

"Westerns? You mean John Wayne? Guy rides off into the sunset after he chooses his horse over the girl?"

"Yeah, but more like Alan Ladd in George Stevens's *Shane.*"

I thought to myself, *The gunfighter trying to start over and have a new life.* That was interesting. I had just learned something that I was pretty sure was true about Darius. I decided to ask him another question. "Okay, then, what's your all-time favorite movie?"

"Disney's animated classic, *Bambi.*"

I quit there. I admit, I didn't know what to say after that. We sat for a long while, just being together as the fire sputtered and crackled. Eventually most people left the Library Bar, and the room was hushed except for an occasional clink of a glass as the bartender filled an order. Darius and I whispered rather than spoke. The nearness of his body felt warm and good. We held hands, and he stroked my fingers. We talked of sunrises we had seen and places we had been. We shared a preference for wandering through the quiet backstreets of old Italian cities, stopping in shops where no tourists ever went. I had bought licorice in Venice; he had found an olive shop in Rome. We both had climbed live volcanoes and marveled at their power, sat in awe on the marble seats of ruined

Roman amphitheaters and felt the presence of all those
who had been there centuries before us. He didn't talk
about the details of his life, and neither did I about mine.
It seemed to me each of us was hiding a great deal, yet we
were alike in so many ways—except for the crucial one I
hid from him: He was human, and I was a vampire. And
I could never change.

Finally we both knew it was time to go. Darius walked
me out and hailed me a cab. He gave me a lingering kiss
on the lips that ended all too soon. "Stay alive," I said
with all my heart.

"You too," he whispered as he reached out and tenderly touched my cheek before he closed the cab door. I
looked back and watched him until the taxi turned the
corner. I hoped it wasn't the last time I ever saw him.

CHAPTER 9

The best laid schemes o' mice and men
Gang aft a-gley,
And leave us naught but grief and pain
For promised joy.

—Robert Burns

The hours between midnight and dawn provoke melancholy and grief that find no natural outlet, no relief. They are the hours when nocturnal creatures hunt, bringing death quickly to innocent creatures in their bowers and beds. And these are the vampire hours that since the beginning of time have evoked humans' deepest fears and most secret desires when they long for a vampire's exquisite kiss and gift of immortality. For human beings have always been drawn to forbidden acts that titillate and tempt. Jung described this dark side as the shadow self. Deny it not; you have it. And I live it.

Yet as I waited in my apartment for Benny to finish her evening with Louis and call me, my own night wanderings covered only the intimate territory between the living room and bedroom. I vacuumed under the couch and rearranged my sock drawer. For me, performing these mindless tasks recalls Sisyphus pushing his great stone up the mountain, only to have it roll back again in endless repetition. Housework numbed the mind and stilled the emotions, and I hated it and loved it both. Tonight it kept my thoughts from spinning off to Darius. Almost.

When I finished vacuuming, I put an old October Project album in the CD player. Listening to those lyrical, haunting songs made me sit down and stare at the wall, thinking of Darius. I remembered how his eyes looked when he smiled, soft and warm and filled with laughter. They never held the hardness and frost of J's. I remembered how he had reached out and taken my hand in his and looked at my palm as if it held a priceless jewel; how he had lifted it up to his lips and kissed it. I remembered how he laid his cheek next to mine and whispered poetry into my ear. He told me I was beautiful, that I shone like the moon in his own secret sky. The things he had said to me earlier tonight suggested his feelings for me were growing. As for mine, I was afraid of the intensity of my emotions when I was with him. I didn't want to acknowledge how strongly I cared for him. This relationship was becoming far more than sex, and I knew it. I was sure he knew it too.

Sometime after two A.M. Benny phoned and soon afterward arrived at my door without Louis. She came in, all brass and shine, bringing cool air and fresh energy with her. We adjourned to the kitchen, where I made a pot of herbal tea. As we sat at the breakfast bar, she asked what I thought of Louis.

Diplomatically I didn't say that I thought he could be bisexual and that there was something really weird about his eyes. I didn't blurt out that for some reason he made me want to check to see if my wallet was still in my purse. After all, he did offer to help us, so I said, "He seems nice."

"I had a good time with him," she said, pouring her tea and blowing on it with delicate red lips to cool it. "There aren't any vampires I can go out with who live in Branson. I'm the only one, and believe me, that's something I know for sure. Sometimes vampires come to town to play a gig in one of the highway theaters. And you know what that means—they're usually rockabilly stars; don't ask! I can't discuss foreign films with *them*. The only things that those yahoos talk about is NASCAR, how much they're making or how much money they're getting screwed out of—like any of them was ever making that kind of cash working in Wal-Mart—or how much beer they can drink without passing out. One guy used to show me how well he could belch and fart. He thought he was impressing me. It's a desert out there, sugar. Your Darius is a dreamboat, though."

"And he's not a vampire," I said with sadness in my voice. "So where does that leave me? Nowhere. It's not like I can bring him home to meet Mother. How could I explain her?"

"Lots of mothers look very young, Daphy. Maybe he'd buy the story that she was a teenage mom."

I rolled my eyes at her. "He's not stupid, Benny. Once she started talking about hanging out with Abbie Hoffman and how cute his son America was as a little boy and wasn't it awful how the feds set up the Black Panthers, that would be the ball game. She doesn't even look old enough to have been a gleam in her daddy's eye back then. He'd either think she was nuts or know something just wasn't kosher."

Benny laughed and said, "Nuts wouldn't be so terrible. You could tell him she has mental problems."

I thought how that would go over with Mar-Mar if she ever found out. It wasn't a pretty thought. "I don't think so."

"Well, Daphy," she said, looking into her teacup and not looking at me, "if you ended up really loving a guy— I don't necessarily mean Darius—you could . . . you could, you know . . ."

"Turn him? Make him a vampire? I vowed I'd never

do that. Besides, it doesn't work out in a relationship. The person is too traumatized. You've taken away his identity and given him one he never asked for. He might still love you with part of his heart, but his resentment at what you've done . . . it changes his feelings to ashes sooner or later. Usually sooner."

"Yes, that's true," she said, staring even harder into the cup as if reading her own tea leaves. Then she said so softly I could barely hear her, "But what if you *asked* him first? What if someone loved you so much he was willing to convert for you?"

"Benny, you are so romantic," I blurted out. "Think about it. First he'd have to know what I was and accept me. That's a stretch of the imagination right there. Then he'd have to choose to become a monster, an outcast of society, a hunter of blood . . . and a hunted creature himself, all at the same time. I don't think it's ever happened."

Benny sighed and finished up her tea. Then she looked at me with a terrible sadness written on her face. "You're probably right, sugar. I just think about it sometimes. Our only choice then is to find another vampire, like Louis. And Daphy, I know he's . . . well, *flawed*, but he is smart and lots of fun. And not bad-looking either."

I thought, *Not bad if you're turned on by someone who looks like he plays rhythm guitar for the Rolling Stones, shoots heroin as a pastime, and never held a job in his life, which I'm sure Louis hasn't.* I said, "He does have beautiful eyes, so green."

"Exactly!" Benny said. "He wants to see me again tomorrow. So you don't think I'm making a mistake? I do like him a lot."

"Time will tell, Benny. As long as you're having a good time, what's the harm? Just don't lose your heart too soon." I laughed. "And I need to take my own advice. But

Benny, men aside, how are we going to handle tomorrow? Did you think about us acting on our own and forgetting about whatever J may or may not be doing?"

"Yes, I thought about it, and I hashed over my ideas with Louis. Is that okay?"

I figured that as usual Benny had thrown our vow to secrecy to the winds, but in this case I couldn't see how it was a problem. "Sure," I answered. "Maybe he can be a big help. Is he willing to transform?"

"He said he would. I don't think he minds becoming a bat as much as some of us do. I got the impression he likes it," she said brightly.

"Terrific. A serial converter," I said with a grimace.

Benny made a face at me. "Daphy, don't be snide. He just said he'd take vampire form if we needed him to do it. I thought that was really nice of him," she said, sounding agitated.

I figured I'd better shut up about Louis. I didn't want to upset Benny. We could use the muscle, and we didn't have the luxury of giving job interviews. "What I was thinking is that we're there. We don't know if J or anyone else is around. He is supposed to be listening—if Bonaventure hasn't found the bugs. But how close is he or his team? Who knows? I think we have two areas of concentration. First we need to watch Bonaventure and make sure he doesn't get his hands on the art he wants."

"Why?"

"It's a long story, Benny. The short version is that they're magical, and I'm worried they would give him supernatural powers no human should have."

"Oooohhh," she said, her big eyes growing even bigger. "Okay, then, that's one of us watching Bonaventure."

I went on with my ideas. "And someone needs to follow whoever drops off the diamonds and picks up the key. I think we can count on more than one person doing the delivery." Benny, with her life experience, knew, I was sure, that when it comes to huge sums of money, most humans can't be trusted. 101 times out of ninety-nine, a single person finding himself alone with $250 million worth of diamonds, would never show up at Bonaventure's. He'd take the money and run, open a Swiss bank account of his own, and pick out a villa on Capri. Even if he feared he'd be pursued, that much money can buy a lot of protection. So I knew we could count on two and probably three people making the delivery.

"I agree," she said. "And after what you said about J—and we don't know beans about any backup—I don't want to run the risk that these guys can get away. I think we need to follow them ourselves and find out who they're working with. Maybe we can discover if they know when the weapons will be picked up. It won't take *us* hours or days of interrogation." She grinned.

"Okay, then. Are you willing to follow the delivery-men?" I said, getting excited that things seemed to be falling into place.

"Sure," Benny agreed. "Louis will help me. I told him to stand by for my call."

"Good. I'll watch Bonaventure. And Benny, there's another thing I should mention."

"What's that?" she said.

"When I was in the apartment I discovered there's this woman, Catharine, with him. She's in love with him, I think. I also have this gut feeling she's some kind of prisoner of his. It's not relevant to our mission, but it bothers me. I just don't like to see any woman enslaved to a man, physically or emotionally. If she ever asks me for help, I'll give it. I just wanted to alert you to the situation. Anyway, while you go after the diamond guys, I'll find a way to watch for Bonaventure to leave, then go after him. J said we aren't supposed to stop him. But Benny, I can't let him get his hands on that art."

"Daphy, if you have to tear the guy to pieces, do it," Benny said, her sweetness gone and the hidden strength inside her putting a knockout punch in her voice. "Don't take any chances. You know and I know that evil needs to be eliminated. So much suffering and hate in this world. This guy is vermin. Get him."

A bad feeling came over me. I had worked for decades to commit myself to nonviolence and resist my blood appetites. Now I was choosing to become a warrior, a soldier, and maybe a killer. I hid my unease by flippantly reciting the old saying, "But Benny, killing someone because they've killed someone because killing is wrong. . . ."

"Oh, Daphy, don't go all philosophical," Benny countered. She had made up her mind and my flip-flopping seemed to be annoying her. She faced me squarely, looked into my eyes, and said, "What's to think about? If someone is a predator of the innocent, just turn him into hamburger and be done with it."

"Benny, girl, you surprise me," I said. "You're probably right, and I probably won't have a choice. Oh, one more thing. When you arrive at Bonaventure's try to keep the maid, Tanya, busy for about three or four minutes, away from the kitchen. Can you do it?"

"Is the pope Catholic?" she said.

I went to sleep soon after Benny left, finally awakening Sunday evening. I was still fired up, my dreams having been filled with nightmares of skeletons chasing me and the New Guinea masks laughing as I screamed. Sunday night passed with interminable slowness. I watched the phone. The one time it did ring it was Benny. "How are your nerves?" she asked.

"Lousy. How are yours?"

There was a little pause before she answered. "To be honest," she said, "I feel more alive than the undead have any right to feel. Now that I know it's going to happen, I just can't wait to get into the action. I've often been so bored. Now I feel excited, expectant."

"You are something else, girlfriend," I said. "See you tomorrow night."

"'Byeee, best girlfriend in the whole wide world," she drawled, and we hung up.

Needless to say, Darius didn't call. I watched old movies and infomercials all night long.

I slept hard all day Monday, again tossing and turning. This time I was running down endless corridors toward some distant destination that I never reached. In truth, I wasn't born for death but for a ceaseless wandering, and I began sobbing in my sleep. Then suddenly, in my dreams a nightingale sang, the same song perhaps heard by the homesick Ruth when she stood in tears amid the alien fields of Judah. The song called to me with magic notes, a silver bell tolling me back from forlorn thoughts, reminding me of beauty and peace and the hopes that pulled me onward. As long as I could round another bend in the road, what lay ahead as much a gamble as a throw of the dice, I had the strength to go on. Pain and loss could be waiting there, but so could unutterable joy.

Never fear the unknown. Hop onto a raft in the river of time and let it carry you along, the white water and perilous rocks all part of the adventure. You cannot stop the flow. Better, so much better, to be swept with its swiftness into the great churning sea of life, come what may.

When I awoke at twilight, I felt ready and strong. The phone rang before I left. It was Ringmaster, for Hermes. I felt a stab of anger and distrust.

"Everything's in place," he said.

"How do I know that?" I said.

There was silence for a moment. "Because I'm telling you it is," he said, as if I had some nerve even asking. "Are *you* ready?"

"Yes, but I have some questions about details you seem to have overlooked," I said, my voice as prickly as barbed wire. "Number one, how do I arrange the so-called delivery of the art?"

"You don't," J answered quickly. "Tell Bonaventure it will be brought to him the following day."

"What if he doesn't go along with that, J? Did you consider the possibility that if he makes payment, he may want immediate delivery?"

J's voice snapped back at me. "Use your brains. Tell him to be reasonable. The pieces need to be properly packed for shipment."

"No, J, you use yours!" The words slipped out before I could stop them. "I can't tell Bonaventure what to do, and he would think something's fishy if I try. Is the art really going to be there for him to get? Schneibel said he'd never let Bonaventure have the pieces." My hand was gripping the phone so hard it hurt.

J spoke very slowly and deliberately. "What Schneibel wants or doesn't want isn't your concern. Don't worry; if Bonaventure buys the art, he gets the art. And we can use this as an opportunity to plant surveillance devices in those pieces."

I felt like J just didn't get it. "You don't understand," I said, my voice getting higher and more agitated. "Bonaventure must not get his hands on these things."

J snorted. "You can't believe that black magic stuff Schneibel talks about."

"I do. And you should too." I was nearly shrieking at him.

He had the nerve to laugh. "Look, Daphne, the phantoms

I worry about are the ones holding a detonation device. And that's all you should be concerned about. And don't get any ideas about playing hero. You don't have all the facts."

I didn't answer.

"I mean that," he said, his voice stern. "Our people *are* in place. Just do your part and no more than that. That's a direct order."

"Aye-aye, sir," I said.

"I'll be in contact with you," he said.

Silence again on my end. Even the sound of his voice pissed me off.

"And Hermes," he said in a voice softer than any I had ever heard from him.

"Yes."

"Everything's a go in part because of the bugs you planted. You did good. Take care of yourself tonight."

I dressed casually for this evening, wearing a pair of black slacks with a blue cashmere turtleneck, Jimmy Choo half boots with ungodly high heels, and a black wool coat embroidered with flowers. I would have liked to have worn a good pair of Nikes, but they didn't go with my image. If I transformed later, it wouldn't matter what footwear I had on anyway.

I left the apartment as shadows fell on Manhattan. I walked aimlessly through the streets, ending up on Broadway in the Seventies with its storefront restaurants and neon-lit pharmacies. I found an unoccupied bench in the center island and practiced a form of mediation, a traffic mediation, I called it. No thought. My focus concentrated on car after car anonymously passing by. I wasn't very successful. My mind wandered back to my conflict over whether or not I should kill that night. I do hold all life, in any form, sacred. I have the ability to kill as easily as humans squash a bug. However, might doesn't make right. I especially have "issues," you might say, about humans' callous treatment of animals. I agreed with my mother on that. Their irrational hatred of bats tops my list of outrages.

Finally I hailed a cab. Bonaventure's apartment lay on the other side of Central Park, and it was a swift ride with few traffic lights. I arrived on time and didn't see any sign of J or his team—no commercial vans parked in the area, nobody disguised as a Con Ed worker digging up the street. Maybe somebody was stationed in an apartment across the avenue. I guessed I shouldn't be able to spot a professional surveillance setup. I did half expect Louis to be leaning against a No Parking sign hiding his face behind a copy of the *Daily News*. Perhaps he was coming with Benny.

The doorman announced me and sent me up in the elevator. Tanya greeted me once again. Suitcases filled the hall when I entered Bonaventure's apartment. "Somebody going somewhere?" I asked the unsmiling Tanya.

"The master is waiting for you," she said, and didn't answer my question.

Bonaventure was in the library, agitation or excitement evident in the tenseness of his movements. He wore no tuxedo this time, but still looked impressive in riding pants and high boots. He greeted me with a white-toothed smile, looking like a fat wolf waiting for Little Red Riding Hood. Neither Issa nor the odious Bockerie was in attendance, which bothered me. I wondered where they were.

"Miss Urban, come in! Sit! We have much business to attend to and, my apologies, not a great deal of time."

"You're traveling tonight?" I asked.

"Yes, yes. My country estate. I may need to discuss that with you later. But first, here are my bids."

He handed me the file with the photos. I looked over his offers on the back of each. As I expected, he wanted them all. I was slightly surprised at the amount he offered. He wasn't taking a chance that Schneibel, if the old man could be tempted by money at all, would refuse. The total for the sixteen items was $50 *million*.

"Can you confirm Mr. Schneibel's acceptance immediately? The offer will stand only until nine P.M. tonight. After that it will be withdrawn," Bonaventure said.

"He's waiting for my call," I said, knowing full well that this transaction was in the hands of the U.S. government, not Schneibel's. I assumed they had instructed him to be available tonight. I pulled out my cell phone. The icon for "No Service" appeared.

"Unfortunately, my mobile phone doesn't have reception," I said.

"I apologize, Miss Urban, but my security devices interfere with cell phone transmission. You may use a house phone. Let me have Tanya escort you to one you may use in privacy."

"Thank you. That would be perfect," I said.

Tanya took me into what I assumed was Bonaventure's office. It held a modern desk that was merely a kidney-shaped slab of glass atop a stainless steel pillar with no drawers, a fax machine, a computer, and a bank of telephones. The walls were covered with large photographs of the Ukraine and Croatia by a photographer named Wilton Tifft. The pictures swept like a panorama around me; the images of miners and priests, churches, rustic cottages, misty hills, icons, and graveyards were as poignant as they were beautiful. They left no doubt that Bonaventure's heart remained in Eastern Europe.

The room offered no opportunity for snooping: The only files, if any existed, were in the computer. Except for a blank notepad with a pen beside it, not so much as a sheet of stray paper lay anywhere in the room. Either Bonaventure was a neat freak or he had sanitized the place before my arrival. I dialed Schneibel's number.

The old German answered. "Yessss?"

"This is Daphne Urban. Mr. Bonaventure has kindly let me use a phone in his apartment."

"Yessss," he said.

"He has made an offer. All the items, fifty million dollars. You had told me you need some time to consider it. Unfortunately, Bonaventure needs a reply quickly. May I phone you back in, say, an hour?"

"Yessss," he said.

"Thank you, Herr Schneibel," I said. He didn't answer but severed the connection. I admired his professionalism. I needed an excuse to hang around the apartment until Benny arrived so I could open that service door for Darius. Without knowing about my scheme, Schneibel went along. He played the Great Game exceedingly well: Our conversation was in all certainty being monitored by Bonaventure. Schneibel did not betray me, or himself.

I reported back to Bonaventure. "That is most satisfactory," he said. "I have other business this evening as well. Would you be comfortable waiting in the living room? Feel free to choose something to read, or you can watch the television in there."

I took up residence in the deep cushions of the white brocade couch in front of a sitcom on TV and surreptitiously kept checking my watch. Tanya ferried drinks and sandwiches in and out of the kitchen. At one point I thought I heard a woman crying. I had no chance to slip into the maid's area and unlock the service door.

Before too long Tanya rushed to the front door and let three men enter. They wore badly fitting suits and cheap Eastern European shoes. Their complexions were swarthy and Middle Eastern–looking, but they could have been from anywhere between Greece and Islamabad. One of them carried a valise that looked like a doctor's bag. They looked over at me, their faces worried and tense. Tanya skipped any introductions and hurried them into the library, where Bonaventure was waiting. Even through the thick walls I could hear an excited voice say very loudly, "At Port Newark"? Something Bonaventure said silenced them. I heard no more.

Next at the door was Benny. She looked gorgeous in a red power suit, classy but sexy enough to turn the head of even a dead man. She avoided glancing in my direction as she came in, all nervous and aflutter, a ditzy blonde in a dither. "Oh, honey," she said to prune-faced Tanya. "I hate to be a bother, but I am just about desperate. I just know you must have handled intimate deesasters worsen than mine, but I am just about frantic. The back of my bra strap just snapped. I am about to spill out into the fresh air. I wouldn't want to see Mr. Bonaventure like this. Can you and I go into the little girls' room and maybe you all can pin it or put a quick stitch in it," she said, all innocent and childlike.

Even on dour old Tanya, Benny's sweetness was a charm. "*Da,* do not worry, I fix it quick. Come." And they disappeared down the hall.

My heart pounding like a trip-hammer, I hurried toward the kitchen. I paused for a moment and opened the refrigerator as if I just couldn't wait another second for a drink. I softly closed the refrigerator door and slipped off my boots, praying that Darius had been able to take care of the security cameras. On silent feet I rushed through the kitchen with its slippery Italian tile and down the dim back hall. It was a little after eight thirty. I found the service door without incident and undid the bolt, freeing the iron bar from its niche. I turned around and ran like a rabbit back to the kitchen. I was holding my breath the entire time, and let it out in a whoosh. I scooped up my boots and got them back on. Then I walked casually back into the living room and sat down. If the cameras in this part of the apartment were operating, I hoped I looked unremarkable. But if any were working, I bet dollars to doughnuts they were aimed at Benny's bosom in the bathroom. I smiled in spite of myself.

Minutes crawled along slowly, and my pulse rate dropped to normal as I slid down from my adrenaline rush. Finally Tanya approached me.

"The master asks if you would make your phone call at this time."

I got up and followed her back to Bonaventure's office. I dialed Schneibel again.

"Herr Schneibel?"

"Yes."

"Will you accept Bonaventure's offer?"

"The deal is in your hands. What must be done is in mine," he replied with a voice like shattering glass, cracking with emotion and pain.

"I will arrange for delivery, then."

"Yes. As you wish. It is finished." The phone went dead.

Tanya showed up as if on cue at the door. "Master will see you now."

When I entered the library, Bonaventure sat there with Benny. The large valise was sitting open on the floor. It appeared empty. On the white table, two piles of uncut diamonds sat on blue velvet cloths. They looked like dull little pebbles to me, but there sat a king's ransom.

"Miss Urban, this is Miss Polycarp, a representative of my diamond broker, who unfortunately had an emergency overseas. It was my good fortune that Miss Polycarp was available to handle my needs tonight." He leered at Benny suggestively as he explained to her,

"Miss Urban is the agent for the gentleman whose art I am purchasing with this." He gestured toward the slightly smaller pile.

I acted confused. "You mean you're paying Herr Schneibel in diamonds?"

Bonaparte laughed. "Not at all. These diamonds now belong to the finest gem brokers in New York. Miss Polycarp has brought, at my request, a cashier's check for fifty million dollars, which she will hand to you, if Herr Schneibel accepts my offer."

"He does."

"Miss Polycarp, the check."

Benny opened a folder, slid out the check, and passed it to me. I folded it once and tucked it into my pants pocket. Then she expertly wrapped each pile of diamonds in its square of velvet, put the little packages in the valise, and snapped it closed.

"Thank you, Miss Polycarp," Bonaventure said. "As I have your other check right here," he said as he patted his jacket pocket, "our business is concluded. Now, I regretfully must ask you to depart. Under other circumstances I would love to have you stay for a nightcap. I apologize for the rush." He ogled her openly. She seemed to bask in the light of his attention. Greater men than Bonaventure would have taken the bait and been reeled in. "When I return to New York, I hope you will accept my invitation for a longer talk—and perhaps dinner."

"Why, Bonny, sugar, I would just love it. Now be sure you really mean it. I will be waiting for my phone to ring and hoping to hear your charming voice on the line. It's certainly been a pleasure." She stretched out her hand to shake.

He took it and brought it to his lips. It must be reflex action with Benny and men. If anyone slobbered on mine like "Bonny" just had, I'm sure I'd gag. Benny just gushed. "Bonny, you are the sweetest thing."

He picked up the valise and handed it to Benny.

She said, "Thank you, sugar," and took possession of more than $250 million worth of uncut gems. Diamond dealers carried huge sums all the time, and to watch Benny, you'd think she was getting nothing more valuable than Chinese takeout. As if summoned by a hidden bell, as she probably was, Tanya appeared at the door, holding it open. I knew Benny had to hurry to catch up with the three deliverymen who had disappeared while I was phoning Schneibel, but she left languidly and even gave "Bonny" a final wink.

Immediately after Tanya closed the door behind Benny, Bonaventure turned to me. "I wish to take possession of the art tonight."

I countered, "Herr Schneibel needs time to crate them. He says you can pick them up at nine tomorrow."

"No." His voice was harsh. "I'm leaving the city for my country home tonight. I cannot delay. I'll bring my men and we'll crate the items ourselves. Phone Herr Schneibel back and tell him we are coming."

Again I protested. Bonaventure took off his velvet gloves and put iron in his voice. Finally I said I would make the call. I did as instructed, telling Schneibel that Bonaventure would be arriving before eleven. I hoped he'd pass the message on to J. Schneibel answered in monosyllables again, giving no resistance, yet I felt a terrible foreboding as I hung up the phone.

I took a deep breath and began to turn around, but I never made it.

My neck was gripped violently from behind. I flung my hands up and clawed but I couldn't reach the face of whoever was behind me. Soft leather gloves, the fingers in them very strong, dug in on both sides of my neck just above the collarbone, where the carotid arteries branch upward. Pressure there blocks the blood flow to the brain.

I hadn't a chance to transform. I had time for only two thoughts. One was that something terrible was going to happen. The other was, angrily, that Bonaventure had won. Then I spiraled down into darkness and a place of no dreams.

CHAPTER 10

Childe Roland to the Dark Tower Came.
—Robert Browning

I regained consciousness with the strange notion that it was raining. I slowly opened my eyes and tried to make sense of what I was seeing. It was a spa quality Nautilus machine, the kind with four stations at the compass points. I must be in Bonaventure's exercise room somewhere in the apartment. I was bound by duct tape as I sat astraddle the bench of the machine. My hands were extended over my head, and when I looked up, I saw they were affixed by duct tape to the lat pull-down bar.

I didn't realize all this in a great sprint of cogitation; it was more of a slow wade through molasses. My throat hurt, and I had a splitting headache. I was still looking up at the bar, trying to figure out what happened, when *ping,* a big wet drop hit my cheek. *Ping, ping.* One hit my neck. Another whacked into my forehead. I frowned. I shook my head. I looked up again at my hands, which felt numb and dead. With that something wet again hit my cheek.

I turned my head sideways in the direction where the "rain" seem to originate. Benny Polycarp was duct-taped to a treadmill, her red power suit askew. She was all puckered up, about to launch another lugie at me.

"What the hell!" I yelped. "Benny, stop spitting on me!"

"Shhhh! Don't make noise. I was just trying to wake you up," she said with a small giggle. "I couldn't think of any other way to get your attention."

"Why the hell didn't you just transform and get loose?" I said. My arms hurt, my head hurt, and I wasn't about to be polite.

"Now, don't get all cranky on me. Back home we always say, 'Don't get mad. Just scratch your butt and get glad.'" She giggled at me again. "Think about it, Daphy. If I changed or went ahead and freed myself, you'd still be human. If anyone returned they'd see me, and you wouldn't be ready to fight beside me. Even if I could handle them, you could have been hurt. Besides, I didn't want to start the party without you, for a few minutes anyway."

"I guess," I said, realizing I should be feeling grateful for Benny's help and thinking that I really wanted to locate some tissues. "How long was I out?" I stage-whispered to her.

"I don't know. You were unconscious when they brought me in here. I've only been tied up for five minutes or so, and the bastard who hit me could still be in the apartment."

"Well, let's get out of here," I said.

"Now you're talking," she said.

My captors had pulled the pin from the weight stack, leaving a pull-down weight of over three hundred pounds. Whoever tied me up must have figured no woman—even one on steroids—had the muscle for that kind of weight. But whether in human or bat form, any vampire did.

So I pulled down on the bar and snapped the duct tape with ease. "Assholes," I said as I ripped the tape off my wrists. "This frigging hurts. I lost my circulation too. And where the hell is my purse?" I said grumpily.

"It's over there on the floor, Daphy. They must have tossed it in the room," Benny said.

"Well, that's a plus," I said as I started rummaging through it and found a Wash'n Dri packet. I cleaned up, then I slipped off my clothes. I can't tell you how many of my favorite outfits I've had to abandon over the years. Once I was naked I began to transform. My human self fell away as the vampire inside me emerged; my eyeteeth lengthened, my fingernails became clawlike, my wings burst free from my back with a sharp crack mingled with a deep thrumming, like the string of a bow when an arrow is loosed. Every time I hear that great unfolding, my heart leaps. It banishes the hurt and sadness of the day, sending grief fleeing like a gray thief into the night. As I changed, the colors around me throbbed and intensified, whirling like a kaleidoscope. The room's overhead light became a small sun, hurting my eyes. Too bright, too bright. I craved the darkness. I felt strong and alive, empowered and free.

"Damn it all to hell, Daphy. I just broke a nail," Benny said as she peeled the duct tape off. She stripped down too. A breeze hit me as her wings unfolded with a whoosh. As they stretched out, quivering, I could see they were dark, but her lithe body was golden fur, all glistening and light. She was a natural blonde after all.

We both stood there a moment, adjusting to the change.

"You know what?" Benny said. "Louis is supposed to call me. I'm taking my cell."

"Good idea," I said. "Me too. Can you take our clothes? We might have to change back." Benny's handbag had been bandolier style across her torso even when they tied her up. I was beginning to realize that the woman thought of everything.

Benny rolled her eyes at me. "My purse isn't that big. I can only carry the essentials. But, hey, it's New York. I don't think anyone would even notice if we walked naked down Broadway."

"Benny, *you* they'd notice," I said. I fooled around with the strap on my large Louis Vuitton Noe bag until I figured out how to make a sling that fit snugly over my shoulder. As I started stuffing my clothes into the purse, I asked, "How did you end up here? Who grabbed you?"

Benny was bouncing up and down on her toes and flapping her wings a bit. I guessed she hadn't transformed in a while. She was examining the undersides of her wings while she talked to me. "As soon as I left the apartment, my cell phone rang. It was Louis, and he was in a cab following the deliverymen. He said he'd call me back when they got to their destination, and that I might as well hang around to make sure you got out okay. Then a limo pulled up. Bonaventure and a pale young woman— she looked kind of peaked, you know—left with a ton of suitcases. I thought it was strange that you hadn't come out first. I didn't know what happened to you."

I motioned her over to the window. It was stuck, and I struggled to get it open. She went on with her story as I worked.

"As soon as they pulled away I went back and convinced the doorman to let me go back upstairs. Tanya opened the door, but I didn't get more than a few feet into the apartment when somebody whacked me on the head. Whoever it was just don't know nothing about big hair and hair spray. I didn't really pass out, but I pretended real quick. Some muscular yahoo brought me in here, tied me up, and left. He took the diamonds, by the way. What do you want to bet that Mr. J is going to be throwing a hissy fit about that. It's just my luck. As my mama always said, 'If it was raining soup, I'd have a fork.' Anyways, you were already here. Even though you were out cold, I was really glad to see you. Then I tried to get you to wake up." She paused and said, "You know, Daphy, I think we'd better skedaddle."

I gave her an exasperated look. "Why do you think I'm trying to open the window?"

"Well, you should have asked me to give you a hand." She helped me give it a mighty push, and it slid upward.

"After you," I said. She scrambled onto the sill and looked down. It was a long way to the street. "Where to?" she asked as she jumped.

I stuck my head out the window and yelled to her, "I think we should get to Doug Schneibel's loft as fast as we can. I'm pretty sure that's where Bonaventure was heading. I have a really bad feeling about what's happening there."

She hovered outside the building while I hopped up on the sill. The cold night air rushed by me, fluttering the draperies. The yellow half moon was large and low. I leaped outward with a surge of joy, and I sailed off into the dark sky above the city. Benny was just a second behind me.

In silent flight we swooped around the dark towers of Manhattan that pierced the heavens like the pointed spires of cathedrals. We sailed above the avenues, skimming rooftops and brushing by buildings. In one window the blue spurt of a match lit the face of a red-haired woman smoking alone in the dark. She looked out the window with sadness in her eyes, sucked on the cigarette, and stared at my passing shape with no emotion at all. In another window a small boy sat on the sill, his eyes growing wide as my wingtips nearly touched the pane before him. Would they remember me in the deep recesses of their dreams years hence as the sum of all their fears, or as an angel of the night? A church bell struck the hour

with long, mournful notes, ten times over. The east wind
blew.

And then my cell phone rang.

"Damn!" I said as I fumbled to get it out of my purse.
I couldn't open the damned bag too wide or I'd have the
contents raining down into the street below. Grabbing the
cell phone with my talonlike nails was no picnic either.
"Hello?" I said.

"Hey, Daphne, it's Darius. You okay?"

"I'm fine. You?" I tried to sound normal as I barely
missed a flagpole poking out from the upper floors of a
department store.

"Was that Saks?" Benny yelled.

"Did you say something, Daphne? I think we've got
bad reception. Where are you?" Darius asked.

"Uh, I'm headed downtown," I bellowed into the
phone.

"I can't hear you very well," Darius said. "Are you in
a cab? Is the window open? There's a lot of noise."

"Uh-huh. The cabbie has the windows open. Sorry."
What the hell could I say, *I'm flying twenty stories above
Fifth Avenue?* "Where are you?"

"Taking care of business, you know," he said, and it
was just the kind of answer that ticked me off.

"I mean, did you get into the apartment? I left the door
open. Did everything go okay?" I asked.

"Yeah. Thanks. What you did was perfect. Hey, Daphy,
I . . ." He said something softly, and I couldn't make out
his words over the rushing wind.

"What? I can't hear you," I yelled.

"It's not important," he said more loudly. "I just
wanted to hear your voice. Know you were okay."

"I'm okay," I said.

"I gotta go. I just wanted, you know, to tell you I'm
thinking about you."

"I'm thinking about you too." Well, I was right now, so that wasn't a lie.

"Be careful. Remember we have a date," he said with a laugh.

"I won't forget. You be careful too," I added as I dodged an empty window washer's scaffold somebody had left hanging on the side of a building.

"'Bye, pretty girl," he said, and I thought I heard the sound of a kiss as I clicked off, but it was hard to tell with the wind. Benny was giving me one of those looks, grinning like a Cheshire cat.

"What?" I called over to her.

"Was that Darius? I think he likes you," she yelled back at me. "He *really* likes you."

"Shut up," I said, and as I thought of Darius, I tasted his lips, remembered the touch of his hands on my breasts, and felt the ancient thirst for blood consume me. I wanted to drink from him deeply, fully, until he filled me with his life. I pushed that thought away, but my heart was dancing and I was almost laughing as we flew.

At the end of Canal Street, the Holland Tunnel opened like a gaping maw into the bowels of the earth, leading a stream of cars westward to the barren wasteland and stinking meadows of New Jersey. Near the tunnel, Schneibel's warehouse sat like a heavy box, square and squat. We landed on the window ledge where his hand had once reached out to drop me the key. The huge, wire-meshed window wasn't locked. I opened it. And from the first I could smell the blood.

We scooted through the window and dropped down. The gallery lights were on and illuminated a ghastly scene. Smashed masks littered the floor. A few of the stat-ues made of bones, hair, and wood had been knocked off their pedestals and were hacked to bits in an insane fury.

A spray of blood arched across one wall, red dots against the white like a Pollock painting. And lying with an ax buried deep in his chest was Herr Schneibel, his white hair drenched red, his eyes staring lifelessly toward the ceiling.

I was too late. Schneibel had tried to destroy his collection but not quickly enough. Most of the pieces were gone. Whoever possessed them now had powers no human should wield. These items came from death and brought its dark shadows with them to spread out across the land.

"Who did this?" Benny said.

"Bonaventure, I think," I said.

"It's bad," she said.

"You have no idea how bad."

Benny was walking around the perimeter of the room, taking care not to step in the blood. "Daphy, come over here," she said.

I joined her on the far side of the loft near the door. Pieces of packing excelsior were scattered around the floor. A box cutter lay discarded amid the trash. A pair of men's Ray-Ban sunglasses sat forgotten on the table. I picked them up and put them in my purse. Maybe they'd tell me nothing, but I had hopes that they might help reveal what happened to Schneibel. After all, a lottery ticket isn't a worthless piece of paper until you're sure it's not the number that means you've won a fortune.

"See anything else?" I asked.

"No. It looks like they took the art and got out fast."

"We going to call nine-one-one?"

"I don't think so. Nobody can help him now. Let's just get out of here," I said as I looked back at Schneibel's body. A tiny white head peeped out of his pocket. "Gunther," I said.

"Who?" Benny asked.

"Schneibel's pet." I walked carefully over to the body and gently picked up the rat. He squeaked and looked into my eyes. He was trembling. Blood stained his feet. I stroked his head. " 'Wee, sleekit, cow'rin,' tim'rous beastie, O what a panic's in thy breastie!' " I whispered, quoting Bobby Burns. "Don't worry, little one; I won't leave you here." I opened my purse, made a nest of sorts in my clothes, and gently put him in.

"Wait a sec," Benny said. "Let me call Louis."

She flipped open her phone and punched in the number. "Lou, sugar? Benny here. Where are you? Okay. Say it slow. Okay. No, we can be there in ten minutes. Anybody else show up? No? Hold down the fort. Yeah, just wait. We'll go in together. See ya." She clicked off and looked at me. "He followed the three guys over to Jersey City. They went into the first floor of a row house. It's not far from the river. I think we can find it. Let's go kick some ass!" she said, and laughed.

"Sounds good to me," I said. I took one last look at the corpse of the old man amid the shattered masks. As I stared, the broken bits of bone around him shimmered and grew whiter; and before my eyes the blood began to congeal. A wall mirror reflected my dark form. I looked in it and it cracked from side to side.

Black against black, we flew across the glistening dark swath of the Hudson River, our sleek, winged bodies erratically swooping and gliding like kites jerked along on an invisible string. The wet air added sparkling droplets to our fur. I thought no thoughts. I existed only in my sensations. Cold wind. The sharp smell of water. Pale lights shining through frost on the far shore. I followed Benny's swift flight westward.

Louis, transformed, stood in the shadows outside a rusty wooden house on a ghetto street in Jersey City. A leafless sycamore tree filtered the light from a street lamp, its limbs moaning in the wind and making moving shadows on the sidewalk below. The weather-beaten boards of the facade affected me like a human face, bearing traces of the hard lives and lost dreams of those who lived within. Despair hung over the place like a dank fog.

We should have made a plan before the three of us, our phantom shapes moving silently, flew down the narrow space between the row houses. We slipped into the weedy backyard and burst through the rear door. But we didn't talk amongst ourselves at all before we went in. I can only blame myself for what happened.

The same three men who had delivered the diamonds to Bonaventure sat in the kitchen, where a radio on the counter blared Arab music and a pizza box gaped open on the table surrounded by cans of Coke. All this registered clearly as the scene unfolded in slow motion. Screaming, the men all pushed back from the table. One pulled a gun and fired wildly, the bullet twanging against the refrigerator as he scrambled toward the door. Louis was on him instantly, his claws raking a terrible wound down the man's back, his fangs descending and sinking into the man's neck. I couldn't stop Louis, and besides, I had my own opponent to deal with. Yelling incoherently, the short, swarthy man in front of me grabbed a knife from the table and slashed the air, missing me by a mile. "Fool!" I hissed, and blocked his thrusts with one arm, sending the knife flying toward the sink while my other fist smashed into the bridge of his nose. A torrent of blood poured out of his nostrils, but I felt no hunger, just the white-hot rage of battle. He went to his knees. I kicked him under the jaw and his head snapped back. He fell over like a bowling pin going down.

Meanwhile Benny reached her long arm toward the cowering heap of humanity in front of her. He hadn't even tried to fight or run, just fell down in terror. She squeezed his neck as expertly as someone had recently squeezed mine. The man's eyes rolled back in his head and he slid down onto the floor, unconscious. She pulled the radio's plug from the wall and ripped the cord free. She jerked the man's wrists behind him and tied his hands to the pipe of the kitchen radiator. She took some of the napkins from the pizza box and stuffed them in the man's mouth. Then her eyes caught mine in a silent message. We both knew what Louis had done, and it was too late to intervene.

The third man's body lay limp in the vampire's arms. He let it drop lifeless to the floor with a sick thud. Louis turned toward us then, his fangs dripping red. His green eyes were luminescent and frightening; his lower lids drooped. He looked drunk and cruel. His face reflected a combination of diabolical desire and hellish glee. "Are they dead?" he hissed at us. "This one filled my belly but I can drink more."

"No! Get back, Louis. Get back. No more blood," I shouted, putting myself between the unconscious body at my feet and the rapacious vampire. "We need these men alive. They need to be interrogated. You must not touch them."

"Too bad," he hissed. "Too bad." He stood there, his sides heaving, his head hanging like that of a thorough-bred horse winded after a race.

I had to make a decision right then about what to do and who to call. I couldn't handle this alone. Finally I flipped open my cell phone and called J's number. The answering machine picked up and I left a message giving the address of the Jersey City house. I told him to get out there fast. I didn't tell him one man was dead.

I looked over at Benny. Her attention was riveted on Louis, and he was staring back at her. It was as if a magnet were pulling them toward each other. I remembered the desires spawned by battle, by killing, by the adrenaline surge of power. I wanted out of there.

"Benny," I said. "These men cannot die. Do you understand?" I had real doubts it was safe to leave them alone.

"Yes," she whispered. "Go, Daphy, just go," she breathed.

I glided to the door, my wings unfurling, my feet ready to leave the bonds of earth. I glanced back to see Benny going into Louis's arms and him pushing her against a wall, the lust unmistakable as if he were about to take her there, and I suppose he was. I didn't stay to find out, but soared up into the night.

The darkness embraced me as I ascended high, wanting the air to wash me clean, wanting to forget the look of horror on the man's face before Louis bit him, wanting to forget the mad passion of Louis pushing Benny against the wall. The far shore of New Jersey seemed to move away behind me, and I did not know whether I was riding the wind, or the wind was riding me. There, above the waters, I was suspended between heaven and earth as time passed. The lemon-hued moon shone on the river. I sailed with the currents of air. Empty outside, empty inside, I touched the stars.

And I thought of Darius. I would not have felt this ache inside my heart had I never met him.

The night was lengthening into the wee hours when I decided to go back to Bonaventure's penthouse. Perhaps I could find out what Darius had done there, or if nothing else, maybe I could find the location of Bonaventure's country place.

I reentered Bonaventure's apartment the same way I left, landing silently on the window ledge and gliding in over the sill. I saw no reason to retain my bat form and fell down on all fours as the energy drained from me. In less time than it takes to tell about it, I became human once more. Carefully moving Gunther from his nest, I took my clothes from my purse and dressed quickly. The cashier's check for $50 million was still in my pocket. Then I left the room, fearful of what I might find, but expecting nothing.

As soon as I stepped from the exercise room, my fears proved valid. The smell of fresh blood permeated the apartment. I followed the scent and walked into the living room. Nothing there, no mess, no signs of a struggle. I went into the kitchen. The smell was stronger. I entered the maid's room. A half-packed suitcase lay open on the bed. The dour-faced Tanya lay facedown on the floor, a crumpled rag doll. Blood spread out from beneath her head and stained the hardwood floor like dark red wine. Taking care not to tread in it, I went over to her and stooped down, grasped her shoulders, and gently turned her over. Her blank eyes stared upward; her throat had been slit. It was neatly done, the way a commando would eliminate an enemy sentry standing post outside a camp. Something squeezed tight in my heart. Could Darius have done this? Gently and with a whispered prayer, I laid Tanya back as I had found her.

I decided to go into the entrance hall and search near the telephone for some information on Bonaventure's country place. Perhaps J already knew the information. But I hadn't been too impressed with the quality of his dossiers. And perhaps Darius knew. Yet finding out on my own would not only be deeply satisfying; it would allow me to proceed on my own. I have my own motto for living: *It's far better to beg for forgiveness than to ask for permission.*

I walked back through the kitchen and entered the

dining room with its ostentatious gilded chairs and huge
statue of a blackamoor, his hand outstretched with a tray,
standing to one side. He seemed to grin at me in a disconcerting way. The room suddenly tilted wildly. I stumbled and nearly fell. I must be light-headed, tired from the
long flight, or more deeply affected than I wanted to
admit by Louis's murderous bite and Tanya's death. I
grabbed the back of a chair to steady myself. The sweet,
cloying smell of blood still filled my nostrils, and it wasn't
coming from Tanya's room.

I took some deep breaths. I am a very strong person,
emotionally as well as physically. I was sure no faintness
had overcome me. No, I was certain evil had been here.
Evil had left its mark here. I headed toward the vestibule,
steeling myself for what awaited me.

Close to the front door lay Issa, spread-eagle, his throat
cut with military efficiency just as Tanya's had been. His
mouth was drawn back in a grimace, showing his
crooked teeth. I didn't approach him; I didn't touch him.
I stood immobile and tried to reason out what had happened here tonight.

I was reasonably sure Issa had been the "muscleman"
who hit Benny—if she had been hit. It crossed my mind
that Benny could have fabricated her "capture," after
killing these two—if she wanted the diamonds for herself. I had independent wealth, but Benny didn't. Vampires are a greedy bunch in every way: hedonistic, driven
by pleasure, and with a lax to nonexistent moral code. I
didn't hold that against Benny in the least, but I had to at
least consider her a suspect. And Benny had had on a red
suit, which might have hidden any blood splatters. On the
other hand, it would have been difficult to tie herself to
the treadmill, and I had no reason to believe she would
have killed in this manner. No vampire would have
wasted this much blood. A vampire would have left the

classic puncture wounds, unless, of course, the slit throat was to disguise them. I shook my head. This kind of thinking was too arcane. Another of my mottos is, *Trust everyone but always cut the cards first.* But I knew and liked Benny. Even though I didn't entirely trust her, my instincts are rarely wrong. I was tempted to say "never wrong," but never say never.

I continued to puzzle out what had been the most likely scenario. When Issa and Tanya were killed, Bonaventure and Catharine had already left. Benny was tied up with me in the exercise room. That left only two likely people to have committed the murders: the scary black dude from Sierra Leone, Bockerie, or Darius. Was Bockerie here at all last night? I hadn't seen him in the apartment. Had he been out and come back, walking in on Issa and the diamonds? Of course, I hadn't seen Issa either, and evidently he had been here all along.

And I still didn't know what Darius's purpose was in the apartment. Had he been looking for something? Or had he entered in order to terminate these two? It would bother me if he'd killed them, especially in Tanya's case. She may have been a slavish attendant to Bonaventure's needs, she may have personified the dark Slavic temperament, but she hadn't committed any crime that I knew of. Why kill her?

Then my thoughts went back to the diamonds again. They were gone. Someone had them. Bonaventure didn't take them. My guess was that Issa had hit Benny and grabbed the valise, on impulse, without thinking it out. Then he panicked. Maybe he offered to split them with Tanya. Maybe they decided to take the money and run. Then someone stopped them, and—I would wager the farm on it—whoever stopped them had the diamonds. They were a powerful motive for getting rid of Issa and for silencing Tanya. I sighed. I had pretty much made up my mind. Bockerie. I would place my bets on the cruel, amoral General Mosquito as the one to have murdered these two people without hesitation. I hoped I could prove it. Killing wounds the soul. It numbs the heart. I knew that all too well. I wanted Darius to be a good guy, a white knight, and I hoped my conclusion wasn't just wishful thinking. It would be so much more straightforward to assume his orders were to "terminate with extreme prejudice."

I stopped pondering at that point and started to go through the drawer in the telephone table. There was nothing there except a Manhattan phone book, a pad, and some pens. I took out the pad and started writing down the numbers programmed into the phone's speed dial. The first few were in Manhattan. I copied them down, deciding to check them out later, but they weren't what I was looking for. I hit the buttons and up popped a few foreign exchanges, and bingo, a number with the area code 570, which sounded like a possible. I jotted it down and quickly finished off the rest of the entries.

Next I scrolled back through the caller ID to see who had called here recently. The only call within the last twenty-four hours was a local number that had also been on the speed dial. I made a private wager with myself that it was a car service confirming an appointment for a pickup. Maybe Issa or Tanya had made it, but I'd like to find out who had actually taken the ride and where they went.

I found the hall closet and retrieved my black embroidered coat. I felt glad for the first time that evening. I loved this coat, and I had written it off as lost for good when Benny and I took off out the window. Then I returned to the exercise room and got my handbag. I checked on Gunther. Poor little guy was curled up sound asleep. I don't know how much he understood of what had happened to Schneibel, but animals have a greater intellect than humans believe. Gunther knew about fear, pain, suffering, and death. He knew love. He also knew loss, and I had no doubt he was grieving. In the animal kingdom violent death is commonplace. Gunther didn't judge, but he did feel.

Taking the time to fix my makeup, straighten my clothes, and adjust my attitude, I left the apartment by the front door. I was extremely careful not to walk through any blood as I left. I wasn't going to leave evidence behind or ruin my Jimmy Choos. I wasn't worried about fingerprints, as I had been there legitimately that evening. I was concerned that it was after five A.M. I needed to get home before dawn.

I exited the elevator into the small street-level lobby, taking care not to rush. A different doorman was on duty, a young Spanish fellow, who had his feet up on a desk while he watched a Spanish station on a portable TV and sipped on a bottle of Snapple. I asked him to hail me a cab. He gave me a wide smile and a knowing look. "Oh, that Issa," he said, "he know how to pick 'em." Let him think what he wanted. I didn't need the police to come looking for me, though. I'd better report to J and see if he could handle the damage control.

As soon as I was in the cab, I dialed the office. J answered.

"Ringmaster here. Where are you, Hermes?"

Unexpectedly I felt really happy to hear J's voice. I had been so confused about whom to believe and whom to trust. Now I felt as if he offered a safe harbor. I began to think I could count on him. I hoped I was right. "In a cab," I said.

"Don't say anything," he said. "Report to the office as early as you can this evening."

"Roger," I said, "but listen. This can't wait. We have a

maintenance and repair job to do at Bonaventure's. Structural damage. You need to get a cleanup crew in there, fast. Use the service entrance. Got it?"

"Got it. How many pieces were broken?" he asked with as little emotion as if windows, not people, lay broken there.

"Two," I answered, and my voice broke as I said it.

"Right. It's taken care of," he said, and again his voice reassured me. "Now get some sleep, Hermes," he told me.

Before he could hang up, I blurted out, "Oh, one more thing. What about Jersey City?"

"Done," J said cryptically, then added, "I'll debrief you tonight."

"Okay," I answered, unable to think of a way to ask him who was still alive when he got there.

"Hermès," he said, his gruff voice breaking into my thoughts.

"What?"

"Watch your back." And he clicked off.

I stumbled through my apartment door, wilting from fatigue. I peeled off my clothes, leaving them in a trail across the floor. I went into the kitchen and poured water into a bowl for Gunther. I took him out of my purse and set him on the counter. His little red eyes blinked in the light. I searched for something to feed him and came up with McVities Digestive Biscuits. I get them sent over from England once a month. I offered him a piece of the cookie. He took it in his tiny rat fingers with care and nibbled on it like a society matron.

While Gunther finished his meal and took a drink from his bowl, I downed a small bottle of Pellegrino. The fizz made me burp. *Real ladylike, Daphy,* I thought. I opened the refrigerator and scanned the contents. I had some raw chopped sirloin in the meat drawer. That would have to tide me over. I was too tired for a meal. I downed a patty, then scooped Gunther up. As the first rays of dawn stained the sky pink, I grabbed yesterday's *New York Times* in one hand and my new pet rat in the other, and I headed for my coffin. I told Gunther to use the newspaper if he needed to pee; then I climbed into my satin-lined crypt. I had some memory of Gunther curling up by my shoulder before I tumbled down into a dreamworld where my ghost self took wing and sailed toward a lemon moon.

CHAPTER 11

Fallen flowers do not go back to the branch.
> —Zen saying

In the early winter, snow is the seasonal blossom. I stepped out of my apartment building as streetlights turned on in the deepening dusk. A sudden flurry blew soft flakes against my face, and a stiff wind sent a dusting of white dancing across the avenue. I descended into the subway. I had some anxiety about coming face-to-face with J again. Our meetings invariably exploded into emotional fireworks. Underlying everything was the sexual tension that he denied existed and that I wanted to forget ever had. Unfortunately, denying or ignoring reality doesn't make it go away.

I had dressed down for the meeting in hip-hugging jeans and a pair of Western Frye boots in a funky turquoise with red trim. I still hadn't gotten my ring back from Benny, and made a mental note to ask her about it. I put on a big hunk of Italian gold holding a deep red coral stone from the Amalfi coast. Coral signifies long life and good luck. I had the former. I certainly could use some of the latter. I topped off my outfit with a deep yellow leather jacket that I picked up during my last trip to Florence. Yes, the trip *was* in this century. I took a vacation in Italy last October for my birthday. Unfortunately all my old friends there had been dead two hundred years. Time passes. People I care about age and die. I remain the same. As I've said, that's my cross to bear.

Before I left the apartment I made a cage of sorts for Gunther out of an empty aquarium and a piece of window screen. I put an old silk blouse in there for him to curl up on. I added a tiny bowl of water, and some sunflower seeds. After I woke up from my daily slumber, I had gone online and ordered the most elaborate and beautiful rodent house I could find, bedding, and superdeluxe rodent food. Only the best for my little guy. I let him sit on my shoulder while I worked on the computer. But unlike Herr Schneibel, I couldn't carry him around town with me. Having a rat peek his head out of one's purse would probably cause a panic in the subway. Then again, this was New York. Maybe no one would even notice. Either way, I was disinclined to become known as the girl with the white rat. So I said good-bye, told him to be a good boy while I was gone, and left the apartment.

But not before doing one more thing. I took the cashier's check for $50 million out of my pants pocket and left it in my computer desk drawer.

On the subway ride downtown, I reviewed what I found out during my time online during the predawn hours. I did a reverse directory search of the numbers I took from Bonaventure's phone. The foreign exchanges were to someplace in Georgia—the Georgia in southern Russia, not the Peach Tree State. I figured those numbers connected to Bonaventure's home base or office. And I had guessed right about the local numbers. One connected to a limo service, no doubt how Bonaventure made his exit from the city. That fact opened up a can of worms. What did he do, take the limo to Schneibel's loft and ask the driver to wait while he played Lizzie Borden?

Did he meet Sam Bockerie there? Did he get there after General Mosquito had axed Schneibel and step around the blood to pick up his art collection? I decided I'd have to see Bonaventure himself to get the answers. And speaking of seeing Bonaventure, the 570 area code was a direct hit. The reverse directory gave me an address on Tunkhannock Avenue in Exeter, Pennsylvania. Bingo— Bonny's country place.

The call on the caller ID did turn out to be from a car service, probably confirming a regular pickup. I still needed to find out if anyone took that ride after killing Issa and Tanya . . . carrying $250 million in uncut diamonds. I hoped it was Bockerie. I made up my mind that the person who grabbed that ride just couldn't be Darius.

As I came up the subway stairs next to the Flatiron Building, the light snow covered my cheeks with soft kisses, but the wind was cold enough to make me shiver. As it pressed its icy fingers around my neck, I remembered all too clearly the fingers that had dug cruelly into my flesh the night before.

All the way down here, I tried to get my head together about what things I needed to discuss with J and what things I had to keep to myself. Should I tell him about the phone numbers I copied from Bonaventure's phone? Did he know about Louis? I wasn't about to rat on Benny if he didn't. Was he pissed about the dead delivery man? Most likely. Did he think Benny or I had done it? Probably. He seemed to have a pretty low opinion of us, especially me. Could he give me any information on who killed Schneibel? Did he even know Schneibel was dead? Did he know who killed Issa and Tanya? Come to think of it (and I'd rather not think about it), it had been a four-body night. A frigging massacre. I hadn't seen that much killing since Easter 1916, and that was an entirely different set of circumstances. Damn the Black and Tan. I don't forgive or forget easily, and I don't change my loyalties. Ever.

These thoughts raced through my mind as I took the slow, old-fashioned Flatiron elevator to "my" office, where I hadn't spent so much as one minute since this whole assignment began. When I walked in, J stood in front of the window, much as he had the first time I ever saw him. His posture was ramrod straight, his clothes impeccably clean, his shirt freshly pressed, his pant creases razor sharp, his shoes spit shined. No one could miss the fact that he was military. My stomach lurched, and every muscle in my body tensed. I had been enraged with this man and hated how he had treated me. We growled at each other like two dogs pissing on the same tree. My reaction to him came straight from my solar plexus. Intellect has nothing whatsoever to do with the love or hate between two people, and that's the truth.

"Hermes," he said, and his voice was tired, "have a seat." He didn't sound teed off. Well, that was a plus.

I took off my jacket and slid into a chair. I hadn't written up a report on last night. I wondered if I should have. But I would have had to tell too many lies.

J came over and sat on the edge of the table. Something had changed in him, and I could see it in the way he looked at me. The anger and hostility were absent. His emotions were still locked down, and he still had eyes of frost and blue marble. But now he reminded me of a young Gregory Peck in that old movie *To Kill a Mockingbird*: rangy, honest, incorruptible. Of course, he might just be a genius at manipulation, playing with my emotions like a puppet master.

He began talking, his voice low and kind. "First off, I want to say that as much as I opposed the creation of team Darkwing, I admit that, without you, we probably wouldn't know the information we do now without you.

To be frank, the agency didn't get anyone to Bonaventure's before the delivery last night. They were supposed to be there. Communications fouled. If you and Benny hadn't tracked those men to Jersey City, we would have blown it."

"Uh, I'm sorry about the casualty," I said. It didn't sound as if he knew about Louis. Better that way. If Benny wanted to tell him, that was her business.

His voice was reassuring. "You did what you had to do. We're not playing by any rules here. We're playing to win. We have to win. There is no alternative. We have the other two diamond couriers alive and well. They are, however, terrified by what they saw when you burst into the house. They haven't even tried to withhold what they know. They just never want to see the 'demons from hell' again." J gave me a funny half smile, half grimace when he said that. He had seen a demon from hell too.

I shifted uncomfortably in my seat as he went on. "They've given us names and addresses of the members of the terrorist cell who were behind the transaction with Bonaventure. We've known for some time that the weapons were coming inside a container into Port Newark. Now we know something else, and yes, we suspected it all along."

"What's that?" I said, fear creeping into my voice.

He got up and went back to the window, staring out at the night. "The weapon is what they call a suitcase nuclear bomb, and the clock is ticking, Miss Urban." He was silent for a moment as his words sank in. Then he turned to face me again. "Our plan is to follow the terrorists to the pickup. It's risky. It's taking the whole operation down to the wire. But if we pick them up, and we miss even one, he could get there and set the weapon off before we knew what hit us. We need to make sure we get to the container simultaneously with them. Our suspicion is that they're going to load the weapon into a truck to leave the port, then transfer it into an ambulance and drive into Manhattan, or stay on the Jersey side if the tunnels are too well guarded. We have to stop them as they get to the container. Not before and, God help us, not after."

My pulse was racing, and I felt as if I were going to break out in a sweat. "We?" I asked urgently. "Who do you mean by 'we'? You and the agency?"

J gave me a long, hard look. "Me . . . and *you*. And not just you, but Miss Polycarp and Mr. O'Reilly as well. The whole Team Darkwing. You've proved yourself. You have my total confidence. You got that when you delivered the deliverymen, so to speak." He almost chuckled, but stopped himself before he really laughed. I guess that was as close as J ever got to a joke.

"When is this going to happen?"

"We don't know for certain. Maybe tonight. Maybe tomorrow. We picked up some chatter that targets tomorrow, so I think that's the most likely scenario. I can assure you that our people are in place. All the key terrorists are being followed twenty-four/seven. We're watching their safe house in Englewood Cliffs, New Jersey. As soon as they start toward the port, we will get you, Miss Polycarp, and Mr. O'Reilly on your cell phones. We need you to get to the port the quickest way you can. They have to drive about twenty-five miles to get to Port Newark. Depending on time and traffic, it will take them no less than forty minutes. You have a maximum of thirty minutes to get in place."

I broke in. "You know the only way to get there that fast from Manhattan is . . . is . . . ."

"To fly. I know. Look, we're positive they can't risk entering the port during the day. Our information all along has been that this will happen at night. We have a backup daylight plan if we're wrong. But if ever an operation needed Team Darkwing, this one does."

He got up and went over to a PowerPoint presentation and flipped it on. A screen, which had been set up on the far side of the table, lit up with a map labeled PORT NEWARK CONTAINER TERMINAL. He took a laser pointer. "Here," he said, "are the large yellow stands called 'Portals.' They are passive detection-system devices that scan for explosives, specifically nuclear ones. No vehicle can leave the Container Terminal without passing through them. On the far side of each portal is a traffic light. If the vehicle is clean, the light is green. If it's red, the vehicle is supposed to stop and wait for a customs officer.

"Obviously the terrorists are not going to stop. We will have men stationed there in a failsafe position should Team Darkwing be unable to apprehend the terrorists when they arrive at their container. But our plan is to have all three of you vampires waiting near the entrance to the port, here." He moved the laser pointer. "It's on Kellogg Street." He clicked to a photo. "This is what it looks like. If you were able to reconnoiter, that would have been optimal. However, at this point in time it's way too risky. We will direct you by cell phone when the terrorists are on the move. We have tracking devices planted on all their vehicles. Any questions?"

My head was spinning. I didn't know how to get the questions out fast enough. "You mean you want us to let the terrorists actually get to the container? We're just following them, is that right?"

He nodded yes, and I went on, "And what do you want us to do when the terrorists get to the container?"

"Stop them."

I felt a great anxiety wash over me. Was J telling me to kill these men after they led us to the bomb? After all,

Darius said his people intended to do just that. I didn't want to misunderstand his meaning, so I asked him straight out: "Do you mean terminate them?"

J chose his words carefully. "That will be an on-the-spot decision. Optimally we would like to interrogate them. What happens at the rendezvous, however, is unpredictable. They must not get the opportunity to use a detonation device. If we set up an ambush using conventional weapons, they might push the button. However, if Team Darkwing swoops down on them . . . well, if they do anything before they die, it will be saying a prayer for their immortal souls."

My whole body was vibrating with tension. I was strung as tight as a piano wire. "J, this a tremendous responsibility that you're giving three vampires, who are not known for being the most reliable creatures in the world. Beyond that fact, one of the three is a gay wannabe Broadway dancer, one is a ditzy blonde from Branson, Missouri, and the other is, well, me. Now you're telling me that the lives of hundreds of thousands of people will depend on us."

"Millions, probably."

"Oh, that's just great," I said, starting to freak out. "And what . . . what . . ." I sputtered, "what about Bonaventure?"

"What about him?" J asked, as if he couldn't understand my question.

"Where is he? What do you want me to do about him?" I was starting to sound frantic.

"Bonaventure has left Manhattan. As for what you will do about him, for now, at least, nothing. He's out of this," J said with a finality indicating that this part of the conversation was over.

"But," I blurted out, "he killed Schneibel!" I stood up and was actually wringing my hands, I was so hyped.

"Miss Urban, get hold of yourself," he said. "Sit back down. Schneibel's dead. That's all we know. We don't know who killed him."

I sat down, but I couldn't sit still. "It had to be Bonaventure. I just know it. And now he has Schneibel's collection. J, please, this is a very bad thing."

"Look, Miss Urban," he said, leaning on the table with his knuckles and thrusting his jaw toward me. "A nuclear bomb is a *bad* thing. Forget about Bonaventure. He's not part of this anymore. All you need to worry about right now is stopping the terrorists."

I didn't seem to be able to let what had happened with Bonaventure go. Maybe it was easier to deal with than the potential for a bomb destroying most of New York. "But J, what about Issa and Tanya—you know, Bonaventure's maid."

J clearly was getting annoyed with me. "That's been cleaned up," he said brusquely.

"But who killed them?" I asked.

"Miss Urban, for the last time, it doesn't matter. It has nothing to do with you anymore. Let it go."

I still had questions eating at me; I wasn't ready to let it go. I had been through hell in the past twenty-four hours, and I was tired of J not paying attention to what I thought was important. Didn't I deserve to have answers? Wasn't I important enough? I went ahead and asked another question: "Well, what about the diamonds? It wasn't Benny's fault, you know."

"Miss Urban, drop it. The jeweler is insured against the loss, even if Bonaventure cashes the two-hundred-million-dollar check. You can, of course, return yours."

I had forgotten about the cashier's check that Benny gave me. It was home, where I had put it in my computer drawer. Last night seemed like a hundred years ago. My old habits of lying and deceiving resurfaced before I thought out what I was doing. I said, "Uh, I'm afraid I can't give it back. I don't have it. I was choked unconscious and tied up. When I woke up the check was gone. I don't know who took it." At that moment I couldn't explain why I lied, or why I kept the check. Perhaps I did it because J was in control of everything else, and I could control this. And perhaps I did it because I knew I could safely walk away with $50 million. As of yet, J hadn't answered any of my questions. I was so frustrated, I could have screamed. But now I asked one that I knew J wasn't going to like.

"What about Darius della Chiesa? Did he have anything to do with this?"

J's face tightened. His eyes got hard and shone with a brittle light. "You would know more about that than I do, now, wouldn't you? Your boyfriend may have killed Bonaventure's bodyguard and maid, Miss Urban. It's what he does for a living. He may have been behind the communications foul-up that kept us from being at Bonaventure's to intercept the deliverymen. Someone fed us false information that weapons had been already found at Port Newark, and ordered the whole squad out there. Mr. della Chiesa has his own agenda, Miss Urban. I told you that." J was yelling at me now, his voice shaking. "And for your sake," he shouted, "for all our sakes, stay away from him. Now Miss Urban, you're dismissed." He spun around and went into the office and slammed the door.

I didn't get to ask my last question. Who was Darius working for?

The first thing I did when I left the Flatiron Building was to huddle out of the wind against the building and check the voice mail on my cell phone. When I heard Darius, my heart did a little flip. "Hey, girlfriend," he said. "Just checking to see how you're doing. Call me ASAP. Thinking of you. 'Bye."

After listening to Darius's message, I wondered what his words really meant. My female psychoanalysis started with *girlfriend.* Did he mean it as a casual way of referring to a girl friend, or did he think of me as his girl-friend? *Thinking of you.* That was definitely a phrase loaded with caring. It put the *girlfriend* in the relationship column. All in all, it wasn't an *I just called to say I love you* message, but it wasn't business either. *What the hell,* I thought, and I immediately speed-dialed his number. Darius answered on the first ring.

"Hi. It's Daphne. I just got your message. You doing okay?"

"Sure. How are you?"

"Pretty good . . . now. What's up?"

"You want to take a ride to Pennsylvania?"

"Bonaventure's? How did you know—"

"Do you want to go?"

"When?"

"Now."

Oh, crap, I thought. *Now? I can't leave Manhattan. What if J calls and says that the terrorists are on the move?*

"I can't," I said in a voice filled with regret.

"Yes, you can. I promise you J won't call you before you get back."

Once again my mind reeled. It seemed as if Darius had been listening to my meeting with J. Well, maybe he had.

"Look, Darius, we're on a cell phone. I can't say much. Do you know for sure that I'm not going to be needed tonight?" It would be terrific if I could go. I really wanted to get those shaman totems and black art back from Bonaventure. And I really, *really* wanted to see Darius.

"I wouldn't be leaving myself if tonight was the night. I can swear that. The stakes are much too big. And yeah, Daphne, I do know more than J does. And something else I know: He just got a call that nothing's going to happen until tomorrow night, at the earliest. If you don't believe me, phone him yourself."

I stood there in the street, the cell phone at my ear, weighing what I should do. I believed Darius. Finally I said, "Okay, I'll go. Do you want you to meet you someplace?"

"Yes. From Twenty-Third Street, walk down Broadway to the Strand bookstore at Twelfth. Wait on the corner. I'll drive up in a Ford Taurus, blue. Fifteen minutes."

"How do you know where I am?" I said, feeling shaken.

"Just an educated guess, Daphy." He laughed.

But doubts crowded into my head. Was it an educated guess? Was he watching me? Had he followed me? Had his people followed me?

"See you soon. Better get walking," he said, and clicked off.

I grabbed a cab. Hoofing it for eleven blocks in these boots would kill my feet. Men don't think about those things. They have no clue. They actually think shoes should feel good.

I stood on the street corner at Twelfth Street, hugging myself against the cold. The snow had become a light drizzle, and the streets were wet with rain. I was in a state of high anxiety and kept moving around, stamping my feet and scanning the traffic. I had a lot of questions to ask Darius. I just didn't know if I would or could or should—or if he'd answer if I did. Asking Darius a question was like throwing sand against the wind. The wind blew it right back again.

A dark blue Taurus pulled up and stopped. I hopped into the passenger seat. Despite all my suspicions about him, my hormones trumped my reason. I leaned over, and he gave me a quick kiss on the lips. He smelled of sandalwood and citrus. His long hair was clean, his face freshly shaven, his muscular arms and chest defined by a Ralph Lauren sweater in black cashmere. He wore a single Native American earring that dangled a bear claw from a short chain and was studded with a piece of turquoise. I had to admit he looked good. No wonder my brain didn't work very well around him.

"Hey," he said. "It's good to see you." He pulled out into traffic, and after some maneuvering to get onto a westbound street, he headed for the Lincoln Tunnel in Midtown.

"Hey, you too," I said, suddenly grinning like an idiot. I caught myself, told myself to be cool, took a deep breath, and said, "So how far is Exeter, Pennsylvania?"

He laughed. "I figured you'd know where Bonaventure went. It's only about three hours away, maybe less. We'll be there by ten."

"Shouldn't we discuss some sort of plan before we pull up into the driveway and go knocking on the front door? I mean, I know why I want to go there. I don't know why you do."

"Why do you want to go?" he asked, avoiding my question.

"I believe he killed Herr Schneibel and took that New Guinea witchcraft art I told you about. I intend to get it back. Period. And you?"

"I have some unfinished business with him," Darius said, his jaw getting tight and his eyes sliding off mine and staring straight ahead.

He obviously wasn't going to tell me anything. I felt like I couldn't trust him all over again. I got very quiet and stayed that way through the tunnel. Shortly after we came out in New Jersey, the lighted skyline of Manhattan lay before us on the other side of the Hudson. I looked toward the place where the Twin Towers once stood. I remembered that Darius and I were working on the same side to prevent another tragedy like that one. "Darius," I said. "I have to ask you about something. Will you answer me?"

As we headed through heavy traffic toward Route 3, which would take us westward, Darius kept his eyes on the road when he answered. "I'll try, Daphne. I can't promise. It depends. But ask anyway." His voice was gentle.

"You said you did get into Bonaventure's apartment last night, right?"

"Yes, I said that. And yes, I did get in," he said, and glanced over at me.

"You said you did what you needed to do, right?"

"Yes," Darius said, and didn't add anything. He sounded as if he were being interrogated on a witness stand and I was the prosecutor.

I took a deep breath and said, "Did you kill Issa and Tanya?"

"No," he said. And that was it, just plain *no*. It was what I wanted to hear, but was it true? I went on: "Were you there when they were killed?"

He didn't answer quickly. He put the car on cruise control and fiddled around for a minute. Then he looked at me hard. "Yes, I was there." I gasped. "But there wasn't anything I could do to save them," he added.

My voice was louder, more insistent, when I asked, "Do you know who killed them?"

"Yes," he said in a flat, toneless voice.

"Well, who? Tell me, Darius!"

He absolutely refused to look in my direction, although I had moved closer to him and my face was just inches away. He said, "I can't answer that. Next question."

I felt sick inside. Then I asked, "Did you take the diamonds?"

"No, Daphne, I did not take any diamonds. And I say in all honesty that I never laid eyes on a diamond, an emerald, any kind of gem whatsoever. I didn't swipe the silver either."

He didn't seem to know about the missing valise. I went on: "Can you tell me now why you needed to get into Bonaventure's apartment?" I hoped he'd give me an answer I'd believe.

He looked at me then, and suddenly grinned. That threw me completely off guard. "What are you smiling about?" I said.

"Girlfriend, where did *you* get Bonaventure's address?"

I frowned. What was he asking me that for? "I used a reverse directory to identify the phone numbers I found on the speed dial of Bonaventure's hall phone."

"Bingo! So did I."

I felt like I had to connect the dots. "You mean you needed to get into the apartment to get phone numbers?"

"Among other things."

Yes, I thought, and he had no intention of telling me about those other things. He expected me to be satisfied with a small part of the truth. I felt hurt by Darius's games even though I told myself I shouldn't let them do a number on me. "Darius, I'm not stupid. You didn't just go in there for phone numbers. And are you telling me that none of the U.S. intelligence agencies knew the location of Bonaventure's country place?"

"That's exactly what I'm saying, Daphne. My agency didn't. Yours didn't. Nobody even knew he had a country place in the U.S. until he mentioned it to you and we picked up the conversation with the bug you planted. That's not as crazy as it sounds. He could be using a place belonging to someone else. He could have bought it using a lawyer and a dummy corporation. Believe me, Exeter, Pennsylvania, is not a town where international arms dealers normally hang out. I don't know what he's doing there or why he went there. But I know he *is* there. That's all I care about."

"Do you know if he brought a truck or a van? Do you know if he could possibly have brought an art collection with him?" I pressed.

"No, I didn't have access to any of that information. Sorry."

I made a disgusted sound, sort of like "pah," and said, "You act as though you know everything."

He raised his eyebrows and looked at me. "Do I detect some hostility, Miss Urban? As a matter of fact, I know only what I have to do. I don't care about anything else. As for the art, wasn't it just a phony deal you set up? And why do you care so much that Bonaventure has it?"

"First of all, the deal wasn't a fake," I said with sadness in my voice. I explained to Darius about Schneibel's collection. I told him that Bonaventure could use the statues to bend others to his will. Bonaventure could make others sick if they didn't do what he asked; he could even kill them without lifting a finger. What else could he do? I wasn't sure. Maybe some kind of mass hypnosis that could give him hundreds of followers, or even millions. Bonaventure could be king of a country, and that wasn't far-fetched at all. Saddam Hussein controlled Iraq without black magic. But with the masks, Bonaventure might someday take over the world. When I finished talking, I watched for Darius's reaction. J didn't believe those statues and masks had any powers. I wondered how Darius would react.

"So," I said as I finished my story, "I intend to destroy the art if I can. Will you help me do it?"

Darius had listened very carefully to me. "If these things can do what you say they can do . . ."

"They can, Darius, they can. I don't know if you believe in occult powers, but they exist, Darius. That I know."

"I don't doubt you, Daphne. As Shakespeare said, 'There are more things in heaven and earth, Horatio, than are dreamt of in your philosophy.' I've seen too much of evil not to know at least some of it isn't human. I know there are occult powers. I know there are ghosts." He paused there, and then said, "And I know there are vampires."

I felt like I had to respond carefully. "Maybe there are, Darius. At least I'll keep an open mind about it." I kept my voice from shaking, but his words were so heavy with hate and loathing when he said that, that it sent a sharp pain shooting into my heart. If he hated vampires, he hated me and those I loved. I couldn't even look at him. I felt tears welling up in my eyes. I was trying to keep my breathing even. But just after he finished saying what he did, he reached over and took my hand in his.

"You're cold," he said. "I'll get you warm." Keeping one hand on the steering wheel, he put his other arm around my shoulders, pulling me close like teenagers do. I snuggled against him and put my head on his shoulder.

We drove through the night, our bodies pressed tightly together and our fingers entwined.

CHAPTER 12

Frost at Midnight

Driving westward I felt happier than I had for a very long time, but anxiety underlay my bliss. I focused on the moment, because I knew the good feelings couldn't last. Darius hated vampires. I was a vampire. Sooner or later the irresistible force and the immovable object would meet. My heart would be left in the wreckage; that I knew. I just didn't know how bad the collision would be.

After an hour or so we crossed the river into Pennsylvania. and drove through the tollbooth at the Delaware Water Gap. I sighed and sat up. "We should talk," I said. "How are we going to handle this? Obviously I need to burgle the place and remove over a dozen crates of art, ranging in size from around twenty to fifty pounds each. Is that even going to be possible? And we don't know who else is there besides Bonaventure and Catharine. Do you have any ideas?"

"I always have ideas," Darius said, doing a Groucho Marx imitation with his eyebrows and wiggling an air cigar.

"I'm serious," I said, giving him a playful poke in the ribs.

"Okay. I'll be good. Yes, I have an idea, or maybe two," he said as our blue Taurus slipped through the night, going deeper into Pennsylvania. I saw the exit for Stroudsburg. It crossed my mind that I might need a rest stop before too long.

Darius continued talking: "Plan A. First we case the joint," he said, using a really bad Brooklyn accent.

"You know, I don't think you're serious enough," I said. "Okay, we look around the exterior and find a way to enter. Then I go tiptoeing through the interior searching for a big pile of crates containing witchcraft items. When I find them, I make a huge noise hoisting them out the window—and then what? We need a truck or a van. Damn it, I should have thought this out before we left." I felt down on myself. I had focused on my feelings for Darius and been a total asswipe about what should be primary in my thoughts. If this expedition brought me to grief, it was because of my own poor choices, not bad luck.

"Daphy, don't get upset," Darius said, looking over at me. "Think outside the box. If the art's there and we can't get it out, what's the alternative?"

I was feeling frustrated, and Darius's "quizzing" had a patronizing edge. I started to get an attitude with him. "Why don't you just tell me? I'm not in the mood for twenty questions."

"Hey, I'm just trying to be nice," he said. "The best way to get rid of anything 'on site' is to burn it where it sits."

"Crap. That's major. What about Bonaventure? What about that woman who's with him, Catharine? What if there's any hired help? Or pets? Catharine has a cat." My concerns swam through my mind, and to tell the truth, I have an instinctual fear of fire anywhere but in a nice cozy fireplace. It's my animal nature. The whole notion of setting a raging inferno gave me the beginnings of a panic attack.

Darius must have seen the fear in my face. "Daphy, I've done this before. I can handle it. If the art is there, we'll flush everyone out of the house. Then we'll torch it. Does that work for you?"

Once again I felt like a spy who didn't know anything about the hands-on side of my craft. Over the centuries I had gravitated to the bohemians of the world. I'm an expert at sobering up drunk writers, rescuing suicidal painters, or comforting bad actors who just got panned, but aside from some street fighting with the Fenians, my criminal activities had been largely the white-collar kind. I hated feeling stupid, and I said testily, "There's still big enough holes in this plan to drive a truck through, but I can go along with it. Now, Darius, it's your turn. What about your reason for coming out here?"

"While you're looking for the art, I'll take care of my business. Don't worry about it."

"For cripes' sake!" I exploded. "If I hear 'don't worry about it' one more time from you, I'm saying to hell with everything. Look, I'm going to be in that house with you. What about that whole speech you gave me about keeping each other out of the cross fire? How we need to share information so we can cooperate? Why do I do all the giving, and you do the taking?" Steam was coming out of my ears by the time I finished.

"Whoa, Daphne. Sorry. I didn't know it was such a big deal to you."

"Yeah, it's a very big deal. And I *do* think you knew that. Now be straight with me."

"Look, it's not complex. My agency is worried that Bonaventure knows something about the area we don't, and he's setting up another base of operations for his weapons dealing. I mean, nobody figured Buffalo, New

York, as the location for an Al Qaeda cell, but it was. Back in the early 1970s, the Weathermen had safe houses in Pennsylvania, so it's not out of the realm of possibility. I was going to plant some listening devices. But burning his house down will save me a lot of snooping. If Bonaventure leaves the area afterward, then he was only on vacation. If he rebuilds, we can assume he has reason to stay. What's the reason? Why did he go there in the first place? It's not a resort area. No, something else is going on besides R and R."

Everything Darius explained sounded believable. So why, in my heart of hearts, didn't I believe him? My gut told me he wasn't telling me everything, and I wondered what he was leaving out. "So that's it?" I said skeptically. "That's why you had to run out here tonight when we've got such a crisis situation in New York?"

"It was a window of opportunity, that's all. We have until tomorrow at least before there's going to be action in the city. And Daphy, in case you haven't guessed, I had to see you." He took one hand off the steering wheel and pulled me closer to him once more. "I like to feel you touching me. I don't seem to be able to stay away from you. So I came up with a way for us to spend time together." He put his hand back on the wheel and watched the road, then said, "Now, let's fill in the details of our plan."

I wanted it to be true that he couldn't stay away from me, yet in the back of my mind a little warning light was blinking that Darius used sweet talk to manipulate me. However, I agreed that we should hash out the details of what lay ahead, so I said, "And how will we get the people out if we burn down the place?"

"I can set a small, contained blaze. You start yelling, 'Fire!' When whoever is in the house gets out, I'll make sure the rest goes up in smoke—quickly, before the firefighters can arrive. Then we won't risk anybody getting hurt."

"It sounds almost too easy," I said with a great deal of doubt.

"It's never easy," Darius said. "A lot can go wrong. But I'm good at what I do. It's worth taking some chances."

I had to agree. "You're right," I conceded. "Getting rid of that New Guinea collection is worth taking a big chance, Darius. I feel that it's something I have to do."

"Believe me, Daphne, I understand. And I'd do almost anything for you."

I looked at him again. How much of his affection for me was real, and how much was he just using me? From the start he had used me in one way or another. We had great sex, and I didn't think he faked the gentleness. Things weren't all black-and-white with Darius, even if *he* thought they were. Then again, how well did I really know him? Not well at all.

He took his eyes off the road and glanced over at me. "That look you're giving me isn't a good one, Daphne. You think I'm giving you a line, but I have deep feelings for you. I haven't been able to prove to you that I really care, but maybe someday I can. After this is over."

I looked at his face in the flickering lights of passing cars. He looked sad and serious. I leaned over and kissed his cheek. "All right, what about plan B? What if we can't break in? Or what do we do if the art isn't there and we don't torch the place? You were willing to help me. It should be mutual. If I have to sashay up to the front door and charm my way in, I will."

He reached over and touched my hair. "Okay, let's figure out an alternative. If we don't burn the place down, I'll plant the listening devices, and I'll need to do a surveillance of the layout. And yes, that would be a whole lot safer and easier than arson. It will be in-and-out. You distract Bonaventure, I'll do my thing, and we'll get the hell out of there. Sound good?"

"It sounds real good," I said, but deep inside me I didn't think it was going to be that easy.

Sometimes piss-poor planning is better than no planning at all. And that night Darius and I had no plan whatsoever to deal with the internal fires that began raging whenever we got within arm's length of each other. I should have remembered AA's mantra for staying away from triggers that can cause a drinker to fall off the wagon: *People. Places. Things.* . . . Should have remembered the effect of buying a big bag of York Peppermint Patties "just to have on hand" for company the day you start a diet. Should have remembered that Darius and I had decided to "cool it" until all this was over with. Yeah, I should have remembered all of that before I got into the same car with him, feasted my eyes on his hard body, and smelled the tantalizing scent of him that went straight to the ancient, limbic brain that controls desire. I woulda, coulda, shoulda . . . but I didn't.

We drove farther into the wilderness, past Stroudsburg and up over the jagged ridge of mountains that marks the higher elevations of Pennsylvania. Darius's thigh pressed into my thigh. The car heater was blasting out warm air, but it wasn't generating even a tenth of the heat building up inside of me.

We were snuggled together in the darkness. The radio was tuned to golden oldies. John Cougar's "Hurts So Good" started me thinking. Then Chicago came on with "Hard Habit to Break" and pushed me closer to the thoughts I was trying to ignore. But the clincher was Foreigner with "I Want to Know What Love Is"—*I want you to show me. I want to feel what love is; I know you can show me.* By the time the final crescendo finished, I was a goner. I looked at Darius. I could read his mind as easily as he could read mine.

"You know," I said, "getting to Bonaventure's at ten is way too early."

"I was thinking the same thing," Darius said.

"Without a doubt at ten o'clock everybody in the house will be awake. We need to get there, say, at midnight." My voice was coy, and I was stroking his thigh.

"You're right. I think we have to kill a few hours," he responded.

"Got any of your *ideas* now?" I said, and kissed his cheek.

"We can find a truck stop and get a cup of coffee," he said.

"Well, I could use a rest stop," I answered, then hesitated.

"Or we can"—he paused for dramatic effect—"look for a Holiday Inn or Motel 6."

"I think that's a better idea," I said very softly. I looked over at him and down at his lap. I could see clearly that he was hard and ready. "I guess the sooner the better."

We found a Holiday Inn at the next exit. Darius seemed to know the drill all too well. He pulled up in front of the office, went in, and was back with the room "key"—they're just cards these days—in under five minutes. We opened the door, pushed into the room, and didn't bother turning on the light. Enough illumination from the lamps in the parking lot outside penetrated through the curtains, casting everything in a soft gray glow. Darius double-locked the door, slipped on the chain lock, and we began pulling off our clothes. So much for our mutual resolution to abstain. I had been love-starved for so long that my resistance was not just weak; it was nonexistent.

Our clothes dropped hastily on the floor at our feet, we stood there naked, facing each other. We stepped in to each other till our bodies gently met with the exquisite sensation of two lovers touching full-length, face-to-face, breast to chest, belly to belly, skin to skin. His arms pulled me closer to him. Then, unexpectedly, a metal object pressed painfully into my chest and burned my flesh. "Ouch," I cried, and pushed away. "What the . . ."

"Sorry," Darius said, and he unclasped a large golden crucifix, took it off, and put it down on a table. Bejeweled, at least three inches long, and affixed to a heavy chain, the crucifix gleamed even in the dim light. My skin was painfully tender where it had touched me.

Darius took me again into his strong, muscular arms and I forgot everything else except being held by him. His lips came down on mine, feeling hard and soft at the same time. His tongue rubbed against my teeth, pushing in and filling my mouth. He tasted like peppermints and pine forests. The kiss lengthened and ignited the fires smoldering inside us.

Darius picked me up and carried me over to the nearest double bed. He laid me down and looked at me as I rested there on my back, my raven hair spread out behind my head.

"You are so beautiful," he said. He knelt down next to the bed. He kissed my breasts; he kissed my stomach. His lips trailed down to my wet, dark center and began teasing me into gasps of pleasure. His fingers played with my nipples. I burrowed my fingers into his soft hair and held his head. I was dizzy with sensation. I was moaning with enjoyment. I never wanted the feelings to end.

I was panting hard when he lifted up his head and stood up, climbing over me and straddling my body, his knees on the bed on either side of my shins. He lowered himself slowly, tantalizingly. I shut my eyes and waited for his long, hard shaft to enter me. And so it did, as Darius uttered a long, low moan. He went deep into me, joining our flesh as tightly as his kiss had joined our souls, and I rode through the heavens as the rhythm of our bodies moved us as one in an eternal dance.

We climaxed together, breathing hard and calling out in joy and delight. Then he collapsed on top of me for a moment, before rolling off and making us two separate beings once more. But I felt joined to him still, and despite all my reasoning and doubts, he had stolen my heart.

Darius lay there next to me, our arms touching, his hand holding mine. We stared upward into the dimly lit room, not talking. Then he said, "I never expected this. I never knew I could feel this way."

We were quiet for a moment; then Darius went on: "Daphne, I can't promise you anything. Not because I don't want to. But because as long as I'm doing what I'm doing, my first commitment can't be to you. I can't ask you to understand that. I need you to accept it, because right now I can't change it."

"Darius, I don't know if I can ever accept that, but I don't want empty promises from you. I'm glad you're being honest with me." But behind my words lurked the reality that I didn't know that Darius could ever be honest with me, and I certainly couldn't be honest with him.

"Daphne," Darius said, "I know this sounds nuts, and maybe you don't believe in love at first sight, but the first time I saw you, walking through the East Village, I was drawn to you. That didn't make sense to me. You were a stranger on the street, and yet I was pulled to you with a force I couldn't understand. I tried to deny it and called it crazy. After that I couldn't stop thinking about you. You became an obsession, filling my fantasies, showing up in my dreams. When I approached you in front of the jewelry store on Madison Avenue, I couldn't wait to get close to you and touch you. You know that old saying, 'The heart has its reasons that reason never knows.' And I believe in fate, and that I have been searching for you my whole life. It may still be a mystery why I am meant to be with you, but I've seen too much in the war-torn corners of this world to believe in accidents. I survived things that should have killed me and walked away when everyone around me died. There had to be a reason, and perhaps that reason was you."

I wanted to say I had been searching for him my entire life too, but it wasn't true. Even so, I also believed in destiny, and I agreed with him that whatever brought us together, our meeting wasn't an accident. There is some great scheme for all things, some divine hand directing everything, and yes, watching even when a sparrow falls. So I did say what I meant from the bottom of my heart. "I believe we were meant to be together, Darius della Chiesa. Maybe it's just for now, just for tonight, though. I can't say it will be forever, because forever, I know, is a long, long time."

He turned to face me then and looked at me. I looked back at him without words, but we spoke to each other with our eyes, feeling happy at the proximity of our bodies, the closeness of our hearts.

The hours passed in the blink of an eye. To get to Exeter by midnight, we couldn't linger any longer. Irrevocably changed, we returned to the car and drove off into the cold, uncaring night.

Fern Hall, as a plaque on a stone pillar read, was nothing like I expected. It sat way out in the country with no houses visible for miles around. Mist rose up from the swampy landscape as we drove through a tunnel of thickening night. The windshield wipers swept back and forth as the fog closed in until we could see just a few feet in front of us. Then, without warning, our headlights had illuminated the sign for Fern Hall.

Darius and I left the car parked on the side of the road. We got out and Darius went around to the trunk. He opened it and pulled out a large knapsack. It sounded as if it contained tools, because it clanked when he threw it over one shoulder. Then he handed me an old dark sweater. Since the bright yellow of my jacket was not a terrific color choice for cat burglars, I slipped the sweater over my head, and it was so large it hit me at midthigh. We started up the dirt drive, not talking, and Darius gave my hand a quick, reassuring squeeze. Our footsteps didn't make a sound as we continued through the fog up the unpaved driveway. I can see in even the dimmest light, so I didn't stumble. Darius, however, cursed under his breath when his foot hit a stone and he nearly fell down.

After we had gone several hundred feet, the house loomed up like a white phantom, a few lights like candles burning in the windows of the second floor. In the center of the drive the grass was long, uncut and stiff. Now it made a crunching sound beneath our feet that sounded like little animals chewing on little bones. The night air cut right through my layers of clothing, leaving me with a feeling of cold, numb dread. Low fog clouds covered the moon, diffusing what little light there was. Bare tree limbs gently reached out and snagged the dark sweater of Darius's I wore over my jacket as if to pull me back, as if nature were saying, *Don't go, don't go.*

The house, when we got close enough to see it in its entirety, looked old and run-down. Decay covered it like a shroud. A large piazza surrounded by statues of nymphs fronted the house, but most of the sculptures were broken, becoming eerily grotesque figures with missing heads or arms. In some places just an empty plinth stood next to the neglected piazza. Weeds had sprung up between the terra-cotta paving stones. Everything about Fern Hall was silent and dead.

The only thing that gave a clue to the billionaire living inside was the sleek black Mercedes parked in the center of the piazza, its color as dark as the windows on the first floor. The entire scene was drenched in gloom and shadows. A gray cat crept along the foundation and ran around the corner of the house, while a dog howled somewhere far away and an owl hooted. I began to shiver from head to toe. A smell of dampness and fresh dirt hit my nostrils. It was a smell that caught in my throat and reminded me of somewhere else, somewhere I had been long ago.

Nevertheless the house had once been grand. I could see that in its graceful design, even though its stucco was peeling, and a wrought-iron balcony missing some railings sagged crazily across the second-floor facade. The steep roof was slate, crowned by four huge chimneys, one on every side of the house. They looked like cruel black fingers reaching up into the murky sky. The windows were tall and narrow, mullioned and magnificent . . . at least, I guessed the windows were magnificent from as much as I could see of them behind the iron bars that covered every single one, first and second floors. The bars looked new and unbreakable.

Flanked by stone pillars, the front door was also new, metal, and not one to be kicked in. Plan A was definitely fucked.

I looked at Darius. He looked back at me. "Plan B?" he whispered.

I took off the old sweater and handed it to Darius. He stuffed it into the knapsack. I smoothed my hair, raised my chin, and marched up to the front door.

I reached for the brass knocker. It was in the shape of a dragon's head. As I raised the brass ring, the door moved, startling me. It was ajar just a crack. So much for security. I pushed it open. Inside, a spacious hall was unlit, but not pitch black. I could see wide stairs of a dark wood leading upward. A astonishing round stained-glass window formed a backdrop to a landing where the stairs split to ascend grandly on opposite sides. I motioned for Darius to come up to the door. He joined me.

"Let's go in," he whispered.

I had a really bad feeling about all this. He gave me a little push. I didn't move. "After you," I said.

Darius shoved the door wide open and went into the hall. I came in behind him. The smell of dampness and dirt was even stronger inside the house.

To our right, behind beveled French double doors, lay a huge formal living room. Against the far wall a low-watt bulb burned in a Tiffany lamp on top of a grand piano. The upholstered Victorian-style furniture was dark red and overstuffed. Nothing around us moved. No one was here.

We entered through the French doors and crossed the living room. Near the piano a door stood open to reveal a short hall. At its far end was a kitchen. Our feet made a clicking sound as we started down the hall on a bare wooden floor. Except for our footsteps, the entire house was silent as a tomb.

The ceiling of the kitchen soared at least ten feet above us. One wall of the large room contained a gigantic fireplace, its firepit black and deep, like an open mouth waiting to be fed. A double granite sink and granite counters ran the length of the outer wall. Illumination came in the horizontal window above the counters from a security lamp outside. We could see well enough to walk single file through the room to a door at the kitchen's far end.

The old planked wooden door was padlocked. It didn't need a Do Not Enter sign to tell us that it was off-limits. I thought at once that it must be a storeroom where the New Guinea art was stashed. Darius looked at me. I nodded.

Darius put down the knapsack and took out a set of lockpicks. Most padlocks are easy to remove, and he opened it so quickly that it slipped off and fell to the floor with a loud thud.

"Shit!" he whispered, and I looked around behind me, fearful that someone had heard it, even though the walls were thick and the first floor of the house appeared empty.

Darius pulled open the door. There was no room behind it, just the dark, forbidding emptiness at the top of a steep stairway that led down into blackness. The door led to the basement. Wafting through the open door, the dirt smell hit me hard. My brain was buzzing, trying to remember where I had smelled that particular harsh, choking odor before.

Darius replaced the lockpicks in his knapsack, put it back on his shoulder, and moved forward as if he were about to start down the stairs. "Wait!" I said sotto voce. "You're not going down there, are you?"

"Yes," he said.

"No, don't! Let's go back. I think this is a bad idea," I whispered. I clutched his arm, holding him. "Let's go look upstairs."

"You can stay up here if you're frightened," he said, and gently shook me off.

I looked around the gloomy kitchen with its squat six-burner stove and huge pots and pans hanging from a ceiling rack, the yawning fireplace, the black-topped counters. The whole place was giving me the creeps. I thought I heard a board creaking above my head.

All my instincts were screaming, *Don't do this!* but I said "Okay, I'll come with you." I didn't like this whole setup at all. I had to force my legs to move through that battered, ugly ancient door.

Darius started down the stairs slowly, hugging the

wall, trying not to make any noise. I was right behind him, my hands on his shoulders. The air was so dank I could barely breathe. We were about halfway down when I could hear the squeaking. I knew what it was.

"Darius, wait!" I said. "I hear rats! There are rats down here. And there's no light at all." Even my bat eyes couldn't see in absolute darkness.

"Hold still a minute," he said, and reached into his knapsack. He pulled out a Maglite flashlight, the heavy black kind with the long shaft that cops carry because it can also be a weapon. He turned it on and we kept going slowly, one step at a time, down the stairs.

The squeaking was louder at the bottom. I didn't like this at all. Somewhere in the recesses of my brain a memory was trying to emerge. What was it? It had to do with the rat sounds, the dirt smell, the stone walls. Just then Darius shone the light across the cellar. There they were—hundreds of huge gray-brown rats that ran from the light. Unlike cute little pink-eyed Gunther rats, these were river rats, which are as big as cats and have mouths filled with sharp rat teeth to feed an insatiable appetite.

Darius shone the light higher. Stacked against the far wall were wooden crates. No, they weren't small crates that could house the New Guinea collection. They were unmistakable long rectangular boxes: coffins. Dozens of coffins were stacked to the ceiling. Then I remembered the Transylvanian castle where I had seen all this before—this was a vampire's lair.

"Darius," I whispered urgently, "we have to get out of here." I tugged on his arm.

But Darius had already taken a crowbar out of his backpack and was walking over to the coffins, swinging his Maglite back and forth to scare away the rats. I reluctantly followed. He handed me his knapsack and flashlight. Then, using both hands on the crowbar, he pried a coffin open. I screamed as rats poured out of the interior. In the bottom of the coffin was dirt, dank and loamy. Darius pried open a few more. Except for the rats and the dirt, they were all empty. I wanted out of here. This was my own personal nightmare come to haunt me.

Darius, breathing heavily, his shoulders sagging, his arms heavy at his sides, turned toward me. His long hair had pulled loose and blew wildly around his head as a wind came out of nowhere and howled around us. Darius spun his head from left to right, his eyes wildly searching for the source, and he let out a terrible cry in a high voice I had never heard from him before. "He's heeeere! He's heeeere!" He pulled the knapsack roughly from my hands and brandished the crowbar like a weapon with the other.

I quickly stepped away as I cried out, "Darius!" He looked at me, but his eyes were unfocused and open so wide I could see the whites all around them. He didn't seem to see me at all. "Bonaventure! Bonaventure!" he howled in that weird voice that cracked with something like insanity. Darius frantically turned one way, then the other, as if he were looking for the source of the strange, awful wind that tugged at our clothes with a gale force. The crucifix around Darius's neck had come out of the sweater and gleamed on his chest, seeming to possess a light of its own. I took off running for the stairs and barely was able to stay in front of Darius, who was close behind me. My overriding thought was to get out of the house. I wasn't afraid for myself; I was terrified for Darius, who seemed to have lost his mind.

I dashed through the kitchen and down the hall, but when I got to the door into the living room, I stopped and froze. The flashlight slipped from my hands and hit the floor with a crash. Bonaventure sat at the grand piano. He wore a black velvet evening jacket and a white silk ascot. Catharine, in a sheer white dress, lay pale and limp on the red sofa, her blue veins showing through her translucent skin, her golden hair spread out like a halo around her face. Delicate satin ballet slippers covered her tiny feet.

Bonaventure was seated at the piano, his back to me, and didn't turn around to acknowledge me. Instead his fingers crashed down on the keys, playing the opening bars of the overture from Bizet's opera *Carmen*. The notes he played were the "Fate" theme. *Da, da, da, da, dum. Dum, dum.* He repeated them several times as he threw his head back and laughed crazily. Afterward he abruptly stopped playing and slammed the cover down on the keys. He turned to look at me.

"Welcome to my home," he said, and every syllable resonated with a heavier Eastern European accent than he had used with me before. "I am surprised to see you, my dear Miss Urban. I thought I left you . . . indisposed. I'm glad you weren't too inconvenienced by your little rest in the exercise room. I apologize, but a situation arose unexpectedly. It would have been, well, unacceptable for you to witness it. The whole incident was unfortunate, but unavoidable." He smiled a hideous smile and pulled his cape around him, while he hunched down on the piano bench looking more than ever like a malevolent black toad.

"Now, do introduce me to your friend," he said.

Darius moved out of the shadows behind me. "I am Darius della Chiesa," he announced loudly. Bonaventure jumped up when he heard those words, knocking over the piano bench. Darius continued talking: "But I think you already know that, *Bonaventure*."

"Yesssss," Bonaventure hissed, "your reputation precedes you," and he began to transform into the vampire I had realized, albeit too late, that he was.

"No!" I screamed as Darius threw down the crowbar and pulled a stake and a mallet out of his backpack. *"No, don't!*" Before I could stop him, Darius threw himself at Bonaventure, putting the full force of his fury into his charge. He plunged the stake into Bonaventure's heart, and the vampire went down on the Oriental carpet. Darius was on top of him in a flash, the mallet in his hand pounding the stake deeper into Bonaventure's chest. Bonaventure screamed and screamed, and then with a groan his form began to crumble and smolder until only a pile of dust remained on the carpet.

My horror was palpable. My hands were trembling. I was breathing fast. I was shaking from head to toe, trying not to let myself transform. Darius looked at me but his face was blank, his eyes unseeing. He turned then toward Catharine, who had pushed herself back against the cushions, her eyes wide with terror.

"No, please, no," she cried.

"It must be done," Darius said in a voice that sounded flat and disconnected from his body. "You are his creature. You are not human."

"No, oh, please," she said in her little-girl voice, her hands stretched toward Darius, pleading with him. "It wasn't my choice. He took me from my home. I don't want to die. Please, no."

I couldn't bear this anymore. As I stood unseen behind Darius, I tore off my clothes and let myself change. I grew in size as my shape transformed into the great fantastical winged creature within me. The air rushed in a whirlwind around me. Tingles of electric power surged through me. My fur glistened and sparked, shooting light into the room, and a rainbow spray of colors danced across the walls. Darius spun around. I will never forget the look on his face. It was a combination of absolute shock, wide-eyed horror, and—what bothered me most— a look of undisguised hurt, as if I had betrayed him. I had, but he had also betrayed me.

"Do not touch her, human," I hissed. I reached out with one mighty wing and effortlessly batted him across the room. He sailed through the air and crashed into the far wall, sliding down it and sitting stunned on the floor.

"Look at me, Darius!" I commanded. "Look at me!" He raised his head slowly and stared at me. "You need to know what I am. I am one of *them*. I am what you most hate and fear. Yet you kissed and stroked me. Yet you loved me. I am who I am. But you! You are all J warned me you were—a vampire hunter. Worse than that, you are a wanton killer. You think you are destroying evil, yet you are destroying *life*," I hissed. "Bonaventure was a criminal, but it was not being a vampire that made him so. He should have been brought to justice, but not by *you. You* had no right to murder him. And you have no right to kill this woman. To kill *my people*."

I flew over to Catharine and gathered her frail body in my arms. "She is an innocent," I said, turning my gaze upon Darius and pinning him to the wall with my eyes. "You shall not have her; you shall never have her. Or me!" I rose above the floor and flew to the door. Darius didn't rush me. I was relieved at that. I would have had to hurt him if he did. Perhaps he was incapacitated by the blow I dealt him. Unmoving, he remained sitting immobile against the paneled wall. I looked back at him before I took off into the night sky with Catharine. It may have been my imagination, but I thought I saw tears in his eyes.

CHAPTER 13

The blood-dimmed tide is loosed, and everywhere
The ceremony of innocence is drowned;
The best lack all conviction, while the worst
Are full of passionate intensity.

—W. B. Yeats

I didn't fly far with Catharine. I landed in a tree, and hanging upside down as bats do, waited until I saw Darius leave the house, jog down the driveway, and drive away in the Taurus. Bats aren't long-distance fliers, and despite my immense strength, flying carrying a full-grown woman taxed my abilities.

When I was sure Darius was gone for good, I flew back to Fern Hall. Crying softly and not speaking, Catharine had clung to me tightly the entire time. I set her down carefully in the vestibule. I flew into the living room, quickly transformed back to human shape, and hastily collected my clothes. Among them, there on the floor, was the sweater Darius had given me to cover my jacket. He must have flung it out of his knapsack before he left. My heart sank. I picked it up. I put it to my face, and it smelled of him. I hesitated and then tied it around my waist under my jacket. It was all I had of his. I couldn't bear to leave it behind.

Catharine waited patiently in the hall until I reemerged. I closed the French doors behind me. I didn't think she should go back in there, where the dust from

Bonaventure's body lay dry and desolate on the rug. I had noticed that the stake Darius had pounded through his heart was gone.

"What would you like to do?" I asked Catharine as gently as I could.

She looked up at me with tearful eyes. "I want to go home," she said.

"Where's home?"

"Far away. In Dubrovnik, Croatia. But perhaps for now you can take me back to New York? To the apartment?"

"Of course I can. Can you get your things quickly? We don't have many hours until dawn."

"I understand," she said. "It will take me only a few minutes. And I must get Princess. She's locked in the bedroom. Bonaventure didn't like her hair on the furniture. She wasn't allowed to come downstairs."

With that she rushed up the stairs. I sat on a bench in the hall and tried to think, and tried not to think. I wanted to just sit and sob my heart out, but this wasn't the time or place. I had to stay focused on what I had to do next. Right now that was to drive Catharine back into the city and get home by six A.M. It was already nearly two. I hoped I didn't get a speeding ticket on the way.

When Catharine came back down, she looked less like a frail victim than I had ever seen her. She had changed into a pair of jeans. She wore a jean jacket over a black turtleneck. Her long hair was pulled neatly back. She didn't look more than sixteen years old. She had a cat carrier in one hand and a small valise in the other.

"Catharine," I said. "I need to ask you something, and I need you to tell me the truth."

She looked at me with wide eyes. "You saved my life. I owe you everything. I will tell you anything I can. I am so grateful. So very grateful."

"Where are the pieces of art from Herr Schneibel?"

"I don't know. We didn't get them. We tried, but they were gone."

"What do you mean?"

"We took the limo down to Canal Street. Bonaventure had arranged for a small truck to meet us there. When we arrived, there was no truck. Bonaventure left the limo and ran upstairs. He was gone for only a few minutes. When he came back, he was enraged. I was very frightened then. When Bonaventure is angry, I try to stay away from him, but there was nowhere to go in the limo."

"What did he say? What did he do?"

"He didn't tell me anything, but he made a call on the car phone. I think it was to his bodyguard, Sam Bockerie. Bockerie was supposed to be driving the truck. No one answered, so Bonny left a message on the machine. He told Bockerie to bring the art to Pennsylvania. He said Bockerie had forty-eight hours to deliver the art. If he didn't, on the forty-ninth hour he would die. Bonny's voice was chilling. I could barely breathe while he was speaking. It was terrible, the way he said what he did. I can't describe it. It wasn't a warning. It was a curse." She began trembling.

"It's okay, Catharine. Bonaventure is gone. He's gone forever. I'm sorry about what happened tonight."

"Don't be sorry, Miss Urban. It wasn't your fault. I will miss Bonny, but I am free now. I am no longer a prisoner. I can go home."

"Let's get out of here," I said. She handed me the keys to the Mercedes. "Thanks," I said, and I took them and her valise too. We went quickly out to the car, and I drove away as fast as I dared.

I didn't want to turn on the radio. Listening to love songs would be pure masochism after what had happened tonight. I did want to cry until the tears couldn't come anymore, but that would have to wait. I needed to drive, and wanted to avoid wrecking the car. It had been such a terrible night, and yet it had been such a happy one. For a few minutes I had had everything I ever wanted—a man to love and one who loved me. Then within hours it had all vanished, and I was left with this huge emptiness inside.

When I thought of Darius, I felt betrayed and disappointed. I was angry with myself for not believing J, and I hated Darius for killing Bonaventure, for being a vampire hunter, for not being the man I wanted him to be.

To distract myself I turned to Catharine, who was crying quietly in the passenger seat, soaking through Kleenex after Kleenex. "Do you feel like talking?" I said. "It might help you to get it all out, and it might help me to listen."

"I guess you of all people would understand," she said, her eyes swimming with tears. "Who else can, except someone who knows what Bonaventure was?"

"That's true," I said. Only another vampire can truly understand what the life of a night stalker means. "Did you ever care about him or were you forced into the relationship?"

She sniffed into the tissue. "Oh, no, I loved him so much. When we first met, I was a waitress in a beautiful Dubrovnik restaurant, the Konoba Pjatanca. It's outside the Ploce Gate on Kilocepska Street. From its terrace you can see the old port and the city walls." Catharine's voice became dreamy, nostalgic. "I was still in school, but I needed the money, you know? He came in frequently and always sat at my tables. He ordered caviar, champagne. The cost meant nothing to him. He flirted with me. He was so charming. Finally, after coming in a few times, he asked me if I would go out with him."

Catharine was whimpering just a little now as she

focused on memories instead of the present. "I was so flattered. He was a very important person. One night he had come in with Putin. I didn't wait on them. They took a private room in the back. Another time he was with the French prime minister. What is his name? I can't remember. But they all treated him with respect. And this important man who dined with heads of state wanted to go out with me, a student, a nobody."

The roads were virtually empty of traffic as I steered the Mercedes toward the interstate. The way was well marked, and I was relieved. The car was big and comfortable, and having to drive kept me from thinking. Keeping Catharine talking helped too, so I asked her, "How old were you?"

"Seventeen. Just seventeen," she said, and began to cry again. "So young and innocent. I had never even been with a man."

I reached over and gave her hand a comforting pat. "What happened when you went out with him?"

"He took me to a café for cocktails, and afterward we walked along the old wall of the city. It is so beautiful in Dubrovnik. Like a fairytale."

"Yes, I know. I've been there." And I had been, both before and after the terrible shelling in 1991 from the Serbian and Montenegrin forces during the Balkan conflict. Since then that pearly city of marble sidewalks, palaces, bell towers, and green-shuttered houses had been carefully restored. Dubrovnik has been called the "Venice of the Adriatic," although it's much older than Venice. It is a breathtakingly beautiful city.

Remembering that and feeling in my heart what Catharine was describing, I paused, then said again, "Yes, I've walked along the Dalmatian coast for miles. Its waters are so clear you can see schools of silver fish darting by. It reminds me of the Mediterranean as it used to be.

The breezes are clean and pure. Cypress trees tower above, nightingales sing, and everywhere are wildflowers. It is a very beautiful place."

"Oh," she said, and clapped her hands. "You know! You understand, then, how much I love it. And you will understand too the romance. Bonaventure and I walked through the Old Town. He held my hand. We'd stop and kiss in doorways. He asked me if I would go back to his hotel room. I hesitated. He said we would do only as much as I wanted. That he respected me. If I just wanted him to hold me, that was all he would do. I trusted him, and I said yes."

"But of course, trusting some men is a bad idea," I said sadly.

"I don't know," Catharine said, "about other men. But at first, when we got there, he kept his word. I was light-headed from the drinks I had at the café. I was very dizzy—drunk, in fact. I couldn't seem to think clearly. He sat me down on his lap. I put my head on his shoulder. He began stroking me. I didn't stop him; God forgive me, I didn't stop him. He asked if that was okay. I said yes, that he could do what he wanted. That I wanted him too. But I didn't really know what that meant.

"He stood me up and began to unbutton my blouse. I felt a little scared but I let him do it. Before I realized what was happening, all my clothes were off. When he started to undo his trousers, I got very scared. I told him no! I had changed my mind. But it was too late. He told me that. It was too late. He grabbed my arms and pushed me down right there on the floor. He pushed himself into me. It hurt. I screamed and he covered my mouth with his hand. He pushed and pushed. Finally it was over. Or I thought it was over. That's when it happened."

"What happened?"

"He lowered his mouth to my neck and bit me. He

began drinking my blood. I couldn't believe what was happening. I tried to get away, but he kept drinking until I passed out.

"When I regained consciousness, I was in a big bed. I was still naked, and I felt very weak. Bonaventure came into the room and asked how I was. I told him I was tired. He came to me and brought me a cup of tea. He sat on the edge of the bed while I drank it. After I finished I began to feel very strange. I think the tea was drugged.

"He took me again then. I couldn't resist. He was rough with me. And when he finished he lowered his mouth to my neck once more and began to drink. I don't remember much after that. Days seemed to pass. I don't know how long. I was delirious. I remember him coming to me again and again. He did things to me. I can't talk about them really. He said he was teaching me about love. Sometimes he tied me to the bed. Sometimes he hurt me, not much, just a little. It was so strange. The pain increased the pleasure, and when I told him that, he laughed and told me I was a good pupil. And always he drank from me. At last, though, I felt stronger and different somehow, powerful and new. And by then, when I finally felt better, I didn't want to leave him. I was bound to him by the things we had done, by what he had shown me, and by the blood we shared."

My heart felt like stone as I listened to her. I pitied her. But I couldn't change what had happened. She went on, her voice more excited now, almost happy in remembering.

"He gave me beautiful clothes to wear and expensive jewels. He told me he was married, but that he loved me. He said he had left his wife, and that she had filed for a divorce. He told me we were going to America, where I'd be very happy and have a wonderful life. When I was lonely during his absences for business, he went and bought me Princess. He wasn't all bad, Miss Urban. He could be kind, and I do think he loved me in his own way. His servants adored him. Tanya loved him, I think. All of them were completely loyal, and that says a great deal."

Yes, I thought, *it says money can buy loyalty.*

"And Bonaventure was telling me the truth. Anything I asked for, he gave to me. But I didn't understand what he was. One day I gathered up my courage and asked him about drinking my blood, why he had done that. I asked him what happened to me."

Listening to Catharine's story I felt so terribly sad. For her. For myself. Even for Bonaventure, that damaged, stupid man. He thought you could force a person to love you, and that he could possess Catharine's heart by drinking her blood. He wasn't the first vampire to make that mistake. "And what did he tell you?" I asked her.

"He said he was a vampire, and that he had been a vampire for a very long time. He said by biting me he had given me a wonderful gift: that I could never die—by natural means anyway. It also meant we could be together forever, literally forever. He said there was nothing wrong with what happened between us and apologized for his impatience in taking me by force that first night, but that he adored me. To face an eternity without me would be torment, that's what he told me. He didn't tell me, not then anyway, that he had to drink blood to live and paid poor souls to sell their bodies to him. Sometimes he drank too much and they died. He had people who helped him bury the bodies. Families were paid off. No one complained or stopped him. In Croatia they called him a great man." She began trembling uncontrollably then.

"Catharine," I said sharply, "it's over. You are safe." I wondered if I should stop the car and try to help her, but she rallied and, shaking, but less so, she continued.

"And he didn't tell me that I had to drink blood too.

But I was soon driven to it. I tried not to, but the hunger overwhelmed me. He brought me young men mostly. They were very sweet, really. They knew what I wanted and they let me do it. It seemed to excite them so much. I don't like to think about it. That's when I began to drink vodka, starting in the morning until everything was hazy and beautiful. I drank to forget and tried to stay drunk. What shall I do now, Miss Urban? Will I die? Will I have to go out wandering the streets looking for blood? I don't know what to do." She began to weep again.

"I'll help you, Catharine. There are other ways. I'll send you to my mother. Stay with her until you can go home. She'll show you how to live without killing. You can trust her. She's helped others before."

"I don't know how to thank you. You've done so much for me. I hope you don't think badly of me for not hating Bonaventure. I know he was a bad man. I know he made his fortune by selling weapons. I know what he did to me was wrong. But I loved him. At least, I loved him once."

I understood her more than she could ever know. Pain struck me like an arrow through my heart. When I answered her, I was fighting back the tears. "We don't love with our reason and intellect, Catharine. We love with our souls. It doesn't always make sense. Women love bad men as well as good men. We sometimes can't help loving them even when we know it will bring us pain. We love them even when we know we shouldn't." I thought of Darius then, the memories flooding my mind, remembering him telling me how much he felt for me, and then remembering his shock when he saw who I really was. Tears spilled over my lower eyelids and rolled down my face. I would never be held by him again. It was over. And I would never stop wanting what I had lost.

Before we got back into Manhattan, I made Catharine write down Mar-Mar's phone number. My mother may drive me crazy, but there's no better person to have in your corner when the chips are down. Mar-Mar knows everyone—everyone of importance, that is. She has connections that reach into the highest circles of governments all around the globe, and she always has, starting back when she lived in the Vatican hundreds of years ago.

Mar-Mar may look silly, with her hippie clothes and peace signs, but my mother is one of the shrewdest manipulators I have ever met. She has run great businesses as far back as the merchant guilds in medieval Europe, and probably countries, too, although she won't usually talk about it. From what I have found out about her, I know she was always behind the scenes, pulling the strings, and more than once she told me what Margaret Mead said: "Never doubt that a small group of thoughtful, committed citizens can change the world. Indeed, it's the only thing that ever has." I wouldn't want to be her enemy, but if I weren't her daughter, I would be proud to be her friend.

I planned to give her a call too, explaining what Catharine probably wouldn't tell her—that this fragile woman needed some time in detox, and rape counseling too. When Catharine got her head together, Mar-Mar would help get her back to Croatia and set her up in a nice villa. Prices have skyrocketed there, but money wouldn't be a problem for Catharine. Even if she merely sold all the jewels that Bonaventure had given her, she'd be set for life. And she had confided in me that he had made sure she had safe deposit boxes filled with gold coins and ingots. She might not think so now, but she could be happy. And Mar-Mar could help her find a purpose in life too. Her country needed rebuilding. She could become an important woman there, a respected woman. When I told her what I was thinking, her eyes no longer were filled with tears.

We pulled up in front of the Park Avenue apartment house, and the doorman came out to open the car doors for us. Catharine told him to put the Mercedes in the garage, so we left it running while he called someone on his cell phone. I was so exhausted I was running on fumes by this time. I didn't have much time to get home before six A.M., but Catharine said she could find Bockerie's address and phone number for me. So I took the elevator up to the penthouse with her.

When we got in, she went right over to the phone table that I had searched last night. I hadn't found anything except blank pads and pens. She pushed a button underneath, and son of a gun, a secret drawer popped out. She copied down the information and handed it to me.

"Come with me a minute," she said. "I want to give you something. But first let me let Princess out." She stooped over, opened the cat carrier, and Princess went scampering down the hall. Then Catharine led me through the apartment. She stopped in the dining room and opened the doors of a built-in cabinet. She took out a blue box from Tiffany's and handed it to me. "I bought this," she said. "Not Bonny. I thought it was beautiful and wanted it."

I opened the box. A huge opal in a platinum filigree setting hung from an intricate platinum chain. Catharine reached into the box and took it out. She stretched her arms up and slipped the necklace over my head. "Please," she said. "Take this to remember me. A girl whose life you saved. A girl who will never, ever forget you."

"Thank you," I said. "It is so kind of you. It is magnificent." I had learned long ago that to accept a gift gracefully is as important as giving one. I understood Catharine felt she was in my debt, and so I accepted her generous present with my whole heart.

I hugged her, and her thin body felt as delicate as a bird's beneath my hands. It was then I noticed that Princess was pacing back and forth in front of the door to the library. She was meowing and making a fuss. The door itself was ajar, and the lights inside were on. The apartment had been dark everywhere else when we entered. I wondered why that room was lit. A chill passed over me. I had a terrible foreboding.

"Catharine," I said. "Stay here. I want to look in the library."

"Is something wrong?" she said nervously.

"Probably nothing. But let me look."

I went into the library. I walked past the table where I had sat with Bonaventure not so very long ago. As I rounded the table I saw it. There on the pale pink and cream of the Chinese rug was a wooden stake lying amid a pile of dust. I inhaled sharply. Who? What?

That was when I saw the glitter of gold in the dust. I stooped down and picked it up. It was my ring. My precious, beloved panther ring. An awful realization washed over me.

"Oh, noooo," I cried. "Benny! Dear, sweet Benny." Tears flowed, and rage filled my heart. I shook my fist at the fate that had brought me to this point. "Darius!" I screamed. "You bastard! What have you done! What have you done!" I ripped his sweater off from where I had tied it around my waist and flung it across the room. Then I sank to the floor, covering my face with my hands and weeping, sobbing, and swearing, "You will pay for this, Darius della Chiesa. I will make sure you pay for this."

CHAPTER 14

*If you can look into the seeds of time
And say which grain will grow and
which will not,
Speak then to me . . .*

—Shakespeare
Banquo, *Macbeth*, Act I, scene 3

I slept, but I got no rest. *What's done cannot be undone.* I tossed and turned and dreamed fitful dreams. In one I was phoning Benny on my cell phone, but the number was out of service, and the phone melted in my hand. In another I was hiking on a trail through a thick forest and a sign read BENNY, THIS WAY. But when I followed the arrow, she wasn't there. Instead I heard Darius's voice, calling my name. I ran toward the sound and saw him being attacked by dark figures, fighting alone, screaming to me to help him. I couldn't reach him. I couldn't move. I could only watch helplessly as he was struck again and again and fell down. It was a terrible nightmare, and I awoke with my heart racing. I was filled with guilt over Benny's death, for it was I who had brought Darius to her. My grief spilled over into helpless tears that drenched my satin coffin.

As evening fell and I arose, doubts battered against my conscious mind like a moth at the windowpane. Should I have refused to become a spy? Would it have been better to have perished on the spot than to undergo this pain? The words pounded through my brain. *What's done cannot be undone.* But I have never been one to wallow in self-pity. "Get on with it," my mother always said. "Don't put your wishbone where your backbone ought to be."

Now I needed to survive and do what I had started out to do—use my gifts, my strengths, my intelligence to protect others. I clung to that idea, wanting to extinguish the desire for revenge that was already beginning to eat away at my soul. Yet blind rage overtook me when I thought of the stupidity and waste of Darius's misguided quest, and the taste for getting even stayed with me, burrowing down into some place deep in my heart.

I checked my phone messages. As Darius had predicted, J had called the evening before to say there would be no movement that night. He sounded incredibly angry that he couldn't reach me. I didn't call him back. My mother had also phoned, wondering where I was and would I please contact her. I would phone her soon to tell her about Catharine. If Catharine didn't call her, I knew with certainty that Mar-Mar would show up at the Park Avenue apartment with a tote bag filled with organic veggies and a load of good advice.

I dialed Benny's number, hoping against hope it had all been a terrible mistake. As in my dream I could not reach her. Her answering machine picked up on her home line, and her cell phone went straight to voice mail. I fought back tears. I wondered if J knew she was dead. I didn't want to tell him or have to admit he had been right all along about Darius, and about endangering the entire team. I should have listened. Right now I couldn't bear even one "I told you so."

The night hours stretched before me like a long highway to nowhere. I could sit here waiting for the phone to ring and tell me that it was time to go out and stop some terrorists, or I could do *something*. Gunther hopped up on my shoulder and squeaked in my ear. I put Bach on the CD player. I sat down, took out my Waterford crystal, and dined on my "victimless" blood-bank blood. Then I went to the corner of the living room I had made into a meditation space.

A retired military man once told me that when you are suddenly hit with a crisis and get the urge to jump right into action, stop! Sgt. Harry DePew had looked lazily at me with his dark eyes barely visible under his hooded eyelids. He tipped back in his desk chair and folded his ashy dark hands over his still-trim belly. He spoke slowly and deliberately, just the way he did everything. "Don't panic; remember the *Titanic,*" he said. He went on with his advice. "You get the call that all hell's breaking loose. The ship's going down. Or the enemy's circled the fort. Your heart starts doing a tap dance. You want to run for the lifeboats or grab your gun and head for the door. Don't do it, brother. Instead, sit down. Put your feet up on the desk, and *think*. Even if you only take a minute to do this, and five minutes are optimal if the situation allows it, you will make a better decision and probably avoid one hell of a mistake." That was what Harry told me. I've done my best to follow his advice.

With no imminent crisis looming over me, I took five minutes and fifteen more. I sat down in the lotus position. Gunther sat by my knee and proceeded to wash his face with his little pink hands. I touched my forefinger to my thumb in the classic mudra. I opened my mind, I emptied it of all thought, and I let guidance come to me.

I accepted that I had made mistakes. I focused on the knowledge that I had two tasks before me that I couldn't screw up. Number one, I still needed to find Schneibel's art and destroy it. If it were in Sam Bockerie's hands, that was a very bad thing. Bonaventure was greedy and venal, but Bockerie was a psychotic killer; of that I had no doubt.

And the second task: With Benny gone, I had to be there to help intercept the terrorists. Just the two of us remained standing, and Cormac O'Reilly could never handle the situation alone. Perhaps a steel resolve lay hidden beneath his self-absorbed butterfly demeanor. I hoped so, but I could not allow the lives of millions of people to rest on his fluttery wings. No, this was a job for Daphne Urban, Vampire Spy. I walked over to the CD player and switched the disk to "The William Tell Overture." Perfect. The Lone Ranger rides again. Or flies again, as it may be.

Sam Bockerie, a.k.a. General Mosquito, lived in Brooklyn—legendary Brooklyn with John A. Roebling's Brooklyn Bridge leading in from Manhattan at its mouth and the Verrazzano Bridge stretching out to Staten Island at its asshole. Brooklyn: Williamsburg, Coney Island, Dyker Heights; Flatbush and Bay Ridge; old Jewish ladies speaking Yiddish on Thirteenth Avenue, asking the counterman for whitefish and just a little lox. Brooklyn, the third-largest city in the United States.

I went back there now. I had dressed for comfort, not fashion. I pulled on an old pair of black jeans, black turtleneck, black leather jacket. I finished it off by putting on my workout Nikes, leather gloves, and a hat with earflaps. I slipped a can of Mace into my purse. This was New York at night, and I'd rather use a conventional defense if someone tried to mug me. Clawing out someone's eyes would surely attract unwanted attention.

I left my apartment building and headed for the subway. I took the BMT, catching the N local. I got off in Brooklyn at Forty-fifth Street and Fourth Avenue. There is no lonelier place in the world than a New York subway station in the dead of night. The sounds of my footsteps on the dirty cement platform echoed off the white-tiled walls. I felt oppressed by the smell of urine, the dingy yellow light. I emerged up the stairs into a Spanish neighborhood and started walking as fast as I could to the great warehouses that line Gowanus Bay, the Brooklyn waterfront.

I found Bockerie's address. The square, plain corner building looked like a fortress, with wire mesh covering the small panes of its factory-type windows. I stepped inside the building. According to a label scrawled in Magic Marker over the mailboxes in the vestibule, Bockerie was on the fourth floor. The entrance door was secure, hard as steel, and locked up tight. *Shit and double shit.* I had no choice. I removed my clothes in the little antechamber and transformed.

Afterward I cautiously opened the door and looked up and down the street. Silent as a tomb. I went outside and flew nearly straight up to the fourth floor. I landed on the window ledge and peered in through the dingy panels of glass. I could see a loft space like Schneibel's, but this one was unfinished. Large pieces of milling machinery still occupied most of the floor space. The big, hulking pieces of metal sat beneath flickering fluorescent lights and cast quivering shadows across the gray linoleum floor. A makeshift bedroom had been set up in one corner; it was little more than a battered dresser and a mattress on the floor. Anyone would have mistaken this place for a squatter's quarters if it weren't for the whole arsenal of semiautomatics that were leaning against one wall—and the valise sitting near them. It was the one I had seen at Bonaventure's, and I knew it held $250 million worth of diamonds. *Son of a bitch!* I thought. Bockerie *had* been the one to kill Issa and Tanya. It figured. The realization clicked into place as neatly as the last piece of a jigsaw puzzle. I hovered outside of the window, watching.

Sam Bockerie walked into my line of vision carrying a large suitcase. He threw it on the mattress, unzipped it, and began stuffing clothes into it from the dresser drawers, not doing it neatly, and definitely not folding anything. I could see sweat beading up on his forehead and running down his face. He didn't bother wiping it away. His breath looked as if it was coming heavily. He sat down all of a sudden in a chair, shaking his head, and appeared to be mumbling to himself. He kept looking toward the door, which was out of my sight, somewhere to the left of the window.

I didn't spot the masks or statues, but I could literally feel their presence. There was no point in waiting another second, so I grasped the wire mesh and effortlessly yanked it off the window, letting it drop to the empty street below. I took my foot and smashed the glass out, then crashed through the empty frame and landed like a huge black demon about ten feet from Bockerie.

Bockerie's head yanked up at the sound of the mesh being torn off. When he saw me blasting into the room, I could see his eyes widen in shock. His mouth opened to scream, but no sound came out. Instead he clutched at his chest with his hand and crumpled to the floor. He landed hard and didn't move.

Holy shit! I thought. I've seen all the ways humans reacted to the sight of me. I'd had them faint with terror many times. But the way Bockerie looked in the split second before he collapsed hadn't been a man fainting. It had been a man dying on the spot. I flew over to him. I knelt beside him and felt for a pulse. He was gone . . . to hell, I hoped, to that beyond where he had to face his crimes and his victims, where he would truly pay for his sins. On the other side he would face a justice more terrible than anything man could bring on him.

And even if the official cause of death turned out to be a heart attack, I knew what had really happened to him. I looked at my watch. Two days ago, nearly to the hour, he had double-crossed his boss. He stole the diamonds and he grabbed Schneibel's collection. He had to know what Bonaventure was. Even a psychopath or megalomaniac would fear Bonaventure's mortal power as well as his immortal abilities. On top of that, the vampire had cursed him. Bonaventure had given him an ultimatum, and if he didn't meet it in forty-eight hours, Bockerie was to die on the forty-ninth. That was why he was watching the door. Well, right on time death came calling. Only it didn't knock; it came flying in through the window.

But my hands were clean. I had no doubt Bockerie had killed himself with fear. Bonaventure's curse had kicked up all the superstitions and fears of Bockerie's African tribal heritage. He expected to die. When he saw me coming for him, his fears took physical shape and overwhelmed him. The mind is a powerful weapon, and he had turned it on himself. Good riddance to bad rubbish, I say.

I left the body lying there and flew through the loft. I quickly found the crates containing Schneibel's New Guinea collection, or at least most of it, the things Schneibel hadn't been able to destroy before Bockerie arrived. I don't know how Bockerie tolerated being so close to them. They radiated malevolence. Perhaps his own twisted cruelty fed on their evil. Schneibel, I believed, had been protected by white magic, for he seemed unaffected by their powers. But what in the hell was I going to do with them? Torching this large building would be unconscionable. Innocent people or firefighters could be hurt or killed. Instead I needed a way to get these crates out of here and to someplace I could dispose of them.

I couldn't call J. He'd want to turn them over to the agency, and I feared that a government would misuse their magic. I don't care if we're the guys with the white hats. Power corrupts, and absolute power corrupts absolutely. So that avenue was out.

I couldn't move these myself, at least not in the short time I had available. J could be calling at any minute and I'd be out of here. So I did the only thing I could do under the circumstances.

I called my mother.

Having learned from Benny's example, I had begun to take my purse and cell phone with me when I transformed. Therefore I had mine handy. I had no problem calling Mar-Mar, and she was home. There was a lot of noise in the background, but I didn't ask who was there keeping her company. I was relieved that she didn't ask any questions when I told her to show up in Brooklyn with a pickup truck and a change of clothes for me. My own clothes were downstairs in the little anteroom in front of the inside door, and I didn't think it was a great idea to risk tiptoeing down there to get them. Anyone walking in and seeing my abandoned black leather jacket would have taken it. It's New York, where finders are keepers most of the time.

My mother had heard the urgency in my voice and said she'd be there as fast as she could. Even if she rushed, it would still take her two hours from Scarsdale, and at that she'd have to be traveling at warp speed. Meanwhile I transformed back into human shape, because otherwise I'm so big that it's uncomfortable in any confined space except maybe a castle in Transylvania. That left me prancing around naked until my mother showed up, unless I found something to wear. There wasn't a snowball's chance in hell I'd put on anything of General Mosquito's. I decided to see what was in the boxed-off part of the loft housing the bathroom, and was disappointed to find only a stall shower, a sink, a commode, and some filthy towels. Commandeering the plastic shower curtain wasn't appealing, but there were heavy green velvet drapes over the windows. I ripped them down, found a safety pin in the medicine cabinet, and made myself a toga. It felt okay. I slung the swag from the curtains over my shoulders like a shawl, as I was feeling chilled to the bone. I had to stay barefoot, though, and I hated walking on the dirty floor. My feet were already grimy. I made a mental note to book a pedicure when this was all over, and then laughed at myself. Even in the midst of trying to stop a terrorist attack, I'm vain.

Going back into the main loft area, I began a methodical search, starting with Bockerie's body. It's always best to get the worst jobs out of the way first. He lay sprawled out on his back; his eyes were wide open and staring without sight. I pulled the Ray-Ban sunglasses I had found at Schneibel's out of my purse and slipped them on him. That was much better.

With two fingers I gingerly pulled his wallet from his pants pocket and flipped it open. Along with several hundred dollars in American cash, there were leone, the currency of his native country. I guess he thought he was going home, and I suppose in a way he had. There was also a yellow Post-it note with R530 written on it. I left the money and put the note in my purse. His wallet also contained an American Express card, a New York driver's license, and a local supermarket discount card. That was it: no photos of family; no proof of health insurance.

I stood up and looked around. I dumped out the contents of his suitcase onto the mattress. Nothing but clothes. I went through his dresser. It was virtually empty. I pulled each drawer out, looking underneath on the off chance that, like my mother, Bockerie hid things by taping them under drawers. Lo and behold, when I pulled out the bottom drawer a brown nine-by-twelve envelope was taped to the underside.

I pulled the envelope off, opened it up, and pulled out a number of pages. I scanned them and realized they were Revolutionary United Front, or RUF, records of the diamonds they'd confiscated from Sierra Leone's diamond mines. If there is a hell on earth, it is where the blood diamonds of Africa originate. Blood diamonds . . . the name refers not to their color, but to their cost in human lives, particularly those of children who are used as forced labor. Those diamonds, legitimately sent or smuggled through the United Arab Emirates, Dubai in particular, can buy anything, and the dealing is largely unrecorded, anonymous, and effective. Terrorists have made diamonds their currency of choice. It was ironic that some of the most beautiful gems on earth financed death. Yet if I think back over history, perhaps it has always been so.

The envelope felt hot and heavy in my hands. Here were the secret records of millions of dollars in diamond transactions, including names of buyers and dates of purchase. Most of the buyers were Arabs, and even I recognized some known members of Al Qaeda. I would turn these papers over to J, who could use them to identify both terrorists and their financiers. If the money behind terrorism could be stopped, the whole chain of human misery, which began with the kidnapping of African children to become slave laborers, might be broken. Along with stopping Bockerie's theft of the New Guinea art, I felt better that the violence and dying of the past few days—may poor Benny rest in peace—had proved to be important. And silently I promised her spirit that I would make sure the threatened nuclear attack could be stopped too.

My search of the rest of the loft turned up some gold coins in a plastic bag in the bottom of the toilet tank. I left them. The medicine cabinet held bottles of prescription painkillers, a muscle relaxant, and Prozac. I guess General Mosquito had a bad back and felt a bit depressed. I reminded myself that humanity is frail, and its immoral monsters are not completely evil. Even Hitler liked dogs. But everyone makes choices, and those people who choose to hurt others out of greed or psychosis make the worst ones humans can. General Mosquito chose cruelty and war. Now few, if any, would mourn his death.

My searching over, I decided to sit down and meditate until Mar-Mar showed up. Wherever I was going, there I was—specifically I was in a factory building on Gowanus Bay with a dead man lying twenty feet away. I faced the large factory-type windows, sat down on the floor in my green velvet toga, and emptied my mind.

Time passed unnoticed until a commotion in the hall outside the front door stirred me from my zazen. Mar-Mar had arrived, and she hadn't come alone. Someone pounded on the door. I opened it just a crack. My mother stood there, holding the clothes I had left downstairs in the vestibule and a paper bag. Behind her stood a gang of six aging hippies, punk rockers, and Goths—all male— who looked like escapees from the seventies. I wondered if she had driven through the East Village and just picked up people off the street. Nah, I thought these were Mar-Mar's Save the Trees people, no doubt.

"Ma!" I hissed through the crack in the door. "I've got a dead body in here."

"Did you kill him, sweetheart?" she asked, unfazed.

"No, he had a heart attack, I think."

"Then not a problem. People!" she yelled. "Don't step on the corpse when you go in."

"Right on," they yelled back.

"Dear, I think you need to let us in. We can't stay in the hall," she said softly, as if I were five years old.

I widened the door and grabbed my clothes from her hands. "Come on in. Don't touch anything!" I yelled to the troops. "Just wait by the door. I have to talk to your fearless leader."

"You silly," Mar-Mar said. "We aren't a hierarchy. We vote on everything."

"Whatever! Ma, I need to talk with you. Alone," I whispered.

Mar-Mar and her gang of six came into the loft. They stayed bunched together and glanced around the huge space. "Nice place, dude," one gray-haired pothead with a ponytail said. "Love the industrial look."

"It's not mine." I glared at him. I thought he looked vaguely familiar. I must have met him at one of Mar-Mar's "dos." He was eminently forgettable. I pulled my mother off to the side.

"Look, Ma, I can't explain everything right now, but the short version is this. This guy was into witchcraft. He has some really bad stuff, masks and statues, in crates stashed in here. They need to be buried or burned ASAP. Don't keep them. Don't stay around them too long. Don't dump them anywhere. No one should get their hands on them ever again."

Mar-Mar again was diplomatic and unquestioning. "I know what to do, dear. Don't worry about it for a minute. I'll figure something out. With witchcraft items, burning is preferable, but an open fire without a permit presents difficulties." She paused for a moment, thinking. "Hmm, I have a funeral director friend with access to a crematorium. Well, just don't worry. I understand. We have a truck, and these nice strong boys can take the crates on downstairs. Do you want us to take the body too?"

"No! I'll call nine-one-one tomorrow morning. He died a natural death. I'm just worried about his art collection. And Mar-Mar, I need you to hang onto these. It's very important." I handed her the brown envelope containing the diamond mine papers and the suitcase containing the diamonds.

She put the envelope into her backpack and took the valise with one hand while she handed me her paper bag with the other. "I don't think you'll need these now," she said.

I peeked in. The grocery bag contained the clothes she had picked out for me: an L.L. Bean insulated royal blue turtleneck, a Pendleton wool shirt of red and black plaid, a black velvet peasant skirt, and a pair of old snow boots that I had left at her house a decade ago. I fervently hoped I wouldn't ever need to wear them. Thank God nobody had taken the clothes I left downstairs. "Thanks, yeah, but I've got my own clothes to put back on." I handed the bag back to her.

"Where are the crates?" she said.

I pointed toward the back of the loft. "Just walk between those lathes and the drill press, and you can't miss them," I told her.

Mar-Mar nodded, pulled her shoulders back, and turned to her helpers. She reminded me of that old Sally Field movie, when Norma Rae gets up on a table in the factory to address the striking workers. "Okay, people, listen up!" Mar-Mar bellowed. "We've got a bunch of crates to get into the truck. They contain really bad mojo, so whoever brought the sage smudge pots, be prepared to get them out. Set them up in the back of the truck while we're loading. And people, we're working under security level Red Alert. When you take the crates down to the truck, leave one person to guard everything. I mean it; this is evil shit. Let's get this done as fast as possible. The briefer our contact with these things, the better. We'll plan a sweat lodge cleansing ceremony for tomorrow. Before we start, does anyone feel they shouldn't touch them at all?"

A skinny guy in a Dracula cape, his eyebrows and lower lip pierced, raised his hand. "I'm dealing with hep C."

"Right, Norman. You do the guard duty and try to stay at least ten feet from the crates. Everybody else okay?"

They all nodded, and except for Norman, who vanished out the front door, the remaining five followed Mar-Mar to the back of the loft. Mr. Ponytail passed me and said, "Bodacious toga. Are you a disciple of Isis?"

"No, it's a Kabbalah thing." I said

"Cool," he said, and followed Mar-Mar into the gloom. He waved at me as he went, and I noticed part of his index finger was missing. Very briefly I tried to remember someone else I'd seen with the same deformity recently, but it didn't seem very important. Of greater urgency was getting back into my own clothes, so I hurried into the bathroom to change.

I shouldn't have even bothered. I had just reemerged from the bathroom, happily in my jeans again and having applied some fresh lipstick and mascara, when my cell phone rang. The guys had already gotten one load of crates out in the hall, and they were going down the stairs making enough noise to wake the dead, although Bockerie still lay there like a stone. I turned my back to the door and answered the call.

"Hello?" I said, my heart starting to speed up. I knew it had to be J.

"Hermes?" he said quickly. "Ringmaster here. It's a go. Move it."

"Right," I said, uncertainty plain in my voice.

There was silence on the other end of the line. I could picture J trying not to lose his temper. When he spoke again, his voice was tight and controlled. "Hermes? Is there a problem?"

I hemmed and hawed for a second before blurting out the truth: "Um, well, I'm not exactly sure how to get to New Jersey from here."

There was something like an exasperated sigh. "Where are you?"

"Uh, Brooklyn," I confessed.

Another heavy sigh came through the phone. "I won't ask why. Look, fly toward the lower tip of Manhattan. You'll see a narrow strip of water between Manhattan and Staten Island; that's the Kill van Kull. Follow it west until it opens into Newark Bay. You'll be going northwest at that point. Call me on the cell and I'll guide you in. Will you remember all that?" He sounded majorly annoyed.

"Yeah, sure," I said.

"And Hermes, move it!" he barked, and hung up.

Shit, I thought, *I'd better not screw this up.* I had to find the container facility in a hurry, because I didn't have a lot of confidence that my old pal Cormac would get there on time. Maybe I was selling the guy short, but he had been late for everything as long as I've known him— and that's been for more than two hundred years. I wouldn't be surprised if he got lost somewhere over New Jersey. This was a job for Superman, all right. Or should I say Superwoman.

I turned around. My mother was standing there staring at me. I wondered if she could hear what I had been saying to J. "Ma," I said. "I've got a little emergency here. I've got to transform. Can you keep your guys in the hall for a couple of minutes?"

She looked serious as cancer when I told her that, but she didn't ask me one single thing. Mar-Mar's always been there when I needed her, and this wasn't the first time. "Sure, sweetheart," she said. "You go ahead. I'll peek through the door before I let them in to finish." With that, she went out into the hall and closed the door behind her.

I stripped down again and left my clothes neatly folded on the chair. I hoped Mar-Mar picked them up, or I might as well say good-bye to them for good this time. Damn, I really loved that motorcycle jacket. Then with a whoosh and a flash of light, I changed into the vampire I am. I slung my purse over my head and made sure I had my cell phone. With that, I hopped up onto the windowsill and leaped out into the sky.

CHAPTER 15

Nothing ever becomes real till it is experienced.

—John Keats

A sou'easter was blowing in from the Atlantic, making flying difficult and churning up the water beneath me into angry whitecaps and choppy waves. A cold, heavy rainfall slowed my progress. The wind pushed me back and forth. This was not a night for flying, even for a vampire with superhuman powers. My fur kept me dry, but the leather of my purse was ruined. I should have taken a cab.

I was swooping well out over Newark Bay when I managed to get my cell phone out and call J. Rain was streaming into my eyes. I give him credit; he did manage to "talk me in" to Port Newark. The facility was huge and lit up with sodium vapor lamps, giving the whole place a glow like a low-burning fire. I landed inside the facility by the service road leading from Kellogg Street. There were security cameras everywhere. I assumed someone was watching me come in.

As I touched down, I could see I was the only vampire there. The original plan was for all three of the Team Darkwing vampires to rendezvous at this entrance to the port after getting the "go" signal from J. I hoped Cormac would be flying in any minute because I knew Benny wasn't going to make it. J said his men were set up throughout the facility with the main contingent near the exit portal. He gave an ETA for the car full of terrorists of about ten minutes. The rain was coming down in sheets. I lurked in the shadows and tried not to listen to my gut, which was telling me that this was a snafu waiting to happen. Somewhere out there in the rows of thousands of containers was a weapon of horrifying power. If dread was a living thing, it was worming its way up into my throat.

My attention was riveted on the service road. It was raining hard, and the drops striking the pavement made a drumming sound, drowning out anything that could have alerted me to movement around me. I never heard a thing when something big and hard hit me from behind and knocked me over. Before I could scramble back up on my feet, a huge tarp was thrown over me, and I was wrapped up in it so tightly I couldn't move. Then I felt something rigid and metallic being tied around the outside of the tarp. No matter how hard I struggled, I couldn't break free. Whoever thought this operation was airtight and under control was dead wrong. The terrorists coming down from Englewood Cliffs must have had people waiting to meet them—and they sure as hell had met me.

Trussed up like a turkey, I felt myself being lifted up by two or three men. They were speaking in Arabic and they sounded scared as shit. They were asking each other what to do with me. They decided to dump me in the water. That was an alternative that held no appeal to me at all, but I was being carried along at a jog. I intensified my efforts to wriggle out of the tarp and was almost free when I felt myself falling a long, long way. I landed with a splash in the cold, oil-drenched waters of Newark Bay.

I sank like a stone. The water was so frigid it took my breath away. I felt as if I had fallen into liquid ice. I went downward, descending into a nightmare. I hit bottom. The tarp was loose enough that I didn't have to break the rigid wrapping, which turned out to be a chain. I was able to wriggle free. The effort left me needing oxygen, and my body was screaming for it. I fought my instincts to take a deep breath. I had to use tremendous willpower to keep from inhaling. I won't go into all the particulars of immortality, but while I can regenerate from injury pretty quickly, I would be out of commission while doing so. Two lungs filled with dirty seawater would knock me out of the ballgame for tonight and possibly for a great many nights.

Kicking free of the last of the tarp, I tumbled along the bottom with the current. *Swim up,* I told myself, and surged toward the surface. When I finally broke through into the night, the rain was coming down so hard I could barely breathe even above the water. As I pushed my head up as far as possible, I gulped down air, then flopped about trying to get my bearings. Waves hit me in the face as I was swept laterally along the shoreline. I realized that I couldn't take off from the water, and my only hope was to get back up on a dock somehow.

But the currents in Newark Bay were strong and treacherous, and they were carrying me away from the spot where I had been thrown in at a pretty good clip. Oil and debris from the dozens of container ships anchored here made the water smelly and viscous, and it was making me gag and cough. Above me the docks were lit up by the pinkish orange of the sodium vapor lamps. They were high, a good fifteen feet above the surface, and should have had emergency ladders somewhere. After all, if there's a dock, people sooner or later are going to fall off. I concentrated on finding one of them.

I had survived for five hundred years on intelligence and luck, and I hoped my luck didn't run out tonight. Precious minutes were ticking away as I swam diagonally toward shore, going in with the waves and getting tugged out again by the tide. Finally a spit of land and a long dock loomed up before me. As the current swept me under the wharf, I was battered against cement pilings until I was finally able to cling to one. It was slippery with slime, and barnacles made it sharp and treacherous beneath the surface. I couldn't hold on long without cutting myself to ribbons, and to make things worse, the cold was making my hands numb.

Soon hypothermia was inching through me, making me feel light-headed and slow-thinking. I couldn't feel my hands or feet. I started to wonder in a dreamy way if this was what death felt like when I got knocked against another cement piling. The sharp pain and the surge of adrenaline that shot through me brought me back from my drift into oblivion. Swiveling my head around I could see the outlines of a ladder extending down from the dock above. It was about twenty feet away. I struck out for it with all my might, giving powerful kicks with my feet and using my wings like great oars. I hit another piling and caromed off. If I wasn't careful I'd be swept completely through the underside of the dock and out into the bay. This was my last chance at getting back to the container facility in time to stop the terrorists.

I swam forward with every ounce of strength I possessed. I reached out with one hand and managed to grab a rung as the waves pulled me past. I felt the force yank my shoulder, but I tightened my claws around the metal and held on. I pulled myself closer to the ladder and finally got my other hand around the rungs. I began to drag myself upward.

My fur was sodden and my wings heavy. I couldn't feel my feet at all. The metal rungs were slippery and I was cold to the bone. I took heaving breaths. I had no choice but to push myself to get to the top, which loomed about fifteen feet above me. I didn't dare let go. One slip back into the water and I could drift until dawn. I might not die, but I wouldn't be conscious of life either. This was it; I couldn't fail.

I could only imagine what it might have looked like, this huge bat shape, dripping with salt water, slowly pulling itself up the vertical metal ladder one step at a time—a true monster from the deep. My progress upward felt as if it took hours, but probably wasn't more than a few minutes. I was nearly to the top, two rungs away from the deck, when my nearly frozen foot slipped on the smooth, wet metal. I fell downward with my feet swinging into air, but I held on to the ladder with one hand. The yank on my arm socket sent shocks of pain through my body. I screamed. I was dangling by one hand, trying to get my feet back into the rungs, bouncing against the ladder and unable to get a grip with my other hand. By that time I was chattering loudly, making whistling bat noises, which happens when I get stressed.

I was clenching my teeth and hanging on with every bit of strength I had when a hand reached down and grabbed the fur at the back of my neck. Then another hand grasped under my armpit. The lift gave me enough of an assist to get my foot back on the rung. Pulled from above, I was able to give a mighty heave and throw myself full length on the top of the dock, knocking my rescuer aside as I did. I lay there gasping, barely able to turn my head to see the good Samaritan who had landed a few feet away. A human in military garb was already scrambling to get up, and as I lifted my head to say thanks, my rescuer turned around and looked at me.

It was my mother.

I thought I was delirious. I must be hallucinating. Had she followed me? Why was she here? How did she get here? It didn't make any sense at all. I started to raise up on my knees when I saw moving spotlights begin criss-crossing the dock, and men's voices were yelling, "Where are you? Did you get her?"

Mar-Mar answered, "Over here!" She clicked on a flashlight, sweeping it up and down as a signal.

Before I knew it, J stood above me, running the light from a large torch back and forth over my body.

"Hey, get that thing out of my eyes," I yelled, and put my arm over my face.

"Are you okay?" my mother whispered close to my ear.

"I'm fine, but what—"

"We'll talk about this later," she whispered, then stood up.

"Can you take it from here, Captain?" she said crisply to J.

"Yes, m'am," he answered, and stood ramrod straight. Then he saluted her. I thought I was dreaming—or having a nightmare. It all washed over me in a moment of sickening realization. I had been manipulated. I had been duped. My mother had engineered everything—my recruitment, the Darkwing squad, the vampire-spy approach to saving the world. I should have known. How long she'd been working in U.S. intelligence, I didn't know, but I did know she was always playing with the big boys. My mind spun in a dizzying whirl of thoughts, and I felt the beginnings of the mother of all headaches.

"Carry on," she said to J, then brushed herself off and ran off into the night with several of the men.

J turned to me. "Are you hurt? Are you able to stand?"

"I'm fine," I said as I got to my feet. I shook myself off like a dog does, sending a spray of water in all directions. Warmth began to flow back into my veins. My breathing returned to normal. Within seconds I was feeling ship-shape, so to speak. "What's going on?" I asked J.

"The terrorists are in the facility. Our men have a tracking device on a car that came down from Englewood Cliffs and are sticking with it, but there are at least two other groups of four or five men each rendezvousing with them. One cadre attacked you, and all of them are somewhere in the port. We think they are heading for the container. You need to get airborne to see if you can spot them. Here's a walkie-talkie to replace your cell phone. I think it is probably out of commission after being submerged."

"Right," I said, and took the device. "What about the other Darkwing members?"

"Cormac got blown off course, but he's here," J said, pointing upward. "He's flying around looking for the mavericks we didn't expect. I don't know where Benny is. She hasn't called in. She may just show up."

"I hope with all my heart she does," I said sadly, knowing it just couldn't be.

J began to sound rushed. "Right. I'm rejoining my squad that's tracking the car. You get airborne."

"What do you want to do if I spot anyone?" I asked quickly.

J was already jogging toward a jeep when he said, "Radio the information to me. Knock 'em down and hold them. Make sure no one has a detonator."

"Is that it?" I said sarcastically.

"You can handle it, Miss Urban," J said, and smiled at me.

"Roger," I said as I leaped skyward with a great bound, swooping gracefully higher on bat wings until I was a huge, dark silhouette against the orange of the sodium lamps. There was something like awe on J's face when I looked back.

Once airborne I quickly spotted Cormac and flew over to him. He gave me a mock salute and shouted above the wind and rain, "Hey, Daphy, want to buddy up?"

"Good idea," I said. "Are you doing a methodical search?" I asked, figuring Cormac was just swooping around willy-nilly, leaving everything to chance or serendipity, as he usually did.

"Never thought of it."

"Let's do a grid. Ten rows, ten containers each row per swoop; use echolocation," I screamed at him, my cry sounding like a whistle in the wind.

"Righto," he squeaked back.

We began swooping one grid at a time as I felt the urgency of the situation squeezing my brain. Working quickly and efficiently, we sent out inaudible signals that bounced back better than any radar man has ever created. One group was pinpointed within thirty seconds. As we descended I saw them fighting with a soldier who was getting the crap beat out of him, but holding his own. One of the terrorists was down on the ground, moaning. Four others were closing in on the lone fighter.

We landed, and our winged bodies cast long shadows across the men. The terrorists looked up and screamed. Distracted by our appearance, they forgot their opponent, who moved in from behind and slit the throat of one terrorist. Blood poured down the man's shirt. When he slid to the ground, the blood poured onto the macadam, mingling with the rain.

The soldier was dressed in camouflage fatigues, a black ski mask covering his face, a commando knife in his hand, and a semiautomatic rifle slung over his shoulder. He grabbed another terrorist by the hair and screamed at him, asking him what container held the weapon. Pushing the man's face toward the dead man, the soldier was screaming, "Give me the number! Give me the fucking number, you miserable bastard. Now, or you die!"

The terrorist looked at him with stark terror, but he

didn't utter a sound. He merely shook his head no. He, like his brethren, was ready and willing to die for his cause.

True to his word, the soldier coolly slit the terrorist's throat and threw the body to the ground. Then he looked directly up at me. He pulled off his ski mask. It was Darius.

Mixed feelings washed through me—love, hate, sadness, anger. The look he gave me was easier to read. It was Berserker rage. Darius was the archetype of a warrior on the battlefield, who throughout the ages has always been consumed with a determination to beat the enemy or go down fighting.

I could have gotten my revenge right then, knocked him down and slit his throat with my claws, no knife needed. I wanted to pay him back for Benny's death. But I didn't want him dead by my hand. I was still looking at him when he arrogantly turned his back on me. He was a bastard. He was bleeding from his shoulder, but he stuck his commando knife in his belt and put his ski mask back on. Then he ran off down a row of containers and disappeared into the night.

Cormac and I grabbed the last two men standing. They trembled in our claws, falling to their knees and crying to Allah for salvation. I radioed to J, and within seconds black-clad figures slipped into sight and retrieved them. I knew they would try to get them to talk, but I didn't hold out much hope.

Cormac and I got airborne again and resumed our grid-by-grid search. Seconds ticked past. We had miles of containers to go. Even working fast it would take hours to cover the entire facility. We needed luck, and we needed it now.

We didn't get it. Instead the sound of automatic rifle fire began a terrific racket nearby, and a ball of fire blazed against the night sky, followed by a great bang. The explosion wasn't the mushroom cloud of a nuclear weapon, but something else. We two vampires zoomed over to the site. A car was engulfed in flames.

I landed next to J. We stood there in the pouring rain, our faces lit by the fire. J was drenched to the skin. His face was as rigid as iron, his brows knit with anxiety, his tension like a wire pulled taut. He looked at me with his agate blue eyes. He was a man running out of time. I could see right into his thoughts as if I were peering into clear water.

"What the hell happened?" I asked.

He shouted over the noise of the burning car, "They tried to make a run past the portal. They started shooting and we returned fire. Then they blew themselves up."

I looked at the black skeleton of the vehicle and could see the charred figures of men inside. "Better them than us," I said without compassion.

J nodded. "Yeah, but we're running out of options. Those men you captured aren't talking. Maybe they will at some point, but not soon enough. Look, get back up there and find the remaining group. Track them to the container. Don't stop them. It's our last chance."

I flexed my legs and stretched my wings, preparing to take off into the downpour. "I'll do my best," I said grimly, and I was about to lift off when J touched my shoulder, stopping me.

He stepped close to me and said into my ear, "Miss Urban, your friend Darius della Chiesa is here." Even the mention of Darius's name cut into me like a sliver of glass, but I gave a small nod and tried to keep my face emotionless as J added, "He's a loose cannon. Watch your back."

"Thanks," I said, and meant it. I looked over at Cormac, who, if I read the grin on his face correctly, was having the time of his life. I signaled to him to take off, and we soared upward once more.

I might make derisive remarks about Cormac, but he had stayed alive as long as I had. If he acted like a twit and a flake, it was just that—an act. I had seen him be selfish, narcissistic, and a dilettante, but above all else he was a vampire, part of a brotherhood that united us with unbreakable bonds. It also meant he had to be smart, tough—and damned lucky. When the dice were tossed for either of us, they came up lucky sevens, not craps. Together we made a nearly invincible team, and that's the truth.

Cormac squeaked at me now with great excitement. He spotted the remaining group of terrorists, and they were on the move, running from cover to cover down a row of containers. They had guns drawn. We stayed behind them, following them in swooping flight. Both of us spotted the lone soldier coming down a cross street toward them unseen, his rifle drawn and ready. He didn't know the terrorists were there. They didn't know he was there either, but in seconds they'd meet. There would be a firefight. At best—and it was a lousy option—the melee would stop them from reaching the container, and we might never find it. At worst, they'd detonate the weapon and end everything, for us and millions of people.

Before I could stop him, Cormac, like a bat out of hell, flew at the soldier. With the claws of his feet he grabbed Darius from behind, sending him sailing through the air. Darius hit the ground hard and slid across the asphalt until the rifle in his hand banged the side of a container and discharged. The noise was deafening. Struggling to his feet, Darius whirled around, ready to fire at Cormac. I swooped down and brushed him with my wing, knocking him to his knees. But it was too late. The gang of terrorists must have heard the shot and rounded the corner, firing their weapons. I charged at them with Cormac pulling up my rear, and we flew like screaming eagles at the men.

Fortunately they carried only pistols, not semiautomatics, and hitting a target with a short-nosed gun at a distance was pure chance and usually a ricochet. Our luck held, and they missed us by a mile as bullets pinged off the sides of the metal containers. The terrorists began retreating, running back the way they had come. I yelled into the radio for J. He answered, and I screamed at him to get over here fast. I told him that I'd go airborne where he could see me. He said, "Just give me the number."

"What?" I didn't know what he meant.

"The location, damn it. Look on the containers. There's a number painted on the asphalt where they're parked. Quick!"

I glanced over and told him it was AB2021. "We're on our way," he barked.

Cormac and I pursued the fleeing terrorists, catching them easily and batting them around with our feet and wings. The five of them went down like bowling pins. Crawling for cover behind containers, some of them kept firing, so we had to go airborne quickly. Others were running down the street between the rows. Like B-2 bombers, Cormac and I circled and got set for our second run.

At that moment J and his squad came screeching up in a jeep. They jumped out with their rifles drawn, with J yelling at the terrorists to get their hands up. One terrorist opened fire. J threw himself out of the way, and a few squad members quickly cut the aggressor down. Blood mixed with the puddles on the asphalt, wet and black. Two other terrorists fired and fell. Finally the last two, who were hiding behind a container, tossed out their pistols and yelled that they were surrendering. They put their hands over their heads and marched into the open. J and his men grabbed them and handcuffed them. They were facedown in the back of the jeep before they knew what happened, and the driver was speeding off.

That was when I heard the moans. I flew over to Darius, who had been left stunned near a container. He lay face up in the rain, his rifle still clutched in his hand. I didn't see much blood, just a small round entry wound in his chest. I felt as if a branding iron were searing my lungs; every breath hurt. Realizing how much my bat form would distress him, I landed and transformed quickly. I stood there in the pouring rain, naked except for my sodden leather purse. I pulled it off over my head and put it down on the ground.

I bent over Darius, taking his head and cradling it in my arms against my breasts. I was crying. My sobs wouldn't stop coming. He looked up at me, turned his head away, and closed his eyes, not wanting to see me even then, when he was dying. I reached down to feel the pulse in his neck. He flinched at my touch. His pulse was thready and weak. The wound looked close to his heart. I had no doubt he had only minutes left to live. Darius had gone down in battle, and he'd die a hero. Karma would catch up to him on the other side, or maybe it already had: a life for a life, his for Benny's. So why did I feel so rotten?

A bat shadow crossed over us. I figured it was Cormac returning. I turned to tell him to get me somebody's jacket to put on. A bat landed next to me. It was blonde, not dark. It was Benny.

"What are you doing here? You're dead!" I said in wonderment, and stared at her.

"I'm undead, sugar, but I sure as hell ain't *dead* dead

yet. I'm just late. Long story. Did I worry you?" she said, but her attention was riveted on Darius, whose life was ebbing away before our eyes. "Honey, what's going on here? That's your guy."

I nodded and choked back a sob.

"Why are you sitting there doing nothing? Save him!"

I just looked at her, uncomprehending.

"Bite him! You don't have much time. Don't let him die!"

I tried to get my mind around her words. It never occurred to me to turn him into a vampire. He'd become the very thing he hated most. It would be the perfect revenge, but it would be a terrible thing to do. I started to explain that, when Benny broke in.

"You think too damn much. How do you know what he wants? Follow your heart! For God's sake, you love him. Don't let him die. If you don't bite him, I will!"

I stopped thinking and started feeling. Naked, I knelt on the cold, hard ground and put my lips to his neck. Something began to burn into my flesh. It was his crucifix. I unclasped it and threw it as far as I could. Then I leaned down once more, tenderly, gently finding his carotid artery with my lips. Then I bit him and began to drink the blood of my beloved. With his remaining strength he tried to push me away. I embraced him firmly and continued to drink. The sensation was exquisite. I was filled with him and possessed him, body and soul. It was better than sex; it was an experience that joined the human and the immortal in a union that was both damned . . . and divine. Darius went limp in my arms, but he did not die. I felt his body stir with life beneath my hands. I broke the kiss. He turned his face toward me and slowly opened his eyes. In a voice barely more than a whisper he said, "Why? Do you hate me that much?"

I looked at him, and I had never before felt such a

mixture of sadness and joy. He'd live now, but he might never forgive me for turning him into what he hated most. "Please believe me; I don't hate you, Darius. I bit you because I love you." His body was heavy against me. I hoped I'd always remember how he felt beneath my lips. I laid him down softly onto the ground and stood up.

J came running down the street. Keeping his eyes level with mine, he never looked at my naked body. He thrust a paper bag and a dry towel at me. "Here," he said. "The commander said you might need this." Then he was screaming into his radio for a medic. I don't think he had seen what I did to Darius.

I looked into the bag. *Crap.* It was the clothes my mother had brought to Brooklyn. I thought she did this on purpose; I really did. As a soldier came running up to him with a medical kit, I left Darius's side. I walked over to the shelter of a container and quickly wiped myself down. I got the clothes out of the bag, put them on, and felt like a refugee from Woodstock. My mother had even placed a collapsible umbrella in the bottom of the bag— the Mary Poppins touch. I opened it and looked at Benny. She was biting her bat lip, trying not to laugh at me.

Another jeep drove up, its tires squealing. Men jumped out and lifted Darius by his armpits and feet. They put him in the back of the jeep and took off. I watched him go, knowing he would live, not knowing if he'd be glad that he did or if I'd ever see him again. I wanted to cry my eyes out.

J walked over and barked at Benny. "Miss Polycarp. Where the hell have you been?"

"Sir, I'm so sorry. I was in the sauna. The cell phone got all messed up from the heat, so I rushed down to an all-night place to get a new one, but having the number switched over took absolutely forever and—"

"Never mind!" J boomed. "Miss Urban, get your butt

over here! Mr. O'Reilly!" he yelled. Cormac came swooping down. Two huge vampires, one pissed-off captain, and a Mary Poppins wannabe huddled in the rain for a conference. "Look, we have a desperate situation here. We've stopped all the terrorists, but others may be involved. They may know where the container is and just waltz in here at any time, and either remove the weapon or detonate it. We need to find it now. Sealing off the port will cost millions in lost revenue and disrupt the economy. It would give the terrorists a victory. We need to find that weapon ASAP. Any ideas?" He was clearly grasping at straws. How the hell would *we* have any ideas if he didn't?

Just then a small, slim figure appeared at his side. Mar-Mar had arrived. "Thank you, Captain," she said, her authority unmistakable, even though she looked like a teenager dressed up for a paintball contest. "Let me handle this.

"Daphne," she said, looking at me. "When you were at Bonaventure's or at Bockerie's earlier tonight, did you find anything that might give the location of the container? Think! Was there any paper with a number-and-letter combination on it? It might not have meant anything to you then. Was there anything?"

"Yes!" I said. "In Bockerie's wallet. A Post-it note."

"Do you remember the number?" she queried.

"Of course I remember." I ran over to my purse. "But better than that. I have the note." I rushed back to the group while pulling out my wallet. "Here," I said, handing the paper to her.

"R-five-three-oh," she read it out loud so everyone could hear. "Captain, alert the bomb squad. Get them over there! Let's roll 'em!" she yelled.

Cormac and Benny took off flying. I jumped into a jeep with J and Mar-Mar. We tore hellbent for leather down rows of containers looking for R530. As we pulled up, dozens of trucks and jeeps converged on the scene. Men rushed over to the container's door and started applying detecting devices, looking for a safe way to access the space. I guessed Darkwing's job was done here.

Benny and Cormac had landed behind a nearby container, out of sight. The fewer people who knew of their existence the better. As I walked over, Cormac said, "Girlfriends, I'm outta here. I have a date waiting, believe it or not, and he's such a sweetie. He's cooking dinner for me. I just gave him a jingle and told him to warm up the pot roast. But it's been a hoot! I'll give you guys a call. This has really been a blast. I can't remember when I've had such fun. 'Byeee," he yelled as he leaped skyward into the night.

I turned to Benny. "I thought you were dead. My ring . . ."

"Oh, sugar! Your ring. I didn't have a chance to tell you. That creep Louis. He stole it from me! I'm all apologies. I just know he took it. Me and him, we're history, sugar, that's all I have to say. When a boyfriend starts stealing from you, why, there's just no trust. And with no trust, there's no relationship, I always say."

I'd heard that line before. She sounded as if she'd been talking to my mother.

"After that little incident in Jersey City—and honey, I know you didn't like it, but oh, that was a hot night; I admit I'm just not a lady about some things—I thought me and Louis really had something. I knew he could get a little out of control, but, no man is perfect, you know? We went back to my place, and I really did think he was going to move in. We had some incredible night, I tell you."

"So what went wrong?"

"He left while I was sleeping! The creep! I woke up

with the bed empty, the apartment empty, and Louis gone. So was your ring. I tried to find him, I really did. I looked the whole damned night last night. Even his mother hasn't heard from him. What a jerk!

"All he cared about was money, you know. He kept talking about the plantation his family once had, and some vampire named Lestat. He kept asking me about Bonaventure's diamonds and all. Then he left without a word. He didn't even give me that old sorry line, you know, 'It's me, not you.' I'm sorry, sugar, I really am, about your ring and all."

I decided right then and there not to tell her Louis had been staked. Let her be left righteously angry. If I told her he was dead, he'd become a martyr or a hero. He probably went to Bonaventure's knowing the place was empty and was looking for stuff to steal. I still think it was Darius who staked him, but maybe I'll never know what really happened.

I gave her furry form a hug. "Benny, don't worry about it. I got my ring back. He returned it to me."

"He did?" she said, astonished. "What did he say?"

I crossed my fingers behind my back because I was about to tell some whopping lies. "We didn't talk. He just left it where I could find it." Well, that was the truth, just not all of the truth.

She stood up straighter and her fur bristled. "That makes me feel a little better about him, but it's still over. He walked out on me once, and no one gets to do that to me twice."

I nodded in commiseration, all the while biting my lip, trying not to smile at her. She was fired up, and since she was in vampire form, her wings kept flapping in agitation. It looked pretty funny to me. "You're right," I said, "I think he's gone for good. Maybe he just wasn't ready for a commitment and didn't know how to tell you."

"The hell with him, sugar. I don't wait for anyone. You know what my mama always said: 'Weight is what broke the wagon down.' And you know something else? Men are—"

I broke in and we finished in unison. ". . . just like streetcars. Another one will be along in a minute."

"You bet," she said, and giggled. And with that she began to transform. In the twinkling of an eye she stood beside me naked as a jaybird. Christ, she'd cause a riot if she walked out in the open looking like that. She crowded under the umbrella with me. "Let's see if we can get something for me to put on," she said. "I'm colder than a well digger's butt."

We peeked out from the side of the container to see who was around. A young soldier stood by a jeep. Hurrying through the driving wind and rain, we ran up behind him. He turned around and gave us a stunned look. Cute as a bug and young, maybe twenty or twenty-one years old, he had dark hair, round cheeks, and green eyes that were about to pop out of his head when he was suddenly face to face with two young women, one of them starkers.

"Can you all do a lady a favor?" Benny drawled.

"Yes, ma'am," he drawled right back at her, and tried not to stare at her 34 DDs.

"Do y'all have a blanket or a jacket in the back of that there jeep?"

"Yes, ma'am, I have both of them," he said, and immediately began rummaging around. He pulled out a green army-issue rain poncho and handed it to her.

She slipped it on, and it covered her down to her knees. She turned to the young soldier and flashed him a brilliant smile. "Thank you for being such a gentleman," she said.

"Any old time," he said, and grinned back, showing two deep dimples and lots of country charm.

"Now, I can't help but notice you're not a Yankee," she said as she hopped up into the seat of the jeep, sat facing the young GI and made a show of crossing her legs.

"No, ma'am, I'm not," the soldier said as he watched her. Then he reached into the back of the jeep again and pulled out a blanket. He opened it up. "May I tuck this around you, ma'am? You look a mite chilled."

"You are a fine Southern gentleman." She twinkled. "Where all are you from, Rebel boy?"

"Belfry, Kentucky," he said, looking at her and forgetting I even existed.

"Why, I'm from Branson, Missouri. Now isn't that just a coincidence? What's your name, if I'm not being too bold in asking?" She laid her well-manicured hand on his sleeve.

"Larry D. Lee," he said, tipping his hat as he told her.

"Why, what's the D stand for?" she said, shamelessly flirting.

"Damn you," he answered with a straight face.

"Damn you? Why ever so?" she said, her big brown eyes wider than wide.

"It's 'damn you' 'cause every time my daddy called me, he said, 'Larry, damn you, get over here!' So my Mama said 'damn you' was my middle name, and it just stuck." He made the word *stuck* into two syllables.

I figured I was a fifth wheel and excused myself. They were talking a mile a minute and never seemed to notice I was leaving. I walked toward J, smiling to myself. Benny wasn't going to sit around carrying a torch for Louis. I don't know if Larry D. knew what he was getting himself into, but I could see right behind that innocent act. Those country boys can handle themselves. Benny had found a match made in heaven . . . at least for a couple of weeks.

Now I had some things of my own to face.

CHAPTER 16

Everything is determined, the beginning as well as the end, by forces over which we have no control. It is determined for the insect as well as for the star. Human beings, vegetables, or cosmic dust, we all dance to a mysterious tune, intoned in the distance by an invisible piper.

— Albert Einstein

I crossed the wet, dark asphalt, my old snow boots splashing through the puddles, the long velvet skirt sodden at the hem and tangling around my feet. I didn't see Mar-Mar anywhere and figured she was off reporting to the president or something. As I walked over to J I was almost fainting with fatigue. My head was pounding, my lips were quivering, and I knew my face must be blue with cold.

J could see I was shaken. "You look like you can use some hot coffee, Miss Urban," he said. Taking my arm, he marched me over to a jeep, opened the door, and took the umbrella from my cold hand. He lowered it, shook off the water, and stuck it behind the seat. Then he helped me in before he went and got in the driver's side. After he slammed the door, he pulled a thermos out from a bag on the floor and poured coffee into its red plastic thermos top. I took it gratefully, and the first sip told me it was hot, creamy, and very sweet. I usually drink my coffee black, and made a face.

"The sugar helps stop you from going into shock," he said, guessing what I was thinking. He was studying me intently.

"What?" I said to him, looking at him over the cup of the thermos top.

"Miss Urban, you did good. You did real good. I just wanted to say that. And I wanted to tell you I was wrong. About a lot of things. But especially about you."

I didn't know what to say. My emotions were all jumbled up inside. He didn't know how badly I fucked up, in so many ways. But I kept silent.

J looked away from me then and stared at the windshield, where droplets of rain ran down in rivulets, like the tears that I still needed to shed. "I got a call from the medics," he said. "It looks like Darius della Chiesa is going to make it. They don't know how he lived. The bullet nicked his heart. He lost a lot of blood. He's in surgery, but the outlook is optimistic. I thought you'd want to know."

"Yes, thanks. I appreciate your telling me. But it's over between him and me. You were right, you know; he is a vampire hunter," I said, trying not to cry. I looked over at J and gave a bitter smile. "Things ended badly with us. And he thinks I hate him."

J was silent for a moment before he said anything. "It's none of my affair, Miss Urban, but if you have unfinished business with him, maybe you need to go talk to him. As Yogi Berra said, it ain't over till it's over. . . ."

"I don't think he'll see me. Once he found out what I was—and I found out what he was—well, we're just too far apart. And I can never accept that he killed vampires, exterminated them out of pure vengeance, without understanding or compassion, without knowing what he was really doing."

"Miss Urban," J said with a funny sound in his voice. "I don't like Darius della Chiesa, but I respect him. He's a good soldier. As for him hating vampires, I did too. If I changed my mind, maybe he can. After what I've seen . . . well, vampires, I figure, are just another level of beings, somewhere between humans and the angels, I guess. I didn't know that before . . . before you changed that day. . . ."

"Oh, sorry about that." God, this was getting embarrassing. I remembered the kiss I had given him. I remembered how he bent his head in submission and how I could have taken him right then.

"No, let me finish. I'm not a talking kind of man, so don't cut me off. I want to get this off my chest," he said, his hands tight around the steering wheel and his eyes avoiding mine. "Before you changed that day I didn't know what the hell I was talking about. You weren't what I thought—a monster. And you've proved to me you are a natural warrior, amazing, really. And beyond that, you are"—he stopped and coughed—"a good person. I'm sincerely sorry if Darius della Chiesa hurt you. You didn't deserve it. And if he rejected you because you are a vampire, he's a fool."

"Thank you for saying that. It helps." I paused for a moment and decided I couldn't bear to talk about Darius anymore or I'd burst into tears. So I said instead, "Now about my mother—"

He cut me off. "Look, I'm not at liberty to discuss your mother, not even with you. If you have questions, you need to talk directly to her. Sorry, but I have orders."

I suddenly felt as if I had to lie down. Everything that had happened this night had drained my strength. "Sure, J, I understand," I said in a weary voice. "Can you help me get home now? As you can see, I'm in no condition to fly." I gave him a weak smile.

"Are you going to be okay?" he said, giving me a worried look. "I can get a medic over here."

I bowed my head to hide the tears that had suddenly overwhelmed me. I gestured with my hand that I was all right. "I just need to rest," I choked out.

"I'll find a soldier to drive you into the city," he said, and started to open the jeep's door. Then he shut it again and turned toward me. He reached over and put his hand under my chin, turning my face toward his. With great gentleness he wiped away the tears running down my cheeks with his fingers. Before either of us realized what was happening I was leaning toward him. Our lips met in a brief kiss. It was sweet, I still felt a tingle of our old chemistry, but the world didn't rock. Then he pulled away and got out of the jeep.

Before he shut the door, J looked at me. "I should have done that in the office, that night. It would have been against regulations, but what I said to you was far worse than breaking any rules. I apologize. When you're ready, if you ever are, maybe I can make it up to you. But it's your move, Miss Urban." He winked at me, and then, all Gary Cooper in *High Noon,* he turned around and walked away, tall, proud, and a hero.

I wasn't ready for J to be part of my life, but what he said had helped my head. My heart was beyond help at the moment: It was breaking because of Darius. I didn't know what I'd do next. But I'd worry about that tomorrow.

When I finally got back to my apartment, I stripped off my ridiculous clothes and tumbled into my coffin. Then I slept the sleep of the dead, or the undead, as it may be. I got up as purple dusk was fading into night. My thoughts of Darius made me feel like a cat batting at a moth behind a window shade. I couldn't stop thinking about him, but I couldn't resolve anything.

I called the hospital to see how he was doing. He was still in the ICU, and only his immediate family was allowed to see him. Was I his wife? the receptionist asked. No, I said, just a friend, and hung up.

The next thing I did was phone my mother.

"Mar-Mar, we need to talk," I said in place of hello.

"Do you need to vent?" she said innocently.

"You might call it that," I said through clenched teeth.

"Would you mind coming up here, sweetie? I have a meeting later tonight, so I can't come into the city. I would come down there if I could. If you can come to Scarsdale, I'll fix you something to eat." She was speaking quickly, knowing I was about to lose it.

"Don't bother cooking for me," I said, envisioning a stir-fry of tofu and things that grow on the bark of trees. "I'll be up there by seven. What time's your meeting?"

"Much later. Come on up," she said. "Love you."

"Yeah, me too," I said, although I didn't feel very loving. I felt betrayed, lied to, and thoroughly pissed.

I dressed simply in a long straight dress with a shawl collar, and put on low boots. I was all in brown. Once again the sober color fit my mood. But before I left the house I added a wide deep-purple suede belt I had bought in Positano that was studded with brass and rhinestones. It added a hint of whimsy and lightness, although I felt anything but whimsical. I took a car service and arrived in Scarsdale on the dot of seven.

Mar-Mar answered the door wearing one of her Janis Joplin outfits: floppy hat, Mexican vest, peasant blouse, and bell bottoms. Her tiny feet were bare, except for the toe rings.

She stood up on tiptoe and kissed the air on either side

of my cheeks. Then she took me by the arm, leading me inside. "How are you?" she asked. "You did take quite a chilling dip last night. Do you think you're coming down with anything? Let me get you a cup of herbal tea with echinacea," she said as she hurried away from me into the kitchen.

I followed. "Mar-Mar, we need to get some issues settled."

"Yes, sweetheart, I absolutely agree," she said, keeping her back to me.

"You meddled in my life. Again." I stood there, tensing up as my anger started to build.

My mother turned around and looked at me. "Yes," she said, "and it was high time I did." She handed me a handmade pottery mug filled with the steaming brew.

I took it over to the kitchen island and sat down, working up a whole speech to lambaste her with. I didn't get a chance.

Mar-Mar was already talking: "And before you say a single thing, I want you to know, I believe you did a splendid job. You far surpassed the expectations we had for your performance. Except for getting involved with that . . . *person,* you handled your mission with nearly no mistakes."

She had just pushed about ten of my buttons, and I fumed. "Just a minute; let's back up here. First off, who are *we*?"

"That's classified. Let's just say it's the U.S. government," she replied calmly.

"Would you mind telling me how the hell you are mixed up in this, as much as my security clearance allows?" I said sarcastically.

"Daphy, dear, please don't take it personally, but any information about my role in the intelligence community is on a need-to-know level."

That frosted me. I stood up and leaned toward her, practically spitting as I spoke. "Ma! If you don't want me to walk out of here and never come back, you'd better believe this is on my need-to-know level."

She sighed, reached for the teapot, and poured some more herbal tea into her mug. "Okay, sweetie. I can tell you this much. I had been out of the loop, so to speak, for a few decades. Oh, I kept up my contacts, but I had dedicated myself to the peace movement. I was tired of the Machiavellian approach to world affairs. Then September eleventh happened. Certain old friends came to me and asked me to get back into what we used to call 'The Great Game,' only it's an endgame now."

"So your whole peace, love, hippie thing is just a disguise, a mask?" I said in a nasty voice. I don't know if I had spoken to her in quite those tones before; I never would have dared, but this time she had topped anything she had ever done to me.

She reacted with vehemence, her voice getting louder. "Absolutely not! I truly believe that war is not the answer. Violence never solved anything. But this nation and our way of life are under attack. Until this mess can get sorted out diplomatically, I intend to ensure that a tragedy such as September eleventh *never* happens again."

"That's what *you* wanted to do," I began, shouting. "Why did you drag *me* into this?" The angry words had poured out like rushing water.

I could see her taking off the velvet gloves. Something inside me cringed. The steel behind the magnolias was about to cut right through my thin skin.

"*Drag* you into this?" she practically snarled. "It was about time something was done with you. You've been mooning around over that . . . that *poet* Byron for almost two hundred years. When you went to Ireland at the beginning of the last century, I thought, *Good, my daugh-*

ter is finally using her talents for something of value and thinking of something bigger than herself. But no, that didn't last. Off you went to join that lunatic James Joyce in Paris and got lost in the wildness of the 1920s. Once again acting frivolously, you spent your time in cafés and indulged in fashion and fads. Even World War Two didn't change you. Although you did your little part as an ambulance driver in Spain, you still managed to get mixed up with those literary types, and they're so ... so *sensitive.*"

My mother and I were polar opposites in so many ways. Always an extrovert, she had a head for business and politics. That wasn't me, and I always felt she was a hard act to follow. Now she was putting down things I had done and people who had been very important in my life. It absolutely infuriated me, but she was still my mother, so I pulled back on expressing my rage, quietly seething instead. "Ma, I don't consider Ernest Hemingway to be a *sensitive* guy. He was perceptive and he drank too much, but *sensitive* he wasn't."

"I'm not going to argue that with you," she said primly. "The point is, you have wasted your special gifts for centuries. I hate to say this, dear, but you have been shallow, self-absorbed, and of no use to anyone. I love you, but I haven't been very proud of you, and I do hate to say that to you."

I suspected she had always felt that, but hearing her say it hurt like hell—even though I knew she was right.

Mar-Mar got up and walked back to the sink and started cleaning up. She was always in motion and never sat still for long. With her back to me, she said some other things I didn't want to hear: "Daphne, you seem to think that if you found your soul mate, the right man, your life would change. If I ever tried to teach you anything, it is that love is *not* the answer. At least *eros* isn't. *Agape* is a different story. But, as I was saying, my point is that spending your life focused on lost love or finding new love is simply selfish and self-destructive. My Scottish friend Thomas Carlyle wrote something a hundred years ago that has always stayed with me. You don't go looking for happiness. You find it by the wayside—while you are pursuing your ideals and your principles. And that applies to love too. You may find it, but you can't go looking for it."

I put my head down on my folded arms, feeling defeated and depressed. "So this whole spying job happened because you set me up?" I moaned.

She turned around and looked at me. Mentally I could hear the words she wasn't saying: *Sit up straight, Daphne. Put some steel in your spine. Never let the bastards get you down. You are a vampire. You're special, and you must never forget that.* As I kept my eyes tightly closed and my forehead against my forearm, what she did say was: "Daphne Urban, I *chose* you. I knew a team of vampires could be a tremendously powerful weapon in the fight against terror. You are the smartest vampire I know, present company excepted, and you have another quality that makes you especially valuable."

I have to admit, she had me hooked with that. I peeked up at her and asked, "And what's that?"

"Courage. You will go after what you know to be right no matter the cost. I've seen that in you since you were a child. You were born with bravery in your very bones. I've never seen you run from a fight. No matter how frightened you might be, your fears have never stopped you."

I sat up then. I pulled my cup of herbal tea closer and circled my hands around it, swishing the leaves back and forth at the bottom. Neither of us said anything for a moment. Finally I spoke. "Look, you're right. I am just very upset that you used deception instead of being open and honest with me. How do you know I wouldn't have voluntarily joined the Darkwings if you had simply asked me?"

She stared down at her hands, which held the dish towel she had been using. She was silent for a hard moment, then she walked over and put her hand lightly on my shoulder. "I was wrong," she said, and kissed the top of my hair. "I am so used to being dishonest and sneaky, wearing masks and playing mind games, that I behaved that way with my own daughter, my own flesh and blood. I shouldn't have done that, and I hope you will forgive me. I had the best of motives, but the ends don't justify the means. They never do, and I should know better. But change is difficult. I can only promise you that I'll be better in the future. I hope you will stay with Team Darkwing. They need you, and this country needs you. And Daphy . . ."

"Yes, Ma?" I said, still trying to digest the fact that she had apologized to me for the first time in my life.

"I need you."

I was stunned. People have always depended on Mar-Mar, and she has never admitted to *needing* anyone, even my father. I turned my head and looked into her eyes. The ancient wisdom of a very old soul shone there. Despite her very youthful appearance, so at odds with her inner self, Mar-Mar was an elder, a wise woman, an amazing creature who had helped direct the history of Western civilization for over a thousand years. I had only a vague idea of what had happened when she mingled with kings and popes, but I am quite sure they needed her, and not vice versa.

All that went through my mind in an instant. Then I said to her, "Yes, I intend to stay with the Darkwings. You were right about my being lost. I think I am finding my-self at last."

"And what about Darius della Chiesa?" she said boldly, throwing down the gauntlet once more.

I didn't flinch or back down. "There are some things, Marozia, that really are none of your business," I said. "Let's say *that* information is classified."

To my surprise, she smiled broadly. "Quid pro quo. I deserved that. Well, just don't get your heart broken. And if you need to talk, I can listen, you know. And I'm al-ways here for you."

I smiled back at her. "I know you are."

"Now, dear, one more thing."

I frowned. What the hell was she going to tell me?

"You have a meeting tonight at midnight. Your office. Don't be late, dear."

I really didn't know if I could handle my mother also being my boss. Only time would tell. But at that point her doorbell rang. She went and answered it. Her "people" from the Save the Trees group came pouring in.

The old hippie with the gray ponytail was among them. He smiled when he saw me. "Shalom!" he yelled out.

That threw me for a moment, until I remembered I told him I was into the Kabbalah movement.

"Shalom back to you," I answered. He looked strangely familiar, and I felt I had seen him someplace else, besides in Bockerie's loft the other night.

"Mar-Mar," I said to my mother, "I'd better be going. I told the car service to pick me up at eight, and they're out in front."

She gave me a quick hug. "Godspeed, Daphy," she said. Then she hurried over to her CD player and put on a Loreena McKennitt album. I left with the haunting deep horns of "The Mystic's Dream" following me out the door. The notion occurred to me that this whole adventure was all a dream from which I'd awaken one day. A cold feeling passed over me as I left.

Midnight. Not a sound on the pavement.

I arrived at the Flatiron Building shortly before the witching hour, after stopping off at the apartment for a meal and to pay some attention to Gunther. He wasn't happy about being left behind every time I went out, but *c'est la vie.* I fixed him a nice snack and left the television on in front of his cage. I don't know if he really watched it, but I put on the Discovery Channel for him.

I had a message on my answering machine from Benny, who told me she'd catch me later at the office. I wondered if setting midnight as the time of the meeting was J's idea of a joke. I immediately nixed the thought since from what I'd seen, a sense of humor wasn't one of J's attributes.

I came into the meeting room, and it was empty. I passed through and opened the door to my own little office. It was bare and impersonal. I made a mental note to brighten up the walls with some pictures from home and to spend some time here, maybe writing up my reports as if I had a normal job. It wasn't much, but it was mine own. I walked back into the meeting room and took a seat at the table.

Benny came breezing through the doorway a minute later. She gave me a big girlfriend hug, and her very presence cheered me up. After you think you've lost someone forever, to have them back in your life is something wonderful. I was even glad to see Cormac when he came fluttering in.

"Oh," he said as he pulled out a chair and sat down. "I'm so nervous I could thread a sewing machine with it running."

"Why are you all jittery?" I said.

"My agent called. I have an audition. For a principal part on a new HBO series. This could be my big break." His face was lit up like a Christmas tree.

"That's just wonderful, Cormac, honey," Benny gushed.

"I thought you were a full-time spy?" I said dryly, having heard about Cormac's possible "big breaks" before, like the time he got called back for the part of the houseboy in *Birdcage,* only to lose it to a young Puerto Rican actor. "But I *do* Spanish," he had whined plaintively to me. "Yeah, and you do Greek too," I answered, and he didn't speak to me for weeks.

Now he said, "Why, Daphy, you know as well as I do: 'Never give up your day job.' Of course, it's a night job in this case, but you know, I'm not independently wealthy like you. So few of us are," he said waspishly.

Before I could think up a snappy comeback, the door crashed open. We all stared at it. A big fellow wearing a John Deere Tractors hat, a denim jacket, and mud-crusted Timberland boots filled the space without coming in. His face was red, his neck was red, and he had the beginnings of a beer belly hanging over his jeans. He looked like a construction worker. I figured he was with the maintenance staff.

"Hey, you all," he boomed. "Is this here where the vampire meeting is? I'm supposed to report in. I'm the newbie!" He gave us a huge grin.

We all looked at him with our mouths open. Benny, always a lady, recovered first.

"Why, yes, you're in the right place. You just come on in and sit yourself down." She pulled out a chair for him right next to hers. "Now, what's your name?"

"Bubba," he said. "That's what most folks call me anyways. And you must be the little lady that Larry D. is seeing. He's my cousin twice removed, and I want to thank you for telling him about your job. He called my mama, and that's how I got hooked up with these folks."

Benny did blush when he mentioned that she'd told Larry D. about us. Keeping secrets sure wasn't her long suit. J must have been superpissed when he heard about it . . . if he had heard about it.

I figured now I had heard *everything:* a vampire named Bubba. "Well, Bubba," I chimed in, "have I deduced correctly that you too hail from Belfry, Kentucky?"

"Ma'am, I'm not real sure what you're asking, but hell, yes! I'm from Kintucky. Anybody who cain't tell that I'm a redneck is either blind and deaf or dead . . . drunk!" he said, his belly rocking with laughter.

With that J entered the room. "I see you've met the new member of Darkwing. Welcome to our team, Mr. Lee. I'll be brief. The hour is late." He didn't give me a wink or even a hard look. J was back to being all business.

"Our last mission was accomplished. Although the government cannot give any of you public recognition, be appraised that Langley has noted your valor. You have proved that Team Darkwing can be an invaluable addition to this nation's security. I wish I could say that your job is over, but in fact we have just begun. Mr. O'Reilly, you will remain in place at Opus Dei."

"Oh my god, more Gregorian chants. I may go mad, I tell you." Cormac always was a drama queen, pun intended.

J continued. "Miss Urban and Miss Polycarp, you will receive new assignments by the end of the month. Meanwhile, we are pleased to grant you two weeks' leave. Get some R & R. Miss Polycarp, if you would like to get back to Branson, we can arrange military transport. Just give me a call. And Miss Polycarp, there *is* a note in your file you need to read. Mr. Lee, I'll be meeting with you during the next week. We have a special assignment for you that may dovetail with Miss Urban's and Miss Polycarp's. I think you will work well together."

I thought, *He's got to be joking.*

"And now I want to distribute to the original team members your first wage and earnings statements. Congratulations." With that he passed out three white business envelopes. "And you're dismissed."

"Wait a minute!" Benny cried. "What happened to the terrorists? What happened to Bonaventure?"

J gave me a quick look and slid his eyes away. "The terrorists are undergoing interrogation. We have made a thorough search of their safe houses. The information we obtained will help us stop any future acts of terrorism. And that is largely thanks to the Darkwings. As for Bonaventure, he is out of the picture, and that's all I am at liberty to say."

Benny wasn't about to quit. "What about the diamonds that got stolen from me? I'd just as soon have lost myself than have let go of those gems, although my mama used to tell me I'm never lost, 'cause someone's always telling me where to go."

"The diamonds have not been recovered, " J said. I almost fell out of my seat when he said that, since I had put them right into Mar-Mar's hands. "But as Bonaventure never cashed the larger check from the diamond broker, only the fifty million dollars remains missing. The terrorists were the big losers on the deal, and they aren't in any position to complain. As for the uncut diamonds themselves, we assume they were stolen by a person or persons unknown. Although we've turned the matter over to the Treasury Department, it's unlikely they'll ever be found. Any other questions?"

I had one, but it was personal. I'd wait until the others left.

"No? One more thing, Team Darkwing . . ."

We all looked at him.

"I'm proud of every one of you. You did a fine job. You saved millions of lives—and the city of New York. This country owes you a great debt. Now, soldiers, you are dismissed," he barked, and gave us a salute.

With that team Darkwing got up to leave. Benny whispered that she'd catch up with me later. Cormac rushed out blowing kisses and waving good-bye. Bubba Lee tipped his hat and said, "See ya," as he lumbered back through the door, and I lagged behind, needing to speak to J.

"Yes, Miss Urban?" J said, maintaining a totally professional tone.

I felt uneasy about what I wanted to ask, but I plunged on. "I have a request. I don't know if you can help, but I'd appreciate it." He nodded at me, so I went on. "I'd like to get into the hospital to see Darius. Right now his visits are limited to family."

I couldn't read his reaction; his face remained totally expressionless, but his voice was tight when he answered. "I'll see what I can do. I'll let you know. Is that all?"

"Yes. I mean no, I want to ask you one more thing," I said. He raised his eyebrows, and I sensed a desire to end the conversation. I plunged on, saying, "I spoke with my mother."

"And?" he said with clear impatience.

"I hope I'm reporting to you and not to her," I blurted out.

His words were clipped and brief. "I'm in charge of Team Darkwing. Is that it?"

"Yes, thank you," I said, and then with a rush of gratitude I reached out and touched his arm as lightly as the landing of a butterfly, saying, "Thank you, J, for everything. I mean that with all my heart."

I pulled my hand away, and he responded in a gentler voice, "That's quite all right, Miss Urban. Get some R and R. I'll be in touch on the hospital visits."

"Good, great," I said, hastily picking up my things and hurrying out the door. As I was going down in the elevator, I opened the envelope J had handed out earlier. Inside was a form from the United States Government indicating that $1,036 in net earnings had been deposited in my bank account, that I had accrued one vacation day and one sick day, and that the government had started a Thrift Savings Plan and pension for me. Suddenly I felt damned good.

CHAPTER 17

Fire does not wait for the sun to be hot,
Nor the wind for the moon, to be cool.

— the Zenrin Kushu

Christmas was only a few days away, but the holiday spirit was eluding me this year. Overshadowing everything was the issue of seeing Darius again. I called every day to check on his condition. Yesterday I had learned he was out of the ICU. Today I had discovered he had been transferred to a different hospital. They wouldn't tell me where. If he had gotten word to me that he wanted to see me, I would have moved heaven and earth to get there. But he didn't. I remembered all too clearly that with his dying breath, he refused to look at me. That still hurt, and I thought it always would.

During my days of R & R, I had treated myself to a facial, pedicure, manicure, and Parisian peel. Another Buff 'n' Glo had eliminated my pallor. And I shopped, which is the best therapy a woman can buy. My Bloomingdale's charge card was smoking. When I got back to my apartment after every spending binge, I sadly looked at my purchases and wondered if I'd ever wear most of them.

And there was one more loose end I sewed up, and wished I hadn't. I called the number from Bonaventure's caller ID, the East Side car service. I identified myself as a police officer, a deception that I suppose will just be tacked onto my long list of sins one day, and I questioned a dispatcher about that call.

"Yes, we have a record of that service," she said.

"Do you know who actually took the trip?" I asked.

"I can ask the driver. It's been a while, but he may remember, especially if it was a regular. Can I get back to you on that?" Yes, I said, and gave her my cell phone number.

"One more thing," I said as my heart thumped heavily in my chest. "Do you have the address of the destination?"

"Why, yes. It's right here. The party went to Grand Central Station."

That bit of information didn't help me any; it just confused me. Catharine told me that Bockerie had been driving a van, so it wasn't him who took the ride. When the dispatcher called me back, she told me that the driver had expected to pick up Bonaventure's maid, as he usually did, but that wasn't who came downstairs and got in the car.

"Who was it?" I asked.

"Two young white guys. One of them had a blond ponytail," she said.

That information left me confused all over again. Evidently Darius had entered the apartment with an accomplice, and he had kept that information from me. Although I had proof that Bockerie took the diamonds and assumed he killed Issa and Tanya, there might be another scenario: Darius had been part of an execution squad and Bockerie had arrived after the murders and helped himself to the gems. I wondered if I would ever know the whole truth. Troubling as it was, especially if I contributed to those deaths by opening the door for Darius, the only option was to file the problem away for now.

J called on the evening of the fourteenth day after the

Charge of the Vampire Brigade, as Cormac had dubbed our adventure when he phoned with the good news (he got the part in the HBO series) and the bad news (he got killed off in the first episode). J told me that Darius had been sent to a private hospital out on Staten Island. After giving me the address, he told me a visit had been arranged for me that night at nine P.M. if I wanted it. I said I did and thanked him.

J murmured something like, "You might not thank me after you see him," and hung up.

Choosing from among my recent purchases, I dressed simply in a long wool skirt and pink cashmere sweater. My short coat was really a suit jacket for the skirt. It was classic Chanel. I wanted to look sophisticated, not sexy. I sprayed on a scent to match. Then I took a car service out to Staten Island. It was a long ride all the way down Richmond Avenue toward the Outerbridge Crossing. I had a lot of time to think. When I got out of the car on the tree-lined street of an older block, a dusting of snow covered the ground, and Christmas lights on nearby front porches cast colors across the white. As I started up the sidewalk I saw a cat's paw prints. They looked like fallen plum blossoms.

The "hospital" seemed more like an office building than a health-care facility. There was no plaque giving it a name. The front door held the building number in plain gold numbers and nothing more. It was sturdy as a prison and locked tight. I had to ring a buzzer to get in.

The door opened into a waiting room that held some plastic chairs and a table with a few magazines. An artificial Christmas tree sat in one corner, looking forlorn. A guard's station behind heavy glass filled one wall. I walked over and spoke through a circle cut in the glass. I soon discovered just how tight security was in this place.

Automatic rifles were held by two of the three guards behind the glass, and the one unarmed guard now checked for my name on a list. Obviously no one got in without prior approval and the appropriate security clearance. I was buzzed into another room. The two armed guards came out, leaving the third man inside the glass box facing the entrance. I was quickly fingerprinted, photographed, given a name tag, and told where to go to find Darius's room. The guards were very nice to me; I have to say that. I must have looked tense and unhappy.

"He's going to be okay, miss," the older of the two said in a kindly way. "The doctors say it's just a matter of time. He looks a whole lot worse than he is, they say."

That didn't inspire much optimism in me. "Is he conscious?" I asked.

"Right now? Don't know. He's wide-awake sometimes. Mostly at night anyway. We walk by his room, and he's got the TV on. He sleeps a lot. He was pretty banged up. He always sleeps through the days. Light seems to bother him. He has a lot of bad dreams too. They've sedated him, so if he's real quiet don't let that worry you none. It's normal, you know. He'll answer questions, but he doesn't seem to want any conversation. It's not unusual with soldiers coming back from a war zone. PTSD, they call it—post-traumatic stress disorder. We've got shrinks to help him, and getting a visit from a pretty miss like you is sure to cheer him up."

I wouldn't count on it, I thought. They opened the inner door for me and pointed the way down a shadowy corridor.

I marched out feeling like a prisoner going to my doom. My heels made a *tap-tap* sound on the green linoleum. The place seemed empty. Everything was painted in institutional green. This was strictly government-issue, I thought, and it must be a safe house for agents. Most of the doors I passed were shut tight. I rounded the corner and saw that the door to Darius's room was ajar, but not open. Stopping in front of it, I could see the flickering light of a TV turned on without the sound. My heart was racing, and I dreaded going in.

Darius was asleep, turned on his side, his face toward the doorway where I stood. Even in the dim light his skin was paper white, but he looked like an angel lying there, innocent and young.

I said a silent prayer of thanks that he was asleep, because that would make what I had to do so much easier. As much as I wanted to talk with Darius, my most urgent reason to see him was to bite him again. I had given him the "kiss of life" there in the rain at the container facility. But it takes more than one bite to ensure a complete transformation from human to vampire. It would be truly tragic to leave him in some limbo state, not human and not vampire either. I wanted him to have the same powers I did, the same wings to soar on, the same gifts. Such wonderful abilities would make it easier for him to accept who he now was. And he'd have to accept it, for he had no other option. I hoped he'd come to that realization sooner rather than later. At some point he had to decide whether to hide his transformation from his employers or choose a different life. And seeing the empty bag of plasma hanging from an IV rack on the far side of the bed, I knew he was still being given blood transfusions. Later on he would need help in learning what to do about feeding, avoiding daylight, and all the myriad things a vampire is forced to do to survive.

Gathering up my courage, I came quickly into the room and closed the door tightly behind me. Even amidst my anxieties, my desire was increasing and a wetness had begun between my legs. My breathing quickened as I carefully crept onto the bed next to Darius. Feeling his body next to mine made my heart lurch. I ran my hands over his bare shoulder and cupped his neck as I leaned down. I found the sweet spot on his throat and bit quickly, beginning my long, deep drink. I was soon in ecstasy, swooning with the sensations that coursed through my veins as his essence flowed into me. I didn't notice that his eyes had opened until I had finished and lifted my bloody mouth.

Before I knew what happened, his lips came up to mine in a hard kiss. With surprising strength he roughly turned me over on the bed and got his hand up under my skirt, pulling down my panties and yanking them off. So fast I barely knew what was happening, he entered me and began thrusting hard into me again and again. I was stunned, but not surprised. A vampire's bite is as arousing for the victim as for the vampire, and his drive for sexual release would have been overwhelming.

I moaned and welcomed him. Darius pushed into me again and again and again. I was rising up to meet his excitement, wanting him to stay with me, in me, forever. I opened my eyes just once and saw him glaring down at me, with eyes filled with anger and pain, but not love. I closed mine tight and sought his mouth, using my own strength to hold him with a kiss. He rammed into me until I couldn't stop myself and began to come; then he climaxed and stopped moving.

He rolled off me then, leaving me empty and forlorn. He didn't embrace me. His eyes were open wide when I again opened mine.

"Darius?" I said, my voice breaking and the tears welling up in my eyes.

"Did you get what you came for—my *soul*?" he asked bitterly.

"Please let me explain," I pleaded.

"There's nothing to say. I accept what you did, but I

will never forgive you for doing it." He shifted away from me, turned his head, and stared at the television while he spoke to me.

My voice was trembling and my heart was breaking as I tried to tell him, "Look, the change is difficult at first. I know that, but I couldn't let you die. I did what I did because I love you."

"I don't think you know what love is," he said. "It wasn't love to make me into a monster. Like you."

His words were like a dagger thrusting into my breast. When I was bitten centuries ago, I remember being confused, but with that was also a tremendous excitement at having the heightened sensations and the magnificent strength of the vampire race. Of course, it had been different for me, since I didn't hate vampires, having been born from one's womb. Now, trying once more to reach him, I cried out softly, "Darius, please try to understand. You are immortal now."

Darius still didn't look at me. He just stared toward the flickering TV screen while he said slowly and deliberately, "Look, just get out. Leave me alone. I don't want to see you. Don't you get it? I don't want to have anything to do with you. Get out of here!" His words were hard and cruel.

I touched his shoulder with my hand. He shrugged it off and pulled away. Now I spoke the last things I needed to say to him. "You don't want to hear this, but there are things I need to tell you. Listen to me: You don't have to kill to get blood. I'm leaving my mother's number here. You can always call me, but in case you don't, please call her. She'll set things up for you. You can trust her. I swear it."

I rolled off the bed. He still wouldn't look at me but was looking blankly up at the ceiling now. His face was like a mask, wooden and unmoving, his lips silent. I straightened out my skirt and slipped out the door. I nearly ran down the hall, never looking back. If I had, I would have seen that Darius was openly crying, and that he held the black wisp of my silk panties clenched in one hand.

CHAPTER 18

Consciousness determines existence.
Cogito, ergo sum.

—Descartes

I left the hospital, desolation in my every step. I heard the lonely sound of a chestnut dropping beneath a tree. I stopped. The sound struck me in my soul. Awakening. *Satori*. Everything changed.

Suddenly I picked up my chin and straightened my spine, realizing with full force just how heroic Team Darkwing had been. We had made history and saved lives, and I myself was different, proud of what I had done. I had succeeded, never shirking from a challenge, never running from danger. My head was high. I wanted to yell to those passing cars: *A vampire walks here! She is strong and fine. She passes you on the street. You don't recognize her, but she is here. She lives!*

The moon peeped out between the snow clouds in the night sky. I could soar toward it if I wished, like a bird, just as humans have wanted to do since time began. They merely dream of flying, but I could do it. I was who I was, and for the first time in my long life, I didn't wish to be anyone else.

No matter what Darius had said to me, with a diamond-hard surety inside me, I knew it was right to have saved his life. And it was meant to be so. He was now an immortal. I was his conversion on the road to Damascus. I had transformed him from a persecutor into the persecuted, from a killer into a victor who could fight and win—and yet never kill again.

I believed, and I had witnessed it again and again in all my years on this globe, that we are given our fates in life; we don't choose them. To be bitten by me was Darius's destiny. Everything he had done had been to bring him to that night in the rain, to the bullet that ricocheted and struck him down, to that wet, hard asphalt where he fell, his mortality ebbing out of him. And everything I had done had brought me there to his side, with Benny showing up like an angel dropping out of the weeping sky, returned from the dead, or so it seemed to me. She arrived like a miracle, just in time to urge me to bite him. The ends had made a circle, tied neatly, bringing it all together. We met. We loved. I bit him. Nothing is accidental.

Now, with a bone-deep longing, I wanted Darius to forgive me and to see that what had happened to him was a beginning, not an end. His transformation meant we could be together now, without lies. It might be foolish of me to hope, but if we could be a couple again, we could stay together forever. We could wander under moonshine and travel the world. I envisioned taking him to my beloved Ireland, where I had known Yeats and proudly worn the green, traveling the land from Dublin to Dingle where the bay lies placid under the stars. And in the warmth of an Irish pub, we could raise a pint and sing "rebel songs" to the mandolins and guitars played by the apple-cheeked members of local bands.

Swiftly, without warning, the memory of the first time Darius had kissed me, there on Madison Avenue in front of the jewelry store, washed over me. Had I listened carefully, I would have known that my heart was telling me from the first that he was meant to be my mate. Now I could only hope that *his* heart would find its way back to me after the storms of anger had passed. Then, like a cold wind, reality crashed down on me. My reveries stopped with a rush of deep hurt and the knowledge that in all truth I probably had lost Darius forever. As a sob escaped from my lips and blackness threatened to overwhelm me, I looked up and saw a lighted Christmas star atop a church. Pulsing white and beautiful, it seemed to shine for me, sending me a message—or a promise—that love conquers all. I needed only to have faith.

And at that moment snow began to fall lightly, fragmenting the glow of the Christmas star into hundreds of fairy lights that sparkled all around me. I did have faith in love. And I also felt jubilant that the vampires of Team Darkwing were protectors, not destroyers. Walking more quickly now, feeling strong and ready to wend my way home, I paused for a moment by the church. The doors stood open, and the inside was crowded with worshipers. A rosy light spilled out across the snow, and from within the sound of a choir rang. As I stood there, the words they sang reached out and embraced me: "For unto us a Son is born, For unto us a Child is given." A vision of the young virgin Mary with her baby flashed into my mind. A certainty came upon me that I was on this earth for a purpose. I couldn't foresee the future, but I could face it courageously. With Darius or without him, I would fight for what was right and good, and one day he might return to my arms. If he didn't, I might mourn his absence each day and night, but I would take one step at a time, and go on. . . .

All your favorite romance writers are
coming together.

SIGNET ECLIPSE

COMING JULY 2005:
Much Ado About Magic
by Patricia Rice
Love Underground: Persephone's Tale
by Alicia Fields
Private Pleasures by Bertrice Small
Lost in Temptation by Lauren Royal

COMING AUGUST 2005:
Home at Last by Jerri Corgiat
Bachelorette #1 by Jennifer O'Connell
Dangerous Passions by Lynn Kerstan